THE VARLET AND THE VOYEUR

RUGBY SERIES BOOK #4

L.H. COSWAY

PENNY REID

THE VARLET AND THE VOYEUR

RUGBY SERIES BOOK #4

L.H. COSWAY

PENNY REID

COPYRIGHT

This book is a work of fiction. Names, characters, places, rants, facts, contrivances, and incidents are either the product of the author's questionable imagination or are used factitiously. Any resemblance to actual persons, living or dead or undead, events, locales is entirely coincidental if not somewhat disturbing/concerning.

Copyright © 2018 by Cipher-Naught; All rights reserved.

No part of this book may be reproduced, scanned, photographed, instagrammed, tweeted, twittered, twatted, tumbled, or distributed in any printed or electronic form without explicit written permission from the author.

Made in the United States of America

ISBN: 978-1-960342-06-5

PRINT EDITION

ONE
JOSEY

@JoseyInHeels: First world problems—when you're thinking about eating your restaurant leftovers all day and you come home and your mam had them for lunch. ☹

@THEBryanLeech to @JoseyInHeels: Maybe. . . don't live with your mam?

"We have something we need to tell you, Josey."

I glanced up from my textbook, finding my mam and dad standing just inside the living room. My father's hands were clasped together in front of him and he wore his favorite green and red striped jumper, his balding gray hair a pile of haphazard fluff atop his head.

It reminded me of the Forgotten Old Word of the Day I had for him: pilgarlic, which was what they termed a bald head in the sixteenth century, because it resembled peeled garlic. We were both obsessed with historical English words nobody used anymore, and created our tradition of Forgotten Old Word of the Day a couple of years ago to celebrate our shared appreciation.

I set my pen down. "Oh, are you two finally going on that trip to Machu Picchu? Because you definitely deserve a break."

"No, love," Mam said, glancing at Dad in a way that appeared nervous. "We aren't. In fact, none of us will be going on any trips for quite some time."

I frowned. "What on earth are you talking about?"

"We're broke," Dad blurted. I'd never seen him look so ashamed. My heart clenched.

"Broke? But how?"

Neither of my parents had what you'd call proper jobs. My dad wrote books about Medieval history, hence his obsession with old words, and my mam taught art classes to the elderly part-time. They both, however, had a large inheritance from my grandparents on both sides. We Kavanaghs came from money, but my parents weren't snobbish, the exact opposite. Compared to most of my relatives, we lived downright humble lives. We didn't flash our cash around, which was why none of this made any sense.

"Your father and I decided to invest our savings in some shares, and well, the company went out of business. We lost everything, which means we're going to have to downsize."

I gaped at them. "You're selling the house?"

"With the way prices are going up and up, especially in this neighborhood, it's a good time to sell," Dad put in. "We could buy a small two-bedroom apartment, then keep the rest of the money to live off until I'm finished my next book."

My worries died down slightly. This wasn't so bad. When you thought about it, we were simply downsizing from a house to an apartment. No big deal.

I exhaled a heavy breath. "Okay, well, I guess it's not the end of the world. This house is too big for the three of us anyway. A two-bedroom will be cozy, and of course I'll take the smaller room."

"Josey," Mam said. She looked like she was steeling herself to continue. "You won't be coming to live with us."

I stared at her. "What do you mean?"

"You're almost twenty-six years old, darling," Dad said. "We both feel it's time you branched out on your own."

As soon as he said it, tears welled in my eyes. "But…but…we're the fearsome threesome," I sputtered. "We stick together. Always." It was a silly little skit we used to do, but I still loved it. It broke my heart to think they wanted rid of me.

Mam's eyes turned sad. "Yes, and we always will be, but you're not a little girl anymore, Josey, and if you don't try going it alone now, you never will."

"We don't want you to be forty and regret spending your entire life with us two old fogeys," said Dad. "Your mam and I have discussed it, and we think this is a good thing. We realize we've been holding you back from living a full life. We want you to enjoy being young."

"I am enjoying being young," I protested, but in the back of my mind I knew it was a lie. I spent most nights sitting in with my parents, watching TV before hitting the hay at the reasonable hour of 9:15 p.m. Maybe that wasn't what most twentysomethings considered living it up, but I was happy.

Wasn't I?

I frowned, feeling sad. Maybe I wasn't living life to the fullest… but on the other hand, sleep was key to good health.

Dad cleared his throat. "Also, we're not going to be able to pay your college fees next term."

Like the flick of a switch, my sadness turned to worry and I jumped to my feet. Not pay my fees? The veterinary program was literally all I had going for me right now. If they took away their support, I'd be aimless again. I couldn't go back to that.

"This is unbelievable," I breathed out.

"Darling, we don't even know if you'll see the course through, and we can't take the chance of spending thousands on fees when next month you might decide you want to become a hairdresser instead."

I scowled at my mother, hurt by her bringing up the fact that I'd switched courses three times already. But I knew becoming a vet was my calling. In my gut, it felt right. "Fine. I'll—I'll manage. And I'll be out of your *hair* within the hour."

With that I grabbed my textbook and stomped out of the room.

"Oh Josey, don't be so melodramatic," Mam called as I climbed the stairs to my room. "We just want what's best for you."

I opened my wardrobe and pulled out my suitcase, then started shoving clothes inside. Rocky, my dog, hopped up onto my bed, stole a pair of socks from the pile, then scarpered. Unfortunately, I didn't have time for a game of chase today.

When I looked up, both my parents stood in the doorway, arms folded, expressions grim. Rocky returned with his mouthful of socks, expression all *why you not chasing me, lady?*

"We didn't mean you had to move out right this minute," Dad said.

"Yes, take a few weeks to find a place," Mam added. "Perhaps there's some student accommodation you could avail of."

I shook my head. "You want me gone, so I'll go. I wouldn't want to hang around, ruining your plans to reinvigorate your sex lives once you're free of the third wheel."

"Josey!" Mam gasped, while Dad's mouth twitched in amusement. That twitch irritated me to no end.

"We can take care of Rocky until you find an apartment," Dad said, and I scowled like I'd never scowled before.

"Oh, you'd just love that, wouldn't you? No way am I leaving Rocky here. He's my dog. You just want to keep him for yourselves."

"We're only trying to make things easier for you."

"Easier? Yeah, right. Well, don't bother. You might have the power to kick me out, but you'll never take Rocky." With that I zipped my suitcase shut. "I'll be back for the rest of my things tomorrow."

* * *

"How are you today, Miss?" asked the handsome chugger.

I struggled down the busy, crowded street with my giant wheelie suitcase in one hand and doggie carrier bag under my arm, the very definition of frazzled.

Charity worker + mugger = chugger.

That's what we called those people in high-vis jackets, who stopped you on the street and asked for your bank details. They were always intimidatingly good looking, as if that might lure plain Janes like me to stop and hand over my well-earned cash. Normally, I'd brush them off, say I was in a hurry and be on my way. But not today. Today I was in the mood to TALK. I stopped walking, leaned my weight on the handle of my suitcase and emitted a long, woe-is-me sigh. Rocky, my trusted min pin Pin companion, sat dutifully in his carrier.

"Do you know what? I'm doing horribly. In fact, I've had a terrible day."

The chugger frowned a perfectly empathetic frown. "I'm sorry to hear that, but if you could spare a moment, I'd like to tell you about the starving children in—"

"My parents are broke and have to sell their house," I continued. "The very same house I grew up in and still live in, by the way. They've known this for months and have only taken it upon themselves to tell me today. *Today.* I mean, I should've been told as soon as it was decided. And to make matters worse, I'm going to have to drop out of the veterinary program I just started, because they can't afford to help me out with the fees and it's a private college so—"

"That's awful," the chugger interrupted, "but I'm sure it'll all work out in the end. Now—"

"No, that's the problem, you see, it won't. Have you any idea how high rent is in Dublin these days? I'll have to pay almost two grand a month for an apartment, and that's if I can even get one with all the competition out there. Did you see that documentary last week about the immigrants paying to live in death trap houses? My goodness, there were ten people in each bedroom, sleeping in bunk beds with only one bathroom between over thirty people. It's just not sanitary. Oh my God, do you think that's where I'll end up? I might not have a choice…"

"Well, it could be worse. Did you know there are almost seven million children suffering from malnutrition in East Africa, including over one million who are severely malnourished and risk dying by the end of the year—"

"Yes, but the problem is, I need my space. I'm not picky, but I simply can't function without at least having my own bedroom. I could try a house share, but what if there's some nut job living there who tries to Single White Female my life? I couldn't be having that. Some girl going around with the same hairdo as me, or turning up wearing the same jacket I bought on sale at M&S. No, that just won't do."

"Miss, if I could just…"

"Or worse yet, they could be a serial killer. Or one of those cannibals who get into people's heads and convince them to let them fry up their private parts with some garlic and onions for dinner. Oh! Can you imagine?" I laughed. "Joke's on them, though. My privates are covered in cobwebs."

"I think I'm going to go now." The chugger turned away.

I realized how self-centered I was being and reached out to catch his arm. "Wait. I'm sorry. Here I am, rambling on about myself and I haven't even asked how your day has been."

"My day would be a lot better if you'd let me talk to you for a moment about the starving children in East Africa," he said kindly. The man obviously had an endless supply of patience.

"Right. Yes. Starving children. Hit me with it."

Ten minutes later, I walked away having filled out a form agreeing to donate five euros a month to the hungry babies. I might be broke and homeless, but they needed the money more than I did. One less latte for me meant 40 children could go to school and drink clean water, how could I say no?

My mind wandered back to earlier, when I'd arrived home from a long day of lectures. I had a happy, carefree smile on my face when my parents had found me in the living room, taking me by surprise. How naïve I'd been.

I was lost in my thoughts all through the tram ride and walk to my best friend, Eilish's house. She and I went through a bit of a rough patch a while back, but we'd since made up. She also had a spare bedroom, so I knew she wouldn't mind if I stayed a few nights. Just until I figured things out. Plus, her little boy loved Rocky, and my dog was fully house-trained, so at least I knew he wouldn't be leaving any unexpected surprises for my hosts.

I lifted my hand and pressed the doorbell. A minute later, I was greeted by Eilish's smiling face.

"Josey! What a nice surprise." Her smile fell when she saw the suitcase and dog carrier. Maybe she wouldn't be so happy to have me as a houseguest after all.

"Hey, uh, you don't happen to mind if Rocky and I stay here for a few nights, do you?"

Her frown transformed into a look of concern as she ushered me inside. "Not at all. What happened?"

"It's a long story."

Eilish nodded. "I'll put the kettle on."

TWO
WILL

@FinleyIRE to @WillthebrickhouseMoore: I think you broke my nose during drills today.
@SeanCassinova to @FinleyIRE and @WillthebrickhouseMoore: Yeah, but did you die?

B ryan looked at me. He took a deep breath, like he wanted to say something, ask a question probably. Instead, he breathed out and shook his head, seeming confused. But also like he thought something was funny.

I understood his amusement. From the outside, I could see how my situation was funny, in a way.

This was the first time I'd been called into the administrative offices for negative reasons. Usually, they pulled me in here when they needed to remind folks that the team still had good guys on it. They'd send me out, dressed in a suit that was too tight, to shake hands and smile all polite. In their defense, I'd never met a suit that fit. They were all too tight.

Bryan made a sound, kinda like a laugh.

I scratched my jaw. "Just say it."

He shrugged, smiling a little. "I have no idea what to say. I'm . . ." He shrugged, laughing again. "I'm shocked. There"—he lifted his hands, like he surrendered—"I admit it. Of all the blokes I know, you were the last one I'd peg for a—" Bryan snapped his mouth shut and dropped his eyes to the conference table between us. I watched him swallow, waiting for him to finish.

He didn't, so I supplied easily, "A pervert?" I wasn't afraid of the word.

"No," he said, now grinning uncomfortably. "Not a pervert."

"You think I'm a pervert."

His smile dropped. He frowned. His eyes cut to mine. "Will, you're not a pervert."

Now I shrugged. "I know what I am," I responded flatly.

He was right. Rationally, I knew I wasn't a pervert. I didn't need him, or anyone else, to tell me that. Nevertheless, I used to think of myself that way, especially in my youth, when I'd *watched* for the first time.

Bryan glared at me, but didn't get a chance to speak because we were interrupted by the entrance of Ronan Fitzpatrick—our team captain—and Brian O'Mahony, head coach. I'd expected more people: lawyers, representatives from human resources, folks from marketing and media services maybe.

Shutting the door as soon as they entered, both men looked grim as they took their seats at the conference table.

"Will. Bryan." Ronan nodded his head at each of us, not quite meeting my eyes. But then I hadn't expected him to. "Thanks for coming."

"To get straight to the point"—Coach leaned back in his seat, and glared at me—"this situation has put us in a real bind, Will. As stated in your contract, your personal life is your own, except where it reflects poorly on the Club, or undermines your image and credibility."

I nodded, ready to accept the consequences of my choices. "I'm ready to step aside."

Ronan and Coach swapped a quick look of confusion, with Ronan asking, "Step aside? You mean, leave the team?"

I nodded again.

"No!" Ronan was looking at me now. "No. Absolutely not. Not an option. With bloody Sean retiring this year, we need you."

I ground my teeth, a flare of guilt burning my esophagus. He was right. They needed me. My actions had brought shame to the team and now they were trapped, stuck with me. I didn't like that.

I felt Coach's stare and met his searching expression. "Will, nobody is talking about cutting you loose. It's damn awkward, but not career ending. Obviously, this isn't the first time one of our players has had an image problem," his eyes flickered to Ronan and Bryan, and then came back to me, turning thoughtful. "Still, I've never seen a frenzy like this before. They're out for blood."

Bryan scoffed. "Such bullshit. It's not like he did anything illegal. Why are the paps making this such a big deal? In my heyday, I'd done a thousand times worse and no one blinked an eye."

Coach looked reluctant to respond, so I said, "Because it's weird. What I've done is weird."

It wasn't illegal. It wasn't unethical. But it *was* unusual.

"You're notoriously private, quiet, stoic in interviews," Ronan said, crossing his arms. "You don't drink, you don't date, you don't go out. You have no social life outside of the Rugby Club and volunteering with the Dream Foundation as far as the media is concerned. You're—well—this makes you look like a loner with a history of—of deviant behavior." After stumbling over the phrase *deviant behavior,* Ronan grimaced and looked to Coach Brian. "I spoke to Annie about it."

Ronan was referring to his wife, Annie Catrel. She was a media consultant to the rich and famous and had helped Ronan rebuild his image a few years ago. Now he was the most vendible member of the team with sponsorship deals for millions.

"What else did Annie say?" Bryan glanced between Ronan and me.

"She said, if Will had a history of being a party boy, man about town, having affairs, no one would care about his—uh—proclivities. But it's the very fact that he's so reserved that's the problem. He's been put on a pedestal by the public, never makes a misstep." Ronan gave me a bracing smile. "She's willing to come in and help. She's in New York right now, but suggested a conference call today whenever you're available."

"I think that's wise," Coach nodded, glancing at his watch as he stood. "I have to meet with the board. They're going to want answers and an action plan."

"Do you want me to be there?" I asked, also standing, wanting to take the fallout burden from my Coach. "I'll take full responsibility, obviously. Deal with all the questions."

Coach gave me a tight smile that looked sincerer than I'd expected and clapped a hand on my shoulder. "You're a good kid, Will. I think I can manage the board. You three"—he glanced at Ronan and Bryan—"call Annie now—while I meet with the higher-ups—and get me that plan."

Coach left, shutting the door firmly behind him while Ronan pulled out his cell, sparing me a sympathetic look.

"Don't worry, mate," he said. "You'll get through this. Annie is a genius."

"It'll all blow over, you'll see. No big deal." Bryan added around a big yawn.

Ronan lifted an eyebrow at Bryan as he brought the cell to his ear. "You were yawning during drills earlier, and for the last few days. Eilish was also dragging when she worked on my shoulder. What's going on? Need a new mattress?"

Eilish was the physiotherapist for the team and Bryan's fiancée. He and Eilish had a young son together named Patrick.

Bryan shook his head, his expression darkening. "No. It's one of Eilish's friends."

"One of Eilish's friends is the reason you haven't been getting sleep?" Ronan smirked.

Bryan rolled his eyes. "She's staying with us and woke the house up at three in the morning, thought she saw a spider and screamed her bloody head off.

Then, the next night, her dog started to bark, woke up the neighbors, so—get this—she makes everyone a batch of cookies and invites them to tea." Bryan pointedly glanced between us, like he was letting this statement sink in. "At three in the bloody morning! The woman is driving me nuts." He shook his head. "Luckily, Patrick slept through the whole thing. Nothing wakes that kid up."

"How long is she staying?" Ronan pulled the phone from his ear and pressed a button on his screen.

"That's the worst part. She was living with her—"

"Hello?" Annie's voice on the other side of the call sounded over the speaker. "Ronan?"

"Hey love. It's me, Bryan, and Will. We're calling about—" he breathed out, frowning, blinking a few times. "We're calling about that thing I discussed with you earlier."

"Yes, I assumed as much."

I'd met Annie several times over the last few years, usually at Club events or parties Ronan had thrown for the team. She'd always been nice. But now, she sounded detached, businessy. I didn't know if this was because we were talking to her in an official capacity or because her opinion of me had changed.

If her opinion had changed, I had no bitterness about it.

"Will, I want you to know that this is a judgment-free zone." Her tone softened a little as she addressed me. "My job here is to help the public see you for the person you are, not the person the media is making you out to be."

"What if I am the person the media is making me out to be?" I glanced at my hands.

This seemed to give Annie pause, and Bryan grumbled something indistinct.

Finally, she said, "The worst of the stories leaked to our agency this morning—which will be printed no later than next week—called you a sexual deviant and implied you prey upon prostitutes, pay them to have sex with each other while you watch. Is that true?"

My hand curled into a fist, a burst of fury igniting in my chest, though I'd never show it.

With a steady voice, I responded, "I've never paid a prostitute. I'd never pay —*would never* prey upon—anyone. As to whether I'm a sexual deviant . . ." I told myself to relax my hand. "I guess it depends on who you ask."

She made a small noise, it sounded sympathetic. "Will, I know you. You are not this person they're making you out to be. If you feel comfortable doing so, please explain the situation to me. Who are the Gallaghers?"

"They're a married couple. I met them on a website. I've been watching them when they—when they're intimate." I wasn't embarrassed for myself. But as I looked at Bryan and Ronan, and I witnessed their discomfort, I was embarrassed for them.

"Okay. How long has this been going on?" Annie didn't sound embarrassed. She sounded professional.

"Two months."

"And was any money ever exchanged?"

"No. It was a mutual arrangement. They enjoyed being watched so we all got something out of it. But there was another couple, before the Gallaghers. The O'Farrells. I didn't pay them either. I've never paid anyone."

"You didn't pay them? But you watched?" Annie sought to clarify.

"Correct. The O'Farrells approached me, wanted me to watch. They actually wanted to pay me at first, but I didn't take the money." I glanced at Ronan, found him studying me with interest. "The arrangement worked for all of us."

Annie paused, then asked, "How long did that go on?"

I hesitated, but then said firmly, "Three years."

"Three years," Annie repeated, like I'd surprised her. "You and this other couple—the O'Farrells—you watched them have sex for three years?"

"Yeah." I looked at Bryan. His hand covered his mouth and he was staring at me with wide eyes. I met his stare evenly. I wasn't ashamed. I defied anyone to find a single exploitative or shameful thing about what we'd done.

They were consenting adults, as was I.

They were already married.

They liked an audience.

I liked to watch.

Annie cleared her throat, her tone becoming official once again. "Where would you do this? Where did this happen?"

"At my apartment."

Bryan's eyebrows jumped, likely because—before he and Eilish got together—Bryan and I shared an apartment.

"What happened? Why did you stop?" Annie asked.

"The O'Farrells moved to Galway."

"Wait, I have a question," Bryan interrupted, looking incredulous. "Why did you say yes in the first place? To the O'Farrells? Why consider it at all?"

Staring at my teammate evenly, I debated how best to answer. *Should I tell them?* I wasn't exactly proud of my past in this regard.

"This is a safe place, Will," Annie said softly. "Any information you can give me about your history, something to give me context, would be helpful."

"I've done it once before," I said on a rush, my stare dropping to my hands. "When I was fifteen."

The room fell silent and I thought I heard Ronan try to quietly clear his throat.

"What happened?" Annie prodded.

I rubbed my forehead. "We had a . . ." I shook my head, disbelieving that this was actually happening, that I was actually saying these words. "The county where I lived had a fall festival."

"In Oklahoma?" Annie was typing or clicking her mouse on the other side of the call.

"That's right. I was in the barn, drinking tequila with a friend, Carlos. A couple came into the pen across from where we were and . . ." *Do I really have to finish?* "Anyway, I couldn't see them clearly, I never found out who they were, but I saw enough, and heard enough. And I liked it."

"That's kind of hot," Bryan muttered, and both Ronan and I tossed him a glare.

"What?" Bryan held his hands up. "It is. And, don't feel badly about it, mate. I don't know a single fifteen-year-old boy who would've done differently."

"Why do you know *any* fifteen-year-old boys?" Ronan teased.

"Fuck off." Bryan rolled his eyes. "You know what I mean."

"Okay. That's helpful, Will. Let's get back to the O'Farrells." Annie was all business again. "After they moved, you looked for a new couple? That's how you found the Gallaghers?" She gave me the sense she was writing something down.

"Not immediately. I had no intentions of finding anyone new. I figured I would just stop. So I moved in with Bryan. Sharing a place, having a roommate, meant I wasn't thinking about it as much. But when he moved in with Eilish and Patrick, I started looking for a new couple."

Bryan made a small noise that sounded concerned, whispering, "Christ. I had no idea."

I shrugged. "It's not a big deal."

"If you needed someone to stay with you, a—a sponsor or something, I totally get that." Bryan's usual carefree expression was replaced with genuine concern.

"I don't get it," Ronan cut in. "Is this your kink, then? You like watching people? Why not just watch porn?"

I shook my head. "Pornography and the porn industry objectifies and takes advantage of emotionally unstable and underprivileged populations. It's an exploitative industry and I won't support it."

Ronan blinked at me, flinching like I'd tossed water in his face. "You—you don't watch *any* porn? Ever?"

"Never," I said resolutely.

His stare flickered over me, as though he suspected something. "Are you . . . are you a virgin?"

"Ronan," Annie chided, "that is none of your business."

"I'm not a virgin," I answered anyway, a rare bitterness slicing from my abdomen to my sternum; I hid that too while I avoided Bryan's stare. He knew part of my history, not all of it but definitely enough to have an opinion about my past.

"So you don't like having sex?" Ronan sounded honestly curious. "Just watching other people do it?"

"Maybe he had a bad experience, and doesn't like women anymore." Bryan's tone was casual, but the grain of truth behind the words had me glaring at him again.

"Bryan Leech!" Annie's tone was now stern. "You leave William alone."

"It's fine." I met Bryan's pointed stare calmly. "I don't mind. But before I address that statement, let me ask you this: how many women have you slept with, Bryan?"

Bryan winced a little, not answering.

"And—if you can remember each of those women, each of their names—can you honestly tell me that most of the time, with most of those women, you weren't leading them on? You weren't taking advantage of your fame and position to exploit them? Take what you wanted without giving them a second thought?"

My friend looked ashamed and his eyes fell.

"So, yeah. I liked having sex. But not enough to lie to another person in order to have it."

Bryan mumbled something like "I've never *lied*" but didn't lift his attention from the table.

"What about a relationship? A partner?" Ronan still looked and sounded confused. "Something committed."

I hesitated, because I had very specific ideas about what I wanted from a partner, but now wasn't the time to get into that.

Finally, I settled on, "I've been on dates."

"And…?" Ronan pressed.

"I'm not going to sleep with a woman until I know it's serious. It's never been serious. Like I said, I won't lead a woman on just to have sex with her."

"But you wouldn't need to lead anyone on and you wouldn't need to lie." This objection came from Annie. "You make it sound like all women are cow-eyed milkmaids being led around by sinister male abusers. There's plenty of women who like a good no-strings-attached arrangement just as much as Bryan did once upon a time. Give us ladies a little credit for knowing our own minds."

"Yeah"—Ronan gestured to the phone—"listen to Annie. There's a ton of other blokes out there having good—*fully consensual*—times with the ladies. If no woman wanted recreational sex then recreational sex wouldn't exist."

I shook my head, because I'd had this conversation with myself a hundred times and—based on my experiences—always arrived at the same conclusion. Voyeurism, with consenting *married* adults was the least exploitative solution, the least likely to cause harm or disappointment to anyone involved.

"We're not *other blokes,* Ronan"—I couldn't help but argue—"and you know it. We're famous athletes. There's always going to be an unavoidable imbalance in the power dynamic. With that comes additional responsibilities, not a free pass."

"I agree with Will," Bryan said unexpectedly, drawing our attention. His expression was sober.

"You can't be serious." Ronan glared at our teammate.

"I am serious. If I knew then what I know now, the people I've hurt . . ." His eyes clouded and he appeared to be frustrated by a memory.

"We're getting off track." Annie sighed, and I heard her typing on her computer. "And as much as I fundamentally disagree with Will about the agency of women—"

"It's not about the agency of women," I tried to explain. "It's about—"

"Regardless, that's not the central issue." Some irritation bled into her tone, which she quickly masked as she continued, "Your image is the issue, and how to—moving forward—avoid any further missteps. So I have to ask, Will, you said earlier that having a roommate helped you not think about it, helped you abstain from couple-watching. Do you need a roommate now? To help you from seeking out the Gallaghers or another couple?"

I thought about that, and my instinct was to say no. I had no desire to seek out the Gallaghers. They'd broken the rules.

And I wasn't a child. I didn't need a babysitter.

But then I swallowed the instinctual response and I forced myself to admit that lately things had spiraled out of my control. I thought the Gallaghers and I were on the same page, I was wrong. Aideen Gallagher had refused to respect my boundaries, but I never should have sought them out to begin with.

If Bryan had still lived with me, I probably wouldn't have.

The truth was, even now, I was tempted to seek out a new couple. Since calling things off with Aideen and Kean Gallagher, I'd been fighting the urge on a daily basis. Watching the O'Farrells and the Gallaghers had ignited—or reignited—something in me I couldn't ignore.

I liked to watch.

And it would be so easy to hop online and make it happen. I *wanted* it, more than just an outlet—a safe, well-defined means—for sexual satisfaction.

But voyeurism wasn't an option anymore, not if it brought shame to the team. And I knew that if I had someone at the apartment, someone to keep me focused on what was important, hold me accountable, then I wouldn't look for another couple.

I would stop.

A babysitter . . . I grimaced.

"It can be a temporary arrangement," Annie suggested, "just until the situation can be managed. Maybe a life coach, someone who will check in on you, keep you to a schedule, keep you busy and distracted."

"There's no shame in asking for help." Bryan's statement had me looking at him.

Before I could catch myself, I said, "I'm not ashamed."

"We'll find him a roommate." Ronan said this like the matter was settled and rubbed his hand over his face. "Now what can we do about the rest of it? According to Annie, the headlines that'll be printed next week will call him the *Perverted Flanker*."

"I have some ideas." Annie ceased typing. "I'd like to try to find the prostitute who sold this story to the papers in the first place. If Will is telling us the truth, then her story is false. Perhaps we can convince her to retract it and—"

"No, I don't want to do that," I interrupted firmly. I wanted to put this behind me. I didn't want anyone digging around trying to find the woman. It just felt like prolonging the torture. Once a story was out, it stained your reputation. A retraction wasn't going to fix that.

"But it could really help our cause," Annie argued.

"I said no," I replied, holding firm.

There was moment of awkward silence before Annie got back to business. "Okay, well moving on, the best way to improve a person's character in the public eye is to borrow someone else's credibility. So, Will, how do you feel about dating a few supermodels, musicians, and actresses?"

I grimaced. "I won't lie."

Ronan grunted. "What are you talking about?"

"I won't pretend to be something I'm not."

Ronan stared at me in plain disbelief. "You're going to tell me that you have something against dating supermodels?"

"No." *They have something against dating me.* "I've gone on a few dates with women who are celebrities, and it never worked."

Based on previous experience, I was not the kind of long-term partner a supermodel, musician, or an actress wanted.

"Then it wouldn't be a lie, you've done it before." Ronan's tone was clipped, like he was losing patience. "You just have to take them out to dinner."

But it would be a lie. It would be dishonest because I wouldn't date someone I had no intention of starting a relationship with, or vice versa. And I didn't want to. I would be using them to erase a perceived stain on my reputation, and that didn't sit right with me.

"Ronan, I can't use a person like that. I—"

The team captain cut off my protest, holding his hand up. "Holy shit, William. Will you listen to yourself? You're dating supermodels and that is that!"

THREE
JOSEY

@JoseyInHeels: Quite like a dog, I sweat through the pads of my feet. #interestingfactsaboutjosey
@ECassChoosesPikachu to @JoseyInHeels: That's hot #punintended
@JoseyInHeels to ECassChoosesPikachu: On the bright side, I never have to worry about armpit stains #alsohot

"I won't lie, it's been a stressful week." I sighed as I sat down to dinner with Eilish and Bryan.

Patrick was at the other end of the table, discreetly feeding his peas to Rocky.

"Yeah, you must be tired," Bryan commented dryly.

He was obviously being sarcastic, since I'd woken him up several times this week. But it wasn't my fault there'd been a spider the size of my hand on the ceiling. The next night the neighbors made Rocky bark like mental with their vacuuming, though why they were doing housework at three in the morning is anyone's guess. And let's not forget the fact that Eilish had a full-length mirror at the very top of her staircase. I went down last night for a glass of water and got the fright of my life on the way back when I saw a woman standing there. I screamed at the top of my lungs, like any normal person would. And yes, okay, it was merely my own reflection looking back at me, but how was I supposed to know that?

Needless to say, Bryan's hospitality was wearing thin. Not that it had been very plentiful to begin with. I knew he wasn't my biggest fan, and I didn't blame him. I was a babbling, flustered mess around handsome men.

Okay, sorry. That's not precisely true. I was a babbling, flustered mess around people I didn't know. All people, handsome or not. I always managed to say something to make everyone feel uncomfortable. It was my superpower.

Here I'd known Bryan almost a full year and was only now getting used to talking like a normal human being around him.

I cleared my throat, glancing at Eilish. "I spent this morning searching for studio apartments to rent. I also applied for a bunch of jobs online, so fingers crossed I'll get some interviews."

"Oh, I'm sure you will," she reassured.

"How are you with interviews though?" Bryan questioned doubtfully, and Eilish lightly elbowed him in the side.

"Don't listen to him," she said, her smile strained.

"No, it's fine. I prefer you to be honest with me. Besides, I know I'm not the best at, um, creating a rapport. Now, if only I could *rap* my way to a rapport. Then I'd get all the jobs!" I grinned, hoping to make them smile and remind them of my better than average rhyming abilities, which also happened to be one of my top three endearing qualities. The other two were my dog and my ability to do complicated maths without scrap paper.

"You just need to practice. Everybody gets nervous for interviews."

"Josey gets a little more than nervous, Eilish," Bryan said, ever the truth teller. His expression was almost sympathetic as he went on, "No offence, but sometimes you—inadvertently I'm sure—insult people. And you can come across a little overenthusiastic. When we first met I thought you were a rabid fan who would've sold her grandmother to be seen with a celebrity."

"Oh please, you're hardly a celebrity. You're a famous sportsperson, you're not Benedict Cumberbatch," Eilish teased, and he shot her a narrow-eyed half-smile.

"As I was saying"—Bryan brought his gaze back to me—"what we need to do is find you a job where you don't have to interview."

"Ha-ha!" I smacked the table and snort-laughed, causing Patrick and Rocky to jump. To be fair, I always snorted when I laughed. It was just my laugh, nothing I could do about it!

Still laughing, I sent Patrick an apologetic smile. "Sorry, Patrick. It's just, who's ever heard of a job where they cut out the interview part and just skip straight to the *Congratulations, you're hired* part? Sign me up."

Bryan's eyes narrowed thoughtfully as he ate a bite of chicken, his gaze on me. And then he blinked, as something like an idea or a realization formed behind his eyes.

I tensed. "Why are you looking at me like that?"

"I think I have it," he pointed his fork at me in a way that had me wanting to lift my plate to protect myself. Bryan continued excitedly, "I actually might have a job for you. I'm just trying to decide if you're the right person."

"I'm the right person," I enthused, maybe a little too fervently. "And if I'm not, I'll change so that I am the right person. Seriously, you know how much I need a job. I don't want to drop out of college or defer my course. I'll literally do anything if it means I can earn enough money to pay my way."

Bryan pointed his fork at me again, this time a little less aggressively. "You see, this is what I'm talking about. You come across desperate."

"But I am desperate."

"That's beside the point. If I put you forward for this "job," you can't act like that. Think of the mantra, *be yourself*, and then do the exact opposite."

"Bryan!" Eilish hissed.

"What? She said she wanted honesty."

"Well, you could be a little nicer about it, and why did you put bunny ears around the word 'job'?" She sounded suspicious.

Bryan lifted a shoulder, not looking at either of us when he replied, "It's an unconventional setup."

"As in?"

"William needs a, uh, roommate."

"William Moore? Your teammate who you used to live with? The American?" I asked curiously. I'd never actually met the Oklahoman before, but I'd seen him at one or two events I attended with Eilish. He was always so reserved and polite, but not very approachable. I only saw him speak with other players on the team.

Bryan nodded. "Yep, that's the one."

"Why does Will need a roommate?" Eilish asked. "And more to the point, how is being a roommate a job?"

"Well, it's actually more of a babysitting position."

"Will has kids? How did I not know this?" Eilish exclaimed, dropping her fork onto her plate.

"No, he doesn't have kids." Bryan rubbed the spot between his eyebrows and glanced at his son. Patrick's plate was empty, though I suspected my dog had eaten half of it. "Hey buddy, why don't you open that new Lego set, eh?"

"Can I have cake, too?" Patrick asked as Bryan ushered him into the living room.

Bryan mumbled something, and then I heard, "... I have to check with your mam."

Eilish and I shared a look—she seemed to be mostly amused—and when Bryan returned, he took his seat and exhaled before speaking. "Will is the one who needs to be babysat."

Eilish frowned. "I don't understand."

"He needs a companion, sort of like a sober companion, to keep him on the straight and narrow."

"Okay, this is just getting more confusing." Eilish wrinkled her nose. "Will barely even drinks."

"He has . . . other vices." Bryan's eyes were fastened to his water glass.

"Such as?" Eilish nudged him again gently.

Finally, he sighed, and spoke mostly to himself, "I guess you two are gonna read all about it in the papers anyway."

Both Eilish and I exchanged another glance, this time she didn't look amused. She looked worried.

"Will is into voyeurism." Bryan blurted. "He's been watching other people have sex for years and now some gossip journalists have gotten their hands on the story. It's all going to come out sometime this week, so we're preemptively working on damage control. I was pulled into the meeting today because we're friends." Bryan, still not looking at either of us, crossed his arms; he looked super uncomfortable and his voice pitched higher. "He's not a weirdo or a pervert. It's just his thing. But he wants to stop, so he needs a roommate. He needs someone to live with him, and keep an eye on his behavior, and stop him from making any unwise decisions."

"Oh my goodness," Eilish breathed after several long seconds. "That's so bizarre. I never would've guessed. He's just such a…such a gentleman."

"Being a voyeur doesn't mean you can't be a gentleman," Bryan countered defensively.

"Well, yeah, but it's still surprising. Will never struck me as the kinky sort."

I wasn't surprised like Eilish, maybe because I didn't know him. But I did have so many questions—SO MANY QUESTIONS!—but I daren't ask them. I might've been more comfortable around Bryan now, but I wasn't *that* comfortable.

I cleared my throat, folding my hands on my lap. "So, um, what would the job entail exactly?"

He eyed me speculatively. "You'd have to move in with him, live there in his apartment, check up on him a few times a week, and keep an eye on his behavior. I guess you'll need to check his internet history, since apparently he finds couples online to, you know, *watch*."

"Sounds pretty full on, like a live-in nanny for grown-ups," Eilish commented, and I got to thinking.

Was I the right person for this? It sounded like it'd take a pretty ballsy gal to lay down the law for a 6'5" rugby player who was more than twice my width.

But…but I needed a job.

Plus, this wasn't just a job.

This was a job *and* a place to live.

It's perfect!

But also intimidating. Will was a stranger. A handsome stranger, hot in a wholesome farm boy who could throw you around a haystack in the barn—or the bedroom—without even breaking a sweat sort of way. Plus, a gentleman. Plus, a talented and dedicated professional athlete. Plus, from what everyone said, just a super nice guy.

Plus, he's kinky.

The thought made me smirk. I quickly rolled my lips between my teeth to hide it.

I'd be nuts not to fancy him a little bit already, even though we hadn't even officially met. If I fancied someone, having an ordinary, grown-up conversation was impossible. This was true for me of both women and men. If I met a woman and I thought she would make a great friend, then I was most certainly doomed to say something horrible.

As an example, when I first met Eilish I asked if I could climb her (because she was so tall).

See?

Horrible.

Still, this was too good an opportunity to pass up. I had to at least explore the possibility.

I fiddled with the hem of my shirt. "Do you think Will would be open to meeting with me? Obviously, there'd have to be an interview. No getting around that. I'm more than willing to help, but he would need to decide if I'm someone he could live with," I finished and tried not to look directly at Bryan when I said it.

"I'll run the idea by him." Bryan eyed me, his smile small and hopeful. "If he's agreeable, we'll set up a meeting. You two could go for coffee and have an informal interview."

I nodded, nervous butterflies fizzing in my stomach already.

But I tried to take some of Bryan's advice and endeavored to sound cool as I responded, "Sounds like a plan."

Now I just needed to figure out how I was going to convince William Moore I was right for the job, and not a ridiculous bobble-headed moron.

Easy, right?

* * *

Two days later, I sat waiting in Bewley's on Grafton Street to meet William. It was a large, busy café, so at least if things got weird—I mean, *when* things got weird—there'd be distractions. I was upstairs beside an open window, through which you could hear a guitarist playing an instrumental piece as he busked down on the street. I took this as a good sign. It meant that any awkward silences wouldn't be quite so punctuated.

Not that I ever really left room for silence. I was more inclined to ramble about any subject that popped into my head. Since I was trying my best to be "normal" and not come across "desperate" as Bryan so kindly put it, I had a list of subjects that were off limits.

1. How Rocky once got diarrhea and pooed all over my bedroom.
2. How I had to clean up said poo.
3. How I prefer to use men's deodorant because it works better, but also because it allows me to pretend there's a man in my life.
4. My favorite brand of bandages.
5. That I once had a unibrow, but through the miracle of laser hair removal, I now have two eyebrows instead.

And yes, all of these were topics I brought up in recent conversations, effectively killing the atmosphere.

It was an illness.

I wondered if many other people felt this way, or if it was just me. Was I somehow defective, or did everyone get anxious in social situations? And if everyone did, how come my resultant verbal dysentery was so pronounced? Did I have some sort of vociferous diarrhea gene whereas others had vociferous constipation?

To be honest, I'd take constipation over diarrhea any day of the week. All you have to do is eat prunes and BAM! However, with diarrhea, there's nothing you can do to stem the flow . . . as it were.

But enough about that.

When I spotted William Moore walking up the stairs I stood immediately, thinking he might not know me on sight. He wore a navy shirt that looked like it barely fit around his arms, shoulders, and chest, gray slacks and brown shoes. They looked high quality, probably Italian. I wished I'd made a bit more of an effort to dress nicely, but I'd come straight from my intern position and was in my veterinary scrubs and oversized knit jumper, my hair a knot atop my head.

Anyway, standing was my first mistake, because my leg bashed off the table, knocking over the glass of water the waitress brought me. I winced, both at the pain in my leg and the mess I'd made of the table. Will's eyes came to mine when he heard the kerfuffle. I plastered on a friendly expression and tried to act calm.

"You must be Josey," he said with a small smile as he approached. Even though it was small, it set my heart pounding. He seemed completely confident and at ease. I hadn't even opened my mouth and already I was failing.

"Yes, I am she." I nodded. "Sorry about the water. I'm all fingers and thumbs. That's not a euphemism by the way, hahaha."

Oh, man. This was bad.

At least I managed not to open with *So, voyeurism, eh? What's all that about?* But really, my inner pervert was intrigued. She wanted to know where, why, and with whom he engaged in such activities, but I guessed quizzing him on kink right now wouldn't work in my favor.

Will's mouth did a weird, non-smiling quirk thing, but I couldn't tell if it was a good or a bad sign. Probably bad.

"Didn't think it was," he replied, and I swallowed.

"Oh my goodness, I've offended you, haven't I? It was supposed to be a joke, but sometimes I have a weird sense of humor. Anyway, just pretend I never said it." I held my hand out to him. "I'm Josey Kavanagh and it's a pleasure to meet you."

He took my normal sized hand and shook it in his giant one. "It's a pleasure to meet you, too. I'm Will. Bryan said you're a friend of Eilish?"

"Yes, me and Eilish go way back to our days in the 'hood."

Silence.

Stop trying to make jokes, Josey. They're going down like a glass of cold vomit.

"She's my physio." His eyes got all crinkly and I wondered if maybe he had a soft spot for her. Eilish had her fair share of admirers, so it wouldn't surprise me if he did. She was kind, strong, and smart, beautiful, easy to talk to.

"Yeah, she's great with her hands." I nodded and internally winced. Usually, I had a ratio of three okay statements for every awkward one. Now every single sentence coming out of my mouth was bad.

William—er, Will—didn't seem bothered though, or maybe he was just good at hiding it.

"Can I take your order?" the waitress asked, having approached the table, and I was glad for the distraction. She used a cloth to dry up the spilled water as I replied, "Yes, I'll have tea."

"Black coffee, thank you," Will said.

The waitress left, and Will held my gaze for a second. His eyes drifted along my forehead, then travelled down to my chin. He blinked, his eyebrows inching together.

I stiffened. "Do I have something on my face?"

He shook his head. "No."

I frowned, touching my chin. "Are you sure? You can tell me."

"No."

"No, you're not going to tell me? Or no, I have nothing on my face?" Now I was searching my cheeks with my fingers.

"No, you have nothing on your face." His eyebrows did this odd thing, where they came together and then apart, and then together again, like he was trying to clear his expression.

I squinted at him. "In my teeth? There's something in my teeth." I picked up a spoon and checked the reflection. Unfortunately, it was concave, so I was upside down.

"There's nothing in your teeth." His calm voice held a hint of something I couldn't identify. When I glanced at him again his gaze was still moving over my face in a peculiar way. So I dropped the spoon, unhappy with its distorted reflective qualities, and picked up the knife.

"There's nothing on your face, I promise. It's just—"

"What?" I wiped my nose with the back of my hand because—oh God—I probably had a hanging snot.

"It's just . . . interesting." He said this haltingly and then winced slightly, giving me the impression he hadn't meant to say the word 'interesting.'

I blinked at my miniature reflection in the knife, and then at him. "I beg your pardon?"

"You've got"—he lifted his chin towards my face and breathed out, sounding frustrated—"you have interesting features."

I stiffened.

I knew I wasn't the most conventionally attractive flower in the garden—more like a thistle than a rose—but it wasn't a nice feeling when someone pointed it out. When I was younger I'd get upset, but these days I tried to own it.

Considering him, and his conventionally attractive *everything*, I crossed my arms. "My friend Alice from school used to say I looked like a bug."

Will's brows drew together, like my statement irritated him. "No. You remind me of those big eyes paintings from that movie. Ever seen it?"

"Can't say that I have," I mumbled quietly. *Big eyes?*

I had no idea what paintings he was talking about or what movie. I also didn't want to know, because if they were ugly or weird looking, that meant he thought I was too, and I'd rather live in blissful ignorance of the extent to which my features were "interesting," *thankyouverymuch*.

The waitress came with our drinks and I busied myself adding sugar and milk as I tried to get the conversation back on course. "So, about this job, what sort of person are you looking for?"

Will thought on it a moment, then answered, "I need someone who's honest."

I waited for him to continue, widening my eyes. When he didn't, I prompted, "That's it? Just honest? That's the only requirement?"

He stared at me, as though considering, or maybe struggling to find the right words. Maybe he was one of those verbally constipated people. I noted his eyes were gray-ish green, the color reminded me of granite for some reason.

Abruptly, he said, "Living with Bryan worked because he was sober and attending AA. He had this rigid routine and I followed it. But then he left to move in with Eilish and things went downhill." He glanced at his hands, like they held a memory.

Studying him, I nodded. "So, you need someone like Bryan? Who doesn't drink, smoke or do drugs, who goes to bed at a reasonable hour and gets up at 5:00 a.m. to work out?" Because if so, I was *not* that person.

I loved wine. We were in a relationship.

I did exercise, but mostly (only) because of my dog.

I'd also indulged in a little marijuana every now and again. In fact, my parents were the only ones I smoked it with. Most people thought this was weird, I know, but my dad was an intellectual and my mam was an artist. They claimed it opened their minds, helped them access a higher plane of thinking, but really, they just liked getting high.

Honestly? I liked it because of the snacks. My dad couldn't cook a real meal to save his life, but he made *the best* snacks whenever he was high. My favorite was his fondue. Sometimes I'd pretend to smoke just to get the snacks.

And last but not least, I wasn't a morning person. My alarm going off at 7:00 a.m. was my least favorite part of the day.

"No, I don't expect you to be Bryan." William's eyes seemed to smile, but the rest of his expression was unchanged. "Honesty a-and boundaries." He took another deep breath, his gaze moving over my shoulder. "Someone to"—he frowned, again looking frustrated—"someone to help me resist my worst impulses, and check in on me, hold me accountable." A dark cloud seemed to form behind his stare as he brought it back to me.

"Can you explain that a bit more? What do you mean, 'check in on me'?"

He glanced over my head, squinting. "Be present. Ask me about my day, tell me about yours. Ask me what I've been doing, if I've been tempted to seek out company." His eyes came back to mine. "That kind of thing."

"So, I'll be like a mish-mash between a therapist and a babysitter." *Blarg!* I regretted the words as soon as they left my mouth.

But he nodded, not looking at all perturbed by my description. "Yeah, basically."

"And what if you are tempted?"

"Distract me. Remind me of all the reasons why it's a bad idea, my responsibility to the team, the ramifications to my career." His gaze flickered over me, and he added quickly, "If you think you can do that then the job is yours."

The job is mine? *What??*

YES!

Except . . .

My stomach flipped over.

I really wanted to lie and tell him I was sure I could do that, but I had to be honest. "Cards on the table, I might not be the person you're looking for."

He sat back, his gorgeous head tilting to the side as though he were studying me, his delicious voice a deep rumble. "How so?"

"I'm messy and disorganized. I drink too much wine and I oversleep. I'm not great with boundaries, frequently overstepping, or just saying absolutely the wrong thing. I never seem to know when something is or isn't my business, offering opinions when I should hold my tongue. I also have a dog. He's a bit of a handful."

"I like dogs," Will said, his eyes seeming to smile again. "On the farm we had lots of working dogs."

Rocky was about as far from a working dog as you could get. He was a ball of pampered, energetic mischief, but I wasn't going to get into that right now.

"The fact is, in all honesty, because I have a real problem with honesty—in that I'm always honest and frequently to my detriment, like now—I would absolutely love to take you up on this offer, but I think there are people out there far better suited. You'll have a much higher chance of success if you choose someone else." I paused to give a soft laugh. "Someone who's the opposite of me, basically."

Will didn't say anything for a moment, studying my face in a way that made me start to feel self-conscious again.

Then he said, "You're hired."

My brows shot right up into my forehead. "Have you listened to a single word I've said? I'd make a terrible sober companion, or well, voyeurism abstinence sponsor, I guess."

"I disagree."

What?

I stared at him, incredulous. "Why on earth do you want to hire me?"

"You'll tell me the truth even if it won't benefit you to do so." His gaze was steady. "That's what I need."

Mouth agape, I blinked. Well. . . *wow.*

Did you hear that? I'm what he needs!

And I'd told him the truth, so maybe I was right for this job after all. I felt like doing a little fist pump of joy but managed to keep it at bay.

I lifted my tea and took a sip, and then glanced at William. *Play it cool.* "So. . . the apartment, it's in the city?"

He nodded. "Two-bedroom apartment, you'll get you, a large balcony. There's a communal garden area where your dog can play. Eilish said, uh, you're a student?"

"Yes," I answered distractedly, not sure I believed what was happening. "I'm training to become a vet. Animals are my passion. I have classes every day, late on Tuesdays and Thursdays."

His eyes did that smiling thing again, where his face didn't move otherwise. "A vet? You must study a lot."

"It's going to take a couple of years, but I'm determined to have my own veterinary surgery one day." I was still focused on my jumble of thoughts, which was probably why I was actually answering questions and carrying on a conversation like a normal human.

"That's your dream?" He asked softly, his voice quiet.

"Pretty much." I shrugged, mentally calculating how soon I could move into his place. Also—*maybe distraction is the key! I'm actually doing good with the casual chat. Good job me!*

A pause in conversation ensued, quiet falling between us, but I barely noticed. It was highly out of character.

William broke it, leaning his elbows on the table. "My dad and grandpa taught me all about animal husbandry. If you ever have any questions, feel free to ask."

"I think I'll be sticking with cats and dogs. I don't have the stomach to be an agricultural vet." I eyeballed his forearms. They were—in a word—luscious. *Am I really going to be living with this guy? This hot, seemingly unflappable voyeur of epic attractiveness?* The idea of someone like him watching other people have sex was…interesting to say the least.

"It's not for the faint of heart." William made a small—and I mean very small—sound of amusement, and I realized something about him: William Moore was exceptionally stoic. He didn't talk much. And when he did, he said very little.

And me, being the curious sort, couldn't let him get away with being vague. "I feel like there's a story there."

"The procedure for insemination . . ." He rubbed his jaw, leaning back in his chair, and lifted his cup with a whisper of a smirk, ". . . is one lesson I could never unlearn."

I let out a loud snort-laugh, then slapped my hand over my mouth. I knew my run of ladylike behavior was too good to be true, but then I looked at William and he was laughing, too.

Like, *actually* laughing.

It made me feel less embarrassed about the snort.

"Some people might consider exposure like that a form of child abuse," I said.

"I was never the same after." William grinned.

Whoa. Nice teeth.

I stared for a few seconds at his teeth, wondering if I'd ever see them again. But then I managed to shake myself before it got weird and glanced at the time on my phone. Inwardly, I sighed. I had to get moving if I was going to make my next class.

"Well, it was great to meet you. And I'd love to accept the job if you still want me. I won't be offended if you change your mind." I hitched my bag up on my shoulder and stood, reaching out to shake William's hand.

Once again, I noted the size of it as it dwarfed mine, and it's not like I had small hands. Nevertheless, his was big and solid and warm.

William looked me in the eye, his steady gaze somehow calming. "The job is yours, Josey. I'm not going to change my mind."

Well, how about that?

I'd actually managed to make an okay first impression for once. Eat your heart out, Mam and Dad. I'd just secured a job and a place to live.

For the first time in a long time, everything was coming up Josey.

FOUR
WILL

@SeanCassinova: Today is **@RonanFitz's** birthday? What do you get for a man his age?
@WillthebrickhouseMoore to @SeanCassinova and @RonanFitz: I don't know, but I guess you'll be able to tell us in two months.
@SeanCassinova to @WillthebrickhouseMoore and @RonanFitz: You, sir, are a wanker.

I watched Josey Kavanagh go as she navigated the close-set tables. Twisting to the side to avoid hitting a chair, she hit the chair anyway, and then turned and apologized to the chair's occupant.

The man paid her no attention at first, giving her a short glance over his shoulder. But then Josey kept talking and laughed at something she said. I heard her little snort. Eventually, the man gave her his attention, but he looked irritated by her interruption.

She kept talking.

I took a swallow of my coffee as I watched this exchange. She continued speaking, apparently ignorant to the fact that she was being impolite by inserting herself into the strangers' conversation.

Josey Kavanagh was weird.

My cell vibrated in my pocket and I pulled it out, glancing at the screen. Seeing who it was, I swiped to the right and brought it to my ear.

"Bryan."

"Will. How did it go?" My teammate sounded worried. "Should I apologize?"

My attention moved back to Josey where she stood at the table of strangers. Her sharp cheekbones were flushed pink, she'd rolled her wide lips between her teeth, and she was waving goodbye to them, all the while talking. The couple at the table shared a look of confusion.

I turned the handle of my coffee cup toward me. "I hired her."

Bryan made a choking noise. "You- you what?"

"I hired her."

Bryan was quiet while I followed the progress of Josey's departure. She kept tucking non-existent hairs behind her ears like she didn't know what to do with her hands.

My decision had been uncharacteristically hasty, but I wasn't at all worried. She was what I needed, even though I hadn't realized it until moments ago. She was perfect.

After speaking with Ronan, Coach, and Bryan, I'd resigned myself to a roommate who was something like the prototypical strict Catholic nun. Someone who would hold me accountable with check-ins and a schedule, who was focused on discipline of character rather than distraction.

Josey Kavanagh was not that person, and yet I was certain she would be infinitely better—more effective—than the alternative. She was charming, disarming, distracting. I had no doubt she would be honest and direct, but it wouldn't be brutal. I also didn't doubt that she would hold me accountable, but being accountable to Josey wouldn't be something to dread.

It would be like being accountable to a puppy. I wouldn't want to let her down, I wouldn't want to disappoint her.

"Well . . . that's amazing." Bryan breathed out, as though he'd been holding the breath for a while. "Wait, you're not doing this as a favor to me, are you? Because, as much as I appreciate it—and believe me, I really do—don't throw yourself on the Josey sword unless you actually want to hire her. I mean, I can't wait for her to move out, but I also can't ask you to make a pity hire on my account."

"It's not a pity hire." My shoulders tensed, not liking the way he spoke about her. "I . . ."

"What?"

She *was* strange. I hadn't wanted to admit it, but her features were also unusual. Striking. Her brow, cheekbones, and square jaw were pronounced; her eyes huge; and her mouth was impossibly wide. She had no single defining feature, with every part of her face too big, exaggerated, except her nose. Her nose was perfectly normal, and therefore too small in comparison.

I didn't think she looked like a bug, but—reluctantly—I understood the origin of the comparison.

"She's honest." *I feel comfortable around her.*

This was miraculous. The more I thought about it, the more I decided it was likely because she reminded me of my oldest brother, Thomas. He was always making jokes, always trying to make people laugh, see them smile. Sometimes he succeeded, sometimes he failed spectacularly, but despite his flops, he always tried.

Like a puppy.

Bryan made a sound of amusement. "Yes. She is. Too honest. But"—he rushed to add, maybe sensing I was going to argue with him—"if you're happy with her for the job, then I'm happy for you. I'm also happy to give Ronan a heads-up. He's right here."

"Sure." I narrowed my eyes as Josey walked out of the door, turning to the right. A half second later, she walked back in front of the door, heading left.

I smiled.

"This is incredible," Bryan muttered, giving me the impression he was speaking mostly to himself.

His incredulity was amusing. "Why are you having such a hard time with this, Bry?"

He hesitated, then made a sound like he was clearing his throat or coughing. "I have to point this out—and don't take this the wrong way—you avoid women."

I made a face at that. "No."

"Yes, you do."

I grunted.

"I understand, I do. After what you told me about your ex—"

I grunted again. He knew I didn't like to talk about Eve.

Bryan continued, "Stop making that noise and listen. I understand why—after what happened with your ex—and I was proud of you when you tried dating that tennis player a few years ago. What ever happened there?"

I didn't respond immediately, considering my words. I'd thought dating another athlete would work. Neither of us would be at a disadvantage, we would both understand the demands of each other's job, there was no danger of an imbalance in the power dynamic. I was right about my assumptions, except it didn't work.

Finally, I responded to Bryan's question with the truth. "You can't be a celebrity if no one can see you."

"What does that mean?"

"Exactly what I told Ronan at the meeting with Coach, I can't date celebrities—athletes included." I hated media attention, parties, movie premieres, award shows, and large gatherings, and those events were the lifeblood of supermodels, musicians, famous athletes, and actors.

"Well, ever since the tennis player, with the exception of a very few, you do avoid women. So, you have to give me a minute here to deal with my astonishment that you want to move Josey in."

"I don't avoid women."

"Will, come on! Every party, social event, meetup of any kind, you're hiding behind me, or Sean, or Ronan. Or you're lurking against the wall, hiding in the shadows. If the ladies approach, you disappear."

"That's different," I grumbled. "Those aren't ladies, those are packs of ladies."

Bryan burst out laughing and I ground my teeth.

Let him laugh.

I knew firsthand, people acted differently when in packs, surrounded by a group with like-characteristics. They were more aggressive, bolder but not braver, thoughtless, behaved in ways they wouldn't normally on their own. I didn't subscribe to this group mentality, this diffusion of responsibility, always doing my utmost to be considerate of each individual, even when surrounded by others similar to me.

I followed rules, not peer pressure.

"Besides"—I added, cutting into Bryan's laughter—"I don't think of Josey as a woman." I'd never been as comfortable with a new person as I had been with Josey just moments ago—none of my teammates, not at first—and *especially* not a female.

His laugh tapered off. After a brief pause, he said thoughtfully, "I guess I see what you mean. An annoying little sister maybe, but definitely not a woman."

A little sister. Yeah.

Or a puppy.

* * *

From: William Moore
To: Josey Kavanagh
Subject: Details and timeline

~~Dear~~ Josey,

Thanks for meeting with me yesterday. ~~It was so great meeting you.~~ I want to finalize the details of our roommate arrangement over email ~~so everything is spelled out and we both know where each other stands and there are no miscommunications about what I expect~~ so that expectations are clear.

I propose the following arrangement:

1. You try your best to be at the apartment whenever I'm home (obviously, school comes first and this might not always be possible). ~~I'm most tempted at night, when the apartment is quiet, so feel free to make noise until you go to bed. I read a lot, but I won't mind the sounds you make. Have you ever read A Tree Grows in Brooklyn? There is this one passage where she talks about the world being hers for the reading, that poetry is for quiet companionship, biographies~~

~~are for when she wanted to feel close to someone, and adventures are for times when she is tired of the quiet. I've been reading a lot of adventures lately.~~
2. You live here rent free, and
3. I cover all your school expenses, and
4. I pay you a salary of 3k euro every month for expenses.
5. Commitment / term of 6 months minimum.
Does this work for you? ~~I'll be happy to pay you more if you think you need more pocket money.~~
You should move in this Saturday. I have the day off and will help. ~~Looking forward to seeing you soon.~~
-Will

From: Josey Kavanagh
To: William Moore
Subject: re: Details and timeline

Hiya Will!
Thanks for your email. 😊
It was great to meet you yesterday. I'm excited to move in ~~and get started watching Netflix because you're not going to be watching anything else!~~ 😉 *(Note: the rest of this sentence was deleted because I made a really bad joke, but I didn't know it was a bad joke until after I read through the entire email. Thank God for the delete button!! I wish speaking out loud came with a delete button. How awesome would that be?)*
Regarding your items, I think all of those sound great, EXCEPT item number 3. Free rent is plenty, and I'll accept your offer of covering my school expenses because I'm desperate to continue in the program, but I really want to get a job for pocket money and savings. I've been thinking a lot about my life ~~and I realized I am terrible at interacting with people. I think it's because my parents have always been my main source of socialization, and—let me tell you—that is not a good thing. They love me, have always been supportive, but they never ... taught me how to be normal, you know? Everything I did was just perfectly great, and I think I needed some correction sometimes. Does that make sense? Some boundaries, some instruction, some "Don't tell people about your unibrow! THEY DON'T WANT TO KNOW!!!" Instead I was indulged and encouraged in all things, and in retrospect, I truly think that's been to my detriment.~~ *(Note: a super large paragraph was deleted here because, upon review, it was waaaaaay too much information you probably don't want to know) I believe I need to get out there and practice interacting with normal people. You are obviously a normal person, but you're just one person. If I *have to* get a paying job then I'll be forced to interact with lots of normal people every day. I have an internship and I plan to talk to them about finding a paid position, maybe something including*

receptionist duties, so I already have a lead. And I'm determined to improve my social skills! Practice makes perfect, except with murder, because then you'd have to kill *a lot* of people, and that's terrible (I went back and forth about whether to delete this joke, but decided to leave it in as Eilish confirmed you'd think it was funny).

I'd like to move in on Friday if that's okay with you. I have a paper and two exams on Monday, so I'd like to be settled in for the weekend so I can get some quality study time. Please don't feel like you need to help me move in! I can handle everything myself. All I need are the keys and I can figure the rest out.

Thanks again for taking a chance on me. I won't let you down, I promise!

~~Wishing you the best,~~
~~Sweet dreams,~~
~~Take care,~~
~~G'night roomie,~~
Sincerely, Josey

From: William Moore
To: Josey Kavanagh
Subject: re: Details and timeline

Josey,

Friday is ~~great!~~ fine~~, but I wish you'd let me help you move your belongings~~.

I understand your desire to get another job and meet new people ~~even though I think you're completely wrong about yourself~~. However, if your job interferes with your availability when I'm at home, then ~~we'll~~ you'll have to decide whether you want to stay on here as my roommate and quit the other job. ~~I really need you here in the evenings.~~

The entire point of this arrangement is having someone here when I'm here. Therefore, though I support your desire to interact with more people, ~~even though I think you're great just as you are and shouldn't change a thing,~~ if your job interferes and you decide to quit it, I'll be happy to compensate you for lost wages and give you a monthly salary.

-Will

From: Josey Kavanagh
To: William Moore
Subject: re: Details and timeline

Okay! That's fair.

If the job interferes with my availability and responsibilities to you, then I'll quit and we'll work out a salary—but not €3000. That's waaaaay too much. ~~My needs are simple! And I'm a good bargain hunter, believe it or not. I've always~~

~~been this way, clipping coupons for my mam or finding deals for my dad. Finding the lowest price can feel like a game. The key is to stock up on non-perishables when they're on sale and use a good coupon to get a certain figure off the grand total.~~

I guess I'll see you Friday night. I can make dinner ~~to celebrate~~ if you want, but no problem if you already have plans. If you're free, let me know if you have any dietary restrictions. I make a mean vegan quinoa dream bowl!

~~See you soon,~~

Sincerely, Josey.

P.S. How do I get the key? Should I swing by your work? Or one day after work?

From: William Moore

To: Josey Kavanagh

Subject: re: Details and timeline

I'll give the key to Bryan and make dinner for both of us ~~to celebrate~~ on Friday. You should be studying.

~~Looking forward to seeing you then,~~

-Will

FIVE
JOSEY

@JoseyInHeels: In his last life, my dog was a mischievous pixie sprite who specialized in trouble making, mayhem and general tomfoolery 😑

I had the key to my new digs in my pocket and a spring in my step.
Then I tripped over someone's discarded Coke bottle and almost face-planted into a signpost. I recovered quickly though, chancing a look around to check if anyone saw. There was a couple sitting on a bench who tried to cover their laughter. They'd clearly witnessed my epic fail.

Oh well.

I straightened up and continued to the on-campus kiosk for my usual midmorning snack. I perused the selection of oat bars when my eyes landed on a tabloid newspaper headline: **Kinky Flanker Paid Floozies**.

My heart thumped when I saw a picture of Will leaving the rugby team's training center. His expression was stern, and he definitely didn't look happy to be photographed. I bit my lip and tried to resist the temptation to buy a copy and read all about my new roommate's sexy exploits.

The man on the cash register saw where I was looking and let out a low whistle. "It's always the quiet ones. I read the story this morning. A real eye-opener, I tell ya."

I glanced at him, then impulsively picked up a copy, alongside a pecan oat bar and an energy drink. I needed something to keep me awake during my next class, since I tossed and turned all last night, too excited about moving into Will's place to fall asleep.

Now I wondered what I was getting myself into.

I guess I should just read the story and find out.

I paid for my items and headed to class. I hadn't really made any proper friends in college yet. On my first week, I approached a group of fellow veterinary students and introduced myself. When one of them, Felicity, complimented another, Karen, on her perfume, and Karen replied that it was actually a new deodorant, I launched into my aforementioned speech about preferring men's deodorant over women's.

And yes, succeeded in making things weird. They'd been avoiding me ever since.

It made me feel a little lonely, but I guess I wasn't really here to make friends. Also, since most of my classmates had gone straight from school to college, the majority of them were still teenagers. It was only a couple of years, but it still felt isolating.

I was a Millennial and they were Generation Z.

Perhaps the twain didn't mix.

I took a seat near the back of the room and cracked open my newspaper. Luckily, I had a few minutes before class started, because I was keen to read the article. My emails with Will had been a minefield of *Should I say that? No, don't say that, he'll think it's weird. Oh, just say it, it's funny!*

His responses had been polite yet reserved. I couldn't get much of a read on whether he liked me, or simply tolerated my personality.

Most people fell into the latter category, but I tried not to let it get me down. I couldn't censor who I was. Well, I could, but that would be exhausting.

I brought my attention to the paper on my lap.

This week it was revealed that flanker for the Ireland rugby squad, William Moore, has been engaging in lurid sex acts with paid prostitutes. Our source, who has chosen to remain anonymous, claims she and a fellow sex worker were paid by Moore for their services. Moore brought both women to a hotel room and encouraged them to perform sexual acts on one another while he watched.

Heat rose on my cheeks as I glanced around. The class was starting to fill up and I didn't want to get caught reading the story. I quickly scanned the rest.

She went on to detail how this arrangement continued for several weeks before Mr. Moore informed her he would no longer require her services. She claims Mr. Moore never engaged in sexual acts with either her or her co-worker, preferring only to watch.

"It was definitely weird and very kinky," our source says. "I've never had a client request this particular type of service before, and when I recognized who he was, I was flabbergasted. He told me he'd been doing this for years. I asked if he was worried about being caught and he claimed he wasn't. He said he didn't feel he was doing anything wrong."

I sucked in a deep breath, then closed the paper when my professor entered the room. I folded it up and put it in my bag, but my mind raced. I couldn't stop thinking of Will hiring prostitutes. It just seemed so unlike him. I really couldn't picture him pulling up to the side of the road, some lady wearing a short skirt and thigh high boots leaning down as he lowered the window.

Then I thought of him bringing her and another sex worker to a hotel room and my stomach twisted with unease. I didn't like thinking he had that side to him. Not the voyeurism, but the paying prostitutes part.

Could he be arrested? Or was it all hearsay?

I tried to focus my attention on the whiteboard, where my professor brought up a diagram of a luxating patella. My aunt's Chihuahua had one of those. It's a congenital defect where the groove for the kneecap isn't deep enough, resulting in dislocation. Surgery is the best cure.

I jotted some notes down.

Mostly occurs in toy breeds, less common in cats. Sometimes caused by a form of blunt prostitutes.

I read back what I wrote and, embarrassed, immediately scribbled out the last word, replacing it with "trauma." I really couldn't get this whole story about Will out of my head. It was just so disconcerting.

What if he succumbed to temptation and ended up bringing women home one night? Would I have to come storming out of my bedroom with a broomstick and shoo them from the apartment?

I tried to push the thoughts from my head and pay attention to the lesson. Later that day, Eilish drove me over to Bryan's place. I didn't have much luggage, since I hadn't yet returned to my parents' house to collect the rest of my things. I wanted to give them another week to feel bad about what they'd done. Then I'd go over, forgive them, and all would be right with the world.

Our arguments never lasted long, but this was a big one. Sure, it was juvenile, but my hurt feelings required them to suffer just a little bit longer.

"Did you read the story about Will?" I asked Eilish as she helped me with my stuff. I had Rocky on his leash, and he kept straining, entirely too excited about taking the stairs. Will's apartment was several flights up. There was a lift, but we decided we could use the exercise.

Eilish nodded. "I refuse to believe it. Will's just not the type. He would never hire a prostitute."

"How do you know?"

"He's so strict, such a rule follower. You know how I'm always complaining about how I never have enough towels at work? Well, it's because the guys—the team—they take the towels home. But not Will. He always, *always* brings them back. And he's like that with everything. Even Bryan takes towels, drives me crazy."

"But weren't you surprised when Bryan told us about his voyeurism? Maybe the rule following is all an act."

"Voyeurism is one thing, paying prostitutes is another. Firstly, it's illegal.

Secondly, I can't see him taking advantage of vulnerable women like that. I'm not sure if I told you, but before I got together with Bryan, Will and I actually went on a date. He was a complete gentleman."

I blinked at this. Will's affection for Eilish suddenly made sense, and I got a weird pang in my chest. Not because I wanted him to think affectionately of me, but more because I just wanted *someone* to think of me fondly. Eilish was the sort of woman who unwittingly gained admirers wherever she went. I was the sort to gain suspicion and funny looks and avoidance…and demands I apologize to middle-aged men's girlfriends for presuming they were their granddaughter.

"Well, one date doesn't give you the full view of a person. People can pretend to be one way, then they're completely different behind closed doors."

"True. But, again, I work with him on a weekly basis. I feel I know him almost as well as Bryan does, and they lived together. He once lost a pen from Jenna—the trainer—and he bought her a pack of twenty to replace it. He has the lowest number of fouls—for the season and over his career—in the entire league. I'm telling you, there's something off about that story."

"You think they fabricated it?"

Eilish pursed her lips. "If not all, then at least some of it."

When we arrived on Will's floor, I pulled out the key Bryan gave me and opened the door into a spacious, airy apartment. Aside from the bedrooms and bathrooms, it was completely open-plan. One side of the living area was made up of floor-to-ceiling windows, which led out to a large rooftop garden. There was a big corner sofa in the middle of the room, a flat screen TV on the back wall, with shelving on either side. I let Rocky off his leash to inspect his new digs while I checked out the photo frames.

One showed Will with a man who I presumed was his grandfather. He had his arm around Will and their smiles were closed-mouthed. I always found something odd about people who smiled without teeth, like they weren't comfortable enough in their happiness to smile fully.

The next photo was a group shot, with a farmhouse and neighboring barn in the background. It reminded me of *Seven Brides for Seven Brothers*, because everyone in the picture was male, wearing plaid, and they definitely looked related.

I was so engrossed in studying the pictures that I didn't notice Will had appeared and was chatting with Eilish. I met his gaze and he glanced between me and the pictures on the shelf.

All I could think about was prostitutes, seedy hotel rooms, and kinky fetishes.

I walked over to join them. "Hey, I didn't know if you'd be home."

"I just got back a half hour ago," Will replied. His eyes darting over my shoulder when he continued, "What is that?"

I turned around and saw Rocky jumping off Will's sofa and onto his coffee table before landing on the floor. He picked up a large male gym shoe with his mouth, then darted off down the hallway.

"That's my dog, Rocky. Sorry about your shoe. I'll just go grab it."

Will blinked. "I thought it was a rat."

Eilish elbowed him. "Hey! Rocky's no vermin. He's a delight once you get to know him."

I looked at Will. "I promise he won't be any trouble. He's fully house-trained and he sticks with me most of the time. You'll barely notice he's here."

He scratched the back of his head and I sensed he was torn. When I said I had a dog he was probably imagining a golden retriever or German shepherd. Something that weighed a little more than eight pounds.

Finally, he replied, "Fine."

Eilish gave him another nudge with her elbow. "You rugby men, so eloquent. Listen, Josey, I've got to go collect Patrick from his playdate. Do you need help with anything before I go?"

I shook my head. "Nope, all set."

"Great, call me if you need anything," she said, coming to give me a hug before she left.

The door clicked shut, punctuating her departure. Will and I stood side by side. My first thought was to say something, but I was trying to resist my urge to fill every silence with chatter. My cousin, Grace, told me it was my most irritating quality.

Her most irritating quality was telling it how it was, or more precisely, being mean. Next time, that was going to be my comeback.

"I'll show you your room," Will said, and I followed him down the hallway. We passed by his room and the door was open. The first thing I noticed was his bookshelf. It was impressive, stuffed full with what looked like antique books.

The second thing I noticed was my dog. Rocky stood on his bed, the shoe that was almost bigger than he was still in his mouth. I ran inside, pulled the shoe away, and picked him up.

"Sorry, again. I'll do my best to keep him away from your stuff."

Will eyed Rocky. "What's his breed?"

"He's a miniature pinscher. They were bred from dachshunds and Italian greyhounds to hunt vermin. That's why he's constantly stealing stuff, he has this instinct to be busy. Every month when I clean out his crate I find a whole collection of items from around the house. One time he had a hair comb, a sachet of ketchup, and a tube of lipstick." I chuckled.

Will gave me a small smile. His smiles were never full, always with something held back. I wondered if it was because he was shy or if he just didn't possess much warmth.

He stared at me for a long moment, then cleared his throat. "Your room's this way."

He led me across the hall to a medium-sized bedroom. It was fully furnished with a big window and a glass door that accessed the roof garden. Nice. I did notice there weren't any curtains, though they'd probably ruin the chic, modern look.

"This is great. I better make sure I don't walk around naked. I'll be giving the neighbors a show," I joked.

Will frowned, and there was a beat of silence before he said, "I can have blinds fitted."

I waved him away. "Don't trouble yourself. I'm a pajama girl. Never slept naked in my life."

Stop saying the word naked.

More silence. I shifted in place. Will looked out the window, and then to me. "I should still put up blinds. You'll want to pull them at night. I'll go grab your suitcase."

With that he left, and I walked around the room. "Well, what do you think of our new temporary abode, Rocky? I know, it's much more stylish than Mam and Dad's. Plus, we'll get to stay up as late as we like. No more lights out at ten."

"What was that?" Will asked as he returned with my suitcase.

I flushed. "Nothing. Just thinking out loud. Thank you for bringing that."

"Do you like steak?"

"I love it."

Will nodded. "Good. I'll call when dinner is ready."

He left again, and I flopped down onto the bed. Rocky crawled up and licked my face. I giggled and pushed him off. Then I spent the next half hour unpacking my clothes and hanging them up in the wardrobe. I'd just finished when there was a light knock on the door.

"Food is ready," Will called.

I noticed he liked to use as few words as possible. We were definitely opposites.

I went out into the kitchen to find the table set. Will had made steak with roast potatoes and green beans, a nob of garlic butter melting on top. It looked mouthwatering. Nobody had ever made me a dinner like this before, probably because no one in my family could cook. Both my parents *thought* they could, which was why I grew up eating fancy recipes gone wrong. Burned moussaka and undercooked beef stroganoff. Pasta too much on the crunchy side of *al dente*.

I took a seat and cut into Will's perfectly cooked steak with relish. "Oh my God, this is amazing."

He took the seat opposite mine and I realized my mistake of eating before he even sat down to join me.

"It's medium rare. That okay?"

"Yes, it's perfect. Sorry I didn't wait. It just looked too good."

"Don't apologize."

"Well, you're a really great cook, and the apartment is amazing. I feel like I won the lottery. Plus, you've got one of those huge waterfall showers. I'm so excited to try it out. I've never showered in one of those before. Our house was built in the 1920s and the water pressure is awful. I've been trying to convince my parents to upgrade the pipes for years, but I guess that's a non-issue now that they're selling the place—"

"Josey," Will interrupted.

I swallowed. "Hmmm?"

He looked between me and my abandoned steak. "You don't have to talk if you don't want to."

I gave a shy chuckle. "Oh, well, it's not that I don't want to, it's more that I don't realize I'm doing it."

His expression warmed the tiniest bit. "How about we try something?"

"Something?"

"Let's eat first and afterwards, over dessert, we can talk. Get to know each other better."

His suggestion was offered in a way that didn't seem rude, in fact, there was a kindness in his voice that was unexpected. Like he genuinely wanted to have a conversation, but he also wanted me to enjoy my dinner. It was true that I often talked through an entire meal, then looked down to realize it had gone cold.

"Okay," I replied.

He gave me another of those closed-mouthed, almost smiles. Then, we ate in quiet and it was…lovely. It felt peaceful to eat and enjoy someone's company without falling victim to a bout of chatter.

When we were both done, I stood to bring the dishes over to the sink. Will thanked me, and I heard the pitter-patter of Rocky's little paws on the wood floor. He must've just woken up from a nap because he was full of energy and inspecting every corner of the apartment for something fun to amuse himself.

"I'll get dessert," Will said as Rocky made a beeline for my handbag. I'd placed it on the floor by the sofa. Before I could warn him to keep his snout out of there, he stuck his nose inside and pulled out the newspaper I bought this morning.

"Rocky, no," I said in a panic as he marched off, proud of his find.

"What's he got?" Will asked, glancing over.

Rocky now thought a game was afoot, because he ran around the living room, happy to be chased. I tried to swipe for the paper, but he was too fast. I put on my angry voice, "*Rocky, drop it, now!*"

Just like that, he dropped it and ran off scared. The paper fell to the floor with a swish, and to my dismay, Will came to see what the fuss was about. I hurried to pick it up and hid it behind my back, but when I turned around I knew he already saw.

Mortification set in.

"Will, I'm so, so sorry. I should never have bought it."

His expression was unreadable and his eyes didn't meet mine. "You were curious. It's okay."

I winced. "Is it?"

He blew out a long breath. "I'd prefer you to come to me if you have questions."

"Oh."

A moment passed.

Will rubbed his jaw. "You can ask me anything you like."

His openness was a relief, and I nodded. "Yes, all right. What's for dessert?"

"Apple pie." He almost grinned.

"Really? Did you make it yourself?"

He shook his head. "Store bought, but there's fresh cream."

I reclaimed my seat, and a minute later Will set a plate in front of me. He'd warmed the apple pie up in the microwave and it really made all the difference. I took a bite and chewed. Will was obviously waiting for me to ask my questions, but for once I was tongue-tied. I needed to start out with something light before I worked my way up to the hard stuff.

Opening with *Do you* ever *have normal sex?* wasn't an option.

I glanced at him, but he wasn't looking at me, instead focusing on his slice of pie. He was almost finished already. Man, he could put food away quick.

"Do you know how the story got out?" I asked. I felt that was a good place to begin.

He swallowed and seemed to consider his answer. "I think Aideen must've told one of her friends about our arrangement, and then the rumors spread from there. I know Kean never would've said anything. This type of thing seems to be more embarrassing for a man, having someone look at your wife—"

"Aideen and Kean?"

"The Gallaghers. The couple I used to watch."

"Oh. Right." I processed that. A woman and a man, not a woman and a woman, two prostitutes to be exact, like the paper had said. "The newspaper also said you paid sex workers."

Will's expression darkened. "Lies. I would never exploit anyone in that way. Aideen and Kean were married and consenting. There was no payment involved, that would have been unethical. We all got what we wanted from the arrangement. The newspapers must've caught wind, but it wasn't salacious enough. I'm guessing that's why they decided to put the sex worker spin on it."

Wow. I think that's the most I ever heard Will speak at once. He was clearly angry, and I didn't blame him.

"I have to admit, I'm relieved to hear it's not true."

Will made a low grunt but didn't say anything. He was clearly still stewing on the fact that some tabloid was spreading lies about him. If I was him, I'd be livid, too.

"So, is it always couples that you, uh, watch?"

He nodded. "There was just Aideen and Kean, and one other couple before them."

"Were they married?"

"Yes. I guess an athlete watching married, consenting couples have sex wouldn't sell very many papers."

"Oh, I dunno. It'd definitely sell a few," I teased, and that got a chuckle out of him. I was glad to have lightened the mood.

"I'm not ashamed, but I know it's not…it's unusual." He seemed to be opening up willingly, which I sensed wasn't something he did very often.

"Who's to say what's normal?"

"You're right, but, well"—a huff of breath, a furrow of his eyebrows— "with Aideen and Kean, it wasn't like before. It didn't . . ."

"What?"

"It didn't help. I'm stopping for good."

His statement made me curious. "What do you mean by 'help'?"

"It brought me no relief, no satisfaction. I couldn't seem to enjoy myself with the Gallaghers."

"If you didn't enjoy it, then why did you do it?"

He exhaled slowly, his eyes darkening as they met mine across the table. Something about the way he looked right then revealed hidden layer I found compelling. Compelling and a little bit scary.

"Before I answer, may I ask you something?" His voice was different now, deeper, it held an edge.

A tingle skittered down my spine; the air became heavy, shifted. "You want to ask *me* something?"

He nodded, his gaze still intense.

My breathing came quicker. "Uh, sure. It's only fair."

And then he asked, "Have you had sex?"

SIX
WILL

@**WillthebrickhouseMoore**: Signups for @TheDreamFoundation summer programs are coming up. See their webpage for details.
@**ECassChoosesPikachu to @WillthebrickhouseMoore**: You're such a good guy, Will.
@**WillthebrickhouseMoore to @ECassChoosesPikachu**: We've been over this before…

Her eyes widened, looked right, left, and then came back to mine. "Uh, yes."

I stop myself from laughing at how she whispered her response, like it was a solemn secret. Instead, I asked a follow-up question. "Why do you have sex?"

She made a face, as though she found the question confusing, or as though to ask *Isn't it obvious?*

"Because it—sex"—she whispered the word *sex*—"feels good, right?"

Josey's stare lost focus, drifting to some point over my shoulder, and then she added conversationally, "Well, sometimes it feels good. It felt good with four of the people I've been with, the other four were just disappointing. But really, that's my own fault. Sex isn't a cure for boredom—or so I've discovered—and it never makes people like you more. In fact, sometimes sex seems to make people like you less." She sighed lamentably, her gaze shifting back to mine.

Sometimes sex seems to make people like you less. I could certainly relate to that.

Josey started, a little flinch, like she was surprised to find me there, and then added on a rush, "But I feel like fifty percent is a solid number." She shoved a forkful of pie into her mouth, her cheeks burning red, giving me the impression she was shutting herself up with pie.

At first, I struggled against a smile. Her candor was charming.

Yet, as the full meaning of her words were made clear, this initial instinct was eclipsed by grim resolve. She'd been intimate with four unworthy men. Four.

She deserved better, just like I'd deserved better with my ex, Eve.

But Josey had no reason to be embarrassed. Her answer—more or less—was expected, if not disheartening.

"That's why I watch," I answered plainly. "Because, in the moment, it makes —it used to make—me feel good."

Josey openly studied me while she chewed, swallowed, and took a sip of her water, her outward expression much less timid as she asked, "Let me see if I have this right, you watched people because it felt good?"

"Yes."

"And then you stopped because it didn't feel good anymore?"

"Yes." More precisely, it stopped feeling good because Aideen had stopped respecting my boundaries, and then Aideen had made things impossible for everyone.

"So . . . do you not like voyeurism anymore? I mean, why did it stop feeling good?" Her earlier shyness was now apparently gone, replaced with a curiosity that felt academic.

I hemmed and hawed, looking for a way to explain without getting into the nitty-gritty. "It only feels good if everyone involved is on the same page. The woman, she wanted something different from the arrangement, so I had to end things."

Josey bit her lip, giving me the sense she was trying to stem a flood of questions. Eventually, she blurted, "What did the woman do? What did she want? I understand if you don't want to answer. Sorry."

"It's fine, I don't mind discussing it." *With you.* Which was strange, but true. My oldest brother was the only person who knew all the details, and I felt a similar level of comfort with Josey. Nevertheless, I didn't immediately elaborate, not sure where to start.

She must've sensed my reluctance, because her expression seemed to grow tender. "Hey. I'm the most unjudging person on the planet. I'm here to help you. If you don't want to tell me, that's fine."

"She told me she was in love with me."

Josey's mouth snapped shut and her eyes bugged out.

I sighed. "Aideen—that's the wife—came alone to my apartment and told me she wanted to leave her husband. For me."

"What did you say? What happened? What did you do?" She looked like she was sitting on the edge of her seat.

"I told her no, obviously." An echo of the resentment and frustration I'd felt on that day spiked anew. "She had no right to come here, to say those things to me."

"No right?" Josey looked at me like she thought I was a little nuts. "She had no right to fall in love with you?"

"No. She didn't. I'd been very clear about my expectations and boundaries, and she ignored them. I didn't feel anything for her, not like that. I mean, we'd never even spoken in person, that's not how things work."

"How do things work?"

I glanced out the glass patio doors behind Josey. "The whole point is, we were supposed to be strangers. I worked out the details with Kean and Aideen over email ahead of time, a schedule, rules, consent—"

"Rules?"

"Yes. Rules. Rules must be followed, to establish clear expectations and boundaries, to keep people safe." I considered rules—in all matters—to be the solid foundation upon which my existence had been built. Respect and rules. If I was one thing, it was a rule follower. Always. "Then, every week, they showed up at my place."

"Here?" Josey looked around.

"Yes, here. They came here at the agreed upon time. I let them in. After that, they were supposed to ignore me, not acknowledge me. That's what I preferred, as though I wasn't there, or they couldn't see me."

"Where did they—"

"Have sex?" I looked to her, cutting her off before she could whisper *sex* again.

She nodded, and I was amazed to find her features curious instead of disapproving.

"They used the old bed in the guest room, usually."

She sat up straighter. "My room?"

"Yes, the room you're in now. But I replaced the bed."

"Oh."

I watched her closely as I added, "Once, they had sex in the kitchen, here, on the table. And one other time they did it on the couch."

She blinked, leaning away from the table, and I could see she was fighting against a grimace and mostly won.

Eventually, Josey cleared her throat and said, "I see."

I shook my head, rolling my eyes to the ceiling. "I guess I should get a new couch."

"Honestly, I'm more concerned about the table. We just ate here." Her tone held a teasing edge and when I looked to her, I found her lips pressed together like she was hiding a smile.

I couldn't believe she was taking this so well. Josey was right, she was the least judgmental person in the world.

"So all that—the voyeur stuff—was fine and dandy until she showed up alone and told you—told you she had feelings for you?"

I shook my head. "No. I knew something was off before that. She'd started looking right at me while she was with her husband. I'd emailed them both and said I didn't want that. I said it needed to stop. But she kept doing it. I was planning to call it off, find a different couple, and that's when she showed up."

"So, what did you do?"

"I asked her to leave. I then sent an email to them both and called the arrangement off for good."

"Did you tell her husband? What happened?"

A sense of shame spread its claws into my chest. "No."

I'd wrestled with what to do, and had asked my brother for advice. He told me to sever all ties and not tell her husband, saying it—their marriage—was between the two of them. If I'd told Kean, I'd be inserting myself into their problems.

Josey stared at me, but I got the sense she didn't really see me. Her stare seemed to be focused inward.

Out of nowhere, she asked, "When it felt good, was it better than normal sex?"

I sighed, tired of this subject. "No. Not better. But less . . ."

"Less?"

"There's nothing wrong with what we did. Boundaries are established ahead of time, consent is explicit, the rules are clear. No chance for anyone to get hurt or disappointed as long as they follow the rules, and no one is exploited. Aideen didn't follow the rules, and that's on her."

Josey and I stared at each other, and I sensed she was waiting for me to continue. I didn't. Because *that* was the reason I'd become a voyeur: the lack of exploitation, the rules, the clear expectations, explicit consent, and the minimal chances of anyone getting hurt.

"And?" she prompted after a time, her dark eyebrows lifting over her blue eyes.

"And, that's it."

Josey stared at me. Then her fingers came to her temples. "I'm confused. Let's back up. You just stated that watching people doesn't feel as good as . . . you know. So, you watch people instead because?"

"No one gets hurt." *Or, no one should get hurt, as long as they stick to the rules.* I grabbed our plates and stood from the kitchen table, making my way to the sink. I sensed her eyes on my back as I washed the dishes and placed the plates on a towel to dry.

"No one gets hurt," she echoed, like the words were a riddle.

Finished, I wiped my hands on a towel while glancing around the kitchen, making sure all the food was put away, the counters were wiped down, and everything was clean.

"No one gets hurt . . ." she repeated again, her tone distracted.

"Goodnight." I hung the towel on the rung of the stove, intent on my room and the book waiting for me on my e-reader.

"Oh!" At the sound of my departure, Josey jumped to her feet. "I'm sorry. Was I being rude? Please accept my apology."

"No."

"You don't accept my apology?" She lifted an eyebrow, her voice pitching higher with what sounded like worry.

I crossed my arms, but didn't catch my small smile in time. She was really cute sometimes.

"No, you weren't being rude. No need to apologize."

Josey breathed out, apparently relieved. "Oh. Good. Because, again, I'm not a judger, not about things like this. I mean, I might judge a person for standing on the wrong side of an escalator and blocking people from moving past, or playing their music too loud on their headphones—because that can't lead anywhere good—unless you consider an audiology appointment good." She smiled and laughed, punctuating the musical sound with a snort.

The dog she called Rocky lifted his head at the noise, coming to attention, and then huffed a snort of his own in a sort of snort-ish solidarity. Josey beamed at him, then looked back to me.

Returning her smile with a closed-lipped one of my own, I tilted my head toward the hall and said again. "Goodnight."

"Oh. Yes. Of course. Goodnight"—she stepped forward and tapped my shoulder lightly with her closed fist, and then backed away—"roomie. Goodness, I like the sound of that. 'My roommate and I share a flat. I share a flat with a roommate. I am the varlet to his voyeur. Huh, that has a nice ring to it," she went on as though talking only to herself. "The voyeur's varlet."

I gave a quizzical look. "Varlet?"

She appeared sheepish. "Right, sorry. I'm sort of obsessed with old forgotten English words that aren't used anymore. My dad and I like to find new ones and exchange them with one another. We call it Forgotten Old Word of the Day. A varlet is what they used to call an attendant, which is kind of what I am to you, in a sense. I'm here to attend to you. Well, actually, a varlet was usually a young boy, but when I cut my hair a couple of years ago my neighbor told me I looked like a boy, so it could apply."

She seemed to think on that for a moment and then tilted her head to one side. "Although, I guess I could also be considered the voyeur, since my job—technically—is to watch you, which makes me a voyeur. And the newspapers might call you a varlet because the second dictionary form for the word is a dishonest or unprincipled man..."

She trailed off when she noticed how I stared at her, captivated by her rambling and the openness in her expression. Her smile waned.

"For the record, I don't think you're a varlet." Her look and tone were earnest. "You're no varlet."

I continued watching her, having nothing to say to that. Plus, I liked watching her. She had very . . . interesting facial expressions.

"What?" Her eyes narrowed and the back of her hand came to her chin and she wiped. "Do I have pie on my face?"

"No." I shook my head and moved around her to the hall. "You're right, it does have a nice ring to it, and thank you for teaching me a new word. I hadn't heard that one before. See you tomorrow."

"Yes. Tomorrow. See you then," she called after me, her tone friendly but also with an edge of doubt.

As I walked to my room and shut the door, I decided something would have to be done about her uncertainty. She seemed to always be ready to apologize, to second guess herself. That was unfortunate. Josey was just fine the way she was, and I wasn't the only one who thought so.

That dog.

I pulled off my shirt, tossing it into the hamper in the corner of my room. I placed my phone on my bedside table, and then my pants followed my shirt into the laundry, and then my boxers.

The way she looks at that dog.

Grabbing my e-reader from the nightstand, I reclined on my bed and turned on the device, staring without reading the first sentence on the page.

A few moments passed, maybe more, before I was pulled out of my unfocused thoughts by the chime of my cell. Glancing at the screen, I read the message.

> BRYAN
> It's not too late to change your mind.

I picked up the cell and typed out a quick response.

> WILL
> I'm not going to change my mind.

Not a minute later, he responded.

> BRYAN
> Tomorrow isn't too late either. Nor is next week, or next month.

> **WILL**
> It's not going to happen. She's exactly what I need.

> **BRYAN**
> Is she really, though?

I thought about that, endeavoring to pinpoint exactly how to express why I had such confidence in the arrangement, even after knowing her for such a short time.

> **BRYAN**
> Sometimes you're too nice for your own good. Just say the word and I'll come up with a rescue plan.

> **BRYAN**
> It's the least I can do after what you did for me.

> **BRYAN**
> I've been plagued with guilt.

> **WILL**
> She reminds me of my brother.

Bryan's response took a bit longer this time, but he did eventually respond.

> **BRYAN**
> She's like having one of the lads around?

His statement wasn't precisely right. Regardless, I replied.

> **WILL**
> More or less.

That made me smile. All his complaints sounded like a welcome respite from the deafening silence of the last several months. Since the O'Farrells had left and moved to Galway, and yet again since Bryan had moved out, my apartment had been empty in a way that seemed like a permanent abyss rather than just temporarily vacant.

> **BRYAN**
> She's not driving you crazy yet with her constant talking? She talks to herself, and hums when she does housework, and sings when she takes showers.

> **WILL**
> Don't care.

> **BRYAN**
> She also has no comprehension of social rules, does weird shit and doesn't realize it.

> **WILL**
> Don't care.

> **BRYAN**
> She acts and speaks without thinking.

> **WILL**
> Don't care.

> **BRYAN**
> Okay. Fine. But don't say you haven't been warned.

> **WILL**
> I've been warned.

> **BRYAN**
> When she eventually does something completely outrageous and you're pushed over the edge, give me a call.

I thought he was finished, and I moved to place the phone back on the nightstand, but then he messaged one last time.

> **BRYAN**
> Trust me, it's only a matter of time.

* * *

I was having a shitty day.

Practice did not go well. Sean Cassidy, who was set to retire by the end of the year, had been up my ass, complaining about my break speed from the scrum, complaining about turnovers in the ruck. I wasn't disturbing the opposition's ball, I wasn't putting pressure on the breakdowns, I wasn't attacking the backline. He'd been in my face all fucking day, and I was beat.

After practice, after a lukewarm shower and an awkward check-in with Coach Brian, during one of my first Sean Cassidy-free moments, I'd checked my email and received the message I'd been dreading, the one I was hoping wouldn't come.

Wishful thinking.

To: William Moore
From: Stephanie MacBride
Re: The Dream Foundation

Mr. Moore,
On behalf of the Dream Foundation, we would like to thank you for your continued support of our organization, and express how much we appreciate all the hours and energy you've volunteered over the years. Most especially, the Monday and Wednesday evenings you've spent tutoring the at-risk-youth cohorts and your leadership during the youth rugby camps. We know your time commitment has been substantial as have your monetary gifts. Again, we thank you.

However, it is with a heavy heart that we hope you will understand the impossible situation before us. Due to recent events, the board believes the time has come for you to sever ties with our organization. Our programs are meant to serve disadvantaged and neglected youth, not exploit them. As such, a continuation of your partnership with our organization is no longer possible.

Again, we sincerely thank you for your dedication to our cause and wish you the best in all your future endeavors.
Stephanie MacBride
Director of Operations, The Dream Foundation

Though I was mobbed by the media as I left work, and again when I arrived home, I felt nothing but numb.

I thought this would blow over. I should have known better. This nightmare with the news and paparazzi—less than a week old—already felt never-ending. Instead of heading to The Dream Foundation for after school tutoring hours, my usual practice on Mondays, I went home and tried my best not to think too much about it.

Which meant all I did was think about it, about the kids who would wonder where I was and when I would be coming back.

Fuck.

See? Shitty day.

And now, at present, at the end of this shitty day, I stood rooted in the entryway to the kitchen, faced with the fact that Josey Kavanagh was definitely not *one of the lads*. A reality difficult to ignore as I watched her dump bag after bag of tampons into a pile on my kitchen counter.

There must've been twenty boxes.

I knew what they were only because it said so right on the box in big pink and black letters. All capitalized. Like they were shouting TAMPONS at any innocent passerby. I'd never seen a tampon in person before, only on television commercials. So I stared, frozen in place, not knowing what to do, hoping I wouldn't be seeing one now.

There was enough to keep five vaginas in business, never mind one.

It was only three days after she'd moved in, and the first night she'd come home late. I knew she had her internship on Mondays. Afterward, she said she'd be stopping by the store, so I hadn't been concerned. But I had stayed up, planning to help her bring in the groceries.

Josey glanced up as she dumped the final bag onto the counter—again, nothing but tampons—and gave me a welcoming smile. "Well, hello there, Will. I didn't expect you to still be up. Guess what? You know my internship at the animal shelter? Well, they've decided to bring me on to a paid position!"

"That's great." I was happy for her, I absolutely was. But, things being as they were, my happiness for her did not eclipse the distress of being faced with . . . *so many tampons.*

"I know, right? And it pays well, as much as a veterinary tech. And I'll be interacting with people. How are you?"

I was about to answer, lie and say I was fine, but then Josey ripped open one of the boxes and I choked quietly on air and embarrassment.

Oh God. She's not going to . . . I braced myself. *She wouldn't . . . right here. . . in the kitchen, would she?* My stare jumped between her and the now open box. I wasn't embarrassed by much, but apparently, I was embarrassed by the idea of my new roommate inserting a tampon in the middle of the kitchen.

And wouldn't that be the perfect end to the day? A crash-course in reproductive hygiene. On any other day, I might have taken it in stride. But not today.

Unbidden, I thought back to Bryan's warnings about her, about how he said she was unpredictable and didn't navigate social situations very well. Up until now, I'd assumed he was overexaggerating.

Josey lifted an eyebrow, her grin diminishing but not quite disappearing. "Is something wrong?" She dumped the contents of the box into one of the now empty bags, effectively making it rain tampons.

"No," I said, shoving my hands into my pockets, releasing a relieved breath. Nothing was wrong. I'd jumped to the wrong conclusion. Josey wasn't going to use one, she was dumping them into the bag.

Everything was fine.

Bryan had been wrong.

She wasn't a ticking time bomb of outrageous behavior.

But Bryan had been right about everything else: Josey wasn't quiet. When home, she was always talking to herself, or to her dog, or reading her textbooks out loud, or singing to no one. But that all suited me fine. She filled the apartment with her happy, distracted sounds.

Glancing down at the mountain of boxes she'd created, she picked up another one and ripped it open. "Boots was having a sale." She said this like she was excited, and I should be too. "They're never on sale. Buy one get one, or BOGO, as the kids call it. Best day ever!" Josey laughed, but then abruptly stopped and cleared her throat as she dumped the contents of the second box into the waiting bag. "Anyway, how was your day?"

"Are there any more groceries to bring up?" My voice was tight, so I cleared my throat, my attention shifting to beyond her, hopeful I'd be able to escape the scene of flying feminine hygiene products by making myself useful.

"Nope. This is it."

My eyes came back to her and I saw her swallow, a light pink stain covering her high cheekbones as she reached for another box, opened it, and continued her dumping.

In a low voice she added, "I honestly thought you'd be asleep."

She was now avoiding my gaze

I mentally cursed myself—and Bryan—because, clearly, I'd made her uncomfortable.

Finally, feeling like an ass, I took a step forward. "I waited up. I wanted to help you bring up the groceries." *And make sure you got home safely.*

"Oh." She swallowed again, her attention affixed to her progress of opening boxes and emptying them into the bag. "Well, tampons are very light, so I had no problem carrying the bags. I wouldn't usually buy so many, but these are *never* on sale, and they're the ones I prefer because they're—" she scrunched her face, cutting herself off, her cheeks burning a new, deeper pink.

"Anyway," she started again, "I'll be finished in a moment. The boxes are just too bulky, so I keep them in a bag instead. It takes up a lot less room, then I can recycle all the boxes at once. It just makes things easier. Once I'm finished, I need to take a shower, and then I need to sleep because I have a test on Thursday, so all day tomorrow will be spent at the library."

"The library." I ventured further into the kitchen, my hands still in my pockets, feeling ashamed of myself. Josey had been nothing but kind and generous since she'd moved in, upbeat and positive.

She wasn't crazy, she was kind. She wasn't nutty, she was naïve, trusting. There was absolutely nothing wrong with Josey, and I silently promised I'd never let Bryan—or anyone else—plant seeds of doubt about her again.

"Yes. The library. It's one of my favorite places." Her tone was firm and she'd angled her chin, giving me the impression she was expecting me to say something critical.

"Why is it one of your favorite places?"

Her gaze flickered to mine, and then back to her progress. "Because no one is allowed to talk."

Despite myself, despite the shitty day, I felt the corner of my mouth curve. "*You* like going someplace where no one can talk?"

"Yes." Her eyes narrowed, her mouth formed a pucker. On anyone else, the line of her lips would look pinched, but not on her. Her mouth was too wide, her lips too big.

Not liking her posture, or how succinct her last response had been, I made a decision. I'd been the jerk, acting like an adolescent, making her feel uncomfortable. It was up to me to make things right. Taking a deep breath, I closed the rest of the distance to the kitchen counter, picked up one of the boxes labeled TAMPONS and ripped it open.

Startled eyes flew to mine, growing wider as I dumped the box's insides into the bag. She then watched me as I did it again with another box. Finally, as I did it a third time, the stiffness of her shoulders seemed to lessen as an easy smile, tinged with what looked like wonder, tugged at her lips.

"Why," I asked, keeping my tone conversational, "do you like being someplace no one is allowed to talk?"

Josey shrugged, giving me a self-deprecating grin. "Because then I can't say anything stupid."

I shook my head at her. "I haven't heard you say anything stupid."

She barked a surprised sounding laugh, like a *HA!* and then ripped into another box. "You're very kind, Will." Josey waited a moment, and then added under her breath, "You're a liar, but you're very kind."

SEVEN
WILL

@RugbyMom1973 to @WillthebrickhouseMoore: You are a disgusting disgrace! Go home to the USA with the rest of the perverts!

It happened two weeks later.
   Actually, it happened two weeks and one day later, on a Tuesday. The fifteen days that preceded it had been great. In just the short time we'd lived together, things were much better than before. So much better. Josey and I had fallen into an easy, comfortable rhythm.

Mondays, Wednesdays, and Fridays Josey had class in the mornings, and interned at an animal shelter until the late afternoons, but she was usually home in the evenings. On those days, I made dinner for both of us and we ate together on the new kitchen table. I'd donated the old one along with the sofa, as Josey seemed to avoid both after I'd told her about the Gallaghers.

At first she'd protested my making dinner, but stopped when I explained that I had to cook anyway as I had to feed myself. Cooking for two instead of one—especially since my portions were already relatively huge—was no big deal.

We finally came to a compromise when she agreed to let me cook if I agreed to let her clean the kitchen. It was a perfect arrangement.

It was also how I learned Josey was deceptively messy. I say deceptive because her messiness was incredibly clean. Rocky's chew toys littered the floor, but the tile was always swept and the carpet was always vacuumed, free of dog hair.

She left cooking magazines all over the couch, but I noticed she'd dusted and polished the coffee table and shelves in the living room twice during the first week.

When I saw how spotless the shared living space was, I allowed my curiosity to get the better of me and peeked my head into her bathroom, Rocky dancing around my feet as I entered the space. The counters were covered in woman products, but the marble surface and sink were free of water spots, and the glass of the shower had been wiped clean.

I glanced at Rocky. He glanced at me. Bemused, I chuckled to myself, about to turn back to the door, and that's when I spotted it.

A dildo.

A big, Pyrex dildo.

With ridges.

In the shower.

I froze, blinked, and I stared at it, my brain sluggish. Oddly, I had to remind myself to breathe. Likely because I was . . .

I was—

I was shocked.

I shook myself, tearing my eyes from it and rubbing my chest where an odd kind of pang was spreading mild warmth up my neck.

But why was I shocked?

Why should I be surprised?

Despite my never seeing her that way, Josey was a woman and women have needs.

Don't they?

I hadn't grown up around women—*any* women. My mother died when she had my youngest brother. My grandmother died before I was born. I had no sisters. We lived on a farm, way out in BFN Oklahoma.

Girls—women—and their bodies were sacred lands of the unknown to us Moore boys.

Unbidden—*completely* unbidden—an image of Josey flashed through my mind's eye. Her full lips parted, her big eyes closed, causing her thick black lashes to catch droplets of water before they dripped over her sharp cheekbones. Her head would be lolled back as shower spray melted bubbles of slippery soap, sliding down her bare skin as they dissolved. Her legs would be parted, and maybe one hand would be braced against the wall of the shower while the other moved in a steady rhythm.

Holding that huge, glass dildo.

I swallowed a sudden rush of saliva and, unable to help myself, I leaned closer to the sex toy, examining it and comparing its size against my own.

I was bigger.

But not by much.

And for some reason, this realization made me instantly hard.

Crap.

Of course I knew Josey was a woman, but until this moment, I'd never really thought of her that way. Not even the tampon-mountain drove the point home. Up until this point, she was someone I liked as a person, someone who made me laugh, who was smart and compassionate, someone around whom I felt completely comfortable. A good—no, a *great* companion.

She was still all of those things, except—

Except now I've pictured her naked.

The sound of our front door shutting broke me out of my stupor. Rocky jumped to attention, barking excitedly as he leapt for the hallway.

I flinched, hesitating only a split second before I also spurred into movement, turning immediately for the bathroom exit. For the first time in a very, very long time, I felt a rush of embarrassed heat flood my face, making the top of my ears burn and my throat cinch tight.

I shouldn't have been in her bathroom. I should have held my ground and confessed to what I'd done and apologize.

Instead, I darted soundlessly to my room and quietly shut the door, hastily flipping off my light and holding my breath.

And then I cursed my seditious instinct to hide.

But she was home a half hour early. She'd taken me by surprise. Usually, I'd be lying in bed reading by now. I'd been on my way to my room when I'd walked by her bathroom.

Hopefully, she hadn't heard me. Hopefully, she'd believe I was already in bed. Hopefully, she'd think I was asleep.

I strained to listen, but my heart hammered between my ears. Closing my eyes in the darkness, I forced myself to relax, willing my breathing and pulse to slow. Eventually, it worked.

But I would still have to tell her, I would still have to confess.

Do you, though? A voice in my brain that sounded suspiciously like Josey's asked the question. *Who are you trying to make feel better? Yourself or Josey? If yourself, then telling her would be selfish and it would definitely make her uncomfortable. Let it go.*

Then I heard the real Josey. She was whispering to Rocky, something indistinguishable at first, but then she drew closer to my door.

"Shhh, stop it. Don't wake up Will," she was saying, clearly trying to get the little dog to stop his excited barking. "If you quiet down, I'll give you a treat. Is that what you want? Yep, thought so, tiny manipulator."

More footsteps and whispered conversation, further away this time, and I finally exhaled. Rubbing my hand over my face, I walked further into my room. Slowly, careful to be as soundless as possible, I removed my shirt, placed my cell phone on my nightstand, and then took off my pants and boxers. The darkness precluded me from aiming correctly for the hamper, so I left my clothes in a pile on the floor and climbed into bed. I would pick them up tomorrow.

I breathed in, I breathed out. Resting my head on the pillow, I opened my eyes. After a moment, I huffed a laugh at myself.

My grandfather had always said I had an overactive imagination. He never allowed exaggerations in the house, only complete honesty, no matter how brutal or boring.

Now, surrounded by night, I imagined Josey as she was likely to be right this minute, forcing myself to be brutal about the truth of her.

I liked her, but I'd never been physically attracted to her. Like Bryan had said, she was like a little sister, and it was *not okay* to think about a little sister naked.

So I pictured her dark hair pulled into a disheveled ponytail, tired circles under her eyes, her baggy scrubs stinking of wet dog—and maybe dog piss—her sharp, odd features, hoping it would replace the earlier lurid slideshow.

It worked.

She was Josey.

Just Josey.

Cute, funny, sunny Josey.

I breathed in. I breathed out.

My chest eased. The earlier discomfort in my throat diminished until it was virtually gone. My mind wandered to other things: practice tomorrow, the laundry I needed to do, the next scheduled payment I would be sending to Oklahoma, to the farm, to my family, the upcoming trip to Australia.

I was almost asleep when I heard the unmistakable sound of Josey's shower being turned on.

My eyes flew open. Unconsciously, I strained my ears. Seconds turned to minutes, and I was just on the precipice of relaxing again when I heard a new sound.

The noises were indistinct at first—a soft moan, a sigh, a truncated whimper—but there was no mistaking their meaning.

Groaning, I covered my head with a pillow and tried to picture her again—baggy scrubs, dog piss, tired circles.

It didn't work.

The brutal truth at this moment was: Josey naked, in the shower, wet, hot, skin flushed, using her big dildo.

Josey Kavanagh, unfortunately, was inescapably a woman.

* * *

"How are . . . things?"

My eyes cut to Ronan Fitzpatrick. He watched me while he used the bottom half of his shirt to wipe the sweat from his forehead and neck.

"Good," I said. "How are you?"

Ignoring my question, Ronan set his hands on his hips and looked out over the stadium. "Everything okay?"

I studied my team captain. This was our last practice before our game on Saturday and I'd played well. I knew he wasn't asking me about tackles or line-outs.

"Everything is good."

His attention came back to me. "The papers have been brutal."

I nodded, though I didn't know what the papers were printing about me lately. Weeks had passed since the first story broke, at least a month. I hadn't read any articles since the first, though there was a self-destructive part of me that wanted to. So far, I'd managed to keep it tamped down.

Taking a swallow of my sports drink, I found it wasn't cold enough. It needed more ice. I moved to the refreshments table.

Ronan followed, keeping his voice low. "I spoke to Coach about it yesterday. With each of the stories crazier than the last, they have legal doing some fancy maneuvering, threatening libel for the worst offenders. That should quiet them down a bit."

"Okay. Thanks."

"Also, Annie needs to get you on the line. You need to stop putting her off. She has a few prospects, wants to talk them over with you first," Ronan continued as I filled a cup with ice and poured the sports drink over it.

I glanced at him, not liking the sound of the word *prospects*. "You mean models."

"No, actually. A musician."

I must've made a face because Ronan hit my shoulder. "Get the fuck off it, Will. She's a nice girl, and your new bad reputation will do wonders for hers."

I glared at my shoulder, then at my captain.

"Don't give me that look. It's a symbiotic thing. She needs to dirty up her image, you need to stabilize yours. Everyone wins."

"Everyone wins," I muttered, shaking my head as I studied my drink. I hoped he was right. I hoped she—the musician—would get something valuable out of helping me, something she needed.

Ironically, this musician wasn't the only one looking to capitalize on my new image. Since the story broke, my agent had been approached by an infamously wholesome sportswear brand, wanting me to be the face—or rather, groin and torso—of a new, edgy underwear line.

Their tagline? *Will you watch?*

. . . Get it?

"So, uh"—Ronan turned his attention to the field where the last of our teammates were running drills—"how are things with your new roommate?"

I made no outward sign, but at the mention of my *roommate*, my pulse jumped.

"Josey," I bit out, and then gulped the rest of my drink.

"What?"

Setting the drained cup on the table, I reached for another bottle of Sport-aid. "Her name is Josey."

"Oh, right. How is Josey working out?"

I debated how best to answer as I mentally flipped through memories of our encounters from the last several weeks.

She played with her dog in the living room. There were chew toys everywhere. I couldn't walk five feet without stepping on something that squeaked, had been viciously decapitated, or was soaked with drool.

She had classes on Tuesday and Thursday nights, which meant I didn't see her at all on those days. It also meant I took Rocky for a walk, and played with him, and gave him dinner. I also might've let him sit at the dinner table.

What?

Every time I entered a room he was waiting for me in the play position, rump in the air, tail wagging. I couldn't help being charmed, even if he was barely the size of my forearm.

Josey read cooking magazines that she stole from some doctor's office—the label read *Dr. Khan*—but she rarely cooked anything more complicated than macaroni and cheese.

She told me about her day unprompted—not that I'd get a chance to ask, she was speaking as soon as she walked in the door—from the moment she woke up until the moment we saw each other, a litany of small observations, hilarious anecdotes, and sad tales of animals she couldn't save. She was interesting and insightful and open and expressive. I'd counted eleven different kinds of smiles.

She liked romantic comedies and horror movies, and she giggled at both during our Sunday night movie nights. During which, she also painted her toenails. She seemed to be going through the light spectrum in order: ROYGBIV. Also, her second toe was longer than her big toe.

She sung in the shower, mostly pop music. She also masturbated in the shower, and she came with soft moans and whimpers. She'd done it four times —that I knew of—since she'd moved in. Usually late at night on Tuesdays or Thursdays. And she had no idea that I could hear everything—every sigh, every slap of skin against skin, every song—from my bedroom.

My initial impression, that she reminded me of my brother or felt like a little sister or a puppy, had been annihilated in all aspects except for one. Despite hearing her late-night activities in the shower, despite being plagued by my resultant overactive imagination, picturing her naked and touching herself and—

against my will—enjoying the fantasy, despite noticing that Josey wasn't striking so much as stunning, that her lips were the color of plums and plums were my favorite, despite *all of that*, I was still more comfortable in her company than I was with virtually anyone else.

She'd made me laugh more since I'd known her than I had during the whole of my years in Ireland. She was kind, and good, and honest. She made every room seem brighter, every joke funnier, and every meal taste better. And I hadn't been tempted—not once—to seek out a couple. She filled my apartment with her own brand of sunshine. I liked watching her.

I knew, without a doubt, if she moved out, I'd immediately seek out another couple. I wouldn't be able to stop myself.

In short, she'd eradicated the emptiness, but she'd made the space bigger, fuller, brighter than before. Her leaving would create too large of a chasm, one that I'd feel both acutely and chronically.

But none of that was Ronan's business.

So, I said, "Great," because it was the truth.

His attention flickered over me, as though seeking to ascertain the veracity of my answer. Eventually, seemingly satisfied, he nodded. "Good. That's good. So, what's the plan for Australia? Do you need to bring her?"

I tilted my head to the side, thinking over his question. I'd forgotten about the trip, with everything else going on. Regardless, I couldn't stop my first thought at his question.

Josey should definitely come.

Come to Australia.

Not *come* come.

My neck heated, and I had to clear my throat before I could speak. "Yes. I'd like her to co—uh, accompany me."

Ronan squinted at some action behind me. "Okay, sounds good. Don't forget to follow up with Annie." He pointed at me distractedly and then jogged off toward the field.

Meanwhile, I lowered the cup of ice I'd been holding and pressed it against my groin, forcing a slow exhale as I pushed the memory of Josey's sounds while *coming* last night from my mind.

It's been a while, that's all this is.

I gritted my teeth.

Josey was my friend, I respected her, and we had very clear boundaries. She was my employee, I was her boss. Nothing—no amount of attraction or wet dreams—would ever induce me to willingly cross that line.

Go home. Wait until she's asleep. Take matters into your own hands, quietly.

I closed my eyes and gathered a steadying breath, sending a quick prayer of thanks upwards that my drills were already over.

After practice, I took a much-needed cold shower. And then I took a few minutes to look up the general schedule for universities in Dublin; the week of our Australian trip coincided with most campus's spring break. I ignored the sensation of lightness in my chest, chalking it up to being hungry.

As I left the club I battled paparazzi, and I pushed through a crowd of photographers—most shouting lewd questions—as I entered our building. I couldn't believe they were still interested in this story.

I was tired. But I was also looking forward to dinner and possibly talking to Josey about the trip.

Her new paid position seemed to be going well. Maybe if they let her take time off, she would agree to come—go, she would agree to go—along. The trick would be getting a word in edgewise while she regaled me with her daily adventures, but I had a plan for that.

I'd stopped by Butlers on my way home and picked her up some chocolates. Try as she might, she couldn't talk with her mouth full.

Clutching the box of chocolates to my chest and wearing a small grin, I braced myself for impact as I opened our door. However, neither she nor Rocky met me. The apartment was silent.

Strange.

"Josey?" I called, and then waited.

No response.

I frowned, depositing my bag next to the door and my keys on the console table.

I called again, "Josey?" as I walked further into the apartment. Nothing.

My frown deepened.

She wasn't home. It was Friday. She should have been home. My practice ran late and her shift at the animal shelter had been over at least an hour ago. But she wasn't home.

Pulling out my phone, I typed out and deleted a few iterations of my text message before settling on the right one:

Will: ~~Where are you? Are you okay? Why aren't you here? Where's Rocky?~~ Are you walking Rocky?

Thankfully, Josey answered almost at once.

> JOSEY
> Yes. And picking up a surprise.

Oh.

It was at that moment I became aware of the fact that my heart was beating faster than usual. It didn't take me long to realize the cause: I'd been worried about Josey.

Before I could think too much about this, our doorbell rang. The sound was followed shortly thereafter by a pounding knock.

Still clutching the chocolates to my chest, I moved to the door and hesitated. Our building had two doormen and a concierge, with either the concierge or a key card needed to activate the elevator. The concierge was still on duty, and if I hadn't been called to verify a visitor, that meant the person pounding on my door was either a neighbor or Josey.

So I opened it. And then I rocked back, surprised, because neither of the two angry-looking people standing in the hall were a neighbor (or Josey).

"Can I help you?" I asked the woman, who was standing a little bit in front of the man.

"Yes. You can help us," the man shouted, shouldering in front of the woman and jabbing a finger at the box of chocolates protecting my chest. "And you can start by keeping your perverted hands off our daughter!"

EIGHT
JOSEY

@JoseyInHeels: I love my parents, but sometimes…SOMETIMES *shakes fist*
@ECassChoosesPikachu to @JoseyInHeels: Patrick said the same thing when I made him eat all his broccoli before he could have any custard #spooky
@THEBryanLeech to @ECassChoosesPikachu and @JoseyInHeels: It's true. He also said he can no longer live under such brutal oppression. I'm expecting an uprising any day now #riseofthelittleones

I paused as I slotted my key into the door. I could hear raised voices and they sounded very much like…my parents.

Oh, please no.

This couldn't be happening.

Just the other day we'd made up after our argument, and I'd gushed to them about my new roommate and apartment. They'd been pleased at the time, though a little wary of the fact I was sharing with a man they knew nothing about. I reassured them that Will was a gentleman, and that he was a friend of Bryan and Eilish who simply needed someone to rent his spare room. Just a little white lie.

Okay, a *beige* lie.

"I won't have my daughter living with a…a sexual deviant," my dad shouted when I opened the door.

I wanted to close my eyes and pretend this wasn't happening.

I wanted to become one with the wall and blend away until I could no longer experience the feeling of mortification.

Will stood in the entryway, both of my parents confronting him like the duo of righteousness.

Dear Genie, my first and only wish is that you make this situation go away.

"Mr. Kavanagh, please calm down." Will tried to reason with my dad. I couldn't believe he wasn't losing his temper with the way my father was shouting at him.

"Don't tell me to calm down! I read the papers. I know all about you, and I'll not stand by and allow you to take advantage of my daughter."

"Dad!" I screeched. "What the hell do you think you're doing?"

Both of my parents' gazes came to me, full of accusation, but also worry. "We're here to take you home," Mam replied. She was a little calmer than Dad, but not by much.

"Yes," Dad affirmed and marched toward me. "You failed to inform us that you've been preyed upon by a known pervert."

"He's not a pervert. You're jumping to conclusions."

"He hires *prostitutes*," Mam countered, voice pitched high.

I really wanted to roll my eyes. "No, he doesn't. And even if he did, I'm not in the business of selling my body, so I wouldn't be in any danger."

"Josey!" Mam scolded. "That is not the point."

"No, you're right. It isn't. The point is that you two read some trashy scandal mag and came marching over here like a pair of furious dumbbells. The story that's being circulated about Will isn't true. It was made up by a few lowlifes, presumably out to make a quick buck. You should be ashamed of yourselves." My hands were on my hips and my cheeks were red. I was upset and angry and worked up and embarrassed and *gah*…I just couldn't believe they were doing this.

My parents' faces lost some of their confidence. "How are we supposed to know it's a lie?" Dad argued. "We don't know him from Adam."

I chanced a glance at Will, surprised he still wasn't angry. He looked sympathetic and a little uncomfortable.

"Yes," Mam added. "You're our only daughter, Josey. We can't just sit by and allow you to be taken advantage of."

Oh jeez, I wanted to knock their heads together.

"I'm not being taken advantage of. If anything, Will's done me a favor. Do you have any idea how difficult it would've been for me to find a place to live if he hadn't offered his spare room?"

"Well, sometimes when things seem too good to be true, that means they are," Dad said, still eyeing Will with suspicion.

"All right, that's it. I'm calling Eilish over. She's a good friend of Will's and she'll put you both straight. You two are going to eat your words," I pulled out my phone, ready to dial the number. The next thing I knew, Will was at my side.

"Let's not bother Eilish," he said, then calmly addressed my parents. He gave them his best All-American golden boy impression, which, I guess, was really just Will being Will.

"Mr. Kavanagh, Mrs. Kavanagh, if you'd allow me to explain, I'm sure I can put everybody's minds to rest."

"We just worry for our daughter," Mam sniffed. I think she felt embarrassed that Will was remaining so composed in the face of her and Dad spouting off like a pair of lunatics.

Will glanced at me, his gaze soft. My heart gave a thud. He shouldn't be giving me soft looks. He should be pissed that my parents were chewing his head off for something he didn't do.

"Let's sit down and I'll make us a cup of tea. Then we can discuss this like adults," I put in.

Mam and Dad at least had the decency to look sheepish. I swear to God, once I got them alone they were in for it.

I stood in the kitchen, anxiously waiting for the kettle to boil. From my position by the counter, I could see Will sitting in the armchair, while my parents perched side by side on the couch facing him. It was a ridiculous scene. Nobody knew what to say and the silence was deafening.

I decided the kettle was taking far too long, so this discussion would have to take place without refreshments.

I settled onto the edge of Will's chair, crossed my arms, and leveled my parents with what I hoped was a steely expression, though I probably just looked like a baby trying to hold in a poo.

Will cleared his throat. "Mr. and Mrs. Kavanagh, as your daughter said, I had a spare room I wanted to rent and Josey was in need of a place to live. I also needed to hire someone as my, uh…" he trailed off, stuck for words. We made brief, uncomfortable eye contact before I came to his rescue.

"Will needed to hire a companion to live with him and he thought I was right for the job." I didn't bother coming up with a lie. I wasn't ashamed of working for Will, and I was pretty sure Will wasn't ashamed of employing me. My parents would just have to deal.

"A companion?" Dad questioned, brows furrowed. "I hope you don't mean—"

"A bedroom companion!" Mam finished, high-pitched again.

"Yes, Mam," I deadpanned. "He hired me as his bedroom companion, that's the official job title."

"Oh my goodness"—my mother hiccupped, like she was holding in tears—"you are selling yourself!"

"Josey Deirdre Kavanagh, you best explain the meaning of this," Dad practically growled while Will shifted his weight uncomfortably. I felt bad for riling them, because this clearly wasn't the most enjoyable way for Will to spend his evening. Me and my big stupid mouth had gotten us right back to square one. I sucked in a deep breath as I endeavored to salvage the situation.

"I'm not his bedroom companion. I'm sure he can find one of those very easily without having to pay someone," I said, and elbowed Will in the shoulder. He glanced at me, still tense.

Okay, so that didn't work.

Mam shot her gaze to the heavens while Dad's expression grew even more impatient.

"The story in the papers isn't all false," Will confessed, and my gaze widened. He'd been so silent the last few minutes I hadn't expected him to talk at all, especially not so honestly.

"Christ almighty, I'm not sure I can take much more of this," Dad said, dabbing his brow with a handkerchief. He had a classic case of the stress sweats.

"What Will's trying to say is, yes, he did partake in voyeurism, but he didn't hire prostitutes. He used to watch a married couple."

"Partake in voyeurism," Mam rolled her eyes as she parroted my words, but hers were saturated with hysteria. "Now I've heard it all."

"But I've quit, which is where your daughter comes in," Will explained.

Dad squinted so hard he was in danger of being mistaken for Clint Eastwood. "I'd prefer if my daughter didn't come into it at all."

"Yes, well, it's a pity I'm a grown-up now, so you don't have a say."

"Oh, I have a say," Dad argued.

"You've about as much of a say as Silent Bob," I shot back.

"Bob? Who the hell is Bob?" Mam interjected.

"So long as you're my daughter I will have a say in your safety," Dad stood firm.

Will pushed his hands through his hair, clearly exasperated with our petty grumblings. "I hired Josey to be *here*, to distract me by being present, which will prevent me from going down the wrong path. She's the most honest person I've ever met, which is why I trust her to hold me accountable and check in on me when needed. She isn't shy about discussing things other people might find uncomfortable, which is another reason why I hired her. She's been doing an amazing job, and so long as she's okay with it, I would like her to continue to live with me. As she is a legal adult, that's also her decision to make, though I do understand your concerns as her parents."

We all stared at him, stunned. Will was the sort of person who used words sparingly, so when he gave a speech like that you knew he meant it. I was at once flattered by his view of me and embarrassed for acting so childish. Sometimes my parents just seemed to bring out that side of me. I reverted back to a sarcastic, moody teenager.

"How exactly does she prevent you from "going down the wrong path" as you say?" Dad asked, lips pursed.

I shared a look with Will, silently communicating that I would explain. "Will feels less inclined to indulge in voyeurism when he lives with someone. Living alone means there's no distractions. He needs someone, anyone would do actually, to—"

"No. Not *anyone*." Will sent me a frustrated glare, and then turned back to my parents. "It's Josey. She brings life with her—and light, and joy—wherever she goes, where before there was only silence and . . . absence. I haven't thought about it once—not once—since Josey moved in."

I gaped at Will, and then I gaped at my mother. When I found her gaping at me, I snapped my mouth shut and nodded firmly. A foreign feeling—pride maybe?—suffused my chest and I sat straighter, meeting my parents' stunned gazes squarely.

"There," I said, allowing a trace of superiority in my tone. I figured it was my due. After all, I brought light and joy with me wherever I went, didn't I? "If you don't like me helping Will, then that's too bad."

"That is a very odd arrangement," Mam said, glancing between the two of us thoughtfully, but I'd take it. Thoughtful was light-years better than hysteria.

"I know, and I agree. I thought I would need to hire a live-in life coach, someone who was strict and held me to a schedule, someone who I would report to, someone who demanded access to every part of my life. I was dreading the thought, but willing to do what was necessary to be accountable to the team and make this situation right. I don't *want* to be a voyeur anymore, but the temptation was strong. And then I met Josey, and . . . just having her here, her companionship, it's what works for me, Mrs. Kavanagh," Will replied, his tone respectful.

A few moments of quiet fell and I could see Will had really, really impressed my parents. It was written clear as day on their stunned—and somewhat remorseful—features.

"Well, I'm not thrilled about the situation," Dad finally said, breaking the thoughtful silence. "But I have to accept that Josey is a grown woman and old enough to make her own decisions."

He took my mam's hand and gave her a meaningful look. I knew what that look meant. They'd wanted me to venture out on my own. They couldn't drag me back home just because it wasn't all going the way they'd prefer.

"Your father's right," Mam agreed, gaze settling on Will. "And we apologize for jumping to conclusions after reading those stories in the news. So long as you treat our daughter with respect, and so long as this is a safe place for her to live, then we . . . we'll have to live with it."

"Thank you. And I'm glad to know Josey has parents who care so much for her well-being," Will replied graciously. He was being such a good sport about this. Thankfully, I'd decided to cook him a special dinner tonight as a surprise, because I definitely needed to make it up to him. That was some great foresight right there.

"I'll, uh, let you three sit and visit. I have some errands to run." Will stood, presumably to leave. I had a feeling he just needed an excuse to get away from my nutty parents, but I didn't blame him. I sent him a look of thanks and turned my glare on Mam and Dad once I heard the door snick shut.

"You two have some explaining to do."

"Oh Josey, surely you can understand our concern," Mam said.

"Yes, and at least now we're all on the same page. He seems like a nice man, all things considered," Dad added, albeit grudgingly.

"Oh, he does, does he? Well, if you'd taken the time to call before bulldozing over here I could've explained that to you. Have you any idea how embarrassed I am?"

"William seems understanding. There's no need for you to be embarrassed." Mam wasn't looking at me as she said this, she was looking around the apartment as though cataloguing its contents.

I threw my hands in the air. There was no talking to them sometimes. I just hoped Will really was okay with all this, though I'd completely understand if he wasn't.

* * *

Will returned about a half hour after my parents left. I was in the kitchen, putting a Shepherd's pie in the oven thanks to a recipe I found on the food section of the BBC's website. Fingers crossed it turned out okay because I'd never made it before.

Will gave me a nod hello and dropped his keys on the entry table. I wiped my hands on a dishcloth and went to him, unease making my chest tight.

"Will, I'm so sorry. I can't believe my parents ambushed you like that. I don't know what they were thinking—"

My apology was cut short when he placed his hands on my shoulders. His palms were firm, and I felt a warm zing in my belly at the contact, which only served to heighten my anxiety and make normal breathing impossible. He gazed down at me from his impressive height, his voice gentle.

"They did what any loving parents would do, Josey. I'm not upset. I'm actually glad you have people who care about you that much."

I blinked, taken aback, and also flustered by how close he was. "They still shouldn't have spoken to you like that."

"No big deal."

I met his gaze. "Really?"

"Really."

"Well, you're a better man than I, or uh, woman. You know what I mean. Anyway, are you hungry? I made dinner."

His gaze warmed in that way that always surprised me. It was completely unexpected, but strangely, I suspected he'd come to like me. Well, I more than suspected it at this point, now that he'd basically called me the goddess of happiness. We'd developed a comfortable rhythm living together. I wanted to believe we were…friends.

"Starved. Is this my surprise?"

I nodded. "You've been cooking for us almost every night. I thought it was about time I returned the favor."

He got a cheeky glint in his eye. "*Can* you cook?"

I feigned offence and slapped him on the shoulder. "Of course, I can cook." *I hope.*

"You burned a boiled egg last week. I didn't think that was possible."

I scowled and sought to hide my smile. "Just you wait, William Moore, you're going to eat your words."

Forty minutes later, he did eat his words, or more precisely, my very average attempt at Shepherd's pie. Hey, at least I didn't burn it.

"I didn't have time to make dessert," I said when we were finished.

Will stood and went to grab something he'd stashed over by the door. He returned with a box of fancy chocolates. "I thought ahead."

"Oooh, nice," I exclaimed as he handed me the box.

"I actually have something I need to discuss with you," he went on, retaking his seat.

I opened the chocolates, perusing the options as I absentmindedly replied, "You do?"

He cleared his throat. "The team are traveling to Australia next month for some test matches—"

"That's exciting," I said, and popped a salted caramel in my mouth.

"I was wondering how you'd feel about coming, uh"—he stopped himself, swallowed, cleared his throat, and then finished—"how would you feel about *traveling* with me?"

I'd just swallowed the chocolate when he said the words *with me;* naturally, I coughed on the caramel.

His eyebrows pulled together. I couldn't decide if his expression meant he was concerned about my choking or something else.

I shook my head, reaching for my water and chugging until I was sure I could speak. "To Australia?" My voice was still raspy, my airway coated in caramel.

He looked away, seemed to need a moment to gather his thoughts, and then brought his eyes to mine. "Yes. I believe it would be wise to have you there."

Ah, right. I'd almost forgotten. It was just that living together felt so natural, it was easy to forget this was a job.

"All your expenses would be paid for."

"But I have college."

"It'll be during your spring break, so you'll have the time off," he reassured. He also seemed to be observing me closely for a reaction.

I'd intended on spending those days studying and racking up extra hours at my paid internship. Though I had to admit, the idea of going to Australia with Will and the entire rugby team was exciting. And I didn't feel compelled to go because it was my job. I actually *wanted* to go. Plus, I could study on the plane and in the hotel room.

Finally, I replied, "Let me check with my internship first, but let's—tentatively—sign me up."

He exhaled a small breath, his forehead clearing. Was he relieved? Did he think I'd say no? The way his shoulders relaxed made me suspect I was onto something. Then again, I could be reading too much into it.

"Good. I'll email you details," he said just as his phone rang. He glanced at the number, frowned, then went into the living room to answer. I ate another chocolate, then made a start on the dishes while surreptitiously listening to Will's phone conversation.

"I'm free Saturday night," Will said to the person on the other end. Whatever he was discussing, he seemed reluctant. I chanced a quick peek in his direction and found him watching me. He really did do that a lot. It wasn't just my imagination, I was sure of it. Although, maybe he was like that with everyone, watchful, intense.

He does like to watch, after all.

That thought brought heat to my cheeks, so I returned my attention to the safety of the dishes.

"She wants to bring a chaperone?" I heard him say, sounding confused. A moment of silence fell as he listened. "Okay, a double date could work."

More listening.

"No, don't do that. I know someone." He pushed his fingers through his short hair again. I was learning his mannerisms and recognized this was something he did when he was extremely frustrated. "Okay. Talk soon, Annie. Bye."

Will sighed as he returned to the kitchen, slipping his phone in his back pocket. I glanced at him.

"Everything okay?"

He made a gruff sound in the back of his throat. "I'm going on a date with a singer."

Something about the statement made my heart sink, which made no sense. I tried to muster some enthusiasm. "That's great, Will."

"No, it isn't. It's all fake. Ronan Fitzpatrick's wife, Annie, is a PR consultant, and the team hired her to help with my image. The singer is one of her clients, too, and she needs to—I don't know—gain some street cred by dating a bad boy. It's ridiculous."

"It's showbiz," I countered, making jazz hands, which immediately made me feel silly, especially since I was dripping water everywhere, so I put them down. "I bet celebrities do this all the time."

"I'm not a celebrity," Will grumped.

"Well, you are, sort of. You're a public figure."

He made another grunting sound.

"Oh, cheer up, Charlie. It could be worse. If she's a famous singer, then she's probably gorgeous."

His eyes met mine. "I need you to come with me."

I gave a small snort. "You what?"

"This singer, Ophelia, apparently she's shy around strangers, so she wants her producer to come and make it a double date."

I blinked at him. "And you want me to be his date?"

Will nodded.

I raised an eyebrow. "Are you sure? You know what I'm like with people, especially when I meet them for the first time. I'm awful."

"You're wonderful."

"You need your head examined," I laughed, though I was flattered by the compliment. Will was one of the few people in this world who actually got me. It was such a stroke of luck that Bryan and Eilish brought us together. I'd only known him a couple of weeks, but already I was glad to have him as a friend.

"Will you come on the date?" he asked, sounding hopeful.

"Well okay, but be warned. This mouth of mine is liable to make things very weird very fast."

Now he smiled. I even saw a hint of teeth. "Your mouth is one of my favorite things about you."

NINE
JOSEY

@**JoseyInHeels**: I often think about how Bernese Mountain dogs only live for 6 – 8 years and I become unreasonably sad 😢
@**THEBryanLeech** to @**JoseyInHeels**: If @WillthebrickhouseMoore were a dog, that's what he'd be. Poor giant bastard.
@**WillthebrickhouseMoore** to @**TheBryanLeech** and @**JoseyInHeels**: You know you can ride that dog like a horse, right? #alwaysaplusside

The next day as I was leaving the apartment complex, I was met by a man who I suspected was a journalist before he even opened his mouth. He had that overeager look in his eye. There'd been a few regulars hanging around outside, hoping to get a conversation with Will, but they'd never tried to talk to me. Until now.

"Hello Miss, you live with William Moore, don't you?"

"No comment," I replied. I didn't have time for this since I was in a hurry to get to class. But even if I wasn't in a rush, there was no chance I'd talk to this joker.

"I'd just like to get his side of the story," the guy continued, walking alongside me.

"I said no comment."

"Are you his girlfriend? What do you think about the stories that are circulating?"

It took willpower of steel not to reply.

"I mean, if I were you, I'd be pissed. I can't imagine how humiliating it must be to find out your other half is having sex with prostitutes. Or, well, he wasn't exactly having sex with them, was he?"

I stopped walking and grit my teeth. I opened my mouth, about to put this piece of work in his place, but then thought better of it. He was purposely trying to rile me. All he wanted was a reaction so he could write about it in whatever crappy magazine or website he worked for.

Finally, I said, "No comment, and if you don't stop following me, I'll call the police."

This time when I walked away, he didn't follow. For the rest of the day, I had a knot in my belly. I worried for Will and where all this media attention was going to lead. Surely, if he kept himself on the straight and narrow they'd lose interest over time.

But what really worried me was my own personal feelings on the matter. I'd wanted to turn around and give that journalist a piece of my mind. I'd wanted to defend Will like he was mine to defend, like I actually was his girlfriend and not merely his roommate.

I needed to reel it in and remind myself that this was nothing more than a working arrangement, a friendship at best.

When I arrived home that evening, Will was sitting on the couch wearing his black-rimmed reading glasses, his e-reader on his lap. The glasses were cute, but what was even cuter was the fact that Rocky was curled up asleep under his arm.

It hadn't taken long for my dog to charm Will. Now I was certain he was slipping him extra treats and taking him for walks when I was in class. It warmed the cockles of my foolish heart.

"Hey," I said as I came in. "I have had such a day. I stepped on gum and tracked it into my classroom, and my shoe made that noise—you know, when something sticky is on it?"

Will gave me a nod and a half-smile, listening. Rocky lifted his head, saw it was me, then went back to sleep.

Hmm. Some people's loyalties were easily bought.

"Anyway, I needed to pick it off, but I didn't have anything, and this guy in my class offered me a napkin. So, of course I used it. But then I looked at the logo on the napkin and I didn't recognize it, so I asked him about it and—turns out—it was from a solicitor's office! What kind of solicitor has logos on their napkins? Weird, right?"

"Yeah. Strange." His smile grew and he returned his attention to whatever he was reading.

I went into my room to change into some lounge clothes, stopping short when I reached the threshold. There on the windows were a set of brand new blinds. Will had put them up for me.

For some reason, I felt emotional. I knew it was a small thing, and Will probably would've put them up anyway, but it was just so nice of him to do it. Ever since I moved in, I'd been getting fully dressed in the bathroom after my showers. And I did love to potter around in my underwear from time to time.

I walked back out into the living room, unable to keep the smile off my face.

Will must've sensed my attention because his gaze flicked up. "Everything okay?"

"You put blinds on my windows."

"I said I would."

"Yes, but, well, it was very kind. Thank you."

Will grinned, a full on, teeth showing smile, and it took my breath away. We stayed like that for what felt like a full minute, just grinning at one another like a pair of loons. My cheeks started to heat. I coughed and looked away.

I was having…feelings.

I couldn't tell if they were platonic or romantic, but there was this hot itch under my skin that wouldn't go away. And my stomach was all tense and achy, like I was hungry, but different.

This was compounded by the fact that, well, I noticed him watching me all the time.

If I was playing with Rocky, or folding laundry, or making a cup of tea, he watched. I didn't find it disconcerting, but I did find it curious. I felt like I was Jane and he was Tarzan, studying me so he could figure out what made humans tick, what our facial expressions and body language meant.

Obviously, that wasn't the case with Will because he'd been raised by human beings and not animals in the jungle.

So why did he watch me so much?

For a second, I considered asking Eilish to ask Bryan if Will watched him too, when they lived together, but thought better of it. Bryan would probably say something to Will and then there'd be an *atmosphere.*

I hated atmospheres. Usually because I had a habit of creating them.

"I could wash your laundry," I blurted.

"Pardon?"

"You've got a pile of dirty training gear in the basket by your bed. Not that I was lurking in your room. I just saw them when I was walking by, you know, out of the corner of my eye. I wasn't looking directly through your door, it just casually caught my attention. I was like, 'Oh! Look at that laundry.' *Anyway*, since you put up the blinds for me, you should let me wash them for you."

Will's mouth crinkled at the edges like he was trying not to smile again. "Josey."

"Yes?"

"You're not washing my dirty jocks. This isn't quid pro quo."

I flushed at the mention of his underwear and struggled on. "Well it should be. We're roommates. I don't want to feel like I'm taking advantage."

"Now that would be something," he muttered quietly.

"What?"

He leveled me with an intense stare. "Enjoy the blinds. No return favor needed." He turned his attention back to his book.

Well, I guess that was that. I swallowed. "Okay."

"And Josey?"

"Uh huh."

"Quit peeking in my room. I'm supposed to be the pervert here." His mouth curved into another full smile, a cheeky one this time. I chuckled and lifted a pillow to throw at his head.

"I wasn't peeking! I just noticed the laundry when I was walking to the bathroom."

"Out of the corner of your eye, of course."

I huffed and folded my arms, exasperated yet charmed by his teasing. "That's it. I'm taking Rocky."

I strode forward and picked up my sleeping dog, then marched into my bedroom and plopped him on my bed. He hopped down straight away and ran back out to curl up beside Will.

"Traitor!" I called, and then heard Will's deep, masculine chuckle from the living room.

* * *

I woke up at 2:00 a.m., needing to pee. I went to the bathroom, took care of business, then on my way back noticed a light shining down the hallway. Will must've forgotten to turn a lamp off.

I walked out into the living room and got a surprise to find he was still up. He sat on the couch, fully dressed, laptop open in front of him. My mind put two and two together and came up with trolling for couples on the internet. Will blinked and sat up straighter when he saw me.

"You're online?" I asked, glancing between him and his laptop.

He coughed and shifted uncomfortably. "I was just Skyping with my brother. My dad had an accident on the farm and hurt his shoulder. I needed to check if he was okay."

I narrowed my gaze, not sure if I believed him. "And is he okay?"

Will blinked. "Yes, he just needs minor surgery."

There was a beat of silence while I glared at him, my eyes moving between Will and his laptop. "I should check your history."

His lips parted in surprise. "My . . . history?"

"Your search history and the websites you've visited." I crossed my arms. "I haven't done it yet and it's part of my job, right?"

Will stared at me a moment, his expression unreadable, then held his laptop out for me to take. "Go ahead."

I took it and sat down on the couch next to him. Will watched while I hit CTRL + H. This felt weird and invasive. I wished I never woke up to pee. *Damn you, tiny bladder.* Then again, maybe this awkward encounter was for the best. If he was trolling for couples, then at least this way I could prevent him from doing anything he might regret. This was why he hired me. This was why he trusted me.

What if I actually find something?

I wasn't sure how I'd feel if Will was seeking out couples to watch.

Dammit, Josey, it shouldn't matter how you feel. This is a job, plain and simple.

But it wasn't simple and that was the problem.

I liked him.

It was tough to admit but it was true. Sure, I was aware nothing would ever happen between us.

Will is out of my league.

Plus, he's going to start dating that singer.

I bet he falls for her.

This last thought formed a lump in my throat.

Pushing aside my unfortunate and wholly inconvenient feelings, I scanned down the list of recent websites; Gmail, sports news, a men's footwear retailer where it appeared he'd bought a pair of leather dress shoes. I swallowed when I saw he'd been looking up articles about himself.

"You shouldn't read that crap." My voice was full of empathy. I knew how horrible it must feel to read those articles, how powerless to know you can't stop the lies.

Will shrugged. "I haven't been. But today I was curious."

"Nothing good ever comes from Googling oneself," I said and wagged my finger at him.

He nodded his agreement.

I gave him a look. "Are you okay?"

"Yes."

"Are you sure? I'm here if you ever want to talk."

He stared at me a moment, then gave a slight shake of his head. I pursed my lips and returned my attention to the screen. I was relieved I hadn't found anything unusual yet. Then as I scrolled down, a few web pages caught my eye, not because they were suspicious, but more because they were unexpected. I had to blink to make sure I was seeing them correctly.

Victoria's Secret?

Don't say anything, Josey. It's not a site where he can find couples, and therefore it's none of your business what he was doing on there.

DON'T. SAY. ANYTHING.

"Buying some lingerie for a lady friend, were we?"

Damn you, mouth. Damn you to hell. And vocal cords? You're just as bad. Also, brain? Go to the naughty chair.

Will's posture tensed, and that's when things got awkward. He hadn't meant for me to see this. Maybe he forgot he was on there, or perhaps he didn't delete the history correctly when he thought he did.

"I, ah…"

Oh man, now he was lost for words. I glanced at him and his face was turning red. This was so bad. Why couldn't I have just stayed silent?

I patted his leg, intending it to be friendly, but it just ended up clumsy and stiff. "It's fine. If I were a man, I'd be looking at this site, too."

Actually, I wouldn't. I'd just go check out some porn, but I was trying to make him feel better.

Why didn't he just look at porn?

Lingerie websites were the sort of thing that was titillating to teenage boys. And these days, probably not even. Porn was everywhere and entirely too accessible.

Don't say it, Josey. Keep that trap of yours shut.

"Can I ask a question?"

Will's jaw tensed. "Uh—"

"Why don't you just look up some porn?"

Here I go again.

He exhaled deeply, looking like he wasn't too keen on discussing this. There was a moment of quiet before he answered, "I consciously choose not to support an industry that exploits the poor, abused, or underprivileged."

My mouth fell slowly open. This definitely wasn't what I'd been expecting, though really, I don't know what I'd expected. "Oh."

"I don't condemn anyone who does look at it, but I simply choose not to."

"That's sort of"—I struggled for the right words for several seconds, finally deciding on—"noble."

"For a pervert."

I swiped him on the shoulder. "Seriously! Stop calling yourself that! And don't you dare listen to what those vapid gossip journalists write. You're one of the nicest men I've ever met."

His eyes seemed to dim at my compliment. "You think so?"

"Of course I do. You've been an absolute gentleman to me, even if you do like to spend your personal time browsing women's lingerie," I teased.

That got a surprised, deep chuckle out of him, and it warmed the heart I hadn't even realized needed warmth. "By the way," I went on. "You do realize there are ethical porn sites out there, right?"

Will's brow furrowed. "Ethical porn?"

I nodded. "Yes, that's what I try to watch, though I admit not as often as I should. It takes a little bit of research to find it, but it's definitely available.

There are independent performers who actually enjoy what they do. There are also couples who like to experiment and upload their videos to the internet. They liked to be watched."

He looked genuinely perplexed now. "I…" he trailed off and rubbed the back of his neck. "I honestly feel stupid that I didn't know that."

I waved him away. "Don't feel stupid. Not many people know about it. It's one of those things you have to actively go out and search for, sort of like good indie music." I chuckled. "You also typically have to pay for it, because when it's free somebody's usually being exploited, so I don't mind paying."

"You watch it?" His voice sounded somehow strained, but his gaze was steady.

I grinned. "Sure. Like I said, I'm trying more and more to only watch the independent stuff. I usually find some good videos beforehand, then when the mood takes me, I have a whole playlist ready."

"When the mood takes you," Will repeated my words back at me. He got a far-off look in his eye, and I wondered if he was uncomfortable talking about porn, which, given the fact I'd sort of sprung this conversation on him, was probably true. I needed to start vetting my topics before I blurted them out. Unfortunately, my curiosity often got the better of me.

Getting the sense that Will didn't really want to discuss this anymore, I stood. "Well, I should get back to bed. I hope your dad feels better soon."

Before he had a chance to reply, I was inside my room. I crawled into bed and yanked the covers around me tight, but I was too tense to go back to sleep. My realization that I liked Will in a non-platonic, romantic, hearts and flowers sort of way had me feeling all kinds of conflicted.

This Saturday I had to go on that double date and I really, really didn't want to. Plus, I was traveling to Australia with him next week. I'd be taking myself and all my gushy, girl feelings on a plane to another continent. There'd be no classes to distract me, no Rocky to play with, no interactions at the vet clinic. Just Will to fixate on.

Will with his watchful eyes and understated charm.

Will with his kind gestures and quiet strength.

Will with his handsome smile and perfect body.

I couldn't wait, but I was also dreading it because we'd be spending every day together, which was going to be a torturous lesson in self-restraint. *But* I was determined not to embarrass myself, which meant I was doomed to fail.

But what if…

I blinked into the darkness, an idea forming. A brilliant, brilliant idea.

What if I just decided *not* to like him? He certainly didn't like me that way. What if I decided that I wouldn't allow myself to go down that road? What if I made a sharp left turn and took my crazy brain train down a different track?

I get to decide.

Could it be that easy? Could I just *decide* that I would only have friendly feelings for him? Did feelings work that way?

"Huh," I said to the dark, and then whispered, "My friend and roomie, William Moore, and nothing more."

The idea didn't feel precisely right, but it did feel inspired, and it did feel safe. I figured the key to my success was to act indifferent to him as a man. In fact, I would pretend he wasn't a man. I would pretend he was a woman.

"That might work!"

Rocky stirred and I winced, realizing I'd spoken much louder than I'd intended. Snuggling deep under my covers, I chanted to myself, "My *female* friend and roomie, William Moore, and nothing more."

Maybe if I repeated it enough, I would believe it.

TEN
WILL

@Socialmedialite to @WillthebrickhouseMoore: Hey handsome! Have fun on your date tonight and tell @BroderickAdams I say hi.
@WillthebrickhouseMoore to @Socialmedialite: Hi, @BroderickAdams. There, done.
@Socialmedialite to @WillthebrickhouseMoore: You're worse than @RonanFitz 😑

*N*ice.
Josey thought I was nice.
She'd said so during our awkward late-night conversation, where she suspected I was searching for couples. I was actually Skyping with my brother, but then she stumbled upon the embarrassing fact that I'd visited a lingerie site.

I would never forget to delete my history again.

Glancing at myself in the full-length mirror, I inspected the black shirt I was wearing and the black pants. We—both Josey and I—were getting ready for the double date, and apparently, I'd unconsciously dressed myself as a villain, or a funeral attendee.

Grunting, I unbuttoned the black and searched for something else, finally settling on a dark purple shirt. Annie told me to "dress sharp" but to not wear a tie.

Since I hated ties, that was good news. So why was I in a terrible mood?

You're one of the nicest men I've ever met.

I glared at my reflection, Josey's words sounding more dismissive the more they repeated in my head. I'd been called nice before and it never bothered me.

I'd always prided myself on being a decent and good person. An honorable person.

But . . . now? Nice? Why did it bother me so much?

And her suggestions about ethical porn, watching willing couples online. If anything, that irked me even more than her "nice" comment. I only knew about the voyeur-couple matching website because of the O'Farrells.

How did she know about such things? Did she want me watching other people online? Would it bother her?

Obviously not, since she suggested it.

I scowled, disliking the fact that she watched "ethical porn," and then wondering how often she watched it, and then deciding I couldn't dislike it completely if it was the inspiration for her shower performances, and then growing irritated with myself for even having these thoughts.

It's none of your damn business what she does or with whom.

My scowl deepened.

A knock sounded on my door just before it flew open. I turned towards it, holding the newly selected purple shirt in one hand.

Unsurprisingly, Josey was already speaking before the door was completely open, "I can't decide what to wear, and since you know more about people than I do—and dates, and expectations, and being a normal human—I thought you could help me pick which of these to wear."

I gaped at her for a split second as she stared at me. Her eyes focused on my face were wide and worried, and she held two pieces of fabric on hangers in front of her. But behind the ineffectual wall of skimpy clothes, I could see she was wearing a strapless wine-colored bra and matching underwear. And that's it.

I struggled. "Uh—"

"I know! Right?" She glanced down at the two hangers, her voice full of despair. "I don't have anything to wear to a club. All my dresses are florals, except these two. Unless this club is an Easter tea with the Queen, I can't wear anything else in my closet. This one"—she held up a black scrap of fabric—"was purchased for a pimps and hookers party, and this one" —she held up a dark green scrap of fabric—"was purchased for a sexy superheroes party, but I didn't know it was superheroes, so I was Poison Ivy, and turned out to be *the only* villain in attendance. The worst!"

The rising panic and unsteadiness of her voice had me unthinkingly tossing the shirt to my bed and crossing to her. Not considering much of anything other than wanting to provide comfort, I placed my hands on her shoulders and brought her to my chest, realizing a half second too late that I was shirtless.

Josey let her hands drop and the length of her virtually bare body connected with mine as she allowed herself to be held. Her skin was smooth, hot everywhere we touched, the tops of her full breasts pressing completely against my chest with every frustrated breath she took.

She felt amazing.

Crap.

She shifted, her arms coming around my waist, the delectable friction of her skin sending a shockwave down my spine. Stifling a groan, I struggled to hold on to my original thread of altruism. *Comfort her.*

Comfort. Her.

COMFORT HER RIGHT FUCKING NOW!

"It'll be fine," I said, lowering my voice and saying each word very, very carefully. I imagined it would probably be appropriate to stroke her soothingly, or rub a circle on her back. But at the same time, it was absolutely not appropriate. So I didn't.

"You sound like a robot." She huffed a laugh, her hot breath teasing across my skin. The little laugh soon became a giggle, and she gave me a squeeze. "You're terrible at this. Hugging you is like hugging a warm marble statue. You're so stiff and solid."

I shouldn't even be hugging her.

We weren't friends.

She was my employee.

There were rules—spoken or unspoken—and this was crossing a line.

But I didn't let her go.

What am I doing?

Instead, I swallowed, and breathed out slowly, forcing my body to relax. "Sorry. I . . . don't have a lot of experience with this."

Josey leaned away, lifting her chin to meet my eyes, but kept her arms around my torso. "You don't have a lot of experience with what?"

I couldn't speak.

Firstly, she smelled good. Really good. Like flowers.

Secondly, her eyelids were hooded as she peered at me, and the way she'd lifted her face meant that her wide, wine painted mouth was just inches from mine.

When I said nothing, her eyes widened. She stepped away, guessing, "Hugging? You don't have a lot of experience with hugging?"

I nodded, missing the feel of her immediately. She was right, I was stiff and solid. I had to be. It was my job.

She was not.

She was soft. Everywhere. Her arms, belly, sides, back, hips, the tops of her breasts, everywhere we'd touched was yielding and rounded. Fragments of thoughts, of her softness beneath me, of her stretching and arching as I tasted and touched the heat of her skin—

Crap.

Josey's gaze turned sympathetic, her smile sad. "William Moore, do you need a hug?"

I shook my head, answering with a rough, "Nope."

God. The last thing I needed right now was another hug from Josey. If she hugged me again, I was definitely going to stroke her back and sides. I was definitely going to take advantage of her bare skin. And I was most definitely going to kiss her.

Or try to.

And *that* would definitely be against the rules.

It couldn't happen. When she didn't barge into my room barely dressed, and when she didn't take masturbatory showers, she was the perfect roommate.

If I kissed her, she might leave, and I wouldn't blame her. It was a boundary that didn't need to be explicitly stated. You don't kiss your employees. You don't.

I wouldn't.

But I wanted to.

But I also didn't want her to leave.

I need her.

This thought, plus how she was now regarding me with blatant pity, was enough to sober me from my covetous haze.

I did not need her soft, hot body. I did not need to kiss her big, luscious lips. I did not need to feel her wet tongue sliding over my skin. I wanted it—a lot—but I didn't need it.

I needed *her*. I needed sunny, funny Josey. I needed her to stay. And I needed to behave in a manner that was appropriate for and commensurate to a boss-employee relationship.

So . . . *NO KISSING.*

She moved, like she was going to hug me again, and I stepped to the side and out of her reach.

"We'll be late," I reminded stiffly.

"You need a hug." She followed me, her gaze persistently compassionate, her arms outstretched, a hanger in each hand.

I picked up my shirt and quickly pulled it on as she chased me around my room.

"Come on, Will. It's hug time."

"No. No, it's not." For some reason I was now laughing. My best guess was because I was frustrated.

Thankfully, after two circuits around the room, she stopped and heaved a sigh. "Fine. But I'll get you later. You can't run from my hugs forever."

Rationally, I knew I should now reprimand her. I should tell her that she shouldn't come into my room mostly naked. It was inappropriate, and boundaries must be respected.

I couldn't.

I physically could not force my mouth to form the words. Just the thought of rebuking Josey made something in me crumple and shrink and recoil.

I couldn't do it, but it was definitely time for a subject change.

Swallowing around a thick knot, I hastily buttoned my shirt, and lifted my chin towards her hangers. "Wear the green one." *It brings out your eyes.*

My distraction technique worked and her attention immediately shifted to the dress I'd indicated. "This one?" She held it up to her body and crossed over to the mirror, giving me an unobstructed view of her generous ass.

I couldn't look away, but I did successfully smother another moan.

I want to touch it.

Nope.

I want to bite it.

Nope.

I want to bend her over and—

Nope. Nope. Nope.

Josey spun around, and my eyes darted to her face, a rush of guilt burning my ears. Luckily, she wasn't looking at me.

"Okay. Yes. The green one. I can do this. Maybe I have some green eyeshadow someplace," she muttered as she darted from the room.

Do not watch her walk away.

I stood in place, hesitating for only a single second, my baser instincts and desires eventually winning the war against prudence and integrity. I crossed to the door just in time to catch one more glimpse of her bottom as she jogged down the hall.

When she was gone, I released a gust of air, my lungs tight.

Unfortunately, my pants were also now tight.

Crap.

No. Not "crap."

Fuck.

* * *

We were late.

It couldn't be helped. Josey blamed herself and I did not correct her. But I did make a point of assuring her it was no big deal.

The truth was, I'd had to beat off. I didn't have a choice. I couldn't walk around on a date with a stranger while sporting persistent wood for another woman. Worse, I couldn't finish until I'd allowed those earlier fragments of thoughts to arrange themselves into a solid fantasy: Josey, me, undressing, ripped dress, shower, wet, hot, naked.

Worse still, as soon as Josey appeared from her room, dressed in her ridiculously tight, strapless, and short green dress, I knew I'd be battling a boner all night. Especially since I'd allowed that fantasy to solidify, and that fantasy involved the dress she was currently wearing.

The last time I was like this was in college and I'd been celibate for three years. Frustration and need had built up, and I'd been desperate for relief. It hadn't been attributed to one woman, but rather a parade of co-eds I'd placed firmly out of my reach.

Now I knew there were only two real, lasting cures: voyeurism or getting smashing drunk. The former was no longer an option.

I usually didn't drink at all, and hadn't been smashing drunk since college, but I decided I'd need to make an exception tonight. Something had to give.

I formed a plan.

I'd drink tonight during the double date—not a lot—just enough to get out of my head and relax. But when we made it safely back to the apartment, I'd get smashing drunk. I'd be away from my employee, alone in my room, and free to indulge in oblivion without worrying about what I might say or do—or confess—around my *employee*.

We were not friends.

I don't want to be her friend.

I quickly pushed that thought away, reminding myself—for the millionth time—Josey was my employee. I would never cross that line. Nothing could or would ever happen.

Do you want something to happen?

Ignoring that minefield of a question, I focused on getting through the evening.

We arranged to meet the musician and her producer at a club downtown called Diamond, or Crystal, or something like that. I was a little too distracted by Josey's dark lipstick to remember.

Damn it.

Employee.

I gave our names at the door and we were escorted into the club. I placed a hand on Josey's back, and I only did this because the loud music, dark lights, and general chaos would make it easy for us to lose each other in the crowd. That was the only reason, and I definitely did not notice how good she felt under my palm.

We were taken away from the main dance floor and up a flight of stairs, leading to an area blocked off by a sheer curtain. A big guy—not as big as me, but big nevertheless—stood poised at the entrance and his eyes widened as we came into view. I recognized that look. He knew who I was. He was also sizing me up.

Guys, all guys, do this to big guys. But other big guys are more blatant about it. I grimaced, hoping we weren't going to have a problem.

Josey turned a nervous smile on me, oblivious to the undercurrents of the situation. "Gosh, this place is posh, isn't it? Look at those curtains. I think that's silk, hand-painted by the looks of it. There must be forty yards of it. And this staircase must be an original feature of the building. And that bar"—she tilted her chin towards a long bar at the far side of the room—"looks like something that belongs in a grand hotel."

I nodded, only half listening as she continued. The hostess who'd been escorting us stopped in front of the bouncer and motioned for us to enter through the curtains. Meanwhile, the bouncer's attention moved from me to Josey, his gaze moving over her slowly, unmistakable appreciation lifting his eyebrows. I stiffened, my hand on her back instinctively moving more fully around her body and coming to rest on her hip.

I only did this because . . . *fuck if I know.*

I should have suggested she wear one of her floral dresses.

The dude's eyes came back to mine and he smirked at me as we passed, which for some reason flooded me with the kind of violence I usually only felt on the rugby field.

Thankfully, we were soon past the bouncer and being led toward a booth at the very end of the space. It overlooked the bar and dance floor, but I doubted the crowd downstairs could see us.

As we approached, a man and a woman came into view. Upon seeing us, the man stood, and after a brief moment of hesitation, so did the woman.

"Hey," the man reached out his hand toward Josey, giving her a wide smile. "I'm Broderick. You must be Josey?" He was American, like me, but his accent sounded East Coast.

She beamed at him.

Fucking beamed.

Something hard and cold settled in the pit of my stomach and I blinked, breathing out slowly, and I forced myself to release my hold as she accepted his handshake.

"Yes. I'm Josey. You must be Broderick."

He laughed, apparently charmed by her nervous response.

She scrunched her nose, immediately catching her error. "I mean, of course you're Broderick. You just said you're Broderick." I watched as she swallowed thickly, forcing a brave smile, and turned to the woman—who, honestly, I'd forgotten was there.

"Hi, you must be Ophelia?" Josey extended her hand to the woman and I turned to look at her as well. "I'm Josey, and this is Will."

The woman—who I guess was one of those single-named singers—grinned at Josey and gave her offered hand a good shake.

"It's so nice to meet you." As far as I could tell, the woman sounded sincere. "Thank you for coming along." Her eyes came to me and she shifted back a step as her smile slipped. "Hi, Will."

"Hi." I gave her a nod.

The woman was wearing a black dress. Her hair was long, straight, and strawberry blonde. Her eyes were plain blue. She was tall and fit. She had a pretty face, everything was in proportion. Nothing was particularly interesting or inspiring or eye-catching about it. She was not stunning. *Not like Josey.*

Inwardly, I sighed. It didn't matter if Josey was stunning. I shouldn't be noticing if Josey was stunning, and I should definitely not be comparing my date to my—one more time—employee.

"Shall we sit?" Broderick drew my attention to him, he was giving me a hard smile. He gestured for Josey to proceed him into the booth while glaring at me, his eyes shifting to Ophelia and then back to mine, like *Man, what is wrong with you?*

I didn't know this guy. Ronan's wife Annie set up the date and she said Broderick was a good friend of hers. If Broderick was a good friend of hers, then he was likely a good guy.

But his hard look was on point. I was being rude.

Reluctantly, I turned my attention to this Ophelia person. "Do you want anything to drink?"

Her grin for me seemed forced. "We already placed our order with the server. She said she'd be right back." Ophelia slipped back into the horseshoe shaped booth and slid to the center, placing her next to Josey and giving me plenty of room.

Once we were all sitting, Broderick looked from me to Ophelia and opened his mouth like he was about to say something.

He didn't get a chance.

"I was just saying to Will how swanky this place is. Did you see the silk curtains? I'd like a dress made out of those, to be honest, or maybe a bathrobe. Or maybe pajamas. I also gave them a bit of a fondle as we walked in. I'm not usually a curtain fondler, but they looked so soft. And how nice are these seats? We can see the whole club from here. Is it hot? I'm a little hot." Josey pushed off the shawl she was wearing, revealing an expanse of bare skin.

I looked away from Josey. I had to.

Ophelia's grin slowly reemerged as Josey spoke and she shared a look with Broderick. I tensed, because they both looked amused.

I swear to God, if they're laughing at her, I'll punch them both in the face.

Well. . . maybe not her. I'd just have to punch him twice.

Broderick glanced at me and he blinked, his smile falling away, apparently confused by the aggression I was giving off.

But Ophelia's attention was on Josey. "What do you do, Josey?"

"Oh, me? I'm a veterinary student. I also intern at an animal shelter. I also work for Will."

Broderick's eyebrows jumped, splitting his attention between us. "You *work* for Will?"

"Oh, not like that," Josey rushed to explain. "He pays me to live with him."

Broderick's mouth dropped open and he stared at Josey. I couldn't see Ophelia's expression, but I suspected it matched his. Josey glanced between them, her smile waning as her features became more and more distracted. I knew what she was doing. She was replaying the conversation in her head, trying to figure out where she went wrong.

I said nothing.

Let them think whatever they wanted.

The server arrived. He delivered four drinks—two for Broderick, two for Ophelia, his eyes lingering on the latter—and then turned to Josey. "What can I get for you?"

Visibly flustered, Josey blinked at the waiter as though she hadn't realized he was there. "Uh, I'll take a . . . I'll have what she's having." She lifted her chin towards Ophelia's clear amber martini glass.

"A Manhattan?" The man nodded once and then turned his attention to me. "And you, sir?"

"Agave tequila, any brand. Four shots to start."

"Fortaleza?"

"Fine." I flicked my wrist, dismissing him.

As soon as he left, but before anyone else could speak, Josey straightened in her seat and said, "That sounded bad. It's not bad. And everything you might have read in the papers about Will is wrong. He doesn't hire prostitutes. He doesn't hire anyone."

"Except you?" Broderick asked, reaching for the first of his glasses.

"Right. Except me. And not for sex." Like before, she'd whispered the word *sex*. "I'm his roommate, and that's it." She slashed her hand through the air, but then her eyes came to mine and she added, "That's not exactly true. We're also friends, I think."

Without intending to, I was smiling. I couldn't help it. The way she looked at me, like she was beseeching me not to reject her, compelled me to do so.

What choice did I have?

So I confirmed, "We are friends," even as every rational fiber in my being condemned me for it.

EMPLOYEE! SHE IS YOUR EMPLOYEE!

Shit.

What was wrong with me? Why was I abandoning my principles? Accepting her friendship, confirming it, would lead nowhere good. Bending the rules, blurring the lines, just the thought usually gave me heartburn.

Meanwhile, Josey exhaled, grinning at me widely, her eyes bright, and all I could think was, *bending the rules for that smile? Totally worth it.*

"So *none* of the stories about you in the paper are true?" Broderick inspected me over the rim of his drink as he took a sip. From the looks of it, he appeared to be having either scotch or whiskey.

"I am a voyeur," I responded with forced easiness, my mind still preoccupied by my earlier uncharacteristic behavior. "I like watching people, that part is true."

I sensed Ophelia squirm uncomfortably next to me. I ignored her.

"But he doesn't pay people, and definitely not prostitutes. He's not like that. He doesn't even watch porn because of the exploitation issues!" Josey was quick to explain for me. "The couples he watched were married, and they sought him out. All he did was watch married people get it on, and it's turned into this giant . . . giant . . ."

"Clusterfuck?" Ophelia supplied as she passed Josey the extra one of her drinks, giving Josey and then me a crooked smile free of judgment.

I began to relax, though I still needed to sort through my own behavior.

"Yes! Clusterfuck!" Josey smacked the table, causing the glassware to jump. "Oh, are you sure you don't want this one?" She gestured to the drink Ophelia had just passed her.

"They'll bring you two as well. Since we're having the same thing, why don't we share?" Ophelia bumped her bare arm against Josey's and gave her a wink.

"Oh, thank you!" Josey grinned at our tablemate and then brought the drink to her lips. She took a gulp. And then she coughed.

Broderick reached over and patted her lightly on the bare skin of her shoulder.

Aaaaand now I'm no longer relaxed.

"Are you okay?" he asked, rubbing a circle on her back.

I glared at the movements of his arm, and then shifted my glare to his face. He was looking at me, his expression thoughtful. When he placed his arm behind Josey, along the back of the booth, I glared harder. This made him smile for some reason.

"Thanks for clearing that up, Josey. I have to admit, we were curious. Annie had told me her perspective, which is why Ophelia agreed to the date, but it's nice to have it independently verified." Broderick turned his smile on Josey, and she smiled back. Even in the dim light I could see that she was flushed with pleasure at his words.

That cold lump in my stomach ballooned.

Thankfully, my tequila arrived at just that moment and I distracted myself by downing the first shot. But when the waiter didn't stop until seven more were lined up in front of me, I lifted a questioning eyebrow at the man.

"What the hell is this?"

"Two for one," Ophelia said, drawing my attention to her.

"BOGO!" Josey bounced in her seat, receiving the Manhattans she'd ordered and passing a fresh one to Ophelia. "This is fun. I love buy one, get one. It's literally my favorite thing in the world, other than my dog. And clean underwear. And indoor plumbing. And beds. I really love beds." Josey took another gulp of her drink, I guessed because she was trying to get herself to stop talking. This time she didn't cough, but she did make a face and breathed out slowly, like the alcohol burned.

"Can I get anything else? Are we happy?" the server asked, his eyes on Ophelia.

"No," I answered for everyone, my attention snagging on Broderick's arm again, where it rested behind Josey. My eyes cut to his. Broderick was still watching me, smiling. I took another shot.

"I have an idea." Broderick removed his arm from behind Josey's seat and leaned an elbow on the table. "We have this game—a drinking game in the States—called, *Never Have I Ever*. It's a good way to get to know people, and since that's what we're here for. . ." He lifted his drink and clinked it against Josey's.

Ophelia tucked her hair behind her ear, sending me a quick but friendly glance. "Sounds good to me."

The hint of nerves in the musician's voice caught my notice and I studied her. She was tapping her fingers against the table in time with the music, her posture rigid, and her gaze—though she seemed to try to give each of us equal attention—lingered a bit long on Broderick.

"Fine," I said, pushing my empty shot glasses to one side.

"This is the kind of game you usually play with beer or wine, not cocktails. So I'm limiting Will here to a quarter of a shot each drink, and you ladies to just a sip of yours."

"How do you play?" Josey watched Broderick with rapt interest.

"It's simple. We go around in a circle, each taking turns. The person who is 'it' says something they've never done, like, 'Never have I ever slept in a barn,' or 'Never have I ever gone skydiving.' If you have slept in a barn, or if you've gone skydiving, then you have to take a drink. If you haven't, then you don't."

"Ah, got it!" Josey gripped her glass like she was ready to get started.

"I'll start," Ophelia volunteered, sending Josey another of her crooked smiles. "Never have I ever gone skinny-dipping."

Broderick made a face and then took a drink from his glass.

"Sorry, I already forgot. If I've gone skinning-dipping, then I have to drink? Or I don't drink?" Josey asked, her cocktail lifted halfway to her lips.

"If you've gone skinny-dipping, then you take a drink," Ophelia explained gently.

My pulse kicked up, and I wasn't sure if I wanted her to take a drink or not.

If she did, then I'd likely be fantasizing about that the next time I took matters into my own hands.

In the end, she did drink, and I chewed on my bottom lip to distract myself from the imagery *that* inspired. I didn't even bother reminding myself that she was my employee.

"My turn?" Josey asked, looking to Ophelia. When the musician confirmed, Josey blew out a large breath and said, "Let me see. Um. How about, never have I ever lived alone."

Broderick, Ophelia, and I took a drink while Josey smiled and then laughed at each of us in turn.

"Never have I ever played rugby." Broderick looked at me as he said it.

Of course I drank. I also rolled my eyes. Ophelia and Josey laughed, but then surprisingly, Josey also took a drink.

"You have?" I asked as I watched her bring the cocktail to her lips.

"Yes," she confirmed. "Eilish and I were big fans growing up. We used to play with some other girls at school."

"Who's Eilish?" Ophelia asked.

"She's a friend of mine, and of Will's." Josey's gaze moved over the musician and she suddenly sat up straighter. "In fact, you know, you kind of look like her. She's gorgeous, like you. And you have the same hair color and build, same skin color, too. But she cut her hair earlier this year into a super cute bob."

"Will," Broderick cut in, giving me a pointed look. "Your turn."

I considered what to say, wanting to use the opportunity to learn more about Josey but without revealing too much of myself.

But desire to know her won out, and I blurted stupidly, "I've never been in love." Which was a lie.

Josey gave me a soft smile, as though to say, *One day you'll meet your true love, don't worry!*

But she didn't drink. Broderick drank. Ophelia—her eyes on Broderick—also drank. But Josey didn't.

Maybe it was the alcohol finally taking effect, but for some reason, the cold weight in my stomach disappeared, replaced with a new and spreading warmth. I felt myself relax for real this time, aided by tequila.

Maybe this evening wouldn't be so bad after all.

"Okay"—Ophelia lowered her eyes to her lap—"my turn. Never have I ever had romantic feelings for someone I work for."

My eyes cut to Josey, and this time my heart stuttered. Time seemed to stand still. Would she take a drink?

She smiled, her bright eyes swinging to mine, they shone like she and I were sharing a private joke.

My chest tightened.

But then Broderick—who had just taken a drink—asked, "You've never had feelings for a boss, Josey?"

I licked my lips as I stared at hers, willing her to bring the glass in her hand to her mouth.

Instead, Josey wrinkled her nose at Broderick and lifted her drink in my direction. "Other than Will, and my internship at the vet clinic, the only people I've ever worked for ended up firing me. Honestly, they were all a bunch of stuffy arseholes. So I think it's safe to say, never have I ever had romantic feelings for *anyone* I've worked for. And look, Will didn't drink either."

With that, she leaned across the table and clinked her glass against mine, the sound signaling a bizarre vertigo-like sensation, as though my stomach had abruptly fallen to the floor.

As she righted herself, I glanced at my glass, swirling the golden liquid in a slow circle and reflected that my chest was now full of hot coals. Or at least it felt that way.

I didn't have any right to feel this way.

In desperation, I tried to remind myself again: *Josey is your employee.* It didn't help. That ship had sailed, the line was blurred, I was adrift.

What I was feeling for her was lust, plain lust. Albeit powerful lust.

That's it.

That's all.

I'd get over it.

Or, I wouldn't.

Just . . . *don't do anything you'll regret.*

ELEVEN
JOSEY

@JoseyInHeels: Dates are weird. It's like an interview for possible sex/ long-term companionship/ lifelong marriage where you both get intoxicated and talk about your hobbies.

"So, Ophelia, what part of Dublin are you from?" I asked.

After the whole "never have I ever had romantic feelings for a boss" debacle, conversation dried up a little. Yes, I lied. But in my defense, it was a wee little lie. My plan to treat him like a girlfriend was actually working!

And if I drank, Will would discover I was struggling with some confusing feelings for him. Since I'd already regaled him with stories of my unfortunate employment history over dinner one evening, he knew none of my bosses were the fanciable kind.

"I'm a Northsider," she replied, with a smile. "I'm guessing from your accent you're from the Southside?"

I held a hand up. "Guilty as charged. I'm afraid we're cursed to be mortal enemies."

She chuckled. "Yes, the age-old rivalry."

"What's all this?" Broderick, my date, asked. He was absolutely gorgeous, all suave and cool with a real edgy dress sense. And he'd been smiling at me *a lot* since we sat down. Maybe I'd chase my hearts and flowers feelings for Will away with this sexy piece of ass.

Whoa.
Josey.
Where did that come from?

My gaze flickered to Will. The waiter had just come and refreshed his supply of tequila, and he sat drinking quietly. The more he drank, the less rigid his posture seemed to become.

"Southsiders are considered upper class, posh types," I explained, giving my attention back to Broderick.

"And us Northsiders are more working class," Ophelia finished. I really was starting to like her.

"So, you guys don't mix?" Broderick pointed between the two of us.

"Not necessarily. It's just a stupid stereotype, and we all know those are frequently wrong. I mean, look at me and Ophie. Do you mind if I call you Ophie?"

Those buy one, get one Manhattans were taking effect.

She laughed and shook her head.

"So, between us two, I'm supposed to be the classy one, but I'm sitting here in this slutty dress, yapping away, knocking back cocktails like there's no tomorrow. All the while Ophie's outfit is downright demure, she's reserved and sipping her drinks like a fucking lady. Oh! And I just cursed! You see, the stereotype is wrong."

"Nothing wrong with a slutty dress every now and again," Broderick winked.

Will made a weird gruff sound in the back of his throat before mustering, "It's not slutty."

I waved my hand through the air. "Oh, you know what I mean."

His brows furrowed, eyes on me as he downed an entire shot glass. I shivered at the dark look aimed at me. There was something . . . gah! Sexy about it. And, oh! Maybe dangerous?

Or maybe you're just tipsy, horny, and imagining things.

I focused my attention back on Ophelia and Broderick, because Will was making me come over all peculiar.

"And do you two live over here, or back in the States?" I asked.

"I live in the States and Ophelia is in the process of moving to New York. I came over to help her out."

"That's exciting! I guess it's better for your career to live over there?"

"And for recording," Ophelia added. "We're going into the studio to record my first album next month."

"Oh, I thought you already had an album out." This was so fascinating and I wanted to hear more.

"No, I just have a few songs online. I had a YouTube channel that gained a big following, and that's how the label found me. Broderick was actually the one who really pushed for me to get signed."

I looked at him. "And you're a producer. I bet that's an interesting job."

His eyes were on Ophelia. "It is when you find great talent."

An odd moment passed between them. A *charged* moment. An *atmospheric* moment.

So of course, I opened my big mouth. "Well, I for one can't wait to go home and look up some of your songs. I can't believe I'm out sharing drinks with *the* Ophelia and her supercool producer, Broderick. It's a story to tell the grandkids."

They both laughed, and I was tipsily delighted to have found an audience who enjoyed my silly babble.

"Do you both only go by your first names?" Will asked, glancing between the two. There was something different in his voice, something it took me a second to pinpoint.

He was definitely tipsy, if not drunk.

Though I wasn't surprised considering the amount of shots he'd had.

"Ophelia is my stage name, but my full name is Ophelia Desdemona Burke. My mam was a big fan of Shakespeare."

"And tragic endings?" Will asked distractedly, twisting his shot glass in a circle.

"Pardon?" She leaned an inch closer to him, like she couldn't hear the question.

"In *Hamlet*"—Will gave her his eyes—"Ophelia drowns herself. And at the end of *Othello*, Desdemona is murdered by her estranged husband."

How does he know so much about Shakespeare?

Ophelia didn't let him phase her. "You know your literature. I'm impressed."

Will nodded and took another drink. I decided a change of tone was in order, so I wiggled in my seat. "Okay Broderick, you have to let me out so I can dance."

My favorite Little Mix song was playing and girl bands made me happy.

Ophelia and Broderick shared a look, and he seemed to oblige happily. They followed me to the dance floor, and I was surprised when Will did, too. He didn't strike me as the dancing type, especially since whenever I jived around the living room at home he preferred to smile and shake his head at me rather than take part.

We all danced as a group, not really partnering off. Even though this was supposed to be a double date, it felt more like a few friends hanging out.

Well, it did until I locked eyes with Will. I tried to ignore the way he looked at me. Actually, it was more than just mere looking. He *watched* me. When I turned around, Ophelia and Broderick had blended in with the crowd. They were still dancing, but they'd moved further into the fray.

A second later, a warm hand pressed against the small of my back. "You look beautiful tonight, Josey," Will said, his mouth close to my ear.

"Thanks for helping me pick a dress," I shouted over the music while tingles skittered down my spine. When he touched me, it was a lot to take in.

I needed to double down on thinking of him like a girl. Usually, when I was with girlfriends, I'd compliment their makeup. But he wasn't wearing any.

So instead I said, "You did a good job shaving today. Well done!"

He didn't respond, instead his arms circled my waist, his movements slow and yet somehow perfectly in rhythm. I inhaled a sharp breath. Will was a big guy, and when he put his arms around you it was a little overwhelming. I remembered our hug back at the apartment, how unexpected it was and how amazing it felt, even though he was completely stiff. I'd turned it into a joke, teasing and chasing him around his bedroom. This time though, it was different. He wasn't stiff or rigid like before. Now he was liquid. His entire form melding itself to mine.

I smelled the sharp tang of tequila on his breath when he spoke again, "You're a great dancer."

The music changed to that "Crying in the Club" song and everything slowed down. Now the atmosphere was thick with something I couldn't quite describe. Every hair on my body stood on end.

And then, Will pressed his mouth to the hollow of my neck.

And my brain stuttered to a stop.

Was this a dream?

It had to be.

The kiss was there and gone, a brief but acute sensation. I was so turned on I couldn't think. I struggled and fought to find anything girl-like about him. He was just so . . . male. And sexy. The sexiest man I'd ever known, to be honest. It —he—turned my brain to mush.

Will straightened and his gaze held mine captive. "Are you okay?"

I nodded, mouth dry.

"Are you sure?" He stiffened, blinking rapidly, like he'd just realized where we were. "I'm sorry. I shouldn't have—"

"You are a sexy male!" I blurted, and then squeezed my eyes shut. *Damnit!* "I mean, you're just very man-like. And sexy. You're definitely a man, obviously, but you're also a very . . . sexy man. Who is very male."

AAAAHHHHH!!!!

Why was I this way?

My face still scrunched, I opened one eye to gauge his reaction to my verbal shit-show. I watched as his mouth slowly curved into a grin that could only be described as one of intense masculine satisfaction. It infuriated me how attractive it was, how exposed it made me feel.

"Am I?" He seemed to be standing taller. How that was possible, I had no idea.

"I'm sure you're aware of this." I shook my head at myself.

"Want to know a secret?" His voice lowered, deep and dark.

I hesitated, or I meant to. I mean, my brain hesitated but my head nodded without consulting my brain. *Stupid head.*

He leaned in close again, so close I had to clench my thighs because his closeness made my knees weak, and his mouth reacquainted itself with my ear. "I think you're very"—he nibbled on my earlobe and, I swear to God, I could not breathe—"very"—his hot tongue flicked the spot he'd just nibbled, causing an involuntary shudder of the intensely sexy variety—"very sexy, too."

What?

WHAT?

He thought I was sexy?

Now I was certain I was dreaming. Any minute now a human-sized bunny would walk by eating a giant purple lollipop.

His hands moved slowly down my back and skimmed over the curve of my bottom. My eyes practically bugged out of their sockets when he gave a light squeeze.

Leaning just slightly away, his gaze met mine; he seemed to be assessing my reaction. "Still okay?"

"Yup. Yes. Yep."

He chuckled lightly and his hands left my bottom, arms circling my waist again. I briefly wondered where Ophelia and Broderick had gone, and then spotted them up on the mezzanine. They were talking, thankfully not paying Will and me any attention.

Speaking of Will, he nuzzled my ear again, this time drawing it into his mouth and giving it a light suck. This of course sent equally hot spikes of sensation on a collision course to my underpants.

"Want to get out of here?" His voice was throaty, raspy, eager.

"Sure." I forced myself to breathe. *Breathe, breathe, breathe.* With air came a measure of sobriety and the thought. *He's drunk. And he's going to regret this in the morning.* Leaning away, I added, "I'll go grab the others."

It was clear he was about to object so I moved before he had the chance to say anything, darting through the crowd, up the stairs, past the skeevy bouncer, to our booth, and away from Will. I approached Ophelia and Broderick with a hastily manufactured smile.

"Hey, you two. Will and I were thinking of getting out of here." I feigned a yawn. Badly.

"Good idea. I'm pretty tired," Ophelia agreed, and soon we were on our way out.

For the record, I was shaking a little and I couldn't seem to stop swallowing. My legs were now unsteady and I had to use the handrail as support descending the stairs. But other than that? Everything was great, thanks for asking.

The four of us left the club as a group, with me and Ophelia in front. But then not two steps out the door, the paparazzi came into view. Carefully, I took a step back and hastily maneuvered a bewildered and slightly grumpy-looking Will so that he was standing next to Ophelia. Then I placed her hand in his and forced him to hold it.

The whole point of this double date was for them to be seen together, after all.

And then there was the whole matter of how Will was acting with me.

But maybe . . .

Maybe this was just how he got when he was drunk.

Camera lights flashed in our faces as we climbed into a taxi. Ophelia gave the driver her address and Will was about to give ours when I stopped him.

"I'm hungry. Can we go get food first?" Really, I just needed a little more time before we were alone in the apartment. There would be no one to stop him from seducing me like he'd been doing on the dance floor. Lord knows, I wouldn't want to stop him. Plus, it would give him time to sober up.

"I'll cook you something when we get home." Will's tone was gentle, maybe a little beseeching, and—disconcertingly—not drunk sounding.

I shook my head. "I want fast food. Everything you cook is way too healthy."

"You can't beat a bit of drunk food," Ophelia agreed.

Will didn't seem happy, but he didn't argue either. In fact, he was quiet for the rest of the trip, studying the scenery as it went by. Meanwhile, I was a bundle of nervous energy.

After the taxi driver dropped our companions off, with a promise to meet up again, find each other on Facebook, etc., he headed in the direction of my favorite fish and chip shop. It wasn't too far away, thankfully, which made for a quick trip. It was pretty empty when we arrived, and I walked up to the counter to order. Will hung back, watching me. I wore my shawl now, so I didn't feel as exposed.

"Do you want anything?" I glanced at him over my shoulder.

His eyes were pure heat. "I'll have whatever you're having."

I turned back around, fighting a rising blush. I was being ridiculous. There was nothing salacious about what he'd said, but it . . . it felt like a come-on.

"Two battered cod and chips, please," I squeaked out.

"No problem." The guy manning the counter typed in our order. "You can grab a seat and I'll bring it over."

I slid into a booth, and Will, after a brief hesitation, took the seat facing me. I rested my interlinked hands on the table and studied the menu overhead even though I'd already ordered.

This situation was too weird.

Even for me.

Earlier today we'd been roommates, friends, buddies. Sure, I was developing some feelings for him, but he didn't know that, and I'd been so very close to turning him into a woman in my mind.

Now I wondered if Will was having feelings for me, too. The very idea was surreal. We were opposites in every way, mismatched. If we were words, we'd be antonyms.

On the other hand, we hadn't had a single fight since I moved in with him. None of his habits annoyed me, and miraculously, none of mine seemed to annoy him. *Yet.*

"You are my employee," Will said, breaking me from my thoughts.

I gave him the side-eye. "Yeah...?"

"I've behaved inappropriately." The edges of his stoic expression were beginning to fray; he looked vaguely crestfallen, and he seemed to swallow with effort, his eyes falling to his hands. "I won't—it won't happen again. Please forgive me."

I stared at him. His demeanor had gone from cold and reserved, to hot and eager, and then cold and reserved again, and it was giving me whiplash.

"No," I said.

Will's gaze cut to mine, wide with concern but also something that looked liked acceptance. "I understand. Please, allow me to make this right. I'll—"

I waved away whatever he was about to say. "You misunderstand. I'm not going to forgive you because—as far as I'm concerned—I'm glad about what happened in the club. In fact, all signs point to me being freaking ecstatic about it."

He blinked at me, clearly confused.

So I leaned forward and sighed. "Look, I like you, okay? And not in a *I like my boss* way, I don't even really think of you like a boss, to be honest. I like you in a, *I would not be opposed to making out with you* way. Yes, you are technically my boss, and I am technically your employee, but that doesn't change the fact that I feel what I feel."

"You want to make out with me?"

"Obviously. And more. But I'm not sure where we go from here." I leaned back, satisfied that my point had been made while my gaze swept over him. If I didn't have four Manhattans in my system, I was sure I'd be embarrassed admitting this, but alcohol made me bold.

He studied me intently, the remorse fading, something hot taking its place. "Go out with me. On a date."

Uhhhhh . . .

Right after he said this, our food arrived. Annoyingly, my appetite was gone, my tummy too full of butterflies. I picked up a chip and dipped it in some sauce, while Will's eyes stayed on me, watchful.

Something I'd noticed about him, he never wasted food, always ate every scrap that was on his plate. But he wasn't eating now. He wasn't even moving.

I swallowed the chip, then opened my bottle of water and took a long gulp. I replaced the cap, then said, "I thought you didn't—don't—date."

"What makes you think that?"

"Eilish said you don't, so did Bryan."

He paused, as though considering his next words carefully, finally admitting, "They're right. I don't."

"Why not?"

"Power imbalances. Dating someone who isn't in the public eye, who isn't as wealthy. I worry about leading someone on, hurting them. I don't want to—haven't wanted to—date someone unless I was seriously considering marriage."

I lifted an eyebrow at that, picking up another chip. "How will you know whether you want to marry someone if you don't date them?"

"I wouldn't, but before I dated someone, I would want to believe she and I had a chance at something serious, a long-term commitment."

I munched on my chip, swallowed, and tried not to read too much into his words, or be too freaked out by them.

Will was hot and all that, funny in an understated way, smart, kind, conscientious, but marriage? I wasn't even sure I wanted to get married. Ever. And I certainly couldn't see myself married to William Moore. I was zany, made mistakes often, was too free and open with my thoughts and feelings.

He was emphatically not any of that.

It would never work. A crush was one thing. Having fun together and going on a few dates was another thing. Wanting his hot body was yet another thing. But a lifetime commitment? That was a horse of a different color, the color being a shade of heartbreak with a tint of failure.

"So, you're telling me that you think you and I—that we—have a chance at something serious?" I allowed the full weight of my skepticism to enter my voice.

Will gathered a large breath, frowning, and not speaking. And his silence spoke volumes.

Right.

I dusted off my fingers, feeling alarmingly pragmatic about the whole thing. He didn't want to marry me. We'd been living together for a little over a month, for heaven's sake! What a nutty idea!

"Will, this is what I think." I dabbed at the corner of my mouth with my napkin. "I think, I cannot imagine a future where you would want me as your wife and vice versa. I mean, not you being my wife—because of course you wouldn't be my wife—you'd be my husband. You know what I mean."

His eyes narrowed, but otherwise he made no movement.

I continued, "I don't want to marry you, and you don't want to marry me. So how about this: how about we date but without any expectations? No rules, no pressure. Just for fun. See what—"

Will stiffened, recoiled, and shook his head, speaking before I'd finished my thought, "No. I can't do that." His words and expression were so adamant, I instantly believed him.

And that made me sad.

"Well then, I guess that's that." I sighed, shrugging my defeat and disappointment. "But, for the record, I'm so proud of us, discussing this like rational adults. At least we can still be friends."

But, could we though? *Can I be his friend? Knowing that he wants in my pants?*

What other choice did I have? I wasn't going to lie to get what I wanted—which was in his pants—and apparently neither was he.

Will's gaze moved over me, still hot, and then he said suddenly, "I want to propose something."

"Oh?"

"I like you."

"Yes." Goodness, I liked hearing him say those words. "And, as we've established, I like you."

"What I mean is"—his stare dropped to my mouth and everything about him intensified—"I want you."

Gulp.

Well. Okay. Yes. He'd already said as much, I wasn't surprised. But what he said paired with how he said it meant I was feeling too hot for my shawl.

"And?" I squeaked, promptly clearing my throat.

He ignored my question. "Do you want me, Josey?"

His voice caressed my name and it took me a second to answer, then I said nervously, "Yes. I just said so. Earlier. Before. If you recall." This appeared to please him. His gaze wandered from my neck to my jaw, lingering a moment before he looked me in the eye.

"I propose an arrangement."

I wet my lips, and his eyes zeroed in on the movement. "What sort of arrangement?"

"Dating isn't an option." He was distracted for a second, his eyes seemed to lose focus, and then he continued, "We're going to Australia next week. While we're there, I'd like us to be friends with benefits."

I stared at him, pretty sure my mouth hung open. This suggestion was so unlike Will. And yet, it was very like him to be up front, lay exactly what he wanted on the table.

I looked away, the last of the alcohol leaving my system in the face of Will's sobering proposition. When I looked back, he appeared disappointed, but also resigned.

"You're not interested."

I shook my head. "It's not that, it's just…I have some questions."

"Ask me."

Under the table, I wiped my suddenly clammy palms on my thighs. "So, this arrangement, it would only be for the duration of the trip?"

"If that's what you'd prefer."

"What would you prefer?"

"I'm going to be honest, despite the fact that I'm your boss, so you know where I stand."

"Yes. Okay. Go for it."

"I'd prefer to be eating *you* right now."

I blinked, tried to think of a response and came up empty. Again, it wasn't just what he'd said, it was *how* he'd said it. Goodness!

Will leaned both elbows on the table. "Does that embarrass you?"

"A little. This just feels weird." I couldn't quite meet his gaze and I tucked a strand of hair behind my ear, placing my hands on the table as another thought occurred to me. "I'm worried you're only saying all this because you're drunk."

"I'm not that drunk, Josey." He shook his head, looking frustrated. "The alcohol is giving me enough recklessness to speak candidly, but that's all. Everything I'm saying, I mean one hundred percent."

I flushed at his impassioned words. "Are you, um…"

He reached out and used the tips of his fingers to open my hand and trace a line from my palm to my wrist. "Am I what?"

I steeled myself to ask a personal question. "Are you interested in ordinary sex?"

"No, I'm interested in extraordinary sex. With you."

I narrowed my gaze, while on the inside my heart did somersaults. "You know what I mean."

"Josey, I'm down for whatever makes you feel good."

Oh, man.

His voice.

Those words.

And his face. His gorgeously handsome face.

I struggled onward, not done yet with my questions. "I guess . . . I guess, if you like me, and you want to have sex with me"—I whispered the word *sex*, which seemed to draw a small smile from him—"then why not go with my first suggestion and date for fun? Why are you so adamant about a commitment up front?"

For the first time since the dance floor, he looked uncertain. A moment passed before he began haltingly, "There's something wrong with me. Every time I date a woman, no matter how long we date, I can't bring myself to have sex with her."

My gaze darted over him. "What do you mean?"

"I can't." He shook his head, looking frustrated. "I can't go through with it. I realized a few years ago, I *need* an up-front commitment, clear expectations. I need to know it's going somewhere, or it's going nowhere. And if it's going nowhere, I need defined boundaries, rules. I don't want to be responsible for hurting someone."

"You worry you're going to hurt your date?" I was so confused. Without thinking too much about the question, I leaned closer, lowered my voice, and asked, "Do you have a monster penis or something?"

Will's solemnness immediately fell away and he was clearly fighting a laugh. "No."

"Well," I sighed sadly, "that's too bad."

He allowed himself a grin, but only for a split second before the solemnity returned. "My—my last serious girlfriend, I loved her."

My eyes widened as they flickered over him. "I thought you said, over drinks earlier, that you've never been in love."

"I thought I was. I thought she was, too. I asked her to marry me." He frowned, glancing over my head, his expression tortured. "She wasn't in love with me. And when I asked her to marry me, she broke things off, cut me out of her life. She said things were never serious between us—not for her—and I'd misread our 'relationship.'"

"Oh my gosh, I'm so sorry." I was on the edge of my seat.

"I did not"—his face was scrunched, and he shook his head—"I did not take her rejection well. My dad, he had to—what I mean is—" Will huffed, rubbing his forehead. "I was very withdrawn."

"You were depressed?"

He nodded, not meeting my eyes.

A slight tingle, a suspicion, had me sitting up straighter. "Did you hurt yourself?"

He swallowed thickly. "I seriously thought about it."

"Oh Will," I murmured sadly, my frown taking over my entire face.

"I have to *know*." His eyes, haunted, came back to mine. "I won't hurt someone like that, not if it can be helped. I wouldn't be able to stand myself, especially when it can be prevented with the communication of clear limits. And I won't go through that again, not knowing, being blindsided."

"So, that's why you haven't been able to *do it* with anyone?"

He inhaled, nodding subtly. "Rules, expectations, boundaries, these things are important to me. They're essential. And if someone breaks the rules, there's nothing I can do about that. I've done my due diligence. But I have to have them."

Breathing out, I leaned back in my seat and thought this over. It was a lot to take in. No wonder he couldn't make the magic happen since. The man was scared to death of sex.

No. He's scared to death of being hurt, or hurting someone else.

"She was your last girlfriend?"

He nodded, meeting my gaze, slipping on his stoic façade once more.

"When was this?"

He paused, seemed hesitant to answer, but eventually said, "Seven years ago."

It was a good thing I wasn't eating, otherwise I might've spat out my food.

"*Seven years?* You haven't been with anyone since? I mean, other than watching people?"

He shook his head.

"Not even a hookup?"

"Even before her, I was never someone who believed in sex outside of committed relationships. It's reckless."

"But you do now?"

He made a funny shape with his lips, an almost smile that looked self-deprecating. "I'd like to try."

Hmm . . .

"Why me?"

Will took a moment to reply. When he did, his gaze darkened. "I've already crossed so many lines with you, broken so many of my own rules."

"Really?" This was news to me. "You have?"

"Yes."

I was dumbfounded. "Why?"

"Because I think about you. In the shower. In bed at night. When I'm training and when I'm not. I think about you all the time. I think about all the ways I'd like to make you come. And I'm tired of only thinking about it."

I blinked several times, too hot, flustered and lost for words.

Finally, after a herculean effort to find my scattered wits, I also managed to find my voice. "And when we get home from Australia, what then? Do we just go back to being roommates?"

"If you want."

"What if I don't want?"

He didn't seem to like this question; his jaw ticked and his eyes dimmed; even so, he responded evenly, "Then I'll respect your wishes."

This all seemed way too good to be true. He was saying everything I wanted to hear, and being completely honest, and yet I was still intimidated. I'd never had sex with someone who looked like Will. I wouldn't even know where to start. All my partners had been normal, ordinary-looking people, same as me. Will was a Greek god, made of marble, beautiful to look at but not to be touched.

But I wanted it.

I wanted him.

So I threw caution to the wind—as was my habit—and shrugged. "Okay."

"Okay?" He looked stunned.

"When we go to Australia we can be friends with benefits—" I picked up a chip and pointed it at him. "And just to be clear, that means no commitment, no strings, no hearts and flowers and romance, no *ideas*. It'll be sex—just sex—and that's it." Despite myself, I still whispered the word *sex*, but I needed to hear the words. I couldn't get any *ideas* or let my heart get away from me.

We were not dating. He did not want to date me unless we were on the fast track for marriage. He'd been very, very clear about that, but I was convinced it would be a disaster.

He wanted sex. With me. Just. Sex. And dammit if that didn't sound fan-fucking-tastic.

I was also in very real danger of melting into a puddle of arousal on the floor, so using my sergeant's voice, I added, "Now let's finish eating this food before it goes cold."

Will's smile—*with teeth*—lit up his face and my heart skipped a beat.

What have I done?

Could I do this? Could I climb him like a tree, use his body, objectify him for my own pleasure, and keep the messy feelings on a shelf?

. . . Honestly?

I had no idea.

But I was certainly willing to give it a go.

Endeavoring to put on a calm façade to hide my inner freak-out, I ate another chip. I let my eyes wander over him as I chewed, appreciating the size of his shoulders, biceps, and forearms; remembering what he looked like with no shirt on; pondering whether he was telling the truth about his lack of a monster penis.

I can objectify him. No problem. In fact, I will objectify him so hard, he won't know what hit him!

Friends with benefits.

In Australia.

With William Moore.

Heart locked up tight.

My brain parts were still a bit of a jumble, but my lady parts couldn't wait.

TWELVE
WILL

@ECassChoosesPikachu: I need a hobby other than playing video games. Any suggestions interwebs??
@WillthebrickhouseMoore to @ECassChoosesPikachu: I'm sure @THEBryanLeech has some ideas if you'd ask him.
@THEBryanLeech to @WillthebrickhouseMoore: You're a good friend.

I woke up with the sense that I could conquer the world, like anything I wanted was mine for the taking, like *everything* was possible. I'd broken the rules. I'd admitted to Josey how I felt, and now we had an arrangement.

Life was good.

Josey was still asleep when I left for my morning run. I left a note on the counter letting her know where I was and when I would be back.

The sense of omnipotence extended to my lungs and legs. I could run a hundred miles, so I stayed out an hour longer and ran just over seven miles extra. I could have continued on and on, but I wanted to get back. I wanted to see Josey.

On my return trip to our apartment, I ran past a newsstand setting up for Sunday business. I stopped, searching for what I wanted, and stretching as I reached for the bundle of pink and red roses in a bucket of water next to the papers.

"I'll take these," I said, pulling out a twenty euro note from the small zippered pocket at my waist. My attention caught on a picture of me on the front page of a gossip rag and a headline that bore my name.

Is Dirty William Moore Debauching Angelic Ophelia?

I picked it up, scanning the front page. There were several shots of me holding hands with the musician from the night before, walking from the club, and the subtitle read, *How do Ophelia's parents feel about the rising star's depraved new love interest? And can she keep up with Will's infamously voracious sexual appetites? Page 2.*

Infamously voracious sexual appetites? I snorted. *Yeah. Right.*

Scanning the picture, I didn't remember holding Ophelia's hand as we left, but I did recall Josey pushing me forward to stand next to her and how frustrated I'd been. The musician seemed nice, but she wasn't the one I wanted to be touching.

"You want the paper, too?"

I glanced at the woman operating the newsstand and returned the paper to the rack. "No. Just the flowers."

"Here's your change." She held out a few notes.

"Keep it." I waved the money away, grabbing the flowers and turning back towards home.

Home.

I chuckled, shaking my head at myself. I'd never thought of my apartment as home before. Home was Oklahoma, with my grandpa, father, uncles, and brothers. Home wasn't a flat in Dublin, thousands of miles away from my family.

I glanced at the flowers I'd picked up for Josey and warmth, a sense of rightness, set in my bones. I liked this. I liked having someone to come home to.

No. That wasn't right. I liked coming home to Josey.

I'd never picked up flowers when Bryan was my roommate. I'd never thought of my flat as home when he lived there. I hadn't minded going home, but I'd never anticipated it. Not like now.

With these thoughts circling my mind, I pushed past the three photographers camped outside—one of them shouting at my back, "Are the flowers for Ophelia? Is she up there now?"—and took the stairs instead of the elevator. Arriving out of breath, I unlocked our door, tossed my keys on the table, and pulled off my shoes and socks. I went in search of Josey.

She wasn't in the living room, or the kitchen, but the note I'd left on the kitchen counter was now on the table. Walking into the hall, I stopped abruptly upon hearing the sound of her shower. My heart ricocheted in my chest, jumping to my throat as I strained my ears and closed my eyes.

Please.

Please. Please. Please.

A gasp. A sigh. A wanton whimper.

My feet were moving. Before I knew it, I stood outside her bathroom with my hand on the door. I halted, common sense asking me, *What are you doing?*

She moaned, silencing common sense. I opened the door.

And there she was.

It was . . . everything. She was everything I'd imagined, but more, different, better. She didn't lean a hand against the wall like I'd imagined. No. She leaned her back against the tile, leaving her hand free to roam over her wet body, grabbing and massaging everyplace I wanted to touch, everywhere I wanted to taste.

But, as I'd imagined, her eyes were closed, her head was lolled back, her hand moved in a steady rhythm between her legs, her hips rolled, and steam rose all around her.

Watching her was the sexiest fucking thing I'd ever seen. Sexier, much more satisfying than any of the couples I'd watched. Just Josey, here, alone. So much better. She was perfect.

And I needed—*needed*—to touch her. I needed to be the one responsible for those sighs and moans and whimpers.

I must've made some noise, because her eyes flew open at just that moment, she flinched, and she screeched, "OH MY GOD!"

Josey jumped into the corner of the shower, wielding the Pyrex dildo like a sword.

I froze, instinctively lifting the hand not holding the flowers. Her eyes were wide and panicked. She fumbled for the towel hanging behind her and pulled it in front of her. She held the dildo in front of her as though to warn me off, her face a riot of emotions, but mostly terrified.

And that's when common sense made its return.

What are you thinking?

Clearly, I wasn't.

I should have knocked. Why didn't I knock? What the fuck was wrong with me?

I backed up toward the door. Based on how she was clutching the towel to her chest and blinking at me through the glass of the shower, I covered my eyes. "Sorry."

"Will!" she screeched, turning off the water. But then I heard her blow out a giant breath, followed by a disbelieving laugh, which was followed by a giggle, which was eventually followed by deep belly laughs. And snorts.

I peeked at her from between my fingers.

She'd lowered the dildo and opened the glass door. She was also laughing hysterically at the entrance to the shower, holding her forehead. "Fucking hell, Will," she said between gasps for air. "You scared the shit out of me. I mean, I think I almost actually shit myself."

This confession made her laugh harder and she turned away, her forehead coming to the glass as she struggled against her hysterical laughter.

I could only watch her, feeling repentant and . . . frustrated with myself.

She was making little sounds now as the laughter receded, her eyes watery with tears of hilarity. "Oh my God. I can't—" She lifted the sex toy, looking at it like she didn't know how or why it was in her hand. "*That* is hilarious."

I grimaced. "Josey. I'm so sorry. I hope you can accept my apology."

Her gaze cut to mine as she lowered the Pyrex figure back to her side. Though her smile didn't wane, her eyes told me she was confused. "You're sorry?"

"Yes."

She cocked her head to the side. "For scaring me?"

"Yes, of course. But also for coming in here uninvited and assuming"—I pushed my fingers through my hair—"assuming I would be welcome."

She studied me for a moment, the confusion lingering behind her eyes before they dropped to my T-shirt and arms, and then lower to my stomach, and then lower still to where my shorts hung on my hips, no camouflage at all for the painful erection tenting my shorts.

Her smile fell away, her brows ticked up as her eyes widened, and her lips parted in surprise.

"Oh my."

I scratched the back of my neck.

Josey gazed at me with something that looked like wonder. "You came in here thinking that we would—that we were going to—that I—"

"I don't know what I was thinking," I answered honestly. I was not embarrassed. I was pissed. At myself. "And I'll just—" I reached for the doorknob, turning away as I stepped out of the bathroom, shutting the door behind me.

After our conversation last night, I'd woken up feeling so great. I'd felt invincible, which had only been compounded by the endorphins released after a three-hour run.

But I knew better. I didn't have wings. I wasn't invincible.

And I needed a glass of water, maybe four. And a shower. And relief for this raging hard-on in my shorts. Marching to the kitchen, I tossed the flowers to the counter and retrieved a glass, filling it at the sink and downing it in just a few swallows.

Seriously, I needed to get my head on straight. I'd just invaded her bathroom —uninvited—and scared Josey half to death. I hadn't taken a second to think about my actions. I'd broken my rules last night, and things had ended in my favor. I'd been riding that wave since, and now I'd just crashed and burned.

Weary and sore, I needed food and a nap. I'd run too far this morning. But even so, tired and aching, I still wanted her. Apparently, I wanted her so badly, common sense and decency had happily abandoned me as soon as I heard her moan.

* * *

When I walked into the kitchen after my shower, Josey was there. She stood at the center kitchen island, drinking from a mug and eyeballing the flowers—still in their paper wrapper—where they lay untouched on the counter.

I hesitated, not knowing what to do. I wanted to kiss her, wrap her in my arms and lift her skirt, but after what had just happened, I doubted she wanted me anywhere near her.

My chest ached, and it had nothing to do with the punishing early morning run.

She glanced up from the roses and met my stare. I was relieved when she gave me a warm smile.

"You weren't kidding."

"What?" To keep myself from touching Josey, I crossed to the fridge, opened it, and looked without seeing the contents within.

"You were serious, last night, when you proposed the friends with benefits arrangement."

Glancing over my shoulder, I studied her. "Of course I was serious."

"Well, *obviously,* I know that now." She waved her hand in the air.

"What did you think?" I let the fridge close behind me, giving her my full attention.

"I thought you were drunk, and maybe you'd regret everything this morning."

"I wasn't and I don't," I said firmly, not liking that this was her first assumption. "But if you regret it, or feel as though I've acted inappropriately, then you have to—"

"Stop it with the inappropriate talk, don't bring it up again. As I said, I'm ecstatic about last night's revelations." She held her hands up. "And clearly I now know that you were serious. But that means we have to discuss it."

"Discuss it?" I asked, honestly curious where she was going with this.

"For one thing, the agreement was that the arrangement would be limited to the trip to Australia. At least, that's what we agreed to over fish and chips."

She was right, we'd agreed to start in Australia.

I stared at her, at how clinical she sounded, like we were discussing something academic. I should have been grateful. But the truth was, my body was still primed for her. I wanted her with an unfamiliar desperation, *now* if possible. I wanted to lift her up on the kitchen counter and fuck her senseless.

And Josey wanted to discuss it.

Crossing my arms, I cleared my features of any telling expression. "Fine. Let's discuss terms, rules, and expectations. I want to start now."

She considered me for a moment, her gaze narrowing. "Now until the end of the Australian trip?"

I nodded.

She made a face. "No. I think we should wait until the trip and it should be limited *only* to the trip."

"Why?"

"Because we live here. Together. And not as boyfriend and girlfriend. We live here as mates, friends. Actually, technically, this is my workplace."

That made me cringe. She was right.

Josey was quick to add, "And don't start with the apologies again. I've got on my power panties. I get to decide what I want for myself, so no more of that. It's just that, if we start things here, then it'll make things weird when we stop. It'll be like, 'Oh. Look. That's the couch we had sex on, and the table we had sex on, and the floor we had sex on.' I don't know if that would make things awkward for you, but it *definitely* would make things awkward for me. And if there's one thing I'm an expert on, it's awkward."

As usual, she'd whispered the word *sex* each time she used it.

When I swallowed, my throat was tight, but I nodded. "All right. That makes sense. We won't do anything here."

"Good." She picked up her mug again and took a sip.

"Anything else?" I didn't understand myself. Usually I was the one insisting on rules, they gave me a sense of control, comfort. I'd always needed to know what to expect. But for some reason, right now, I found this conversation exasperating.

She swallowed, and then said on a rush, "No kissing."

I stiffened, staring at her. "Uh, what?"

Josey gathered a large breath, her eyes jumping between mine. "I've been thinking, and I believe we shouldn't kiss. In all the movies where people do this —the no feelings thing—they never kiss on the mouth. And, you know, I've been thinking a lot about it since last night and I think it's an idea that has merit. Like you always say, rules and boundaries are good. They keep us safe and our expectations from hurting us. We're only human, right? So the no kissing boundary feels like a good one."

She ran out of breath and leaned heavily against the counter, as though the words had taken great effort to say.

Meanwhile, I was stunned, and that sense of vertigo from last night—where my stomach dropped—had returned. "You don't want me to kiss you?"

She made a face. "Of course I want you to kiss me, but the point is I don't think we should. Sex is sex is sex is sex, but kissing . . ." Her eyes searched mine, maybe looking for acceptance of this new rule, or a spark of understanding.

I gave her neither.

Instead, my gaze dropped to her perfect lips and a flare of intense regret speared right through me. *I should have kissed her last night, I should have kissed her just now.*

Eventually, she huffed. "No kissing. And nothing before Australia. Do you still want to do this?"

Gritting my teeth, I inhaled, I exhaled, I nodded. "Whatever you want."

"Okay." She nodded, but her voice was small, unhappy.

She was unhappy and I definitely didn't want to make her unhappy.

"Josey."

"Yeah?" She peeked at me warily over the rim of her mug.

I felt my chest ease, then tighten as I looked at her, at her guileless yet cautious expression. I didn't know why I was behaving this way. She was right. We needed to set boundaries.

I softened my tone. "Whatever you want. I want you to be happy, okay? And, you're right. Rules are good."

She nodded, studying me, her lips twisting to the side.

"Is there anything else?" I asked gently.

Josey set her cup down and, staring at me, ticked items off on her fingers. "So, nothing in this apartment. No kissing on the lips. Also, no romance or romantic stuff, so we probably shouldn't hold hands either, or sleep in the same bed."

I felt my blood pressure rise with each item on her list. I swallowed it down. *What the hell?*

At this point, I was seriously considering calling the whole thing off. If I couldn't kiss her, if I couldn't even hold her hand, did I want to do this at all?

"Anything else?" My voice was impressively dispassionate, even for me.

Her gaze moved over me, she looked completely oblivious to my irritation. "Both of us should have a safe word."

That gave me pause. "A safe word?"

"Yes." She nodded enthusiastically. "I'd like to tie you up, lick stuff off your body, blindfold you, if that's okay. And do other things, too."

"You would?" My blood pressure spiked again, but for a completely different reason. *Wait, why was I upset a minute ago?*

"Oh yeah," she grinned, wagging her eyebrows. "I have plans!"

Plans.

Okay. So, maybe I didn't *need* to kiss her. Or hold her hand. Or sleep with her.

Did I?

I was torn. I wanted both. I wanted it all.

Common sense decided on that moment to speak up. *You could always just date her for fun, see where it goes . . .*

A shiver originating at the top of my skull and snaking down my spine had me standing straighter. A forceful, panicked *No!* reverberated between my ears.

No.

I couldn't date—I wouldn't be able to have sex with her while we dated— unless she agreed to a commitment, to something long term. She didn't want long term. She'd made that perfectly clear.

And, if I were honest with myself, I was relieved. I liked Josey a lot. I wanted Josey, also *a lot*. But I wasn't at all sure about marrying her.

This is better. This makes sense. The rules will keep you both safe.

"Okay." I nodded. "But I have a few rules, too."

Josey's eyebrows ticked up. "You do?"

"I do."

"Okay, shoot." She didn't look irritated or concerned, only interested.

I let my eyes drop to her breasts, stomach, lower, and then back to hers, remembering the way she clutched the towel to herself in the shower. "I don't want you to hide your body from me."

Her gaze turned thoughtful. "You want me naked all the time in Australia?"

Yes.

"When it's just the two of us, in the hotel room, yes."

She tilted her head to one side, then the other, her bottom lip pushed out like she was considering this.

"Okay. Fine. That's fair. As long as you do the same."

"Agreed. And—"

"There's more?" She grinned, her eyes bright.

"Birth control. I will buy—"

"Yes! How could I forget to bring that up? You should know, I'm on the pill."

That stopped me. "You are?"

"Yes. For period irregularities, if you must know. The pill helps so much, with the pain and keeping my womanly processes regular."

I tried not to look too discombobulated, and I was pretty sure I succeeded when her smile didn't waver.

When I was able to speak, I said, "I will use a condom."

A wrinkle appeared between her brows. "Why? I promise you, I'm clean. I can go get tested again if you want. And I'm pretty sure you're spic-and-span, seeing as how you've been celibate for *years*. You are, right?"

"R-right—"

"Then there we are. All settled." She sipped from her mug, but then moved it away abruptly as though a thought had just occurred to her. "Unless you want to wear a condom, then that's totally cool with me."

I felt lightheaded at the thought of taking her sweet body, entering her without any barriers, but managed to say, "No. No condom is fine."

"Good."

On an impulse, I added, "You'll be my d—my plus one, to events."

"Hmm." Now she frowned, but eventually said, "Okay."

"And I want to tie you up."

She grinned again. "I was hoping you would. My safe word is Rolodex."

Rolodex? "Rolodex?"

Josey didn't miss a beat. "It needs to be a word you don't use very often. Something jarring that can't be mistaken for anything else. What would you like yours to be?"

That did make sense. I thought a second, then said, "Combine harvester."

Josey chuckled loudly. "Oh man, that's even better than mine."

I laughed, too, relaxing for the first time since I opened her bathroom door earlier. "I'm a farm boy at heart."

She shot me a wink and came around to pat me on the shoulder. "Well, farm boy, I can't wait to get you to work."

Uh...

Before I'd recovered from that statement, Josey downed the rest of her tea and set her mug in the sink, breezing out of the room and calling over her shoulder, "I'm taking Rocky for a walk. If you think of anything else, just make a list and we can discuss before movie night. I hope you like Simon Pegg films."

Not a minute later, the front door closed and she was gone.

She wants you to tie her up.

I exhaled, leaning heavily on the center kitchen island and staring at nothing in particular as flashes of images, possibilities, deep dark fantasies played a greatest hits reel through my mind, and she was the shining star of each.

When my eyes refocused, they settled on a tightly bound assemblage of pink and red. I was staring at the roses I'd picked up for Josey after my run.

They were still on the counter, untouched.

THIRTEEN
JOSE

@JoseyInHeels: Today at work I met a cat called Katy Purry and I honestly think that's the most inspired thing I've ever heard.
@BroderickAdams to @JoseyInHeels: You obviously never met my childhood cat, Maximus Whiskerus Meridius 😄
@JoseyInHeels to @BroderickAdams: We are now best friends.

Those flowers.

I was pretty sure they were for me, unless Will bought them for Rocky, which obviously he hadn't. I'd received flowers from a few boyfriends, but always on my birthday, or an anniversary, or as an apology. Never *just because*. The sight of them had given me all kinds of flutters and feelings.

In short, they were too much of a complication, which was why I didn't accept them, or even acknowledge their presence.

First, Will and I agreed to be friends with benefits in Australia only. Then he walked into the bathroom while I was showering slash…doing other stuff. Then I found a bunch of roses on the kitchen counter.

And okay, yes, the sight of him, standing there watching me was more than a little thrilling. And I enjoyed the idea of him getting into the shower with me. No, that's wrong, I didn't just enjoy it, I freaking loved the thought of it. I wanted it. But that was because I had a high sex drive, and apparently zero willpower where he was concerned (Ha! Get it? "Will" power?).

Liking someone as a person made it difficult to have a relationship with just their body. That's a life lesson for you right there.

When I got home from walking Rocky, the roses were gone. I guessed that

Will had gotten rid of them, which was sad, but necessary if this no strings thing was going to work. From now on, I had to be unemotional.

A difficult task when all I could hear was his voice in my head saying, "Anything you want." And he'd said it so softly, sincerely, like *anything* I wanted was on the table.

Anyway, all the confusion had me in need of a chat with my best friend. I knew Monday was her day off so, on a whim, I took a bus over to Eilish's house after my morning classes. She answered the door, surprised to see me.

"Josey, I didn't know you were coming over," she said and ushered me in. The house was empty, so Patrick must've been at school and Bryan at work.

"It was an emergency."

Her expression showed concern. "What happened? Is everything all right? Is it about Will?"

"A lot of stuff happened. Everything is not all right. And yes, it is about Will."

She worried her lip. "Sit down. I'll make tea."

"Can I have coffee? One of those fancy pods Bryan gets?"

She grinned. "Sure. Now talk. Tell me everything."

I let out a long breath while Eilish pottered around the kitchen. Picking up one on her coasters, I fiddled with it as I spoke, "So, on Saturday, Will and I went on that double date."

Eilish nodded. I'd told her I was going in our texts the other day, and she encouraged me to enjoy myself and let my hair down, though I was fairly sure she meant with my date. Not with Will.

"Well, it was all going fine at first. My date, Broderick, was gorgeous and Ophelia, Will's date, was lovely. I actually got along with her really well, which was surprising since I thought I'd be jealous."

Eilish's head whipped around. "Jealous?"

I waved my hand in the air. "I'm getting to that part. Anyway, we chatted, shared some drinks and I was having a great time, but then Will got tipsy, or well, drunk I suppose. Have you ever seen him drunk before?"

Eilish placed a hand on her hip, thinking about it. "No, I don't think I have. In fact, I don't think I've ever seen him drink."

"Well, when the tequila goes into that man his walls come down, big time."

"Really?" Eilish said, intrigued. "I can't picture him drunk. He's always so controlled."

"Exactly. That's why it took me so much by surprise. And then we started dancing, but Broderick and Ophelia sort of shuffled off, leaving me alone with Will. And let me tell you, there was nothing controlled about him then. Those hands were *everywhere*, and the stuff that came out of his mouth. I was surprised I didn't fall victim to spontaneous horny combustion."

Eilish set two cups on the table, then took the seat across from mine. "Hold up a second. Are you telling me Will came onto you?"

"That's exactly what I'm telling you. I told him I thought he was a sexy male, and he said he thought I was, too. A sexy female, that is."

Now she burst out laughing. "You called him a 'sexy male'? Those were your exact words?"

"Yes! You know what I'm like. I say the wrong thing. It's what I do."

"It's not so much the wrong thing, you just say stuff in funny ways."

"Jeez, thanks."

"It's a compliment, Josey. It's one of the reasons why I love you. You make me laugh."

"Well, that's great for you but I'm the one who has to live it."

She shook her head, incredulous. "I seriously can't believe you and Will have been having a thing and you didn't even tell me. Wait a second, did you sleep with him?"

"No, I didn't sleep with him." *He just watched me pleasure myself while I was in the shower, no biggie.* "And we haven't been having a thing at all. At least not until very recently. That's why I'm only telling you now."

"Okay, I believe you. So what happened next?"

I rubbed my mouth. "We left the club and dropped Ophelia and Broderick off, then Will and I went to get some fish and chips. This is where things got interesting."

Eilish arched a brow. "Oh?"

"He told me he wants to be friends with benefits when we go to Australia."

She put her cup down too abruptly and tea sloshed out onto the table. "What? He did?"

I nodded. "Just for the duration of the trip. He wants my *bod-ay*."

"I can't believe this. I mean, I can believe it, but Will is usually such a stickler for rules." Eilish gave me a look like she wanted to laugh but was also confused. "Why didn't he just ask you out?"

"We talked about that. Long story short, it turns out he has some issues over a past relationship. This is why he doesn't date. We decided it would be best to skip the romance and just have sex. He didn't used to want *just* sex, because it made things complicated, hence the voyeurism. But now that he's met me, he does want it. Can you believe that?"

"I can *definitely* believe it. What did you tell him?"

"I said hells yes. Have you seen his abs? I mean, abs for light-years! And that V-thing that super fit guys have, well he has it! So, again, *hells* yes."

Eilish went silent, her expression thoughtful. "Friends with benefits . . . it might not be as easy as all that."

"Don't you think I haven't thought about that? I know it won't be easy, but I have a plan. If I can just keep thinking of him as a girl, and separate all the sex from my emotions, then it'll be fine."

She didn't look convinced. "Think of him as a girl?"

"Yes, that's what I've been doing so as not to develop a crush. Only it didn't really work, because I do have a crush. On his body, anyway. Therefore, a friends with benefits arrangement is perfect."

"And what if the crush develops? What if you end up wanting a relationship and he doesn't?"

Jeez, Eilish, way to rain on my parade.

I was silent a moment, thinking on it, then said, "Look, I know I'm fooling myself a little, but I have a very high sex drive for a woman—"

"Yes, you've told me numerous times," Eilish interjected before I got too much into it. "But I think you're wrong. I think female. . . urges come in all different speeds. And I don't think yours is strange or atypically high."

She was a bit uncomfortable talking about sex, having been raised by an ice queen mother who didn't discuss such things. Of course, I was one to talk, since I always whispered the word with Will. But I *needed* to talk about it.

Maybe my hormones were out of whack.

"Well, it gets frustrating taking matters into your own hands," I went on. "Sometimes you just want a warm body to use without having to deal with romantic entanglements or long-term commitments. I don't want to pick up his socks or take him to the airport."

"Picking up his socks doesn't sound very romantic."

"But it's all part of it, right? Having a long-term romantic relationship? You get the flowers, but then you also get to listen to his woes, deal with his mood swings, his parents and how you never know what to get them for Christmas. Plus, I'm terrible with birthday gifts, too. I just want . . ."

"Sex," she supplied.

That wasn't precisely true, but instead of clarifying, I said, "Exactly."

Eilish appeared torn and huffed a breath before she replied, "I can understand that. And I guess if you feel like you won't get hurt, and the arrangement will remain purely physical, then great, everybody wins. But other factors could come into play. What if he decides he wants to go out and watch other people have sex while he's still sleeping with you?"

"He's not supposed to do that anyway. That's why I moved in with him to begin with."

"Okay then, how will you feel if you start to really like him and he tells you he's *tempted* to watch people again? You two already get along as friends, and he's been doing great since you moved in with him. I'm just playing devil's advocate here, but you may want to think things through a little more before you jeopardize the good setup you two have going."

Hmm, she did have a point.

Then again, it wasn't like I was going to live with Will forever. This was a temporary arrangement until I had enough money saved to get a place of my own. Since my unpaid internship had become a paid one, I figured it'd take another six months probably. So, if things with Will went south, it'd only be a couple of months of awkwardness before I moved out. Definitely not the end of the world. And I really didn't think that would happen. We were both practical people. We'd shake hands, agree all's well that ends well, and then go on living our lives.

I looked at Eilish. "I'm not going to live with him for much longer. He's been going cold turkey with the voyeurism and I really think that in a couple of months he won't need me anymore. So, if friends with benefits doesn't work, if it makes things complicated between us, then I'm sure we'll be able to manage an amicable parting."

Eilish had her thoughtful face on again. "You really want to try this, don't you?"

"More than I want to eat a tub of double chocolate fudge ice cream while watching *Magic Mike XXL*."

That got a chuckle out of her. "Wow, it's that serious, huh?"

"Yup."

"Well then, I say go for it. Will's a gentleman, and I trust him to treat you right. But if you feel your crush developing into something more, I'm always here to talk things through. Even if something happens when you're in Australia, I'm just a phone call away."

"You're such a good friend."

She smiled. "When you get back we're enacting your Magic Mike chocolate fudge fantasy, so put it down on your calendar."

I laughed. "It's a date."

* * *

The next few days went by uneventfully. Will didn't randomly walk into the bathroom while I was showering, and we didn't talk about "the arrangement." I guessed he was keeping it under lock and key until we landed down under. In a way, I was glad. It meant I could focus on my studies.

In another way, I wasn't glad, because I fretted over whether he'd decided to cancel the whole thing altogether. Maybe he thought it wasn't worth the potential drama, which would be a personal travesty for me because I was counting on that sex.

Or, more precisely, counting down to it.

Not to sound like a moan, but living with a man who looked like William Moore drove my horniness up to eleven. I needed relief and I needed it *SOON*.

My parents were taking care of Rocky while I was away. I think he knew something was up because he kept pacing my bedroom and huffing while I tried to pack. Every time I put something in my suitcase he pulled it back out again. Eventually, I had to get into bed and cuddle him for an hour to calm him down. Well, it was also for me because I was going to miss him like crazy.

The morning of our flight, Will and I took a cab to the airport. He was frowning at his phone for most of the journey, so I let myself gaze out at the city passing us by. In twenty-four hours I'd be in another continent, thousands of miles from home.

When we arrived at Departures, I looked around for the rest of the team but couldn't see anyone.

"Are we early or late? I can't tell," I said to Will as we went to check our bags.

He glanced at his watch. "Neither. We're right on time."

"Then where is the team?"

"Oh, they're not flying out until later today. I usually book my own flights for long journeys."

My brows drew together. "What? Why?"

Will shrugged. "I like to fly first class. It means I have room to move around. Flying economy is a nightmare because my legs are so long. For the entire flight they're squished up against the seat in front of me."

"That makes sense, but don't the rest of the team fly first class, too?"

"They fly business class," Will replied.

I smirked and shook my head. "Fancy-pants."

He scowled playfully. I think he liked it when I teased him. "The team can also become a little rowdy on flights."

"How so?"

He looked reluctant, like he didn't want to rat out his teammates; but then he leaned close and lowered his voice, saying, "McGuire always gets steaming drunk and Donoghue is sometimes handsy with the flight attendants—male or female, doesn't matter. It's all a bunch of drama I'd prefer to avoid."

Ah, now I understood. Will didn't like drama. He preferred order and peace, which was probably why he spent most nights in bed with his e-reader.

We moved forward in the queue when a thought struck me. "Wait a second. I'm flying economy, right?"

Will frowned. "No. Your seat is next to mine."

My brows shot right up into my forehead. "Seriously?"

His voice was gruff. "It's all tax deductible."

I was flabbergasted. "But flying first class to Australia costs *thousands*. That's like, a ridiculous amount of money."

Will seemed annoyed now. Maybe he was one of those people who didn't like to talk about money in public. "Like I said, it's tax deductible."

I folded my arms and shook my head. "It still doesn't sit right with me."

"Josey."

"No. I—I won't."

His expression heated and once again he leaned close. "Am I going to have to tie you up?"

A rush of heat spread up my neck to my cheeks and I tried to glare at him as he leaned away.

For the record, I failed. I didn't glare. I stared. With longing. Because the big guy was grinning at me.

"Your ass will be sitting right next to me, on those big roomy seats. Believe me, you'll be thanking me by the time we land," he said, teasing now as he softly elbowed me. "Plus, it's not like I can get a refund. You'll just have to live with it."

And live with it I did. And I never wanted to fly any other way again. Knowledge can be such a curse sometimes!

We'd just hit cruising altitude and already I was in heaven. I had my own little pod, my seat transformed into a bed if I fancied a nap. I could pull a curtain if I wanted privacy, and there were unlimited drinks and snacks.

I guess you got what you paid for.

Plus, I got a kick out of the entire arrangement. Who would have ever thought, Josey Kavanagh, a "kept woman" flying in the lap of luxury, on my way to a sexcation with a hot rugby player. *What is this life?* I almost burst out laughing at the absurdity of it.

Will was happily reading a newspaper while I sipped on a Mimosa and ogled the very handsome flight attendant. I wondered if they saved the best-looking ones for first class.

As the flight went on, my mind began to wander. I couldn't concentrate on the movie I was supposed to be watching because all I could think about was whether or not Will still wanted to get down and dirty down under. And if so, when?

My gaze followed a woman who walked by our seats, then went into the bathroom. A moment passed. An idea formed. Technically, we'd begun our trip. The woman was just leaving the bathroom when I leaned across to Will's pod and grabbed his shoulder.

"Hey, I'm just gonna go use the bathroom." I gave him a meaningful look.

He barely glanced up from his reading. "Okay."

My message was obviously not received. "Are you *sure* that's okay?"

Will's brows furrowed as he gave me his full attention. "Josey, you don't need to inform me every time you need to use the bathroom."

I tilted my head and made my voice husky. "Or do I?"

He frowned. "What?"

I huffed a long breath and stood from my seat, keeping my husky tone. "I'm going to urinate. You know where to find me." I waggled my brows for effect.

Will had to understand what waggled brows meant. The man sitting on the seat behind mine gave me a funny, vaguely offended look. Great, now I was lowering the tone of first class.

Once I was shut inside the cubicle, which was slightly nicer than the ones in economy, I sat down on the closed toilet seat and waited. I didn't actually need to pee. Obviously.

I waited a full five minutes and still he didn't show. Another five went by before there was a knock on the door.

Finally.

Feeling a fizzle of excitement in my belly, I unlocked the door and poked my head through. Unfortunately, it wasn't Will on the other side, but a slightly annoyed-looking flight attendant. The same one I'd been ogling earlier on.

"Miss, is everything okay in there?"

"Yes, everything's fine. My apologies. I get a bit of a dodgy tummy when I fly."

He gave a sympathetic look. "Would you like some hot water and lemon? Some peppermint tea perhaps?"

"No, that's not necessary. I feel much better now."

I moved by him and the several passengers waiting to use the bathroom. Now I felt bad for making them wait. Stupid Will and his stupid non-understanding of my sexy invitation.

I sat back down in my seat and folded my arms before letting out an irritable huff.

Will glanced over. "You okay? You were in there a while."

I pursed my lips. "I'm fine."

His face showed concern. "You sure? Do you get sick on flights much?"

"Nope. I was just enjoying a nice, long leisurely pee."

Will gave a soft laugh. "Okay."

I exhaled another gruff breath, supremely annoyed.

"Josey."

"What?" I snapped.

"Are you really okay?"

"You were supposed to come meet me," I blurted, cheeks reddening.

There was a beat of silence. "Meet you where?"

"In the bathroom," I whisper-hissed, my embarrassment increasing by the second.

At long last, Will's eyes widened in understanding. Then he frowned. Then he appeared amused.

"Oh."

I threw my hands up. "Finally, he gets it."

His voice held affection. "Joining the mile-high club is not as fun as it sounds, Josey."

"How do you know? Have you done it before?"

"No, but I can imagine. I don't do well in small spaces."

Oh, right. Sometimes I forgot just how big he was. Most of the time we were sitting down next to each other, so it was easy to forget.

He spoke quietly. "I mean, we could do some stuff, sure, but anything else wouldn't be very enjoyable," Will went on. "Though I am flattered that you want to."

"Do *you* still want to?" I asked, and immediately wished the question back.

But the truth was, this whole thing *was* absurd, and it was the absurdity of it that I kept coming back to. What were we doing? How did this happen? And why me?

To be clear, I wasn't being down on myself. I knew I had skillz in bed, just like I knew I said odd things at the worst time and—yes—I kinda looked like a bug. I was just being realistic. I was no more "kept woman" material than I was marriage material for a guy like William Moore. This, none of it, made any sense.

"Do I still want to what?"

Suddenly, I was shy, unable to look directly at him. "To, you know, do stuff on this trip."

He didn't respond right away, so I peeked at him. Will was looking at me like I was a fruitcake rolled in nuts.

"Of course I do. Why would you even ask me that?"

Because you could have anyone. So why me?

I refused to say *that*. So instead I said, "Sometimes you're hard to read."

Will didn't speak for a second. Then, quick as a flash he undid his seatbelt, leaned across to me and grabbed my face in his hands. His eyes wandered from my forehead, down my nose, and lips. They rose back to meet my eyes and his look was fierce. He bent and pressed a kiss to my cheek, then another to my jaw. I trembled all over. He moved like he was going to kiss my lips, but then stopped, exhaling a frustrated sounding breath.

Will brought his hand to my mouth and softly brushed his thumb across my lower lip. "Is this hard to read?" he murmured.

My throat ran dry as I croaked. "Nope. Not at all."

"Good."

With that, he returned to his seat like nothing had even happened. I glanced around, certain we'd have an audience, but no one was paying us any attention. I settled back into my pod and closed my eyes.

Maybe the *why* didn't matter. Maybe I needed to learn to just enjoy myself, rather than always second-guessing everything. Maybe I had mad skillz outside the bedroom, too. Skills I wasn't even aware I had.

Hmm. . .

I couldn't wait until we landed.

***

When we arrived in Sydney, I was exhausted and feeling about as sexy as day-old underwear. Which, as it happened, I was wearing. I couldn't wait to get to the hotel, shower and change into fresh clothes. A car waited for us, which made me feel super fancy and important. Even though he was exhausted, too, Will insisted on hauling my luggage into the trunk.

The hotel was a plush, five-star situation with lots of windows and exotic plants. Will booked us a suite, which felt like our own little home away from home. It had separate bedrooms, a large bathroom, a lounge area, and a small kitchen.

I told him I wanted a shower, and I half expected him to join me. He didn't. When I emerged, dressed and clean, I felt both better and worse. I found Will in the living area, his laptop open in front of him and a big frown on his profile.

"Everything okay?" I asked as I approached. I caught sight of what appeared to be an email, one line catching my attention, *I miss you so much*. He closed the laptop before I had a chance to read more. Something in my chest tightened, but I told myself it was probably just from one of his family members. Surely, he was missed, living so far away and all.

Will ran a hand through his hair, stress lines marring his forehead. "Fine. I'm going to shower. Do you mind ordering some room service? I was going to order for you, but—"

"I never mind ordering room service." I gave him a wide smile.

He gave me one of his small smiles in return, but it was strained, then he disappeared inside the bathroom. I grabbed the menu, trying to decide what to order, my chest still tight. Will's demeanor was definitely off.

Was that email from his ex-girlfriend? The one from seven years ago? Was she trying to get him back? And could I ask him about it? I mean, that was my job, right? To be nosey? To *ask*.

Man, we hadn't even started having sex and already things felt complicated.

I forced my attention back to the menu and decided I'd eat my anxiety away with a slice of Victoria sponge cake.

So much for cutting out carbs.

FOURTEEN
WILL

@FirstFanRugby0101 to @WillthebrickhouseMoore: You should stay in Australia, we don't want your perversions here! Or better yet, get eaten by a shark.

The first email arrived on Tuesday, a quick note, asking how I was coping with all the newspaper stories. It ended with, *Missing you, Aideen.*

I'd ignored it. It had put me on edge for the rest of the week. But still, I ignored it.

Stepping into the shower now, I reflected on my error. I should have sent that first email directly to Kean Gallagher and asked him to intervene immediately. Stupidly, given the benign nature of her initial email, I thought (hoped) she'd take the hint if I didn't respond.

The second message appeared yesterday, just before Josey and I left for the airport. I'd read it on the cab ride. It was much longer and had ended with, *Missing you, Your Aideen.* I hadn't responded, but spent the entire flight with a hollow feeling in my stomach. I'd been fifty-fifty split on whether or not to send it to Kean and ask him to do something.

I didn't get a chance to decide. The third and fourth hit my inbox today—number three was already there when we touched down from our flight, and number four popped up just moments ago—leaving me with no choice but to forward all the correspondence to Kean. I would do so as soon as I finished my shower.

He would not be happy, just as he hadn't been happy when I'd broken off our deal months ago without telling him why.

Frustration and impatience—with myself—hastened my movements in the shower.

The Gallaghers were the last thing I wanted to be thinking about right now. Finally, *finally* we were here, Josey and I. I'd been counting down the days since I walked in on her in the shower, retrieving the memory and reliving it until the edges felt worn and frayed. At this point, I wasn't certain if watching her touch herself had been as erotic as I imagined, or if my recollection was now more fantasy than reality.

Toweling off and dressing quickly, I decided that after I sent Kean Gallagher Aideen's emails, I would put them both from my mind. *Or, I would do my best.*

When I walked back into the living room, I spotted Josey on the floor in front of the coffee table. Her dark hair was long around her shoulders, still damp, and she had a textbook and a notebook on the table in front of her. She glanced up as I approached, giving me a smile.

"Feel better?" she asked, twirling the pen she'd been writing with between her fingers.

"Yes," I responded, distracted, grabbing my computer from where I'd left it on the chair and setting it on my lap as I sat. Flipping it open, I typed in my password. Aideen's email was still up on the screen. I sighed.

"I ordered you a crazy breakfast." Josey cleared her throat, her pen now tapping on her notebook. "Basically, one of everything."

"Thank you." I clicked on the forward button and began typing my note to Kean.

From: William Moore
To: Kean Gallagher
Subject: FW: Call me

Kean,

I received this string of messages from Aideen, the first one is from Tuesday. I haven't responded, but I thought you'd want to know. For the record, I never touched her or led her on in any way.

Please ask Aideen to stop contacting me. I wish you both well, and—
"Will."
—I hope you two are able to—

"Will, I'm sorry to ask this, and I debated about not saying anything, but it's my job, and I want to do a good job and do right by you no matter what. So, what are you doing?" Josey's voice cut into my train of thought.

I answered unthinkingly, "Sending an email."

"To who? Or whom? Whichever of those is grammatically correct."

"Kean Gallagher."

—work things out. I never wanted to—

"Kean Gallagher?"

"The Gallaghers." Again, I answered on autopilot, distracted as I considered how best to say what I wanted to say to Kean.

"The Gallaghers," she repeated. "You mean, the couple you—you used to—to watch?"

Something about the tone of Josey's voice had me looking up. It sounded off, and when I gazed at her, she looked worried.

No. Not worried.

Concerned.

Josey looked concerned for me.

I gave her my full attention. "The wife, Aideen, she emailed me. I'm forwarding the messages to her husband and asking him to get her to stop."

A wrinkle appeared between Josey's brows. "Why don't you just email her?"

I hesitated, leaning back in the chair and crossing my arms. "Her emails are . . ." I didn't know how to describe them. They weren't overtly irrational, but—I finally admitted to myself—they'd left me shaken nevertheless. "Her emails are disconcerting."

"How so?"

Inspecting Josey, I wondered if I'd read too much into the messages. Maybe I was overreacting. Aideen hadn't made any threats, but had rather used phrases like *I don't know what I'll do if you don't talk to me*, and *I can't stop thinking about you*, and *Please tell me you still think about me*.

I was worried about her. I'd been telling myself that, if her feelings had been hurt, it was her own fault. She was the one who'd crossed the line, ignored my boundaries. But, if she did harm to herself, it wouldn't matter whose fault it had been. She needed help.

Josey's eyes grew wide. "Is everything okay?"

"I think so." I scratched my jaw. "Maybe not."

"Maybe not? Are you worried about her?"

I nodded, but said nothing.

"Do you"—Josey paused, took a deep breath through her nose, gave me a smile that somehow looked brave, and started again— "Do you have feelings for her?"

"What? No!" I closed my laptop and set it aside, lowering myself to the floor next to Josey and grabbing her hand. "No. No way. Not at all. The only person I —" I stopped myself with a snap of my jaw, closing my eyes and bringing her palm to my face.

Crap.

Fuck.

"Josey."

"William."

I huffed a laugh, opening my eyes and finding hers on me, bright and guileless.

"I don't know her. But that was the entire point. I don't want to know her, I never have." I dropped our hands from my face and cradled her fingers in mine. Her hand was so small in comparison, soft and graceful.

"But even though I don't know her, or him, I don't want anything bad to happen to either of them."

"You know"—I felt her gaze on me while mine memorized the elegant shape of her fingertips—"if their marriage splits up, it's not your fault."

I winced, but said, "I know."

"But you would still feel responsible." It wasn't a question. I peered at her as she continued, "From what you've said, how you've described things, you were very, very clear about your boundaries. And when they—when she—didn't respect your boundaries, you told them both about your concerns. You are not to blame for their marriage's continuation, or its end, or anyone's hurt feelings."

I lifted my chin, searching her gorgeous blue eyes. "Because I was clear about my expectations and rules?" *Just like Josey was clear about her expectations and rules for this trip.*

Suddenly, my throat was too dry, too tight.

Josey smiled warmly. "Exactly. You communicated the rules, and what she feels—whether real or imagined—is completely out of your control."

She sounded entirely reasonable, and the sentiment echoed what I'd been telling myself since I ended my arrangement with the Gallaghers.

But even so, something about Josey's words filled me with dread.

* * *

Room service interrupted our conversation on the floor. I finished up and sent the emails to Kean while Josey arranged the plates on the table. She was right, she'd ordered me a crazy breakfast.

Bacon and eggs, sourdough toast with mashed avocado, biscuits, sausage gravy, and cheesy grits—which I hadn't had since the last time I was in Oklahoma—with a side of pancakes.

She grinned at me from her spot on the other side of the table and her bowl of granola, yogurt, and berries. Oh yeah, and a slice of cake.

"Is that all you're having?" I lifted my chin to her food.

She shrugged. "I haven't decided yet."

"You haven't decided?"

"I might steal some of yours." She poured herself a cup of coffee. "That's why I ordered you one of everything."

"You can have anything you want." The words arrived sounding rough, with an edge of meaning I hadn't consciously intended to say out loud, so I gestured to the food in front of me and then pointed to her cake, clearing my throat before speaking again, "Just as long as you share your cake."

"What? No. This is my cake." She shook her head and then dug into her modest breakfast.

I stared at her, trying to figure out if she was serious.

She looked serious.

She sounded serious.

So I asked, "Are you serious?"

Josey gave me a once-over. "Yes."

She took another bite of her granola, another drink of her coffee, and then pulled the cake closer to her side of the table. I allowed our earlier conversation—and all the perplexing dread associated with it—fade from my mind in the face of her silliness. Actually, I pushed it away. I didn't want to feel dread with Josey. I didn't want to worry. We were here, together, to enjoy each other. The Gallaghers and everything else weren't invited.

Studying the woman across from me—her lips twisted, like she was determined not to smile—I ignored the rest of the food in front of me and reached for the cake.

She picked it up from the table, holding it up and away. "Back off, Moore. The cake is mine."

I playfully narrowed my gaze. "I want cake."

She shrugged. "So? I wanted to get laid on a plane. You win some, you lose some."

I met her stare, though mine was stunned. And then I laughed. More correctly, I busted out laughing.

Josey giggled a little, placing the cake back on the table. Inspired, I reached for it again. Again, she held it away, but this time she stood as she did so. Defiance glinted in her eyes.

"This is not your cake."

"I want it," I demanded as I stood, not giving a single fuck about the cake.

She backed away from the table. "Too bad."

I stalked after her. "Give me a bite."

"No."

"One taste."

Her eyes brightened as did her grin as she skipped away toward my bedroom, shoveling a forkful of cake into her mouth and moaning, "Oh, it's *soooo* good."

"Josey," I lowered my voice, making her name sound like a warning.

Another bite, another moan. She was in her bedroom now.

"Best cake ever!"

I broke into a run and she squealed, darting around the bed for the bathroom.

But she wasn't able to close the door fast enough and I caught her around the waist.

"Put me down!" More squeals and giggles, the cake now held at an arm's length in front of her.

Her feet were off the floor and I reached for the plate with my longer reach, snatching it from her hand.

"Will!" she protested, wiggling in my arms half-heartedly while laughing.

"I like cake," I nuzzled her skin, placing a wet, biting kiss where her neck met her shoulder and placing her knees on the bed.

Encouraging her to face me, I continued to kiss and lick and bite her neck, until the cake was forgotten. At some point, I must've placed it on the nightstand, my hands coming to her waist to hold her against me.

"You know what I like?" she whispered in my ear, biting the bottom of my earlobe. A shock wave shot down my neck, stopping my breath.

"What?" My words were more growl than voice.

Her hand came to my mine, dragging it from her waist and lowering it to the skirt covering her bottom. "Doggy style."

Fire ignited at the base of my spine. A shudder racked my body as her backside filled my grip.

She leaned a little away, giving me a small, meaningful smile, completely free of vulnerability or doubt, and then turned until her bottom was against my groin. Josey recaptured my hands, bringing one under her shirt until it cupped her breast and the other under her skirt and into the waistband of her underwear.

"Touch me, Will."

"Josey—"

"You seem frustrated. I don't want you to be frustrated." Her words were breathy, distracted, like she was speaking her thoughts out loud. "Use me. Use my body to make yourself feel good. I want you to."

"Fuck."

"Yesss."

Both her breath and mine hitched as my fingers slipped into her, and found her wet. Unable to stop myself, I delved lower, deeper. She was slick and hot, and I felt her sex clench around my exploring finger.

"Fuck," I said again, my forehead hitting the back of her neck. I'd never been this mindless before, this lost to a moment. *Except last week. Except walking into her bathroom.*

Her back arched and she pressed her generous breast into my hand, clenching her inner walls again as I slid my finger out. "Pinch the nipple, hard. And then pull."

"Pinch it?"

"Do it," she demanded.

Swallowing my uncertainty, I did as she instructed.

"Harder." An edge of frustration entered her voice and she covered my hand between her thighs with her own, urging me to add another finger to my invasion and touch her deeper.

I breathed out, my lungs on fire now, my dick pressing insistently against her backside.

"What do you want, Will?" she asked, taking over at her breast and instructing my hand how to best pluck her nipple.

I groaned. I knew what I wanted. I could see it in my mind's eye. But I didn't know how to form the words.

"Tell me." Her voice pitched higher as I found a rhythm she seemed to like, my fingers now soaked with her.

Again, she tightened her muscles around my index and middle finger, eliciting another instinctual groan from me.

"Do you want me?"

"Yes."

"Then say it," she turned her head towards mine, as though to capture my mouth. I sucked in a breath, greedy for a taste of her. Instead, she brushed a teasing kiss against my cheek.

When she leaned away, the words spilled out of me, "I want you."

Josey gave me a saucy grin, reaching for my hands and pulling them away from her body. A protest died on my lips as she pulled her shirt over her head and our eyes met in the mirror mounted against the wall above the headboard. She then unzipped her skirt and shimmied out of it, pulling her underwear off at the same time.

Holding my reflected gaze, she bent forward, now on all fours, and spread her legs. "Take me."

Take me.

I devoured her with my eyes, the curve of her back, the line of her arms, the indent of her waist, the twin, generous orbs of her backside.

"Do what you want," she said, spreading her legs wider. Then, in a quieter voice she added, "I want you, too."

Do what you want . . .

Pulling my eyes from hers, and acting on complete instinct, I bent and bit the curve of her spine, stroking my hand over her ass. She made a soft, hissing noise, arching like a cat. My hands were now moving without me telling them to do so, sliding up her thighs to her hips, my knuckles tracing the soft skin between her legs.

She made a short whimpering sound, but I was too focused to think about what that meant, too busy doing what *I* wanted.

And what I wanted was to taste her.

I swallowed as saliva flooded my mouth, urging her into a new position. I thought I spotted a shadow of disappointment cross over her face, but I couldn't seem to be distracted from my present course.

When she was on her back, lying before me, her arms at her sides, I licked my lips and lowered to my knees.

She made a small noise that sounded like surprise, and I glanced at her. Her eyes were wide and astonished, and she was looking at me like I was very strange.

I began lowering my head and she caught me by the hair. "Wait. Wait, wait, wait. What are you doing?"

"Let go." I turned my head as much as I was able and gave the inside of her thigh a sucking kiss.

She gasped. "Are you . . . are you going to—"

"You said to do what I want, and I want to kiss you here." I traced the pad of my index finger along the inside of her leg to her clitoris, rubbing a slow circle around it and opening her completely to my eyes.

She gasped again. "Oh. Okay." Her fingers lessened their grip momentarily, but then tightened again before I could move. "It's just that, I've never done that before."

I lifted my gaze from her body and met hers. She looked panicked.

Sobered, I confessed, "I haven't either."

Her panic did not abate. In fact, my confession only seemed to intensify her disquiet.

"You—you don't want me to?" I asked.

"It's not that, it's—it's just that—I mean, I've never . . ." She frowned, and then cleared her throat before saying, "Wouldn't you rather just have sex?" Even now, lying naked in front of me, apparently without shame, she whispered the word *sex*.

I breathed out, felt her shiver, and watched as a wave of goosebumps rose on her leg and stomach. Gazing at her, at the delectable expanse of bare skin, I realized that I was still fully clothed. Something about this, the difference in our situations—her brazen nudity, her legs spread wide, my kneeling before her fully dressed—filled me with a needful, thrashing possessiveness.

I licked my lips, turning my head to press a wet kiss to her other thigh, and whispered, "This is what I want."

Threading my fingers through hers, I removed them from my hair while trailing my tongue along the line of her adductor tendon. Moving our clasped hands to either side of her waist, I finally lowered my head all the way.

"Will." My name was a strangled plea.

I licked her opening and groaned, tightening my grip on her hands before letting her go and wrapping my arms around her legs, roughly positioning her, bringing her knees up to give me better access.

She didn't taste good, not like food. No honey or strawberries or peaches, none of that.

She tasted divine, like salt and heat and the realization of illicit fantasies. A little dirty. A little tangy. A little sweet.

Sweeping my tongue out again, I gave her another savoring lick, then another. Then I sucked on her sensitive skin, using my lips and teeth to kiss and nibble. All the while she made these mindless noises, sounds of despair and elation.

Fuck me, I never wanted to stop.

Josey tilted her pelvis, a reflexive movement, and my hips jerked in response.

"Will," she said, like she was in crisis.

I slipped a finger inside her and she gasped, her hips rolling in rhythm to my invasion. "Oh god, oh fuck, don't stop!"

I didn't. And she came. Loudly.

Josey screamed her climax and I opened my eyes to watch her. Fingers twisted into the bedspread at her sides, her knuckles white, her body arched, and then bowed as her interior muscles trembled.

So fucking sexy.

"I need—" she gasped, her hands lifting as though she were going to grab my hair again, to stop me.

Reluctantly, I lifted my head, evading her grasping hands.

Her breaths were labored, like she'd just run several miles. She looked tired, exhausted, spent, satisfied.

But I wasn't.

Standing, I gazed down at her, at her drowsy eyes, her soft curves, her full breasts, and I unzipped my pants.

The sound had her looking at me, her stare growing wide as it dropped from mine to where I was pushing down my boxers. Josey took an unsteady breath, lifting to her elbows, a question behind her gaze and on the tip of her tongue.

I didn't want to talk.

I wanted inside her.

I was close to mad with it, with the need.

Before she could speak, I wrapped my hand around her knee and pulled her closer, down the length of the bed.

"Will," she whispered, falling back to the mattress, her hands searching for purchase.

Placing one knee on the bed, I grabbed her hips, lifted her pelvis, and with one thrust, buried myself as far as her body would allow. And again, it was everything, she was everything, she was hot and slick, silk heaven. I couldn't think. Everything was in fragments.

More.

Josey gasped, closing her eyes, and then moaned, a long, low, keening sound. A raw sound, wild, mindless.

Deeper.

I moved, pistoning my hips, pushing deeper, spreading her wider. She made a sound like a little cry, bowing towards me.

Open your eyes.

I must've spoken the words, because she opened her eyes, a shock of blue, heated and frenzied. Her lips were parted and her gaze dropped to my mouth.

Lowering her hips, I leaned forward above her, grasping her hands and holding them down on the bed on either side of her face, all the while invading her body deliberately, giving her slow strokes, rolling my hips in rhythm with hers.

She was perfect, so perfect. Open and vulnerable. I wanted to last, but I knew I couldn't, not much longer. I'd been thinking, dreaming about this for weeks, and being inside her, claiming her body was better—so much better—than I'd imagined.

Her eyes were wide with some emotion I couldn't read because I was almost there. And her lips were *right* there, just beneath mine, the color of red grapes, of ripe plums.

"Will," she whispered. "Oh god, Will!" She panted, moaned, panted again, and she was coming. Instinctively, my tempo increased in response, and her climax went on and on. Stars burst behind my eyes, a shock of electricity at the base of my spine, a freefall into her arms. I knew my movements were inelegant, clumsy, but I had no control to spare.

I had no thought of rules or boundaries, just of Josey. Rightness, bone-deep satisfaction as I lay on her, our bodies still joined. Maybe it was madness, but a visceral sense of belonging warmed me, feverish in its intensity. Not just that I belonged with her—here, now—but that I belonged *to* her, with no limitations on place and time.

Gathering her in my arms, I rolled to my side, holding her close, my lips at her neck.

Josey sighed, a replete sound that made me smile.

Leaning away—just far enough to gaze into the blue of her eyes—I felt my smile grow.

"Hello," I said, thinking that I must've been crazy when we first met to have believed her anything other than stunningly beautiful. Yes, crazy and stupid and blind and wholly *wrong*.

"Hello." Her gaze and answering smile were warm. She stretched, and I swallowed a resurgence of lust. "And how are things with you, William?"

"Great." I felt my grin spread as my stare dropped to her mouth, my hold on her body relaxing.

Will she kiss me now?

Neither Josey nor I said anything for a long moment, her breathing slowed, as did mine. But my heart didn't. It galloped on, all my intent and focus on her mouth.

I'd just had her, I'd just kissed her everywhere but here, I'd just taken her body, claimed every part of it, except here.

And I wanted it.

I tilted my chin.

Her breath caught.

I lifted my eyes to hers.

Before I could capture her gaze, she pushed against me, twisting and escaping from my lax hold.

"Well," she said, scooting to the end of the bed.

I felt the loss of her, of her heat and skin, at once. Impulsively, I reached for her. But she just laughed, standing from the bed and evading my hands.

"Nice try, but you're still not getting any of my cake," she said, bending to retrieve the forgotten plate from the bedside table and strolling out of the room.

I stared at the glorious sight of her departing back until it disappeared from view. And then I blinked at nothing, because I was so fucking confused.

She left?

After *that?*

How—

"Your breakfast is getting cold!" Josey bellowed from the other room, breaking me out of my stupor. "Come eat something that's *not* my cake or my vagina."

FIFTEEN
JOSEY

@JoseyInHeels: When I retire, I'm going to become a muffin-walloper #forgottenwordoftheday #aspirationallifestyles

@THEBryanLeech to @JoseyInHeels: I've left my muffin-walloper days behind me 😒

@JoseyInHeels to @THEBryanLeech: I didn't realize you were once a Victorian widow who spent her days gossiping and eating cake #youlearnsomethingneweveryday

I slept like the dead for half the day and through the night. Having been awake for over twenty-four hours, I conked out on the luxurious hotel mattress as soon as my head hit the pillow. I'd been so exhausted I didn't even have the energy to relive the mind-blowing sex with Will. And that was saying something, because a well-rested Josey would've been up half the night remembering the exquisite feel of his tongue, hands, and body. The pure, unrivaled masculinity of his face when he entered me, and when he came.

As I blinked awake, the full force of it hit me.

I had sex with Will.

Not just sex. I had the best sex of my life with Will. Maybe the best sex of anyone's life.

My body felt sore in a way it hadn't for ages, and my muscles were deliciously achy. I stretched out in bed, running my hands along the cool sheets as a slim ray of sunshine filtered in through the curtains. Feeling excited for the day ahead, I got up and picked through my clothes. I chose a bright yellow, flower print sundress and some ballet flats.

Once I was dressed and showered, I went out into the lounge. I was shy yet eager to see him. I found Will sitting by the large open window, sipping coffee and eating breakfast, the morning light streaming through his brown hair.

Damn. He really was a sight to behold.

He wore sports gear, a fitted T-shirt and workout pants. There was something incredibly attractive about how they showcased the toned, sleek lines of his body, the athletic way he held himself.

"Good morning," I said, my voice quiet.

Will looked up, stood from his chair, and smiled at me. My breath caught. This new atmosphere between us was a heady sensation. Our eyes met and just like that, my nipples hardened. Memories of yesterday filtered through my head, the details in high focus. I squeezed my thighs together and tried to act normal.

"Morning," Will replied, his eyes on mine. "I ordered breakfast if you're hungry."

"Starved," I said, uncharacteristically lost for words. I took a seat across from him, noticing he waited until I sat before reclaiming his chair.

Will's gaze travelled down my body and then back up. "You're beautiful."

I tucked non-existent hair behind my ears. "Thank you."

Why was my voice so breathy?

"I like your hair," he went on. "I like your hair like that."

I fingered my hastily styled French braid. "I like your…T-shirt."

His mouth twitched as he lifted his mug and drank some coffee. "I have training this morning."

I ignored a pang of disappointment at this news. "Oh, well, I was thinking I would—"

"Will you co—go with me?" He leaned a little forward in his chair, his hand coming to rest on the table halfway between us.

"Uh," I blinked at him. *YES!* "Sure."

He stared at me for a beat, and then added, "Then there's a press conference this afternoon."

"A press conference?" I frowned, worrying my lip. "Will you be, um, asked questions about the stories in the tabloids?"

His lips formed a frustrated slant. I picked up a slice of melon and bit into it. "There's a chance, yes. Coach thinks it's a good opportunity for me to give my side of the story."

"Your side?"

Will exhaled a gruff breath. "I'm supposed to tell them that I regret my behavior, but that I never hired prostitutes. That I'm working on recovery."

I frowned. "Recovery implies an addiction. You weren't addicted. You just liked it. There's a difference."

"Yes, but—according to Annie—when it comes to the press you have to pander a little. They don't want the real truth. They want some version of it that'll sell the most papers." He looked and sounded bitter as he said this, glaring at his coffee cup. "If I didn't have to consider the team's image I'd tell them all where to shove it."

I smirked. "Why Mr. Moore, I do believe I'm rubbing off on you."

He smirked, his gorgeous eyes twinkling, and picked up a slice of toast.

We ate in quiet and I studied him from across the table. He was such a good, honorable person. He didn't deserve to be slandered, let alone answer questions about it. Instinctively, I reached out to squeeze his hand that laid on the table. He glanced to where I touched him, looking surprised by my sudden affection, his gaze heating as it lifted to mine.

Without speaking, he turned his hand and linked our fingers together. A zing of electricity ran through me when his palm met mine. Our eyes held.

"Thank you," he said.

"For what?" *Seriously, what is with me and the breathy voice this morning?*

"You're a good person, Josey." His voice was low, sincere. It hit me right in the pit of my stomach.

"So are you."

His eyes got a little sad, and I wondered about it. Did he not realize how good he was? Will was the sort of person who did favors without expecting anything in return. He was the sort of person who was there for his friends when they needed him. I witnessed it with Bryan and Eilish, and even with me to a certain extent. When he cooked dinner, he always made enough for two. If he went out for a walk, he brought Rocky along with him because he knew I had to study some days and didn't have the time.

Dammit, there went my emotions again, trying to get themselves involved.

I pushed them away into a far-off, dark corner, and tried not to let myself feel too mushy by the way Will was looking at me, and mostly succeeded.

Later that morning, I sat on the sidelines while the rest of the team warmed up out on the pitch. They had the first of three test matches in a few days and I was looking forward to it. I'd attended a few back home with Eilish and there was always an electric atmosphere.

I tried to focus on the textbook on my lap, *Veterinary Parasitology*, but my gaze kept wandering back to the pitch. Will ran laps back and forth with Bryan, Ronan, and several other members of the team. I admired his athleticism, the muscle tone in his legs and thighs, and the sexy, serious expression on his face as he concentrated on his warm-up.

Maybe later, I could order something from room service with whipped cream, convince him to let me tie him up and—

My phone rang, interrupting my naughty stream of thought. Eilish's name showed on the screen as I answered, "Greetings from the land of Oz!"

She laughed. "You sound happy. I take it you managed to sleep off the jet lag."

"You know me. Out like a light as soon as I crawl into bed. I think I slept for fifteen hours straight last night."

"Wow, I'm jealous. Patrick woke me up at 2:00 a.m. He's been sad because he misses his daddy. I had to let him sleep in bed with me."

"Aww, I bet Bryan misses him, too."

"He does. He's been sending text messages nonstop to check in on us. Speaking of my baby daddy, I'm trusting you to keep all those rugby groupies away from him."

"Wouldn't it be some form of betrayal for them to hook up with a player from the opposing team? Then again, forbidden fruit is always the sweetest," I teased.

"Josey! You are not putting my mind at ease right now."

"Oh, come on, Bryan's besotted with you. He doesn't even look at other women."

"Yeah, yeah. Anyway, how's everything with you?"

"I'm great. Better than great." I lowered my voice. "Will went down on me last night and it was *incredible*. I'm all, *cunnilingus, where have you been all my life?*"

Eilish gasped and then giggled as I belatedly realized there was an assistant sitting a few rows away. By the look on her face, she heard every word despite me speaking quietly.

"You two got straight down to business then, huh?"

"Oh yeah. I'm making the most of this trip, for my vagina's sake if nothing else. She deserves it."

Eilish laughed some more while the assistant shot me another dirty look, stood up, and went to sit somewhere further away. Maybe her vagina needed some hot rugby player cunnilingus? *But really, whose didn't?*

Eilish and I chatted for a while, but then it was time for her to go.

"Well, I'm glad to hear it's all going so great for you over there. I've got to go put Patrick to bed but I'll call again in a couple of days."

"Cool! Talk to you then. Say hello to the little guy for me."

We hung up and I endeavored to read to the end of the current chapter in my textbook before I allowed myself another peek at Will. *Come on, self-control, you can do this.* I didn't entirely succeed, but I did manage to get to the end of the chapter. It might've taken me twice as long, but I got there.

When it was time for the press conference, I stood at the back of the room, sipping on an iced latte. It was way too warm for hot coffee. The place started to fill up with journalists and I listened in to a conversation between the man and woman in front of me.

"I can't believe I didn't know about this, and he's going to be here today on the panel?" the woman asked.

"Yes, he'll be here. You should've done your research. Apparently, he's into some serious kink."

Oh no, I knew instantly that they were talking about Will. I frowned so hard at the backs of their heads, I got an ache between my eyebrows.

"Maybe I'll ask about it," said the woman.

"Not if I get there first," the man replied.

A knot formed in my throat. Will was going to get grilled by these journalists and all I wanted to do was save him from the scrutiny.

The chatter died down when the head coach, Ronan Fitzpatrick, Bryan, Will, two other members of the team, and their publicist emerged. Cameras snapped pictures as they each took a seat at the long table.

Will and the rest of the players had changed out of their workout gear and were now wearing sharp suits. Will looked droolworthy in his navy, fitted blazer and shirt, though I did notice him tug on it a little uncomfortably. I remembered him saying something to me about never being able to feel comfortable in a suit, even when it was tailor-made.

Now I felt even worse for him. Not only was he wearing uncomfortable clothes, he was about to face some uncomfortable questions.

The conference began with the usual opening statement from the coach and sports-based chat. It was a lot of statistics and strategies that I wasn't all that enthralled by. I was mostly holding my breath, waiting for someone to address Will. When the coach was finished speaking, the publicist opened the room up for questions. Someone asked Bryan about his leg injury (healing up nicely), and another asked Ronan if he thought Ireland could snag the Six Nations this year (hell yes, he did). Nobody addressed Will, and I hoped maybe time would run out before they got a chance.

My hope was short-lived when the publicist pointed to the male journalist in front of me. He'd persistently had his hand up for a good five minutes.

"I'd like to ask Mr. Moore if he has any comment on the recent stories circulating about his private life."

I saw the coach shoot Will an encouraging look as he leaned into the microphone. My roommate and friend with benefits spoke with a quiet, confident reserve. "The stories have been greatly embellished. I did not and would never solicit prostitutes."

"So, you don't pay people to allow you to watch them having sex anymore?" the guy probed.

Will's expression flattened. "I never paid anybody."

"But those sex workers told the papers—"

"There were never any sex workers. That part of the story is completely fabricated."

"Okay, thank you, Mr. White. I believe we'll move on," the publicist interjected.

But this guy wasn't letting up. "I don't see why they'd lie."

"They lied so they could get paid. I think that's fairly obvious," Ronan Fitzpatrick put in grumpily. He was known for having a low tolerance for nosy journalists.

"Well, isn't that a bit of a lazy stereotype? Maybe these women simply wanted their story heard," the guy continued, clearly happy he was getting a reaction.

"There is no story. Not where they're concerned. I've never met or interacted with any of those individuals," Will said, his face still flat and unreadable. He was very good at showing no emotion. He had to be irritated by this guy by now, but from his expression you could never tell.

"All right, we're moving on," said the publicist, pointing to a woman on the other side of the room. "Miss Sherwood, we'll take a question from you now."

The woman bit her pen, glancing between Mr. White in front of me and the panel. "Actually, I'd like to know how Mr. Moore feels about the public's reaction to his paying those women to perform sex acts for him. Does he believe their outrage is justified?" She paused and looked directly at Will. "By doing so you were supporting an industry that takes advantage of poor, underprivileged women who have few choices but to sell their bodies to survive. What do you have to say for yourself?"

Oh, jeez. This whole thing was taking a turn for the worse and Will's calm mask started to slip. This was a real issue for him. I mean, the man didn't even look at porn because it went against his ethics.

"As I already said, I didn't pay anyone. I've never met or interacted with any of those individuals."

"Oh, come now. We all know behind every lie is a grain of truth. The story didn't come from nowhere."

There was no way these people were ever going to accept any explanation Will might give. They were out for blood and they were going to say whatever it took to create the biggest amount of drama.

"Mr. Moore is no longer accepting questions pertaining to his personal life," the publicist said. "Now, if we could get back to rugby."

"I just want to know what he has to say. Surely, you'll give him the chance to explain himself," the woman persisted. There were noises of agreement from various others present, noises that only grew louder. The publicist looked supremely irritated, but I think she knew every other question was going to be aimed at Will no matter how she tried to steer the conversation back to sport. She exchanged a look with him, then said, "Fine, but this is the last question Mr. Moore is going to take and that's final."

Every set of eyes in the room landed on Will, and despite his calm façade, I got the sense that he was stressed. He probably didn't even remember the question he was supposed to be answering at this point. And I felt for him. I wanted to swoop in and save him from this nightmare, because he didn't deserve this sort of persecution.

A long beat of silence fell, and still he didn't speak. He was drowning up there. I had to help him. My brain was a frantic scramble of thoughts as I tried to think of something, *anything*.

Then, without taking a second to consider the consequences, I shouted at the top of my lungs, "SCROTUMS!"

The entire room fell silent. People glanced around, searching for the source of the sudden intrusion.

The female journalist in front of me turned around and gave a look of sheer disapproval. "What on earth is wrong with you?" she hissed.

I folded my arms, lifted my chin, and looked her dead in the eye. "Didn't you know? It's Scrotum Awareness Day, madam. Good day."

With that, I turned and walked right out of the conference room before any cameras could pan to the back and spot me. As I left, I heard the publicist speak through her microphone. "Okay, everyone, I think that'll be all for today."

Yes! Will was off the hook. I'd saved him with my lewd battle cry. I just hoped he'd be grateful and not mad when he found out it was me. I went to the bathroom and hid in there for a couple of minutes. When I emerged, the first person I saw was Bryan. He grinned wide as he clasped his hands around his mouth and whisper-yelled "SCROTUMS!" then burst into a fit of laughter.

I hit him on the arm. "Someone had to come to Will's rescue. They wanted to eat him alive in there."

He just kept laughing, and I scowled. "How did you know it was me?"

"Oh, come on. That moment of insanity had Josey Kavanagh written all over it. Scrotum Awareness Day?"

I couldn't help smiling a little. Of all the nutty, weirdo things I'd done in my life, this definitely took the cake. "I guess you're right."

He nodded toward the exit. "Come on, we're all going to get food. Will's waiting in the car."

I followed him out of the building, and then climbed into the waiting vehicle. Inside was Will, Ronan, and the two other players who were on the panel. I think their names were Finley and Harris. Everybody got called by their surnames.

I bit my lip nervously as I slid in beside Will. I was worried about his reaction, but when I met his gaze, he was smiling.

"Come here," he said, and pulled me into a hug. I felt him press a soft kiss to the top of my head.

"I'm sorry. I shouldn't have done that. It was inappropriate and embarrassing and I completely understand if you—"

He placed his thumb over my lips, his hand cupping my jaw, and stopped me mid-ramble. His eyes were warm and full of affection. "Josey, thank you."

I blinked, flustered by the touch of his thumb on my mouth. He let it drop, and my voice returned. "Yes, well, I just wish I'd shouted some other word, like jelly or cupcake. News stations all across the country are going to be broadcasting my voice yelling about dangly male body parts. It's not my finest moment, and believe me, I've had some bad ones."

"In all likelihood, they'll edit it out," Ronan said. He sat in the front seat next to the driver. "I mean, someone randomly yelling about cocks and balls from the back of a conference room doesn't really fit into any narrative. It's too weird to be included in a normal sports piece, but too tame to be considered a scandal. If you'd decided to streak, or ran into the room screaming "It's your baby!" then maybe they'd use it. But nah, you're good."

"Jean, our publicist, apologized to the room and explained that you're a team family member who suffers from Tourette's," Bryan chuckled. "I have to say, that woman really knows how to think on her feet."

"You're officially a legend as far as we're concerned," the player named Finley added with a smile. "Those press conferences can be such a bore. You definitely made this one memorable."

Their reassurances made me feel a little better, and I relaxed into Will's side as we headed further into the city. The large chain hotels transformed into shops and restaurants, and the driver stopped outside a funky-looking Mexican place. I could definitely go for a margarita right about now.

Inside, we were seated at a long, narrow table, and I was wedged in between Finley and Will. I ordered the chicken tacos and ceviche. When the waiter returned with a tray of drinks, I had a feeling we'd all be sporting hangovers in the morning. Will didn't drink a margarita, instead opting for a shot of some fancy tequila. I noticed that was his drink of choice and it struck me as odd. He seemed like he'd be more of a beer man. Lager, maybe.

"When did you start drinking tequila?" I asked as I watched him down the shot.

"My neighbors back home were from Mexico. Well, I say my neighbors, but really their farm was miles down the road. I was good friends with their son, Carlos, and some weekends he'd steal a little of his dad's homemade tequila, filling the bottle up with water so he wouldn't notice any was missing." He paused to chuckle. "When his dad figured out what he was doing, he chased him around the cow sheds, holding a cattle prod, fisting the tequila bottle, and yelling out swear words in Spanish. It was the funniest and scariest thing I'd ever seen, but I never did lose my taste for the stuff."

I laughed. "That certainly is something. When I was a teenager we used fake IDs to buy alcohol from the local off-license."

"My nearest liquor store was over an hour and a half away."

"You grew up in the boondocks, huh?"

Will nodded, his gaze moving over my face. "I loved the quiet though. Still do."

He likes quiet? It was a wonder we were still roommates.

"Why did you come to Ireland?" I asked.

Back home, we'd talk for hours in the evenings, but in retrospect I realized that I'd been doing most of the talking. I wanted to know so much about him.

"Well, they didn't play rugby at my high school. I started out playing American football, then when I went to college, in the off-season, I'd play rugby. I fell in love with the sport and I wanted to go professional but there weren't really any teams in the U.S. that I could play for. Since my dad moved from Ireland when he was eighteen, and my mother was of Irish descent on her mother's side, I qualified to try out for the Irish team. I flew over, and the rest is history."

I thought it was pretty brave of him to move to a whole other country all by himself. "That's amazing."

Will gave a small smile. "That might be too strong a word, but I'll take it."

He held my gaze for a prolonged moment. Tingles skittered down my arms. It felt like we hadn't been alone in forever, even though it had only been a couple of hours. I wished for us to be back at the hotel room. I wished for him to be kissing his way down my body until I came apart under his tongue.

"So, Josey, have you done much sightseeing yet?" Finley asked.

Will shot him a vaguely annoyed look, which was strange. I thought he liked Finley.

I shook my head, turning to Will's teammate. "No, actually. I haven't had the chance, but I would like to go see the Sydney Opera House and maybe do some exploring."

"I could take you if you'd like," Finley offered, taking me completely by surprise.

"Really?" It was all I could think to say.

"Sure. This is my first time over here. So I'd like to make the most of it. We might as well do it together." He lifted his glass towards mine, giving me what looked like a flirty smile.

"Josey and I already have some tours for *two* locked in," Will interjected, his voice gruff.

I glanced at him, wide-eyed. "We do?"

"Yes," he replied firmly, looking at Finley. "We do."

"Well, if you find yourself at a loose end, come find me," Finley said, ignoring Will and clinking our glasses together. I nodded, feeling flushed.

I was. . . awkward and exhilarated all at once, and I couldn't pinpoint precisely why.

After dinner, and a number of drinks, we all headed back to our hotels. Will was mostly quiet during the short walk, his hands shoved in his pockets, his face thoughtful. I wondered what he was thinking. I was a little buzzy from the alcohol, and a little swoony at the way he'd thanked me earlier for my outburst at the press conference and cupped my chin in the car, how he'd brushed his thumb against my lips.

When we finally made it back to our room, I was sweaty from the heat and clammy from my roller-coaster of emotions. Will held the door as I entered first and I sighed, grateful for the room's air conditioner.

"I think I'll take a shower," I said, yawning and placing the bag with my textbook on the couch. I stretched my arms over my head, twisting slightly at the waist as I shuffled towards my room.

A vague sense of being observed as I walked from the living room caused the fine hairs on the back of my neck to rise. I shivered, but Will didn't say anything as I left. He didn't make any sound at all.

Truthfully, I was too busy trying to untangle why the conversation at dinner had pleased me so much to fully take note of his watchful silence. The sense of exhilaration from earlier, a giddy kind of happiness, hadn't dissipated one bit.

Stripping as soon as I entered my room, I tossed my dress, bra, and undies to the bed. Once I was under the spray, I closed my eyes and ran my hands down my body, blindly reaching for the soap just before I heard a noise, a soft *snick* of the shower door.

My eyes flew open and my breath caught. Will stood just outside the shower, completely and deliciously naked, his gorgeous cock thick and already erect. He didn't hesitate, stepping inside and closing the door behind him, his hot gaze moving over my body with obvious—and hungry-looking—intent.

A thrill of excitement, amplified by an edge of alarm, had my heart jumping, racing. I gulped, watching his approach, his eyes on my mouth. My knees wobbled and I took an automatic step back. The force of his stare was honestly a little intimidating. The way he looked at me, I felt . . . hunted, like prey.

I must've been an odd bird, because I liked it. I couldn't bring myself to mind.

Not one little bit.

SIXTEEN
WILL

@FinleyIRE to @WillthebrickhouseMoore: Are you and J coming to dinner tonight?
@WillthebrickhouseMoore to @FinleyIRE: No.
@FinleyIRE to @WillthebrickhouseMoore: What's her avatar / handle?
@WillthebrickhouseMoore to @FinleyIRE: @GoF-YourselfFinley BTW sorry about your face.
@FinleyIRE to @WillthebrickhouseMoore: No, you're not.
@WillthebrickhouseMoore to @FinleyIRE: You're right. I'm not.

"Do you want me to go?" I asked, reaching for the soap in her hand, and stealing it.

Her lashes fluttered against her cheek, inky black against ivory white. "You are welcome. In here"—she motioned to the bathroom and shower, and then crossed her arms over her chest—"With me. To stay."

She's nervous.

I swallowed around a sudden thickness in my throat, gaining another step forward. She retreated, her back connecting with the tile.

"Are you sure?" I rubbed the soap between my hands to give them an occupation, so I wouldn't reach for *her*. Determined to not allow this vision of her—wet, naked, flushed—to eclipse my integrity, I kept my eyes affixed to hers.

What I wanted to do was press her against the shower wall and touch every part of her body with every part of mine.

But based on the look in her eye, and the way she'd stepped back when I'd stepped forward, I needed to make sure that's what she wanted, too.

Despite what she'd said a moment ago, about me being welcome in here with her, I felt dread. I dreaded her rejection. I dreaded the moment she changed her mind. I would accept it, if or when it came, but I dreaded it.

Would this be the last time?

Josey licked her lips, her gaze moving over me. A moment later, she stepped forward, meeting me halfway, but left at least two feet between us.

"I'm sure," she said, reaching out and placing her palm on my chest, caressing down to my stomach. I forced myself to hold still as she took another step forward, turning her fingers so that the back of her knuckles grazed my side. All the while, she watched the path of her hand.

"Your body, it's so perfect." She sounded distracted, giving me the impression she was speaking mostly to herself.

This moment—or rather, the possibility of it—had been on my mind all day. Just the two of us, together. Being with her alone wasn't the same as being with her around other people. With other people, we were interrupted, I was expected to share her time and attention, her conversation.

I didn't want to.

I'd never thought of myself as having a problem sharing with others until tonight.

"You're perfect," I said and thought at the same time.

Her gaze, narrowed with something like disbelief, cut to mine. If she expected me to qualify the statement or take it back, she'd be waiting forever.

Josey gave me a mostly flat smile, and I fought an increasingly insistent urge to soap her stomach, sides, breasts, and back, to follow the sudsy trail with my hands. A droplet of water rolled from the side of her neck to her shoulder, and down her arm. I wanted to catch it with my tongue.

If this is our last time. . . I had no reason to believe this would be our last time together. She'd given me no indication that she wanted an end to this arrangement. Even so, I wanted to memorize every detail.

Her hair was dark with water, which only made the blue of her eyes more striking in contrast. Her skin was damp, glowing, and her lips were rosy and wet.

"Will." I met her eyes, found her inspecting me, looking wary yet intrigued. "Can I, uh, have the soap?"

"Or"—now I licked my lips, wishing they were hers—"or I could help you."

Her lashes wavered, not quite a blink, and her breathing changed. "Help?" The single word was tight, high-pitched.

I nodded, watching her carefully. "I'm good with my hands."

She exhaled suddenly. "Oh?" she said, still tight, still high-pitched. Josey cleared her throat, standing straighter, lifting her chin. "Well, then, I guess I—I—I accept. Your help. I accept the help of your hands. Yes, please."

Pure instinct, I advanced on her, backing her up until she was against the wall of the large shower. Her hand was still on me, the flat of her palm on my chest, but there was no resistance there, only connection.

My attention fell to the naked woman, to the opulent expanse of bare skin. I brought my hand holding the soap to her side and slid it around to her back.

"Josey." I shifted closer.

"Yes?" she answered breathlessly.

If this is the last time . . .

"I've been thinking about you all day."

She gulped, her gaze on my neck. "What—what have you been thinking?"

"I want to kiss you."

Her eyes cut to mine, sharp with some emotion I couldn't read.

Before she could speak, I quickly amended my confession, "Your shoulder, your neck, other places . . ."

"Oh." She huffed a laugh. "Yes. Of course. I—oh!"

Instantly, I lowered my mouth to her neck and licked her wet skin, groaning and stepping more fully against her as her taste invaded my mouth.

Josey's breath hitched, her hands pushing into my hair, her fingers digging into my scalp, her body arching eagerly against mine.

I wanted to savor her, the moment. But, just like yesterday, I felt starved. Trailing hungry kisses up her neck to her ear, I separated our bodies just enough to allow me to soap her stomach and thighs, taking special care to avoid her breasts. I pressed the length of my body against hers, my thigh moving between her legs.

I groaned, or maybe she did, it didn't matter. I had no attention to spare for the sounds I made. Licking and biting the still wet skin of her collarbone and shoulder, I dropped the bar and moved my soapy hand to her ass, grabbing it, and the other between her legs where she'd been riding my thigh. I told myself to slow down as I used my knee to spread her open for my fingers.

Vaguely, I became aware of her nails digging into my shoulders and her gasping little breaths as I forced myself to gently circle her clit with my thumb.

Fucking hell, I wanted to be inside her. I wanted to lift her against the wall and bury myself in her body, suffocate on her skin.

Instead, I asked, "Do you want me to be gentle?" *Please say no.*

Not waiting for an answer, I bent to suck a nipple into my mouth, swirling my tongue around the peak and unable to stop a groan. After this, I wanted hours with her breasts, to kiss them, taste them, to learn their weight and color, to test their yielding softness and watch my hands as they filled my grip.

"I want it hard," she said as her hand found me, encircling my length and giving me a rough tug.

I cursed against her skin, my whole body tensing as a string of expletives escaped my mouth. She gave me another stroke as her hips jerked forward, seeking more of my fingers.

"I want you." Her words were again breathless, and she left hurried kisses around my neck and down my chest.

I couldn't speak, I was so close, so close, and I didn't want to come, not yet. Not in her hand.

Unable to vocalize my thoughts, I grabbed her wrists and brought them over her head, rubbing my dick against her belly as I invaded her with my middle finger.

More gasps, her widened eyes staring into mine as her pelvis rolled. She felt so good, so hot and smooth and slick. Unconsciously, I licked my lips, fighting the urge to bring my fingers to my mouth for a taste.

Kiss her.

Staring at her lips, I leaned closer, breathing her air.

"Will." She lifted her chin, moving her mouth farther from mine as the back of her head hit the wall. "I'm—I'm going to—"

"Do it."

She closed her eyes and she did, and she was not quiet. She vibrated around my fingers, clenched and spasmed, her arms strained where I held them against the tile wall. Her beautiful body tensed as she bowed forward, her stunning features once again a riot of emotions.

Christ. I loved seeing her like this. So lost. So mindless. Purely physical, visceral, carnal. My dick throbbed, a spike running from the base of my spine to the head, and I held my breath, willing myself to hold on.

I couldn't.

I came.

I came against her stomach, my cum spilling on the underside of her breasts. And fuck if seeing that wasn't hot, seeing her trembling, flushed body. It was. It so fucking was.

Out of breath, I leaned against her, releasing her wrists and bringing them to my shoulders. I gathered her to me, wrapping her tight in my arms, because the urge to take her mouth was almost uncontrollable.

Touching her, sex, it had to be enough, because I wouldn't give her up. She didn't want romance, kissing, sleeping together, hand-holding, and I accepted that, but acceptance didn't equate to lack of want.

So I held her instead, catching my breath and searching for control, reassuring and consoling myself with the reminder that we had eight more days. Surely, eight more days would be enough.

Those are the rules.

And at the end of those eight days, we would still know each other, right? I would still have her in my life even if I couldn't ever *have* her.

But for now, we would wash off, rinse the sex from our bodies. And then maybe we could do it again. Maybe this time I'd have her against the wall, or I'd take her from behind, or I'd kneel before her and taste my fill.

Wash. Rinse. Repeat.
It's enough.

* * *

"Everything looks so good here." Josey's eyes moved over the menu, her tone betraying her excitement. "I want one of each appetizer."

I wasn't looking at the menu, I was too busy enjoying her animated expression.

Josey and I ditched the team dinner and went to a small Italian restaurant near Circular Quay in a section of Sydney's CBD (the central business district) called The Rocks. More precisely, I'd ditched the team dinner so I could keep Josey to myself.

I didn't feel bad about it.

We'd been eating dinner with the team and their families for three nights, and Finley always seemed to find himself a seat at our table, usually next to Josey. I was tired of his constant interruptions and his attempt at flirting. I was also tired of looking at his face.

But my weariness of his presence had nothing at all to do with the reason why Finley was sporting a new black eye after our drills today.

Nope.

Nothing at all.

He shouldn't have volunteered for the ruck if he liked the bone structure of his face.

Josey peeked at me over her menu. "You think I'm joking, but I'm not."

"Joking?"

"About ordering one of each appetizer. I'm definitely going to do it."

"Do what makes you happy."

"Oh, I *will*." She closed her menu and placed it on her plate, folding her hands over it. "You can have some if you want, but just one bite. We're not going to have another repeat of the hamburger debacle."

My smile was immediate. "You said I could try it."

"Yes." She narrowed her eyes on me. "I said you could *try* it. *Try*ing food does not mean polishing off an entire hamburger in one bite."

Her attempt at a stern expression was impressive. It was also damn sexy. "It was a small hamburger. I thought you were finished."

She made a sound in the back of her throat like a warning growl—also damn sexy—and reached for the fresh bread between us. "I will allot your sample portions, you are not allowed to touch my plate."

"Can my fork touch your plate?"

"Ha! I bet you'd like to fork my plate." She tore her bread in half and bit into one side.

I stifled a grin. "How about my spoon?"

"No." She grabbed her water glass, swallowed, and then pointed at me. "And another thing, I'm getting my own bottle of wine tonight. You are a wine hoarder."

That made me laugh, because she was both right and wrong. "No, I'm not."

She smiled like she couldn't help it, her gaze moving over my face. "Do you deny you drank ninety percent of the wine we were supposed to *share* last night?"

"I do not deny it."

"Then you are a wine hoarder." Josey took another bite of her bread, lifting her eyebrow at me as though to say *Case closed*.

"Hoarding implies I keep the wine and do nothing with it. I don't hoard. I consume."

"You devour." She was squinting at me again, but she was still smiling. "You're a devourer."

"What can I say? I'm hungry." Preoccupied by her smile, I gave her lips my full attention. She'd painted them purple tonight. They were very distracting.

For the first time in a while, I was completely relaxed.

Dread had been a relentless companion, a constant hum, for over a week, retreating and increasing and retreating again. The fear grew louder every time she left after we'd made love. Or rather, after we fucked.

Because that was all it seemed to be for Josey, fucking.

No matter how close I thought we'd become, or how intense things were during, she'd bounce right back to being sunny Josey after, calling jokes over her shoulder as she left the room, or commenting on the weather. And she always left the room. She always left me wishing she'd stay longer.

Admittedly, I didn't have nearly as much experience actually having sex as she did, but each time we were together was meaningful to me. I now understood what people meant when they said *The earth moved* because it moved for me. Every time.

Basically, Josey was rocking my world multiple times daily. Yet, immediately after we finished, it didn't seem to make any impression on her, like maybe we went on a jog instead of spending hours being intimate.

Presently, the server came back and took our orders. Unsurprisingly, Josey did order one of each appetizer as well as her own bottle of wine, making a point of telling the waiter that it was for her and not for me.

I ordered two entrees and a bottle for myself, making a point to tell the server that Josey could share mine, if she wished.

This earned me another narrowed glare, which only made me laugh, which made her smile. This seemed to be our pattern. I teased her, she pretended to be irritated, which made me laugh, which made her smile, which made me wonder: was I teasing her to irritate her? Or was I laughing to make her smile?

"You ordered the gnocchi and the fish," she said just as the server left but before sipping her water.

"Yes."

Josey considered me for a moment over the rim of her glass. "What's your favorite food?"

"Food. How about you?"

Setting her water back on the table, she shook her head. "No, seriously. What do you crave beyond anything else?"

You.

I scratched my neck, beating back the errant thought and an odd stabbing of fear in my chest. "I don't know."

Was it hot in here?

"You must have a favorite food." She considered me, crossing her arms. "Or what about a favorite meal? Breakfast, lunch, or dinner?"

"I like them all," I replied, distracted. The idea that Josey was what I craved above all things was . . . it was . . .

Correct?

No. Preposterous.

"But which is your favorite? When you were growing up, what did your mom make you for your birthday?"

I stared at her, hesitating, not sure what to do. I was still put off by my own thoughts, which meant I was preoccupied, and I never talked about my childhood, to anyone. I'd never wanted to.

But before I realized it, I was speaking. "I didn't know my mom." I shook my head, reaching for my water glass, concentrating on it. "She died giving birth to my youngest brother when I was three. My dad and his father—my grandfather—raised us."

"Oh."

I glanced briefly at her. Josey was inspecting me, her elbows resting on the table, her head tilted to the side.

She is so beautiful.

Would this arrangement really be over in just a few days?

It has to be. Those are the rules.

I took a gulp of my water.

"What did your dad make you for your birthday?"

I shook my head again, trying to clear it. "Nothing."

"Nothing?"

"Correct."

"Your family didn't celebrate birthdays?" Her voice was tinged with sadness, unmistakable pity.

The pity was why I didn't talk about my childhood, and it had a sobering effect. I didn't have it bad, not at all. But I was raised in a house without softness, art, or beauty. Hugs didn't put food in our bellies, art didn't fix the roof, and beauty . . .

We couldn't afford it.

"No." I set the glass back on the table and crossed my arms, meeting her gaze evenly now that I'd caught up with the conversation. "We didn't celebrate birthdays."

She regarded me, her lush, purple lips parted slightly.

As though coming to some decision, Josey took a breath and sat straighter in her chair. "Will you please tell me about your family?"

I hesitated again, but not because I was sidetracked this time. I hesitated because I found nothing wrong with my childhood, but others always did. My attention moved beyond her to nothing in particular. *I'll make an excuse. I'll change the subject. I'll decline to answer.*

Instead, for reasons I could not comprehend, I said, "I'm the third of four boys. My oldest brother has cerebral palsy and has lived in a home since he was eleven. My second brother died in a car accident when I was seventeen, he was twenty-one. My youngest brother still lives on the farm—with my father and grandfather—and recently graduated from Oklahoma State with a masters degree in Agricultural Science. He'll take over the family business, which is good."

My eyes came back to hers. She was still watching me closely, but I found her expression difficult to read.

The waiter returned, opened her bottle of wine and then mine, allowing us both to taste our selections before pouring a full glass for each of us. He disappeared a moment later, leaving with promises to bring our meals as soon as they were ready.

Josey brought her attention back to me. I waited for—and dreaded—a follow up question.

But Josey surprised me by saying, "You read a lot."

"Yes."

"Who reads in your family?"

I thought about that, checking to make sure it wasn't a trick question. "My oldest brother."

"I see. And you're very close to him? You talk to him over Skype, right?"

"I am and I do."

"Other than reading, and helping me empty tampon boxes, what are your other hobbies?"

I huffed a laugh, disarmed by her phrasing of the question, and leaned forward. "Uh, I need to find a new hobby."

"A new hobby? What was your old hobby?" Her gaze skated over me. "You don't mean—"

"No." I waved away her assumption. "I used to tutor at The Dream Foundation, Monday and Wednesday evenings. And I coached their youth rugby league, led the camp, helped them fundraise, that kind of thing."

"That's great! Why did you stop?" Josey picked up her wine and took a sip.

I sighed, smiling for no reason, staring at the basket of bread between us, and then at the table behind her, and then at my wine. "They asked me to stop, when everything happened in the news. They thought it was best if I wasn't around the kids," I finally admitted.

"Oh."

I shrugged, or I tried to, and ended up wiping my hand over my face. I was tired of shrugging about this. I didn't want to shrug it off anymore. I hated that it had infected every part of my life, how people looked at me, how they treated me.

Except Josey.

Josey's hand covered mine, her fingers wrapping around mine and giving a squeeze, drawing my attention back to her.

She didn't look sorry for me, she looked frustrated. "Those fucking arseholes. I wish I could slash their tires and replace their toothpaste with hemorrhoid cream."

I grinned despite myself. "All of them?"

"Every last one of them." She gave me another squeeze before removing her hand. Too late, I tried to tighten my fingers; she slipped out of my grip and withdrew, oblivious to my attempt to keep her close.

"It'll blow over eventually," I said, picking up my glass and taking a long swallow of wine.

"Hmm." Josey was inspecting me again, and I got the sense she wanted to ask me something but, for whatever reason, was hesitating.

"Ask."

"Pardon?"

I took another swallow from my wine, draining it. "Ask your question."

"It might be too personal."

Again, I grinned; she made no sense. "Really? After these last few days, you're afraid to *get personal*?"

"Talking is different than . . . *you know*."

"Sex?"

She breathed in and then out quickly, glancing at the tables to our right and left. I bit my lip to keep from laughing again.

"Anyway," she leaned forward, "let's talk about something else."

"Something else other than what?" I also leaned forward.

"Sex," she whispered.

"I thought you were going to ask me a question that was too personal."

Josey seemed conflicted, her stare focused and then unfocused, her brows pulling together. Eventually, she shook her head and reached for her wine glass, taking a gulp rather than a sip.

"You're not going to ask," I guessed, an ambiguous but potent sense of disappointment settling in my chest.

"You should be proud of me." Her smile looked self-deprecating and completely genuine. "Look at me, I'm changing."

I blinked at her. Change? *Why would you want to change?*

"What do you mean?

"I'm learning how to keep my mouth shut," she said simply, like this was a positive change, and effectively rendering me speechless.

Our food arrived, saving me from having to respond, which was probably a good thing. Because this time, my sense of disappointment wasn't ambiguous, and it felt more like grief.

And this time, when the constant hum of dread flared, it didn't feel like it would ever recede.

SEVENTEEN
JOSEY

@JoseyInHeels: Every night, my hotel leaves a tray of fancy chocolates by my bed as part of their turn down service. When I go home, I will be lost without my bedtime choccies 😢#spoiled
@ECassChoosesPikachu to @JoseyInHeels: This is perhaps the most first world of first world problems I have ever heard #definitelyspoiled

"What are you doing?" Will blinked and stared down at me as I reached for his belt buckle, his voice gruff.

I wet my lips. "Giving you a gift."

We'd just stepped inside our hotel suite. I'd turned around, met his gaze and lowered to my knees. I was feeling brave and spontaneous. Sexy, even.

I had an ache in my chest for Will. Maybe this would help, maybe it wouldn't, but I had to do something. Listening to him talk about his family caused feelings to grow and expand inside me, feelings I'd never had before, and therefore couldn't easily identify or understand. I was *feeling* things. Big things. Hard to swallow things. Making my chest hurt things.

Will's Adam's apple bobbed in his throat. "It's not my birthday."

Flicking open the button on his fly and pulling down the zipper, I shushed him and grinned. "It doesn't need to be your birthday."

My childhood had been so different from his. I'd grown up privileged, never wanted for a thing. I was completely and totally adored by both my parents. It wasn't that I thought Will wasn't loved, but from what he'd said, I felt like he probably hadn't received much affection. Having been given cuddles and hugs by Mam and Dad practically every day of my life, I couldn't imagine a world without them.

Will's stoic, almost stiff demeanor, his lack of smiles and expression now made a lot of sense. He didn't know how to be warm or affectionate, because he'd never been given that by his family. His life had been about surviving, all luxuries cut to the bone.

It made me want to do everything in my power to give him the things he'd been missing. I wanted to make him feel cherished, show him what an incredible human he was.

It wasn't my place, but I wanted to nonetheless

"Yes, but—" His words were cut short when I cupped him in my palm. I watched, savoring his reaction, as he seemed to sway on his feet. I felt weirdly powerful despite being the one on my knees.

I pulled him from his boxer briefs and touched my lips to the head of his cock. His entire body stilled, then he trembled. I smiled as I took him in my mouth. The effect I had on him was a heady thing.

A shaky breath escaped him. "C-combine harvester."

I paused as soon as I heard his safe word and backed away. "Really?"

He quietly swore and ran a hand through hair. "Sorry. I'm an idiot. No, not really."

I hesitated. "Are you sure?"

"Yes, I'm sure. Really sure. Proceed."

His voice was strained, and I couldn't tell if it was because he was uncomfortable or if he just really, really wanted this. I'd given a couple of blowjobs in my time, but no one had ever reacted this way.

"I don't want to make you feel—"

"Ignore me. I'm being an idiot. I just haven't…it's my first time doing *this*."

Oh.

My smile returned. I bent to kiss his tip, then flicked my tongue around it. My voice was soft when I spoke seductively. "In that case, I better make this good."

He squeezed his eyes shut, like he was praying to God or something. Pleasure and satisfaction shimmered through me. I was in the driving seat and, surprisingly, I loved it. I took his cock in my mouth again, this time bobbing up and down. He groaned and reached down to cup my cheek. I swirled my tongue around his head, then went deeper. He banged his head against the wall, his jaw moving as he swallowed. I adored seeing him like this. He looked like it was taking all his self-control to keep it together.

Who knew I could be such a successful seductress?

His hands sifted through my hair, his groans increasing in volume. I moaned quietly, turned on just by doing this to him. He let out a guttural growl before there was a soft knock on the door. I paused, mid-suck, eyes widening. Since I'd pounced on him as soon as we got back, we were a mere foot away from the door of the suite.

There was a second knock and I pulled away from Will. I opened my mouth to whisper, but he put his finger to his lips for me to stay quiet. I remembered we hadn't put up the DO NOT DISTURB sign yet. Then I heard a key card slide in. I dove forward on my hands and knees to grab the handle before any hotel staff came inside.

"Don't come in!" I called out, then winced. I couldn't have chosen a more suspicious collection of words.

There was a pause, then through the door a muffled voice said, "My apologies for the interruption. Would you like your turndown service later, ma'am?"

I coughed. "Um, no thank you. That won't be necessary. I mean, we don't need a turndown service tonight. We'll turn ourselves down." *Real smooth.*

I glanced at Will, and to my surprise he looked like he was trying to hold in a fit of laughter at the sight of me gripping the door handle for dear life. I shot him a scowl, but couldn't help grinning.

"Okay, well, if you need anything you can call down to the desk." The maid sounded curious now, but she didn't push the matter.

"Marvelous! Thanks again!" I replied and shook my head at myself. A little less enthusiasm would've been better. When I heard her shuffle on to the next room, I collapsed on the floor in relief.

It was just my luck that the one time I tried to give Will a blowjob we got interrupted. Will's deep chuckle set me off and I fell victim to a bout of giggles. He joined me on the floor, stretching out next to me. Every time I looked at him, I started laughing again, only sobering when he reached out to tuck a strand of hair behind my ear. Something about his rough thumb on my sensitive skin was a cold splash of water to my humor. Heat started low in my belly, and I knew Will saw it when his eyes grew hooded.

"I love your laugh," he murmured, eyes on my lips.

Instinctively, I licked them, every nerve ending tingling.

Kiss me, my subconscious yelled.

No, that's not allowed, my brain countered.

In an effort to escape the snare of Will's gaze, I pushed him.

He resisted. "Wait."

"What?" Was he going to use his safe word again?

Will swallowed thickly, his breathing coming hard. "Can we . . ."

"Go on." I wagged my eyebrows.

He grinned. "Can we do this in front of the mirror? In my room? I'd like to watch you."

Heat—molten, scorching heat—pooled low in my belly and I nodded wordlessly. Will offered a hand and helped me to my feet. Pulling me behind him, he flipped on the light in his room and moved us to the mirror in front of his closet. Turning to face me, his eyes zeroed in on my lips.

"Where were we?" he whispered.

Slowly, I lifted the skirt of my dress as I lowered to my knees, my back to the mirror, and I watched with satisfaction as his eyes lifted to the reflective surface and flared, his chest expanding.

He'd pulled his pants up when the maid knocked, but I yanked them back down, determined to finish what I started.

"Josey," Will breathed, all husky. I kept my attention on his face, not missing the way his eyes darkened as I closed my mouth over him.

His hips jutted forward, a reflexive movement, and a helpless but extremely male sound escaped his throat. I took as much of him as I could, running my hands up his toned muscles, enjoying the feel of him as I licked and sucked.

"Josey." My name was a strangled sound, and I lifted my eyes to his face once more.

He was watching me in the mirror, but from where I knelt before him, I could see his gaze was dark and hazy with lust.

"Lift your dress."

Slowly, I lowered my fingers to the hem of my dress and slid it up my thighs, higher, over the curve of my bottom, until my backside was completely exposed.

He made that sound of helplessness again, but then demanded darkly, "Take off your underwear and touch yourself."

I frowned, because if I did that I'd have to stop sucking. Seeming to understand my dilemma, Will reached down and gripped his erection, pulling it from my mouth.

"Do it," he said softly, but with an edge of something that sent a shiver down my spine.

So I did.

I pulled off my dress, and then my underwear, leaving me in just my bra and my shoes. I touched myself, opening my mouth to accept him again.

But he didn't give it to me. He backed away, still stroking his cock, and sat on the bed, his eyes skimming down the length of me to where my fingers circled.

"Pull the cup of your bra down," he said, like he was in a trance, "and grab your breast."

My breathing was erratic now and I felt a momentary flash of alarm. But the alarm only served to heighten my arousal, increasing the sensitivity everywhere my fingers touched.

Even so, I hesitated. "Will."

His eyes came to mine, his gaze hard and yet somehow vulnerable. "Do it."

It was the vulnerability that seized my heart, gave it a rough squeeze, and spurred me into action.

I reached for my bra, pulled down the cup, and grasped the heavy weight of my breast, rolling my nipple between my fingers and giving a sharp tug. The look in his eyes as he watched me sent waves upon waves of tingles and sparks under my skin. I felt electrified, exhilarated, and very, very close to coming.

"Bend over," he said, his voice coarse. "Let go of your breast, and bend over."

I did.

His eyes shifted to the mirror and he sucked in a sharp breath, his lids half-blinking as he watched this new view of me as I rubbed myself.

"Fuck," he said on a breath.

Will didn't last long after that, his brow furrowing, his lips pulled back in a mindless—but oh so sexy—grimace. He came with a loud groan, his eyes rolling back as he closed them, gasping for breath.

Fascinated, I watched him orgasm, pumping himself slowly as his seed spurted out over his hand. *Damn.* I'd never seen anything sexier. My sex clenched just watching him as I continued to touch myself. I was close now. A breathy, lust-filled moan escaped me and his eyes opened. He went still, devouring me with his gaze, and my hand sped up. The way he watched me made me feel powerful, like a sexual goddess taking control of her body, unapologetically taking the pleasure I wanted, needed...

"Put your fingers inside yourself," Will instructed in a low, raspy voice.

I did. I was so wet. The fact that he was watching heightened every single one of my senses. I pumped my fingers in and out, and Will emitted a loud, masculine sigh.

"Now circle your clit again, make yourself come for me, Josey."

God, his voice alone was an aphrodisiac.

My hand returned to my clit. I was so sensitive everywhere now. A gust of chilly night air blew in from the open window, tickling at my senses. I rubbed myself, glancing in the mirror once more to find Will's dark gaze trained between my legs. He looked possessed. I moaned again, rubbed faster, and came with a sharp cry. I came harder than I'd ever come before. All because he was watching.

This sort of sexual voyeurism wasn't something I'd ever thought about, but it was freaking incredible. I recognized a need in Will. He enjoyed this. It was his kink, and if it felt as amazing as this every time, then I was more than willing to participate.

My mind raced with the possibilities. A second later, Will was on me. He lifted me up and laid me on the bed, his face a picture of lust. He climbed on top of me, reached for his unbuckled belt and pulled it off. He didn't break eye contact as he brought my arms up above my head, then wrapped the belt around my wrists, securing it tight. My belly flipped and my thighs quivered. He was… he was tying me up. Just like that, I was wet again.

Will kissed my cleavage and belly, planting his lips all the way down until he settled between my thighs.

His expression was pure sin as he looked up at me and murmured, "My turn."

Unlike Will, I didn't utter my safe word. My vagina was well-acquainted with his mouth and there was no chance I'd ever say no to this.

I closed my eyes and floated away on a cloud of bliss and pleasure.

* * *

About an hour later, I lay sated in Will's bed, the soft noise of the shower running as he washed off. I was completely exhausted. And since I was completely exhausted, I decided I could deal with washing my sweaty body in the morning. All I needed was to summon the energy to get up and walk to my room, and then I would pass out.

I heard the bathroom door open, followed by the faint sound of bare feet on carpet. My heart gave a hard thud when Will climbed into bed beside me. He spooned me from behind and pressed a kiss to the crook of my neck.

"Are you okay?" he asked, real concern in his voice.

I bit my lip, enjoying the warmth of his body. "Mm-hmm."

I knew I should leave, I was always really good about leaving right after, but maybe I could enjoy cuddling him for a few more minutes. What harm would it do? Plus, once we got back from this trip, we'd return to our normal routine. I should savor the physical contact while I could, because who knew when I'd next meet someone.

If I found a guy like Will who actually wanted a normal relationship, then I'd be over the moon. Don't get me wrong, the sex was great, but I found myself yearning for ordinary things I'd convinced myself I didn't want. Things like going out on dates, or to see a movie, or shop for groceries.

"You feel so good," Will murmured, his arms locking around me tight.

"So do you," I replied, twisting my head to kiss his chin. It was a natural instinct, and I suddenly realized how close I was to his mouth. All these rules between us really were a minefield.

I turned back around, and a few moments of quiet passed before I asked, "Do you like going to the movies?"

His hand drew circles on my stomach. "Not particularly. I always get stares when I go alone."

"What about when you're dating someone? Don't you like to go then?"

He paused for so long it became noticeable, finally saying, "I haven't dated anyone in a long time, so I've never really thought about it."

"But what if you were dating," I pushed. "Where would you take your lady friend?"

Will's hand paused. "You know why I don't date."

I sighed, while a sense of unease filled my stomach. What was I doing asking Will questions about dates? I was being an idiot. This entire trip, getting close to him, had me feeling far more emotional than I'd expected.

"Did you want to go see a movie?" Will asked, a note of confusion in his voice.

"No," I replied hastily. "I was just wondering because I never see you go out much when we're home. I thought if you don't like clubs, then maybe you enjoyed movie theatres. Anyway, don't mind me. I better get to bed."

I moved to climb out but Will grasped my elbow. "Hey, you can stay if you—"

"Nah," I shrugged, playing it off. "I like my bed better. Yours is too hard and I'm a sleep ninja."

"Sleep ninja?"

"I kick in my sleep, like a ninja."

He didn't smile, and his eyes seemed to be trying to discern my expression in the dim light. "Everything okay?"

I made sure to steady my voice. "I'm fine. Get some sleep. I'll see you in the morning."

With that, he let me go. And I went. But even though I wasn't looking, I could sense the cogs in Will's head turning. Maybe he suspected I wasn't doing so well keeping my feelings out of this whole situation. Hopefully he wouldn't question me about it, because I wasn't sure I could handle that conversation.

I didn't fall asleep right away, despite my exhaustion, and the next morning I was still tired. Nevertheless, I woke up early and decided to give Mam and Dad a call. I needed to see some familiar faces, say hello to Rocky, and remind myself that I wasn't alone in the world. I had parents and a dog who loved me unconditionally.

I sent a text letting them know I wanted to Skype, then a couple of minutes later got a reply that they were ready. As soon as I logged on, my worries melted away and I chuckled. They had the camera at an angle so all you could see was the top half of their faces. Mam lifted Rocky and held him up for me to see.

"Rocky misses his mama!" she greeted as my dog gave the camera a big, slobbery lick.

"Hi Rocky, I miss you so much," I called out, and waved. "Mam, could you wipe the camera? Rocky's licked it and now you've gone all blurry. You also need to angle it down a little, so I can see more than half your faces."

Dad gave a big belly laugh as Mam apologized. "Oh! Sorry! I didn't realize." She wiped the camera with her sleeve, then angled it better so I could see them. It was late at night for them and I was suddenly terribly homesick. It struck me how far away I was, and my worries returned with renewed force, my belly ached with loneliness.

"So, how has everything been going?" Dad asked. "Have you seen a kangaroo yet? I hope you haven't been suffering from any crapulence."

I chuckled at him adding a Forgotten Old Word of the Day into his greeting. "Crapulence, eh? I hope not. It doesn't sound very pleasant."

"Oh, it definitely isn't," Dad enthused. "It's an eighteenth century word for a hangover, or more precisely, intestinal and cranial distress arising from intemperance and general debauchery."

"Give it over, Phil," Mam tutted. "I don't want to hear about crapulence right now. I want to hear how Josey's been doing on her trip."

"It's been going well," I replied. "But I've been in the city so there aren't any kangaroos, unfortunately. I am going to see the Botanical Gardens today and then we're taking a ferry ride and having a picnic."

"That sounds lovely," Mam exclaimed. "I bet the weather's wonderful. How is Will?"

"He's good. He has a lot of training and work stuff, but he's got the afternoon off today, which will be nice. I've been studying a lot, but I've also been—uh—a little lonely."

They both wore identical frowns. "Oh no! I hope it's not too bad," Mam said sympathetically.

I waved away her concern. "I'll survive, though I am looking forward to cuddling Rocky when I get back, and maybe we could all go see a movie together," I said, hoping plans with my parents might erase some of the sadness last night's conversation brought on.

"That sounds great," Dad replied. "I've been dying to see the new Tom Hanks film. It's been getting rave reviews."

I rolled my eyes. Dad had a bit of a man crush on Tom Hanks. I swear he's seen all of his movies at least twice.

"It's a date then," I declared.

Mam leaned closer to the screen, like she was trying to inspect me for any lingering problems I wasn't telling them about. "You look tired. Doesn't she look tired?" she said, the frown line between her eyebrows deepening.

"It's just the jet lag," I said.

"No, it's not that. You seem forlorn, and you're not your chatty self." She paused to look at Dad. "There's something she's not telling us, Phil."

My dad leaned forward, too, his bushy mustache filling the screen. Now I regretted not calling them on audio only.

"What are you keeping from us, Josey?" Dad questioned, putting on his stern father voice.

"I'm not keeping anything from you. You're both going senile."

"I went senile years ago," Dad joked. "Come on now, out with it."

I let out a long sigh. I could never keep anything hidden from them for very long. I glanced over my shoulder, making sure I was completely alone. Will's room was at least fifty feet from where I sat and his door was closed, so he must be asleep. Still, I made sure to lower my voice as I brought my eyes back to my laptop.

"I think I'm starting to like Will," I confessed.

"I knew it!" Mam responded, a bit too loudly I might add.

"Can you keep it down? He's only in the next room."

"Sorry, sorry, I got a little carried away. But that's great, Josey. He's a nice man."

"You didn't think that when you first met him."

"Yes, but we didn't know him then," she said this like it explained everything.

"Mam, you don't know him now."

"A mother knows. And he's been nothing but kind and respectful toward you, and all the stories in the news seem to be dying down."

"Well"—I glanced at my keyboard—"the trouble is he doesn't like me the way I like him."

"Rubbish," said Dad. "Who wouldn't like you? You're delightful."

I shook my head, unable to help my smile. "Not everyone thinks I'm as delightful as you do, Dad. Most people find me annoying."

"Most people are idiots," Mam wagged her finger. "But why don't you tell him and see what he says?"

"It's not as easy as all that."

"If he can't see you're a treasure, then he's not invited to this summer's Kavanagh Barbecue Bonanza," Dad said, like it was a huge punishment. I doubted Will was excited to eat my dad's overcooked burgers and burnt ribs.

I ran my hand through my hair, trying to figure out a way to explain things to them without including all the details. "It's not really about him not liking me back. I know he likes me. It's just that he had a bad experience in his last relationship, so now he doesn't date unless he's guaranteed not to go through all that again, and I don't blame him."

"He's gun-shy. It's understandable. We all get scared that we might be hurt again," Mam replied, putting on what she imagined was a wise expression. Sometimes she fancied herself an amateur relationships expert, but she'd been with my dad since college. She had no clue about being single nowadays.

"Yes, well, I'm still not sure what I'm going to do," I said. "I need more time to think on it."

"Whatever you decide, know you can always talk it through with us first. We're available for calls, day or night."

I nodded, and soon we said our goodbyes. I could tell they were concerned for me, but I didn't know how to put their minds at ease because I still hadn't figured out my next step. I closed my laptop just as I heard noise from Will's bedroom. He was awake. I froze, fearing he'd heard my Skype call.

His door opened and he walked out, looking sleepy.

"Morning," he said, giving me a smile before he went inside the bathroom.

In all likelihood, he hadn't heard since the bedrooms here were pretty soundproof. Still, a measure of uncertainty filled me, and I felt a little exposed.

All day I was in a weird mood. I was much quieter than usual, and Will kept asking if I was okay. I assured him I was fine, but I had a feeling he didn't believe me. We were visiting the Botanical Gardens, and I was annoyed because it was beautiful, but I couldn't seem to enjoy myself.

"Can we move on from this section? It's making me feel insecure," Will joked as we walked by a collection of giant cactuses.

He surprised a chuckle out of me. "You have nothing to worry about in that department," I said without thinking.

Will elbowed me. "Flatterer. And it's good to see you smile."

"I'm sorry, I've just been feeling a little homesick today."

His hand came to my lower back, its warmth soothing. "Don't apologize. I can understand feeling that way. When I first moved to Ireland, I had a hard time."

I frowned, not liking to think of Will all alone in a strange country with no one for company. "Well that's not exactly comparable. I'm going home in a few days. You moved halfway across the world."

"Still, you should've told me you were out of sorts."

"Why? There's not much you can do."

"I can…" he trailed off, and then shook his head. "Never mind. Is it Rocky? Do you miss him?"

I nodded. "Like crazy."

Will smiled. "Me, too. Little dude got to me."

A warm feeling spread through me. "Sometimes I think he might like you better than me now."

"Never. That dog's crazy about you."

We stopped walking because there were some people in front of us taking wedding photographs. The woman wore a long, flowing white gown and I felt a pang in my chest. I wondered if I'd ever get married, if I'd ever wear a dress like that.

And where did that thought come from?

Before now, before right this moment, I'd never given serious thought to getting married. I mean, it was always a thing, there, on the horizon, a maybe-eventually.

And yet all of a sudden, here I was, mooning over a white dress.

What is wrong with me?

I blamed my weird mood on jet lag. Yeah. . .

I glanced at Will and discovered he'd been watching me watching the bride.

Giving him a small smile, I lifted my chin towards the wedding party. "She looks very pretty."

"It's a nice spot for pictures," Will agreed and continued to study me.

"Do you ever see yourself getting married? I mean, I know you said you didn't want to date anyone unless it would lead to that, but do you actually see it happening?" I asked, my attention returning to the couple.

"I hope so." His voice was quiet, thoughtful.

Something about his answer took the wind out of me. I had a vision of him in a suit, standing at the altar. A bride came into view, her face obscured by a veil, her hair color suspiciously close to mine.

AND ROCKY CAN BE THE RING BEARER!!!

Gah!

All my thoughts scrambled.

"I could be your best man," I blurted, needing to change the trajectory of my thoughts. Will and I were never going to get married. I was being crazy. All those very good reasons why it would never work were just as valid now as they had been back in Ireland. So I should just cut any fanciful ideas out right now. "Or well, your best woman."

Will's brows slowly drew together as he shook his head. "I think Bryan has dibs on that."

I forced a smile. "Damn, pipped to the post again."

Will was not smiling. "What about you?"

"Me?" I placed a hand to my chest. "You know, I haven't given it serious thought. I guess . . . I don't think so. Even if the right bloke came along who'd want to be shackled to all this"—I swept a hand down myself—"for life, I don't know if marriage is for me."

Will's face seemed to harden, but his voice was low and sincere. "Any man would be lucky to have you, Josey."

Just not you.

I swallowed down my immense and unnecessary sense of disappointment as the couple and photographer finally moved on, admiring some tall red flowers as I asked Will another question.

"Do you think you'll stay in Ireland if you do ever settle down, or will you go back to Oklahoma?" Maybe I was a glutton for punishment, but my curiosity just wouldn't allow me to drop the subject.

"I haven't thought about it." Will leaned a hip against the stone wall that served as a barrier between the walkway and Sydney Harbor. "When I retire from the team, I might go back to the States. It depends on my situation at the time."

His answer was frustrating. I'd been hoping for something more definitive. I'd wanted to hear him say he couldn't leave Ireland, that it was home to him now. Probably because in my head Will moving back to America was the equivalent of him leaving me behind. Abandoned. Forgotten about.

I know, I was being ridiculous.

"Do you think you'll ever live anywhere else?" Will asked, turning my question back on me again.

"I don't know." I shrugged, moving closer to the red flowers, not wanting to be near him for some reason. "I think I'd miss my parents too much."

He didn't say anything in response to that, and I didn't feel much like talking. So we continued our walk through the pretty gardens, all the while my weird mood persisted. My mind was still elsewhere.

I wished I'd never asked him about marriage, about the future. Even though we'd only known each other a short time, the knowledge that one day he might not be around was painful.

I would just have to redouble my efforts to think of him like a girlfriend when I wasn't—you know—using him for his penis.

Sometimes ignorance really was bliss.

* * *

"Yes!" I jumped from my seat, pumping my fist into the air in triumph as the team scored a try.

I was in the gigantic Allianz Stadium to watch Will's first test match. He wore a number 6 on the back of his jersey and I kept my eyes on him most of the time. There were only a few minutes left and Ireland was in the lead. My mind kept wandering from the game to memories of the other night, after I went down on Will.

He flipped me over and took me from behind after he made me come with his mouth. And then later, how he carefully released my wrists from his belt, kissing and frowning at the red marks left over from the friction.

A shiver ran through me just thinking about it.

I was in a fancy box with a bunch of the players' wives, girlfriends, and various family members. No one really talked to me, since I wasn't part of the whole community, but I didn't mind. Eilish always told me about the gossip that sometimes happened with this lot, and that really didn't appeal to me.

Don't get me wrong, there were some nice people, but there were also some not so nice ones. I understood it to a certain extent, since sport was competitive by nature, and that extended to the social side of it, too. Everybody wanted to have a better-looking partner, or a more expensive car, or a fancier house.

"You're Josey, right?" came a sweet voice, and I turned to find an attractive brunette smiling down at me.

"Yes, hi, that's me."

She gestured to the seat next to mine. "Do you mind if I sit down?"

I shook my head. "Not at all."

"I'm Melanie, Steve Harris's wife," she replied, introducing herself.

"Oh, right. I met your husband the other night. He came for dinner with us. We drank margaritas."

She nodded. "Yes, I heard all about what you did for Will at the press conference. I couldn't stop laughing when Steve told me. I was like, I have to meet this Josey person. She sounds like my kinda gal."

"I definitely have my moments," I said, about to continue, but then I forced myself to stop. It was a new thing I was trying out. When my brain told me to say two things, I said one. When it told me to say four, I said two. That way, I figured I could cut down on my excessive rambling.

"Seriously, Scrotum Awareness Day? I think that's the best thing I've heard all year. Anyway, I just saw you sitting over here and I thought I'd introduce myself. I know it can be a little intimidating when you don't know anyone."

Well, that was nice of her. I smiled. "Thank you. I'm not the best at social stuff."

"I know, right? Who knew small talk could be such a minefield? And if you put a single foot wrong, people talk about it for weeks. I actually had to take a break from going to team events because I'd get myself all worked up about dressing right and saying the right thing."

"I can understand that. Plus, I'm here with Will and I don't want to do anything that might embarrass him."

"Oh, I'm pretty sure that man is immune to embarrassment after all he's been through of late. I really feel for him. I can't imagine how awful it must've been to have all that stuff come out."

"It's been pretty rough. I mean, he doesn't say it, but I can tell the lies affect him, especially since he's so against anything that exploits women—" I stopped myself. One, because I was falling into the trap of saying five things when one would do, but also because I noticed another woman glancing over at Melanie. They exchanged a look, and suddenly it hit me. Melanie wasn't over here trying to make friends. She was trying to get the inside scoop.

Again, I had that feeling of wanting to protect Will, only now that we were having sex, it was so much stronger. I couldn't deny it. Sleeping with him had changed things. I felt like defending him against anyone who wanted to gossip about him or spread more rumors. I would go up against Melanie and all the other rugby wives looking for a bit of scandal to titillate them over their glasses of chardonnay.

Out on the field, the game ended and there were noises of celebration from those in the box. I glanced out and smiled when I saw Will lift Bryan up by the waist and swing him around in victory. My heart swelled in happiness for them, but then my stomach twisted. This all-consuming feeling of care for Will wasn't right. It was far too strong for friends with benefits.

When Will was happy, I felt aglow.

When he was sad, my gut twisted with a need to mend his wounds.

Standing, I looked back to Melanie. "Please excuse me. I need to go use the bathroom."

"Of course," she replied.

I set my glass of half-finished Prosecco on a table and left the box. Sifting my phone from my bag, I sent Will a text.

JOSEY

> Congratulations! So delighted for you and the guys! Feeling a little tired so heading to the hotel for a nap. See you when you get back. x.

It was true that I was tired, but I was also overwhelmed. I needed a couple of hours alone to think and get my head on straight. I needed to regroup and figure out how to proceed with this arrangement without anyone getting hurt.

Unfortunately, a tear had already formed inside me. And where there was a tear, pain was inevitable.

EIGHTEEN
WILL

@**RonanFitz**: I'm going to miss this place. Sydney is gorgeous!
@**SeanCassinova to @RonanFitz:** You should move here.
@**THEBryanLeech to @SeanCassinova and @RonanFitz**: No!!!!!!!!!!!!!!!!!!!
@**WillthebrickhouseMoore to @SeanCassinova and @RonanFitz**: No!!!!!!!!!!!!!!!!!!
@**FinleyIRE to @SeanCassinova and @RonanFitz**: No!!!!!!!!!!!!!!!!!!!
@**RonanFitz to @THEBryanLeech, @WillthebrickhouseMoore, @Finley-IRE:** *Sniff* Thanks guys.

> JOSEY
>
> Congratulations! So delighted for you and the guys! Feeling a little tired so heading to the hotel for a nap. See you when you get back. x.

I read the message again, which made twenty-one times in total.
Josey.

I shouldn't have been focused on a single text message from her when we'd just won our match. I should have been celebrating with Bryan, talking strategy with Ronan and Coach, giving interviews to locker room press, covering post-match analysis.

But I wasn't. I was in the toilet stall, reading and rereading Josey's message.
Feeling a little tired . . .
The last few days had been exhausting—amazing, but exhausting—and not

just because of the morning sex. Or the (daily) shower sex. There was also the bathtub sex, the bending-her-over-the-couch sex, the we-can't-wait-so-we'll-do-it-on-the-floor sex, and, my most recent favorite, the waking-her-up-in-the-middle-of-the-night sex.

Tossing and turning, thinking of her alone in her bed across the hotel suite, wishing she were next to me, I'd finally decided to carry her into my room three nights ago. I woke her with kisses on her neck and shoulders.

Each time afterward, she'd left immediately for her own bed once we were done, and I was alone again.

But no matter when—or where—we had sex, Josey liked it rough. She liked it hard, the more frenzied the better. Every time I tried to slow things down—take a moment to enjoy her body, the sweetness of her sounds, the warmth and feel of her—she'd say, "Harder," or "Faster," or something like, "You can spank me if you want."

. . . heading to the hotel for a nap.

I wasn't surprised she was tired.

Hell, *I* was tired. She'd worn me out. Maybe I would take a nap. Josey and I were set to meet the team for a late victory dinner, leaving me just about three hours to catch up on sleep once I made it back to the hotel.

Or maybe, we wouldn't go at all. Maybe, we'd nap together. . . I frowned at the thought.

The uneasiness that had been simmering on low since our double date with the musician and her producer was now raging. I'd been ignoring it because I wanted her. But our conversation in the Botanical Gardens yesterday had turned it up to boiling. *She doesn't want to get married.*

We'd held hands this past week while we were out, usually out of necessity when navigating a large crowd.

She'd stayed to cuddle a few nights ago after we were together and had almost fallen asleep in my bed, only to get up suddenly and leave after a random discussion about movies.

She'd even bought me a book two days ago as a gift, explaining it away by saying, "It's no big deal, something friends would do, and definitely not a romantic, hearts and flowers gesture."

We'd gone on a few dinner dates—they were definitely dates—just the two of us.

All the rules had been bent if not broken.

Except one.

No kissing.

The real question I should have been asking myself was, *If you know the rules, why do you keep pushing for more?*

She'd made it very, very clear—every time she lifted her chin, turned to give me her cheek, and interrupted my distracted stares with a joke—that kissing her was not going to happen. That was her hard boundary.

I knew this, but I couldn't seem to accept it, just like I couldn't seem to stop wanting to hold her hand when we were out, and I couldn't stop wanting her in my bed at night, and I couldn't walk past a gift shop or a flower shop or a jewelry shop without wanting to buy her something.

Glancing at her text message again, I admitted to myself that I was falling in love with Josey. Furthermore, I'd never been in love before.

Not like this.

I'm given to understand that most people, when they realize they're in love, feel a sense of happiness.

I did not.

Cold and clammy and feverish and sick to my stomach? Yes.

Regret and remorse and dread? Yes.

Happiness? Nope.

Not even a little.

This is a disaster. A mistake.

This was a mistake.

The thought was a new one, a whisper at first, not fully formed, more like an impression. But as I continued to stare at the message, my longing for more with her, the persistent unease, and the whisper matured. They solidified, until they thundered between my ears with each beat of my heart.

What had I done?

I needed her, and if she ever found out that I'd broken the rules . . . *she'll leave you.*

I was still frowning at my phone—half-panicked—when I received an alert for a new email and stiffened when I saw the name of the sender. Tapping on the alert, I opened the message from Kean Gallagher that I'd been waiting days for.

To: William Moore
From: Kean Gallagher
Subject: Emails

I hope you two will be very happy together. She's a selfish twat. You deserve each other.

I reread the email twice, both times trying to scroll lower, searching for more to the message. There was nothing. I hit reply and typed,

To: Kean Gallagher

From: William Moore
Subject: Re: Emails

I have no interest in disrupting your marriage, nor do I have any interest in Aideen. I hope you two can work it out. It was never my intention to hurt either of you. If you are in a bad way, please call someone. The suicide hotline is on the Samaritans website.

After I sent the email, I waited several minutes, my knee bouncing with nerves. I hoped for . . . something. Not absolution, but a sign that Kean Gallagher wasn't a danger to himself. Just as I lowered my phone, another alert announced the arrival of a second message.

To: William Moore
From: Kean Gallagher
Subject: Re: Emails

Save your concern. I'm not as bad off as all that. I know I'm better off without her in any case.

You should know Aideen is the one who called the press about you. She paid a prostitute to spread the story, gave her all the info on you needed to make the lies look real.

How do you like her now?

This news knocked the wind out of me. But before I recovered, he sent a third message.

To: William Moore
From: Kean Gallagher
Subject: Re: Emails

Aideen knew the rules, but she ignored them. You're not interested in her? Good. She deserves what she gets. She made her own bed, now she has to sleep in it. I hope you break her heart and then I hope someone breaks yours.

* * *

After reading Kean's messages, his revelation kept echoing around in my skull, and—in a bizarre way—I was happy for the distraction. Aideen had been the one to sell the story to the press. *Aideen.* I'd been foolish to think I could trust someone I barely even knew.

No, not foolish, I'd been naïve.

When I really thought about it, it all made perfect sense. I rejected her. She wanted to get back at me. I felt both angry and stupid for ever thinking I could put my faith in a random couple I knew so little about.

With my head all screwed up, I didn't want to see anyone.

Except Josey.

I left quietly, slipping out a side entrance, and made my way back, brooding about the revelation and ignoring the warning bells as I drew closer to the hotel.

But when I walked into the room and I found her asleep on the couch, I couldn't escape or distract myself from the truth.

I wasn't falling in love with Josey because I was already in love with her. And I didn't go to my room for a nap because I couldn't bring myself to leave the living room.

This was the first opportunity I'd had to study her while she slept since she wouldn't sleep *with* me, and I wasn't going to be a creeper who snuck into her room at night and watched her in the dark.

Instead, I was a creeper who watched her in the light, in the living room, where no sneaking was necessary.

Much better.

Or so I'll tell myself.

But it wasn't better. It was just one more item to add to the list.

Nevertheless, sitting on the couch across from hers, I indulged myself in the sight of her prone form, my chest and stomach an aching, rioting mess. Everything about her sharp and stunning features had relaxed. The effect was mesmerizing. She was peaceful, the slight rise and fall of her chest captivating. I was reminded of that fairy tale with the sleeping woman kissed awake by a man.

My thoughts were chaotic.

Biting my thumbnail as I leaned back in my seat, I asked myself, *What would happen if I kissed her now?*

Josey was the definition of a sleeping beauty. Like the woman in the story, Josey would definitely wake up. Unlike the woman in the story, Josey wouldn't be pleased.

We had one more full day, a little over thirty-six hours left in Australia, and the thought of an end to us crippled me.

This was a mistake.

The sinking sensation in my stomach returned, quicksand, a heady combination when paired with persistent dread, only heightened by Kean's emails.

Panic.

I felt panic.

I loved Josey. I was in love with her, and I had no right to be. I'd thought I was in love once before. I knew now that I hadn't been. Even so, Eve's rejection had destabilized me. It was not an experience I would willingly submit to again.

But more than that, I *needed* her.

I thought back over the last week and all the times she'd left me after we'd been intimate, how the axis of my world had changed, and how she was always just the same, unfazed, unaffected.

She doesn't love you.

My attention focused on her lips. Whether or not we kissed wasn't really the issue. Even if we kissed, even if she let that happen, *I* shouldn't have been pushing her in the first place, just like Aideen shouldn't have pushed me.

I hope you break her heart and then I hope someone breaks yours.

I knew the rules. I shouldn't be wanting more. I shouldn't be in love with her. I didn't want to just break the rules. I wanted to annihilate them. I wanted to pound them into dust.

I couldn't continue this way. She would leave me and I wouldn't recover this time, I wouldn't be able to—

"Will?"

My eyes darted to hers. She was awake, sitting up on the couch and looking at me with a small smile. My heart jumped to my throat, my chest ached. I felt sick.

Mistake.

"Are you okay?" she asked, scratching her head and yawning. "You seemed deep in thought."

The ever-increasing dread I'd been carrying around for days reached its maximum. I'd been pushing her, and that was the brutal truth. I'd known going into this arrangement that it wasn't going to last, and I'd been fine with that at the time.

But now, I wasn't.

I wasn't fine.

This. Is. A. Mistake.

The dread was now almost completely panic, such that I didn't know where one began and the other ended.

I cleared my throat, pulled my gaze from hers, and focused on breathing normally. This—our arrangement—had been a mistake. A huge mistake. The issue now was how to fix this mistake, how to reverse it, how to change course and make things right.

I shouldn't want more.

What I needed was a plan, with new boundaries and rules.

"Hey, what's wrong?" Josey stood, and the movement drew my attention.

She stretched, her eyes on me, a wrinkle of concern between her brows as she approached. She was going to touch me. I didn't want her to touch me. If she touched me, I would keep wanting more, I would keep pushing, I would work to obliterate rules and boundaries. I would betray her, and myself.

She was closer now, eyeing my lap like she planned to sit on it. "Did something happen after the match?"

"Combine harvester."

Josey froze midstep, just four feet away, her eyes wide with surprise. "Uh, pardon?"

I shook my head and stood, turning away from her. I grabbed my keys and wallet by the front table. I opened the door.

"Will?" she called after me.

I didn't pause. I closed the door. I left.

* * *

"I made a huge mistake."

Bryan squinted at me as though I was speaking a different language. "Uh, hello, Will. Do you want to—"

"I want to marry her, and she doesn't want to marry me." I walked past Bryan and into his hotel room. I didn't sit on his couch. I paced.

I'd been walking around Sydney for hours and had skipped the victory dinner. It was late, and I'd just come from the Royal Botanical Gardens, where I'd replayed the conversation with Josey—when we'd spotted the bride and groom and spoken about the future—several times.

I kept searching for a clue, desperate for some sign that she wanted me for more than just this stupid friends with benefits arrangement. Each time, I came up empty.

She would never leave Ireland. She didn't want to get married. She'd been quiet and withdrawn. She always left.

With each step I'd taken, I'd grown more and more certain that ending the arrangement with Josey wasn't just the right choice, it was the only choice.

Before she finds out.

My friend closed the door slowly, and equally as slowly, he turned to face me. "Are we talking about Eve?"

"No," I snapped. "Why would I be talking about Eve? Eve is nothing."

"Uh—"

"Josey."

Bryan flinched, stood straighter, visibly shocked. "Josey," he parroted, like the name didn't make any sense.

I continued to pace. "Josey doesn't want to marry anyone." The words physically hurt to say.

His stare flicked over to me, disbelieving. "She said that?"

"Yes."

"When?"

"Yesterday."

He flinched again. "You should—why don't you start from the beginning?"

"I made a mistake."

"What did you do?"

I stopped pacing and faced my friend. "I thought I could—we could—have an arrangement."

"Arrangement?"

"No strings."

"Ah." Bryan winced, inhaling slowly through his teeth. "I see."

"It was a mistake." Shit.

Shit shit shit shit shit.

"Yeah," he agreed, scratching the back of his neck, looking confused. "I'm sorry, you need to give me a minute to catch up here. I can't believe you—I mean, you've never—"

"I thought I could."

"With Josey?"

I nodded.

"Will . . ." his expression was somewhere between frustrated and concerned. "She *works* for you."

"I know!" I closed my eyes, irritated with myself for shouting. "I know," I repeated, calmer. "It was a mistake."

"So you keep saying." Bryan sighed. "And now you want more?"

"Yes. No." I set my hands on my hips and opened my eyes, staring at nothing. "Fuck."

My friend studied me for several seconds before declaring, "You want more."

Grimacing, I shook my head. "I shouldn't."

"But you do."

"It doesn't matter." I'd moved on, now grasping on to Bryan's statement.

Josey was my employee.

There.

There was my reason for ending things early without the risk of losing her.

"You're right." I nodded faster as an idea formed. "She was—*is*—my employee. I'm a terrible person."

"No—"

"We had an agreement and I broke it."

Bryan turned his head, peering at me out of the corner of his eye. "Did you coerce her? Into the no-strings relationship?"

I breathed out, my lungs on fire. I honestly hadn't considered that.

"No," I said. But then I quickly amended, "I don't know. I don't think so. I don't know. I mean—"

I licked my lips, they were suddenly dry.

I hadn't.

Maybe I had coerced her. I had a history of not being able to read people, women in particular. I thought Eve had been in love with me, I thought Aideen felt nothing for me.

Everything was chaos.

Pushing my fingers through my hair, I sat on the couch, resting my elbows on my knees and holding my head in my hands. I needed to sort through this, focus on facts.

"Josey works for me, the time has come to end things, it never should have happened in the first place. It was—"

"A mistake," he finished. I glanced at Bryan, he was watching me closely with a wary-looking focus. "What are you going to do?"

"I'm going to make it right. I'm going to do the right thing."

I'd end the arrangement. I'd tell her it's because she's my employee. She'd never know the truth.

She won't leave.

"What does that mean? 'Make it right.'"

"I'll—" I searched Bryan's hotel room, my attention bouncing from his bed to the dresser to the bathroom door. "I'll end things, now, tonight."

He made a choking sound. "You're going to *fire* her?"

"No! Of course not. I'm going to"—I swallowed around a painful knot in my throat—"I'm going to apologize, tell her it was a mistake, that I accept full responsibility, and give her some options."

"Such as?"

"She can... stay on with me, living in the apartment, and things will go back to normal, professional. Or I could pay her a severance and help her find a new place to live."

Even as I said the words, I knew I wouldn't give her the second option. I wouldn't be able to. I would do whatever it took to keep her in my life. I wasn't a good guy. I was dishonest and unprincipled.

I'm... a varlet.

Bryan folded his arms, his eyes hazy with thought. Eventually, he nodded, "That seems fair. But maybe also ask her if she has any other options in mind? Ask her for her opinion? See what she says and go from there."

I nodded even though I had no plans to follow his advice.

If she decides to stay on... I would see her, every day. It would be torture.

But the alternative was unbearable.

NINETEEN
JOSEY

@JoseyInHeels: When your life starts falling apart, cheese is the cement that will hold it together.
@ECassChoosesPikachu to @JoseyInHeels: … what's going on? Call me!

I woke up on the couch to the sound of the door opening. Glancing at the screen of my phone on the coffee table, I saw it was after 4:00 a.m.
Will.

I'd sat up waiting for him for hours, agonizing. Why had he used his safe word? Had I done something wrong? Was he okay? Had something happened after the match?

My head was a mess. My thoughts going a mile a minute.

One voice said, *he doesn't want you anymore, he's come to his senses.*

Another said, *quit overthinking everything and relax. Will is a grown-up. He knows what he's doing.*

And a third said, *of course he used his safe word. Anyone can see you're falling in love with him. He probably wants to run for the hills.*

The third one caused me the most turmoil.

I even called Eilish out of sheer anxiety because I needed someone to talk me down. She ended up texting Bryan, who texted her back to say Will was with him. At least I knew he hadn't been kidnapped and murdered by some serial killer. When he didn't return, I started to worry something terrible had happened to him. And yes, I knew Will was hardly likely to be targeted by predators—given the fact that he looked like a predator himself—but such was the way my mind worked during times like this.

I was surprised I managed to fall asleep at all, especially with all the lights on in the living room. Maybe I conked out from sheer emotional exhaustion.

As he entered the room, my eyes traveled from his shoes all the way up to the top of his head.

Will looked like he had the weight of the world on his shoulders. His hair was a mess, there were dark circles under his eyes and his shirt was rumpled.

When he caught sight of me he straightened, took a half step back, and ran a frustrated hand through his mussed hair. "I thought you'd be in bed."

He thought I'd be in bed?

How on earth was I supposed to just go to bed when he walked out of the hotel after dropping a combine harvester bomb?

"I was worried about you. Did I do something wrong?" I bit my lip to stop myself from the barrage of questions on the tip of my tongue, and then I tasted blood. I was far too edgy for this conversation.

Will didn't make eye contact as he sat down on an armchair. "*You* didn't do anything wrong. But, we need to talk."

Oh no.

Not a talk.

My heart knew what was coming even though my head refused to accept it.

"You want to end things," I blurted, bracing myself by holding my breath.

Will's eyes widened. He hadn't expected that. *Or maybe I'm wrong? Maybe he doesn't want to end things? Maybe I should stop jumping to conclusions? Maybe I have entirely too many thoughts!*

Will scratched his head, visibly perplexed. When he spoke, his voice was scratchy. "Yes, I, uh…" He cleared his throat, then continued quietly, "We should end our arrangement."

I nodded before I knew I was nodding, an involuntary, self-protective movement. Meanwhile, inside my body, mind, and heart, everything was crumbling. The sense of rejection, of being cast aside, hit me like a wallop. He was…he was *dumping* me. Well, not quite, because we were never a couple, but that's how it felt.

I was being dumped by my friend with benefits in the early hours of the morning at a hotel in Sydney, Australia. I couldn't even run to my parents or Eilish for comfort. They were on the other side of the world.

I was mortified. Maybe more mortified than I'd ever been in the entirety of my life, which is saying a lot. One would think I'd be indoctrinated against mortification at this point.

But I didn't want to be mortified. I wanted. . . *I wanted*. . . I wanted to be strong. Resilient. I wanted to rally against it. I wanted to be something else, something different than perpetually embarrassed Josey.

So I smiled.

Now Will looked supremely uncomfortable *and* confused. Maybe he thought I was going to cry and beg him to change his mind. Nope.

In fact, hell no.

HELL. NO.

"I thought you might. Well, that's perfectly fine. I actually had the same idea, so I guess great minds think alike." I was jumping the gun, but I'd rather him think I was on the same page instead of an emotional mess. "Anyway, no need for you to avoid me anymore. It's all good." I laughed and shrugged and sighed. "I get it. No hard feelings and all that." I added a nonchalant handwave, which might have been overdoing things, but oh well.

This was a new experience for me. And really, a poorly executed nonchalant handwave was the least of my problems.

Even though I was forcing myself to save face and accept this, I was so confused. Aside from when he came back to the hotel today, the last time Will and I were together everything was fine. We'd laughed, had amazing sex, been friends.

I struggled to get my feelings under control. The sad fact of the matter was, I was... I was heartbroken. This whole trip, my feelings for him had blossomed. They'd ballooned from a crush into something much more serious. I couldn't lie to myself anymore.

I was falling in love with him.

It was the exact opposite of what I was supposed to do. I was supposed to keep my feelings out of things entirely.

Emotion clogged my throat. I sat there, my eyes starting to water, but I refused to cry.

Meanwhile, Will's earlier expression of confusion had been replaced with . . . nothing. Absolutely nothing. Whatever he was feeling—if he was feeling anything, which was debatable—had been locked up tight behind a stoic façade. I barely recognized the cold, detached look on his face as his dispassionate gaze moved over my features.

"Well, I guess that's that then," I whispered.

Will stared at me a long moment, swallowed, and then said, "Yeah, I guess it is."

Another silence followed as we watched each other. I continued to summon my composure and even managed to paste on a new, small, closed-mouthed smile.

But this time, the silence stretched longer than before. Much, much longer. It became something else, a tangible, physical thing, a heavy shroud. I hated these kinds of silences, and filling them had always been a compulsion of mine. Instead of just struggling against my feelings, I found myself struggling against my feelings as well as struggling not to fill the silence.

Eventually, unsurprisingly, I lost the fight against my compulsion. "This was never supposed to be forever. Like I said, I was thinking the same thing earlier, you know, before you got back, that we should end this. Ending it before we fly home makes so much sense, and now we just have tomorrow. So, no big deal. Good timing and all that. It's the smart thing to do."

Why was I talking? Shut up now, Josey.

Something that looked to me like sympathy flickered behind Will's eyes. I didn't want it. It made me feel like he could see right through my bluster to my true feelings.

He inhaled a deep breath and stood. "Okay." His voice was croaky again. "I'll, um, get out of your hair."

As he passed me by, I reached out to grab his hand before I could stop myself. He froze in place, his entire body stilling.

My gut twisted up in knots, while my brain screamed at me to let go, leave him alone, say nothing.

I wanted to ask him why.

I wanted to know if he thought he could ever feel something for me in the distant, hypothetical future.

Instead, I pushed those questions aside and, looking up at him, I said, "What about my job? Do you still want me to work for you?"

Will's jaw moved, and he stared at the floor. My heart stalled.

With what seemed like great effort, he brought his attention to me and said, "If it's okay with you, I'd like you to continue to live, uh, help me when we get home."

He does?

"You do?" I was surprised. A tiny measure of relief filled me. At least he wasn't kicking me out of his life entirely.

"I do." A pause as he looked me in the eye. "I need you."

That statement sent my emotions on a roller coaster ride. I knew he meant he needed me as a companion, not *me* me. I wasn't delusional, but it affected me nonetheless.

I was lost in thought when he said my name. "Josey."

"Will?"

He stared at me meaningfully. "I would never hurt you. You know that, right?"

I returned his stare, mine blurred with confusion, because his words made no sense. *He's hurting me now.*

Except . . .

Oh.

Oh.

Will really had seen that I was falling for him. That must've been why he decided to end it now.

He didn't want to break my heart. That's what all this was about.

I huffed a little laugh because, unfortunately, he was too late. Not only was my heart sore, everything inside of me ached. Emotion rose to the surface again, and I couldn't push it back down this time. I needed to get out of there before Will saw me cry.

"Yes, I—of course I know that," I finally whispered, and rose from the couch. I gathered my few things and stepped towards my room. "See you in the morning. And again, this was going to happen once we got home anyway. It's definitely for the best that we stop having sex now in preparation for going back to our usual routine. So…uh, good thinking, to both of us."

Oh man. *Stop. Talking.*

I blinked rapidly to stay my tears and hurried inside my room, shutting the door softly behind me. I crawled into bed and pulled the covers over my head, even though it would be morning soon. I closed my eyes and endeavored to fall back asleep.

You don't feel anything.
You don't feel anything.
You don't feel anything.

A single tear fell down my cheek, contradicting my useless inner mantra, because right now I was feeling everything, and too much. In that moment, I knew I'd never had a broken heart before right now. The few breakups I'd been through before and the subsequent feelings of sadness had nothing on this.

This, what I felt right now, was true heartbreak. I was utterly crushed.

* * *

The next day Will had his final test match. I'd planned on going, but decided against it—for obvious reasons. Instead, I hid in my room until I heard him leave for the day. I couldn't stand for him to see my puffy face and reddened eyes from all the crying I'd done last night.

Today, I would sort my shit out.

Today, I would obliterate all the hurt feelings inside me and put on a permanent brave face. Because if there was anything worse than getting dumped by William Moore, it was him knowing how heartbroken I was. We'd set out the rules and I agreed to follow them. It wasn't his fault I'd messed up.

Instead of calling Eilish or my parents, I decided to splurge. I spent the day in the hotel's spa. I had a manicure and pedicure, a massage and a mud bath. I even swam several laps in the pool and spent a half hour in the sauna.

I resolved to play everything cool with Eilish. I didn't want to make things weird between her and Will. She was his physio and they had to work together almost every day. Therefore—for her benefit—it was best to keep my hurt feelings to myself and pretend like all was well. Eventually, it would be.

My strategy was, if I could pamper myself on the outside, then maybe I'd feel better on the inside.

It didn't feel like it was working yet, but I held out hope.

When Will got back from his match, he looked exhausted, the stress lines around his eyes belying his tension. Perhaps he wasn't doing so well with all of this. Despite my claims that everything was fine, I think he sensed I wasn't being entirely truthful. And he was the sort of person to feel guilty about hurting someone else's feelings, even when he had no reason to feel that way.

I was the one who'd fucked up.

Therefore, my broken heart was my own fault.

"How did the game go?" I asked, trying to muster something that resembled a smile. It kinda worked.

"We lost, 13–15," Will replied, not looking at me. *Maybe that was the reason for his tension.*

"I'm sorry."

"Don't be." His voice was flat and he still didn't look at me. "We won the other two. I'm going to take a shower."

I swallowed and nodded, hating the new, reserved tone he was using. It wasn't like his reserve when we first met, either. Now there was a tightness behind it, like he didn't want to show me any kind of warmth. I assumed this was in case I misconstrued friendliness for feelings.

Yeah, he'd definitely suspected I was falling for him. The very idea plunged a brick to the pit of my stomach. I'd just have to redouble my efforts to appear unaffected.

Good luck with that.

All these thoughts scrambled through my head, and I didn't notice Will had stopped midway to the bathroom. He stared at me with something I couldn't identify, a rawness of emotion that it took everything inside me not to react to.

"Josey, I…" his words trailed off.

"Will?" I said, unable to disguise the hope in my voice.

He shook his head, turning, and muttering, "Never mind."

He left, shutting the door behind him. When I heard the shower turn on, I went inside my bedroom. It was only 8:00 p.m., but we had an early flight. I wasn't sure how I was going to survive the journey back to Dublin sitting next to him.

Luckily, I had some audiobooks to listen to.

Now, if only I could concentrate on something other than my self-inflicted emotional turmoil.

* * *

"Would you like something to drink?" asked the smiling flight attendant as I stared blankly around the plane. We'd only been in the air an hour and already it felt like I'd been here for days.

I looked up, hesitated, then said, "Do you know what? Yes, I'll take a glass of Prosecco."

She smiled. "Coming right up."

Maybe getting drunk would make this flight more bearable, since Will was being even more quiet and monosyllabic than usual.

By the time I ordered my fourth drink, he cast a wary look my way. He'd obviously been monitoring my intake. I knew Will didn't like people getting drunk and causing a fuss on flights. It was why he preferred to travel alone rather than with the team. Well, he needn't worry. I planned to be a quiet, miserable drunk, not a spirited, mouthy one.

"You're going to be sick," I heard him say.

I raised an eyebrow, looking in his direction. "Pardon?"

Will coughed and put down his copy of *National Geographic*. "I said if you keep drinking like that, you're going to make yourself sick."

"I know my own limits, and I feel fine. So you can relax."

Wow, where did that snappy tone come from? I barely recognized myself. Maybe I did want to be a mouthy drunk after all.

Will's lips formed a straight line. "I don't want you ill. It's a long plane ride, and being sick when you fly is the worst. We haven't even caught our connection yet."

"I didn't ask for your advice," I replied with false cheerfulness. "And I'll remind you that I wasn't the one who needed to hire a babysitter, so back off."

Will flinched, blinking at me with astonishment. Turning away from him, I downed the rest of my glass, trying not to feel guilty for that last comment, and signaled to the flight attendant for another. She was busy with another passenger, and I was struck with an urgent need to pee. Instead of waiting, I got up and headed for the bathroom. Luckily, there wasn't a queue since most people were napping. I went inside, did my business, and was washing my hands when a knock sounded on the door.

"I'll be out in a minute," I called. Okay, maybe I slurred a little.

"Josey, let me in," came Will's voice.

Oh, man. The one time I don't want him to follow me to the bathroom, he does.

"I'm not interested in another lecture," I said, opening the door after I dried my hands. I was just about to step out when he put his body in front of mine and maneuvered me back in. My bottom hit the edge of the sink as he reached behind himself and turned the lock over.

My brow crinkled. "What are you doing?"

His dark eyes studied me. "What's going on with you?"

What's going on with me?
What the hell did he think was going on?

"Absolutely nothing," I responded harshly. Apparently, I was a mean drunk when the mood took me.

Will blew out a long breath and his entire posture seemed to slump. He looked exhausted.

"You're . . ." his eyes moved between mine. "You're regretting what happened? You're having a hard time?" he guessed.

I ignored his questions, because even though I felt wretched, I didn't regret a single thing. Even knowing what I knew now, I'd do it all over again. Just the same.

Instead, I jabbed my finger into his sternum. "I wonder, do you have any feelings inside that big, hard chest of yours? Or are you made of stone?" I was saying too much, but it was hard to make good judgment calls when I'd had four glasses of Prosecco.

Will blinked, and for a split second I saw a flare of temper.

"I'm made of flesh and blood just like you. And I do have feelings."

I exhaled heavily. This bathroom was way too small for the two of us to be in here. I could smell his cologne, could feel the warmth of his body, tension radiating off it in waves. I'd spent the last two weeks worshipping his naked skin and it was intolerably close. All I wanted to do was pull him to me, have him hold me in his arms.

Obviously, that wasn't happening.

"You're like a robot," I said absentmindedly, jabbing my finger into his chest again, but this time he grabbed it in his fist. I sucked in a shocked breath.

"Just because I don't go around yelling my feelings from the rooftop, doesn't mean I don't have any."

My anger wavered. "Well, what are they then?"

He opened his mouth, but he hesitated. Will stared at me for an extended moment, and then released my finger. His frown seemed to intensify as his gaze moved over my face. He looked frustrated, upset. Angry.

Suddenly, I didn't want to have this conversation.

"Josey—"

"Never mind. I don't want to know. Get out of my way." I closed my eyes and wrapped my arms around myself, shaking my head.

After another pause, Will stepped aside and I unlocked the door. I rushed past him, returning to my seat where a fresh drink was waiting for me. I no longer had a taste for it. I wasn't an angry person, but I was angry. Will had every right to put an end to our arrangement, and yet, I felt hard done by.

Get a grip, Josey.

By the time we arrived in Ireland, it was 3:00 a.m. and I felt worse than I'd ever felt in my entire life. My hair was greasy, my clothes rumpled and stained with plane food, and my body ached with exhaustion. Still, I didn't want to go home to Will's place. I wanted to see my parents, cuddle my dog, and remember that the world wasn't such a horrible place where people decided they didn't want you anymore at the drop of a hat.

"Where are you going?" Will asked when I went to hail my own taxi.

"I'm going to my parents' house. I'll be back tomorrow to resume my duties, but right now I just need to see my family."

If I wasn't so tired, I might've been able to determine the emotion that swept across Will's face for a split second. But as it was, I couldn't. Nor did I want to.

Finally, he nodded. "Okay. Say hello to your mam and dad for me. Here's some money for the journey."

He held out a fifty euro note, but I shook my head. "No, thank you."

Will didn't try to push the matter. Instead, he slid the fifty back in his wallet and grabbed my suitcase to lug into the trunk of the waiting taxi. I slid into the back seat and shut the door, keeping my eyes studiously forward as the cab pulled away.

My parents were asleep when I got to their house. I noticed the FOR SALE sign up out front and my heart hurt. It wouldn't take long for someone to snap up my childhood home. It was a bit of a fixer-upper, but it was in a very desirable neighborhood.

Rocky heard me as soon as I slid my key in the door. He came running down the stairs barking in sheer glee. I bent down and he hopped all over me, licking my face and sniffing me like crazy. His eyes held an accusation, *Where the hell have you been?!*

I smiled for the first time in almost three days and chuckled when he slobbered all over my ear.

A creak in the floorboard had me looking up to find my parents standing at the top of the stairs in their pajamas.

"Josey, you're back!" Mam exclaimed, coming down to give me a hug.

"We thought you'd go straight to the apartment and come to collect Rocky tomorrow," Dad said, joining in the hug.

I sniffed back the need to cry, blinking away the tears. They all smelled so good. Like home. "I was going to, but I just missed you all so much. Is it okay if I sleep here tonight?"

"Of course, your room's just the same as you left it," Mam replied.

We headed upstairs and I fell onto my bed. My heart was still hurting in a million places, but for a moment I felt a modicum of peace. I stripped down to my T-shirt and knickers and crawled under the familiar duvet. Rocky curled up beside me and I was asleep as soon as I closed my eyes.

* * *

"Believe me, Fluffy, men aren't all they're cracked up to be. Between you and me, you're better off without them. I've learned that lesson the hard way," I told the drowsy tabby cat I was comforting. She'd just been neutered, and I was taking care of her until her owners came to collect her.

I'd been back in Ireland three days and was starting to get back into a routine. I still felt depressed as hell, but I was doing my best to keep busy. When they offered me an extra shift at the clinic, I jumped at the chance.

Needless to say, things between Will and me were weird, but we were both endeavoring to get along. We hung out in the evenings, Will cooked dinner, but it just wasn't the same. When I returned to the apartment after spending the night at my parents' house, I apologized to him for the incident on the plane. I'd been a mean drunk and he didn't deserve my salty attitude. He'd told me there was no reason to apologize in a very graceful, very monosyllabic, very Will-like way.

I was also trying to do my job, keep him on the straight and narrow, but it felt like being around one another was a torture to both of us. It was hard for me because I still had feelings for him, and I assumed it was hard for him because he felt guilty for hurting me.

Every day I asked myself how I was ever naïve enough to think friends with benefits would work.

"Anyway, look at you," I said, petting Fluffy softly. "You don't need to be hearing about my woes. You've been through enough of your own."

The cat made a small sound of unhappiness, like she was agreeing with me.

Later that day when I got home, there was a woman waiting in the lobby. She looked to be in her early thirties, her blonde hair in a sleek ponytail.

"Miss Kavanagh," the concierge greeted. "There's a guest here for Mr. Moore. Do you have any idea when he'll be home?"

"He should be back soon," I replied, then looked at the woman. "You're not a journalist, are you? Because he's not giving any interviews right now."

She looked me up and down, eyes narrowing. "Who are you?"

"I'm his, uh, assistant," I lied, and just like that her hostility vanished.

"Oh, well, do you mind if I come upstairs and wait for him? I'm an old friend and this really is important. I promise I'm not a journalist."

I hesitated, because there was something off about her. Her makeup was too perfect yet too heavy at the same time. She didn't have a hair out of place, but there was an eagerness in her eyes I didn't like. "What's your name?"

She straightened and held out her hand. "I'm Aideen. Aideen Gallagher."

Oh damn.

All of a sudden, it was hard to breathe. This was the woman Will had watched having sex with her husband, the one who'd fallen in love with him. I didn't know what to do. I was pretty sure Will didn't want to see her, but I couldn't just turn her away. Plus, it might be good for him to give her closure in person, right?

Conflict filled me.

My belly in knots, I shook her hand. My palm was sweaty as hell. "I'm Josey. I'm just going to call Will and let him know you're here. He might be running late."

I pulled out my phone, but Aideen reached out to stop me. That was the first red flag.

"No, don't do that. I'm sure he'll be back soon."

I stepped aside. "I should still give him a call."

She smiled wide now, too wide. "I'd really like to surprise him. We haven't seen each other for a while."

I eyed her. Even with how things were between Will and I, I wasn't bringing her up to the apartment to ambush him. That was his private space and he got to decide who he let inside.

Her gaze pleaded with me and I swallowed nervously, stalling.

The door to the building opened and relief seized me when Will walked inside. He had his gym bag over his shoulder, his eyes downcast as he read something on his phone. I hurried over to him, spotting two photographers just outside the door.

"Will, there's uh, there's someone here to see you," I said, an anxious quaver in my voice, sending a small prayer upward that the photographers outside would lose interest and leave.

He looked up. "Josey, what are you—"

"Hello William." Aideen stepped forward.

Will froze as soon as he heard her voice, his eyes darting to hers. His expression clouded, no longer the stoic, reserved Oklahoman I knew. A simmering, barely perceptible anger fizzled below the surface.

"Aideen."

The way he said her name gave me chills, and not the good kind.

I was stressed out for him. I knew he'd been struggling over what to do about her emails back in Australia, and now she was here. He was going to have to deal with her and I knew it wouldn't be pretty. Whatever was about to happen, I really didn't want to be a part of it.

And yet, at the same time, the surge of instinctive protectiveness I felt was impossible to ignore. I couldn't—wouldn't—leave him alone with her. Maybe he didn't need my help, but he was going to get it.

One thing was for certain, the shit was about to hit the fan.

TWENTY
WILL

@WillthebrickhouseMoore: I have retired to the growlery
@THEBryanLeech to @WillthebrickhouseMoore: WTF is a growlery? Is that one of @JoseyInHeels's old words?

"I've missed you." Smiling, Aideen took another meandering step towards us.

But my primary concern was Josey. I moved my attention to her and searched her expression. After learning about Aideen's lies and manipulations, I didn't want Josey anywhere near the woman.

I dipped my head, holding her eyes. "Are you okay?"

"Yeah." She nodded quickly, whispering, "How can I help?"

Despite the situation, and the week of misery that had precluded it, I felt myself smile. "I'm sorry." This was the closest we'd been since I'd invaded her space in the airplane, and so of course my attention snagged on her lips.

"About what?" she asked, sounding breathless. Or maybe just nervous.

"About this." *About everything.*

"Aren't you going to invite me up?" Aideen interrupted.

I stiffened, flexing my jaw.

Yeah, no.

That was never going to happen.

My glare cut to Aideen. She tilted her head as her eyes flickered over me, and then to my . . . my roommate.

Acting on instinct, I stepped slightly in front of Josey and crossed my arms. "What are you doing here?"

Aideen laughed, her eyes coming back to mine. "I just told you. I missed you."

"Does Kean know you're here?" I wondered, hoping that they'd reconciled. It was a longshot, given the nature of his last emails, but I hoped.

Her stare darted to Josey again, and then back to me.

"It doesn't matter." Aideen lifted her chin, as though just deciding something. "I left him."

I exhaled through gritted teeth, frustrated.

"William." Aideen took yet another step forward and I watched her slow approach. "I'm free now. We both are. I did this for you, for us—"

"Are you well?" I asked.

She seemed to perk up at this, which meant she misunderstood my meaning.

"What I mean is, are you safe? How is your mental fitness?"

"My . . ." A confused smile washed over her features and she laughed again. "I'm fine, silly. I'm not *crazy*."

Josey made a small sound and I glanced at her. Before I could see Josey's expression, she tucked her chin against her chest, hiding her face.

"I'm not asking if you're crazy." I moved my focus back to Aideen. "I'm asking if you're depressed, anxious. Are you having suicidal thoughts?"

"What? No!" Aideen shook her head adamantly. "I just want to—"

"No." Sliding my hand into the bend of Josey's elbow, I pulled her towards the elevator. "Let's go."

Aideen made a sound of disbelief but apparently recovered quickly. I heard her steps follow us, heels against the marble floor.

"I just want a few minutes of your time." She seemed to be speaking through clenched teeth. "You can't give me a few minutes?"

"No." I pressed the call button for the lift and took a step back, my eyes on the panel display.

Aideen placed her hand on my free arm and tugged. "I can force you to talk to me."

"Hey now"—Josey peeked around me, her voice held a hard edge—"don't you touch him—"

Aideen ignored her, and her own voice turned threatening. "If you don't talk to me, I'll give an earful to those two photographers out there."

"Go ahead." I shrugged the woman off, stepping closer to Josey and biting back the urge to remind Aideen that she'd already paid a prostitute to give the media an earful of lies.

I glanced at Josey again. She was now staring at Aideen, a furious-looking wrinkle between her brows. Josey was clearly and unmistakably angry on my behalf, which caused my heart to give a bizarre, pleased leap.

God, how I missed her.

This last week—ever since our late-night talk in Australia, where she'd called things off between us before I could—had been miserable. The day after, the plane ride back, the night she'd spent at her parents' house, all miserable. She'd been quiet and withdrawn, and then irritable and callous.

But then, and worst of all, when she'd come home after the night with her parents, she was her normal self. Completely normal. Sunny, funny Josey.

As though nothing had changed.

As though Australia never happened.

As though it had meant *nothing* to her.

I'd been swallowing glass every time she smiled or joked, or played with Rocky and laughed at his antics, like her world hadn't ended that night, like it hadn't tilted off its axis, leaving her miserable and shaken. Selfishly, I preferred her quiet and withdrawn, irritable and callous. At least that had given me hope, the possibility that maybe she'd also wanted more.

But no.

And now we were here, and she was glaring at Aideen with fire and fury in her eyes, and I clung to that sliver of a sign.

And maybe I'm pathetic.

Aideen had been quiet for a few seconds, eventually saying, "How can you be so cold? It's not like you."

That statement earned her a sneer. "You don't know me."

"I do—"

"And I don't know you."

"You know me." Her voice seemed to waver, but her eyes were dry. "You know me *intimately*."

My sneer deepened, chagrined by her implication.

Kean and Aideen, quite literally, could have been anyone. That was the entire point of our arrangement.

"Just leave."

As though a punctuation to my words, the elevator dinged, announcing its arrival. Stepping away from her, I led Josey into the lift and pressed the button for our floor. Turning and issuing Aideen a warning glare as she moved to board, I shook my head slowly.

Don't. Don't even think about it.

"I love you." Her chin wobbled, and yet her eyes were still dry.

"No. You don't," I scoffed. What was it going to take for this woman to leave me alone?

She put her foot in the path of the doors, holding them open. "I do!"

"Why are you doing this? Why are you throwing away your marriage? You know *nothing* about me."

"You're William Moore, flanker for—"

I responded without thinking, my temper flaring, "That's not what I mean. You have to know someone to love them."

"But—"

"And when you love someone, you don't hire prostitutes to spread lies to the media and try to ruin their career."

Josey sucked in an audible breath and I felt her shocked eyes on my profile. Removing my hand from her arm, I pulled it through my hair, grinding my teeth and immediately regretting the words. I hadn't meant for her to find out.

Meanwhile, Aideen blanched. Yet, she didn't remove her foot.

Instead, she shrieked, "I'm sorry!"

"No. You're not. You're sorry you got caught. Do you know what your lies have cost? Not me, but the people I care about? My team? My foundation work? My—those kids?"

Fuck. I couldn't focus on this. If I thought about The Dream Foundation, all those people I'd let down because of this woman's lies, I was going to lose my shit.

"It doesn't matter, I can make it better," she begged. "Please."

"No. Even if you hadn't spread lies about me, you knew the rules—"

"Damn the rules! And damn you. I can't help what I feel," she wailed.

"What you feel is not love."

The woman sniffed, lifting her chin again. "What do you know about lo—"

"Love is letting someone go, because it's what's best for them."

"Is that what this is about?" Aideen shifted like she was going to board the elevator, her eyes hopeful. "Are you trying to do what you think is right for me?"

I growled, infinitely frustrated, glaring at the ceiling. "I'm not talking about you."

The elevator alarm made a shrill, beeping sound, reminding us that there was something preventing the doors from shutting.

"When you looked at me, I felt it, I felt—"

That's it.

Overcome with anger, I charged towards her. "I'm not in love with you. I feel *nothing* for you. How can I love you when I'm in love with someone else?"

Shocked silence followed my shouted outburst, with Aideen stumbling backwards and away, her eyes rimmed wide with surprise.

Finally, *finally*, the beeping ended, and the doors slid shut, blocking her from view. If I never saw that woman again, it would be too soon. I exhaled my relief.

My relief was, however, short-lived.

"Will?"

I grew rigid.

Shit.

What had I just said? What had she heard?

"Who. . .?" Josey's voice was quiet, but her tone was unmistakably confused.

Still facing the elevator doors, I shut my eyes, my confession chanting between my ears. *I'm in love with someone else.*

The panic I thought I'd left behind in Australia returned full force, a knife in my chest, and it only expanded the longer we stood in silence.

"Will," Josey repeated, her voice louder, more like a demand.

"It was—" I had to clear my throat to get the words out, "It was a mistake."

"What?"

The doors to the elevator slid open, revealing the hallway to our floor. I half turned, placing my hand in the path of the doors, and gestured for Josey to exit. I couldn't meet her eyes, because then she'd know, and then she'd leave me.

Just the thought . . .

She didn't move for several seconds, and again I felt her gaze on my profile, searching.

Eventually, she said, "After you."

Her words, especially the cool edge of her tone, had me glancing at her. Josey was glaring at me, her jaw set, her arms crossed. When it became clear she wouldn't exit until I did, I sighed and stepped off, but kept my hand in place.

She glared at me as she left the lift, she glared at me as the doors slid shut, and she glared at me as she walked past. Josey pulled her keys from her bag and unlocked the door, I heard their jangle as she tossed them into the basket and walked inside.

I also heard Rocky's excited sounds of greeting and her soothing sounds in return. I assumed—*hoped*—any conversation about Aideen or what I'd inadvertently confessed was now permanently shelved, that Josey was now happily distracted by Rocky and would just let it go.

So I dropped my bag by the entrance, closed the door, locked it, and walked to the kitchen, seeking to subdue the burst of earlier panic. I opened the fridge, swallowing around a tight knot in my throat, and grabbed a vitamin water.

But when I shut the fridge and turned, Josey was there. Her hands were on her hips, and she was once again glaring at me.

"What was a mistake?" she demanded, her tone reminding me of how she'd sounded on the airplane during our flight back to Ireland.

Again, I had to clear my throat before responding, my eyes moving beyond her to everything and nothing. "What I said."

"You're being vague on purpose. What did you say, specifically, that was a mistake?" She took a step forward.

I struggled to draw a complete breath.

"Who are you in love with?" Another demand, another step forward.

I shook my head, staring at the white wall over her shoulder. *If she knows, she'll leave.*

"It's me, isn't it?" She did not sound happy, and I winced, hot pins and needles rushing to the surface of my skin, resisting the powerful urge to fall to my knees and beg her to stay.

Yet I couldn't deny it.

We stood there, her eyes on me while I fought and clawed and struggled to think of a way out of this mess, one where she didn't leave me.

But then she said, "Coward," her voice catching.

Startled, my eyes cut to her face just in time to witness a tear spill down her cheek. I blinked at the liquid emotion. I stared at it, dumbfounded.

What...? "What?"

Lifting my gaze to hers, I discovered with no small amount of wonder that Josey was not only pissed, she was sad. Tremendously sad.

"You are such a coward!" Her face contorted as she charged at me, pushing against my chest.

She didn't knock me physically off-balance, but my head was spinning, and I caught her arms before she could move away.

Greedy with hope, I examined her flushed face, her chin wobbling though she pressed her lips together admirably. More tears streamed down her face and she scowled at me accusingly.

"Josey—"

"Do you know, I cried so much after you broke things off that night, that I used all the tissue in the hotel room? All the Kleenex, all the toilet tissue. I used all the towels, and was tempted to use the edge of my sheet. My *sheet*! I had to call housekeeping to bring me more tissue and pillowcases and towels." She pulled herself out of my grip, pointing at my chest much like she'd done on the airplane.

My heart soared.

She wasn't finished. "And my face was red, my eyes were swollen, and there I was, negotiating the release of tissue with a very concerned member of the hospitality staff, fielding their sympathetic looks and offers for help, all because you were—no! You *are* too much of a coward to take a chance on something— something—"

I reached for her again. "Josey—"

She evaded me, darting around the kitchen counter and down the hall, shouting around her sobs. "Think of the trees, Will! And now I need more tissue, you selfish, cowardly coward! You're killing trees!"

Chasing her, I caught her just inside her bathroom, where she was pulling at the roll of toilet paper and crying in earnest.

"Josey—"

"Oh, sod off!" She covered her face, her shoulders shaking.

I wrestled with my need to touch her, which raged against the quiet voice of common sense telling me to give her space. Unsurprisingly, baser instincts won, and I pulled her against my chest, holding her tightly in my arms.

She let me, but she whispered, "Coward."

Which spurred me to blurt, "I love you," my voice rough and my heart at a gallop. "I'm so in love with you."

"Yes. *Thankyouverymuch*. I already sorted that bit out." She grabbed fistfuls of my shirt, her face against my chest. She seemed to be attempting to regulate her breathing.

Cupping her cheek, I encouraged her to tilt her head back so I could look in her eyes. She was still clearly furious and sad, glaring at me between hiccupping sobs.

I licked my suddenly dry lips. "Do you—"

"You broke my heart!" she shouted, fidgeting a little, clenching her fists as though to beat them against my chest.

It was absolutely the wrong moment to smile, but I did.

Josey huffed, her scowl returning. "You don't have to look so happy about it."

I held her tighter. "I'm not happy. I'm—"

"You are happy. You wouldn't have told me, would you? Unless I asked point blank, right? Were you embarrassed?" she accused, wiggling again, this time to break my hold.

She succeeded, because I was so surprised by her question. "Embarrassed?"

"Of me?"

My smile fell. *Is that what she thought?*

"God no!" I reached for her and she sidestepped, darting out of the bathroom, taking a length of toilet paper with her.

Growling my aggravation, I followed her again, and found her clipping Rocky's leash to his collar. She was fast, but I was faster, and I blocked the door before she could leave.

Rocking back on her heels when she encountered the wall of my chest, she huffed again, crossing her arms and lifting her eyes no higher than my chin.

"Move."

"Listen to me."

"Why?" Her reproachful gaze came to mine. "Because now, finally, you're going to tell me the truth? First you say you want me to be your employee, then you say you want in my pants but nothing else, and now—

"That's not true. I wanted—*want*—to be with you. I wanted commitment."

Her eyes narrowed with obvious suspicion. "Did you, though? Did you really? Because the way I remember the conversation, you only wanted to 'date me'"—she used her fingers to make quotations in the air—"if we were headed someplace serious, like marriage, which we both knew was a total joke. You didn't really want a commitment or marriage with me. And then, BAM! A friends with benefits arrangement saves the day."

Shoving my fingers through my hair, I clenched and unclenched my jaw, because she was right about then, but wrong about now. "You're right, I was relieved *then* when you said you didn't want a commitment or something serious. I need, needed rules, defined expectations, set boundaries."

"You broke all the rules." Her tone was flat. "You held my hand, everywhere. We had those dinners, just us."

"Those were your rules."

"You agreed to them!"

"I hated them." My attention dropped to her mouth, galvanized by the shape and color of her lips.

"Then why did you agree?" Her voice cracked. "Why not just *date* like a normal person? Why make it everything, or almost nothing?"

"Because I thought. . ." Christ, I wanted to touch her, I burned with the need to hold her again. "I thought it would keep me from falling in love with you."

"What is so wrong with falling in love with me?" Her chin wobbled again, and new tears threatened.

I couldn't bare her sorrow. I reached for her.

She twisted away. "No. Don't touch me."

"Josey." I stepped away from the door. "Listen—"

"I'm done listening." She held her hands up.

Rocky danced around her feet, made anxious by her sadness, and sending me quick glares as though to ask, *Are you responsible for this?*

"Please." She didn't want me to touch her, but I couldn't stay away. I followed her as she backstepped around the couch, looking everywhere but at me.

"You are a coward. You say you love me, but leaving me in Australia, using your safe word, returning in the middle of the night and then ending things instead of admitting the truth, instead of taking a risk. That's not love."

"I couldn't." *What if you didn't love me back?*

How could I make her understand?

"Why?" she said on a sob.

"What if you didn't feel the same way?"

"So you said nothing?" Her voice cracked.

"Yes," I seethed, angry, and not able to pinpoint precisely why. "I didn't want—"

"Me?"

"No! I wanted you. But in Australia, you always left me after we were together. I couldn't read you, I had no idea what you were thinking. And since we've been back here, it's like nothing fazes you, you acted like what happened in Sydney meant nothing."

"What was I supposed to do? Beg you to be with me? You're the one who pushed me away."

"No, of course not. But I didn't want to lose you. I can't lose you. I didn't want you to leave me."

"So . . ." she looked bewildered. "You pushed me away so you wouldn't lose me?"

Reaching my wit's end, I turned Josey's question back on her. "Why didn't *you* say anything?"

Her eyes came to mine then, and she huffed an incredulous laugh.

Before she could speak, I challenged again, "You claim I broke your heart, so why didn't you say anything to me? Why didn't you tell me? Why act like you wanted things to end that night? One word from you and I would have—"

"You're joking, right? You said yourself you were worried about an imbalance in power dynamics in any relationship. I'm nobody! I'm *Nosey Josey, head full of posies, mug like a bug, uglier than a pug*. You're William fucking Moore!"

"You're not nobody." I couldn't keep the desperation from my voice, "You're everything to me!"

Abruptly, she ceased walking backward and held my stare, her lips parted in plain surprise, and I could see my last words had affected her. After a protracted moment, Josey broke eye contact and covered her face with a hand, swiping angrily at her tears.

Balling my hands into fists so I wouldn't touch her, I hazarded a step closer, then another.

"Why wouldn't you let me kiss you?"

She snorted derisively through tears, throwing daggers at me with her disbelieving stare. "If you wanted to kiss me, you would have."

That stopped me, and it took me a full moment to respond. "And disrespect your boundaries?"

She shook her head, her anger becoming something else, something anxious and vulnerable. "I don't know, what I felt—feel—is chaotic. The rules made sense at the time, but I hated them too, and I just wanted you to . . . to . . ."

"What?" I whispered, now within arm's reach of her and Rocky, who was alternating between sitting and standing, his anxious gaze on his mistress.

She seemed to deflate, her arms coming around her middle. "I didn't want you to kiss me, if you didn't love me."

Not hesitating even a half second, I reached for her jaw, stroking my palm against it, stepping closer, caressing the indent beneath her cheekbone with my thumb. "I love you, Josey Kavanagh."

"I'm so confused," she confessed softly, brokenly, her words bewildered, but she curled a hand around my wrist and held on, her gaze moving between my mouth and my eyes until I was too close for her to focus on either.

I slid my other hand around her waist.

I closed my eyes.

And, thank fuck, I finally, *finally* kissed her.

TWENTY-ONE
JOSEY

@JoseyInHeels: After a fight, chimpanzees kiss each other to make up just like humans #funfacts
@ECassChoosesPikachu to @JoseyInHeels: … what's going on? Call me! I mean it this time!!

My arms flailed.
    My heart beat twice as fast.
Pleasurable chills encapsulated my entire body.
A galaxy of stars glittered behind my closed eyelids.
All because William Moore was kissing me.
Not a peck on the cheek. Not on top of my head, temple, or jaw. No, this was a spine-tingling, heart-stopping, toe-curling kiss on the mouth. This was a kiss that changed lives.
It was certainly changing mine. The ramifications of our brief exchange were too monumental to process right now.
You're not nobody. You're everything to me!
I love you, Josey Kavanagh.
The deep, masculine quality of Will's declarations echoed in my head while he cupped my face in his strong hands. He slid his tongue deep into my mouth and drank me in—slowly, carefully—like he didn't want to waste a single second. He savored me, and when I finally managed to snap to my senses, I savored him, too.
The suddenness of it all had rendered me momentarily frozen, but now I kissed him back. After waiting so long, his mouth was on my mouth, his lips on

my lips, his tongue against my tongue. And he tasted good. No, he tasted *incredible*.

I whimpered when his hands left my face so that he could wrap his arms tight around my waist and pull me to him. Somewhere close by, Rocky was jumping into the air and barking, whether in happiness and glee at us finally kissing, or merely for attention, I wasn't sure.

Probably the latter.

Unfortunately for him, I wasn't available right now, because I was too lost in THE KISS. It felt like I'd been waiting my entire life for it. Rocky's hyperactivity died down as he gave up and wandered off, leaving the humans to do human things, while I wrapped my arms around Will's neck and gasped when he pressed his erection against my belly.

He was rock-hard.

A moan escaped me. He picked me up, and I squealed as the air went out from under me. A second later, he was kissing me again. It appeared he was an excellent multitasker as he carried me from the living room to his bedroom—okay, a passable multitasker since his shoulder bumped into the doorframe in the process. He swore into the kiss, which somehow made it sexier, then kicked the door shut with a slam behind us.

We were alone.

Will only broke away long enough to lay me down on his bed and shoot me a dark, sensual look. It said he had plans—dirty, sexy plans. I had no complaints as he crawled up my body, took my chin in his hand, and brought my mouth to his again. Right now, he seemed more interested in kissing than anything else, which was fine by me because we had a lot of lost kissing time to make up for.

He was possessed, and I was more than willing to be the recipient of that possession, of the lust that shone in his eyes.

He nibbled at my lips, kissed my chin, the underside of my jaw, before returning to my mouth. His tongue sank inside, caressing my tongue, licking into me with a need fiercer than a hundred-foot wave. Goosebumps covered every inch of my skin.

Between my thighs, I ached. In my belly, I ached. Everywhere, I freaking *ached*.

It had only been about a week since we'd been together, but it felt like an eternity.

My body hummed, floated on a cloud of bliss, as it finally got what it wanted.

At long last William Moore was kissing me.
I loved him.
He loved me.
I felt like I was dreaming.
Wait, had I actually said it yet?

His tongue did wondrous things to me as I backtracked through our conversation. No, I hadn't.

Will told me he loved me, and I hadn't said it back. Sure, he knew I'd fallen for him, but saying the words was important. At least, it was to me.

I brought my hands to his chest, trying to push him away long enough to break our kiss. His mouth slid across my lips and cheek to my ear, where he lazily sucked my earlobe, and my spine arched up in pleasure. He really was way too good with his tongue. His hand wandered to the hem of my skirt, pushed it up and caressed the back of my thigh. My sex clenched from the seductive whisper of his fingertips, so close yet so far.

"Wait, wait," I gasped, clenching his shirt in my fists. He drew away just slightly, but didn't stop what he was doing. It made it hard to think straight. When his hand moved further up my thigh and slid past the seam of my underwear to caress my bottom, I let out a breathy whimper.

"Please don't tell me to stop," Will whispered, begging. He was looking at me now, taking in my every reaction. His eyes absorbed my entire face, seeming to look everywhere at once.

"I...." I heaved a breath. "I h-have something to say. That is, I..." His fingers wandered between my thighs and I squeezed my eyes shut, my voice turning breathy. "Oh my God."

Will let out a deep chuckle. "Is that what you wanted to say?"

"No, no!"

His fingers paused in their exploration. "No?"

"No, I mean, yes. Please, don't stop, I just need to tell you that I—"

"Yes?" Will purred, circling my clit, licking my lips, and making me lose my ever-loving mind. I got the sense he was enjoying this, teasing me, making me flustered. He sucked my earlobe again and I considered giving up. But no, this needed to be said. He needed to hear it, needed to know I was serious about him. Just as serious as he was about me.

I opened my eyes on a gasp. I was going to come and he'd barely even gotten started. Will's gaze held mine as he paused his teasing of my clit to plunge two fingers inside me. I was so, so wet, and my spine arched again, needing more, welcoming whatever he wanted to give.

"Will, I..." A moan cut off my words as his fingers sped up.

"Josey," he murmured. "You're so beautiful when you're about to come. Your eyes captivate me."

His fingers returned to my clit, and I was a hair trigger. I came swiftly, my body clenching, my heart hammering as he gazed at me with a love I couldn't believe he felt for me. I couldn't believe I hadn't seen it before. There was no mistaking his feelings now.

"I love you!" I burst, as the tremors of my orgasm swept through me.

Will blinked, seemed to hold his breath, then a look of pure adoration claimed his features. He caressed my face with his free hand, his voice reverent when he replied, "And I love you. I've never loved anyone until you, Josey."

A glowing feeling filled me up. It was sheer contentment and happiness, a sense of finally finding the person I didn't even realize I'd been searching for. Will accepted me in a way I'd never felt before. Sure, my parents and Eilish loved me, but Will was the other part of my heart, the missing piece in my soul. He was a silly, silly man for not being honest with me sooner, but I understood his reasons.

His fears.

I had my fair share of them, too.

"Where are you?" he whispered. "Stay with me."

"Sorry. I just…I really do love you," I said again. It felt liberating to say the words I'd kept secret, incredibly freeing to be able to feel my emotions instead of pushing them down. It had killed me to be around Will and not acknowledge the fact that he meant everything to me.

"And I love you, I love you." He bent to give my jaw a little nip. "Now I'm going to fuck you."

I shivered. Will grazed his teeth along my lower lip, then reached over to open his bedside drawer. I watched as he retrieved a pair of fur-lined silver handcuffs.

What the…

"Where did you get those?"

He studied them a second, then threw them on the pillow as he grabbed my wrists and lifted them to the headboard. "I bought them for the Australia trip and forgot to pack them."

My eyes grew wide. Anticipation knocked me upside the head with a hammer; I felt dizzy. "You did?"

He held my arms in place, then plucked up the handcuffs and snapped them around my wrists. I swallowed thickly as he studied his handiwork, a pleased look on his face. His eyes darkened when they met mine.

"There. Open your legs."

I did as I was told. Will proceeded to divest me of my clothes, first my shoes, then my skirt and knickers. By the time he unbuttoned my shirt he realized his error. He couldn't get it off without undoing the handcuffs.

I didn't want him to undo them.

Neither did he, it seemed, because instead he merely pushed it open, unwrapping me, and then pulled down the cups of my bra to reveal my breasts. He leaned down, his warm breath giving me tingles as he sucked a nipple into his mouth. He swirled his tongue around the sensitive tip, and even though I'd just come my body cried out for more.

"Will," I moaned, and his gaze flicked to me. He never looked sexier. With his mouth still on my breast, he started to undo his belt. He pulled his pants and boxers down just enough to free his cock, then, without a word he pushed inside me. My body welcomed him eagerly. His mouth left my breast to take my lips in another mind-melting kiss. With my arms above my head, I had no ability to touch him, to hold on, to caress him in return.

Which was fine by me. I wanted him to do whatever he wanted.

He thrust inside me, hips jutting in and out, as he kissed me into oblivion. With his cock inside me and his tongue in my mouth, I felt like I might come a second time.

"I fucking love kissing you," he rasped, and then he was on me again. He was punishing, his strong, sport-honed body unforgiving, as he murmured sweet, sexy words in my ear and worked me to the heights of ecstasy.

When he rose up, eyes on my bound wrists before they swept across my face, breasts, and stomach, I was fit to burst from the love I saw reflected in his eyes. My lips were sore from all his kisses. He kept up a steady pace as he reached down and found my clit.

I was so, so ready to come again.

"Wait for me," he said, breathless, and I instantly got his meaning. He wanted us to come together.

It was so hard to hold out, but when I felt his thrusts slow, I knew he was close.

"Kiss me, please," I begged.

Something inside of him snapped. He leaned down, still fingering my clit, still fucking me, and claimed my mouth. A second later, I felt him fill me.

Maybe he was a good multitasker after all.

I came with a sharp cry that Will swallowed with his kiss. He fell on top of me, his hot body glistening with sweat. He kissed my breasts, trailed his mouth up to my neck, then nuzzled and sucked as we both floated down from our high. I closed my eyes, drifting off a little when I felt him fiddle with the handcuffs. He unlocked them, massaging my wrists and kissing the reddened skin. I didn't even realize I'd been straining, but allowing him complete control like that had been incredible. We'd experimented a little in Australia, but nothing like this.

"I'm going to run us a bath," he said lovingly, then got up. He was still partially dressed, so he took off the rest of his clothes before he walked to the bathroom. I admired the sight of his muscular backside, grinning to myself.

A minute later, I heard water running and I sighed at the idea of a nice, long soak. The bath here in Will's apartment was much bigger than the one in our hotel in Sydney. When the water shut off, Will returned, stripped off my shirt and bra, lifted me from the bed, and carried me to the bathroom where a delectable bubble bath was waiting.

"Have I mentioned yet that I love you?" I said. His deep chuckle rumbled through me as he lowered me into the tub, then crawled in behind me. He pulled me between his sturdy thighs and wrapped his arms around me. His hand cupped my breast and I softly gasped, both at the perfect temperature of the water and the way he plucked my nipple between his fingers.

I moaned and felt his cock stiffen behind me once more.

Relaxing against him, I rested my head on his chest and he kissed my hair. He made a quiet sound of happiness and I closed my eyes. I thought of all the things he'd been through since the story broke, all the anger and hurt and frustration he must've felt. He'd been ridiculed by the public, asked to step away from his charity work, and forced to make great efforts to clean up his image. In a way it was ridiculous, because Will was more honest, more respectable than most. He might've been a voyeur, but in the most moral way possible. He had real values that he believed in, rules he stuck to. Or at least tried to stick to, *until I came along.*

I had to admit, I quite liked being the person he broke his ironclad rules for.

"I can't believe Aideen was behind all the stories about you," I whispered, stroking my hand along his arm. Will let out a long sigh.

"Let's not talk about her. . . ever. There's nothing I can do to change what she did. I just have to try my best to move on from it."

"Don't you feel angry?"

"How can I be angry when this mess brought you to me?"

Oh man.

He was *good.*

I endeavored not to die of swooning, and instead focused on the issue at hand. "I mean, aren't you angry with her? How long did you work with The Dream Foundation?"

He seemed to hesitate, then admitted, "About five years."

"That's a big investment. It's okay to be angry about what you've lost."

"I'm trying not to let it cloud my judgment. Anger causes us to become irrational and make bad decisions. I don't plan on making any more of them."

I arched a brow. "Only good ones?"

His big hand spread out on my belly. "Yes," he murmured. "Starting with you, Josey."

"Starting with me?"

"I don't want anything between us. I want you"—his arms tightened around me—"I need you."

My heart shimmered inside my chest. I was sure if they opened me up they'd see it glittering. That was how Will made me feel.

Like a unicorn cupcake dipped in edible glitter covered in chocolate sprinkles.

I turned a little and tipped my head up to kiss his chin. "Back at ya, homey."

"Homey?"

"Yep. You're my big Okla-homey."

"Josey."

"Yes?"

"You're my favorite person, but maybe never call me that in front of the team, okay?"

I laughed and made sure he saw my wink. "Sure thing. Only in bed. I got you."

He pursed his lips, fighting a smile. "Not in bed either. Actually, never call me that anywhere."

"Whatever. You love it."

His hand wandered between my thighs, cupping me gently. "I love this," he whispered.

My voice grew husky. "What else do you love?"

His hand moved to my breasts, caressing them under the water. "These." It wandered up to my lips, his middle finger dipping inside my mouth. "And this." I closed my eyes when his fingertips trailed across my eyelids. "But most of all these."

"Will."

"Hmmm?"

"Make love to me again."

He made a low grunt.

However, we both must've had our eyes closed because we didn't see Rocky nudge the bathroom door open. And Will didn't get a chance to answer because a second later there was a loud splash of water and I let out a high-pitched squeal.

"Oh my goodness, get out!" I yelled as I opened my eyes and saw Rocky had decided to hop into the bath. Will's chuckle started low, then transformed into a deep belly laugh as my dog wore a delighted, happy smile, tongue hanging out and everything. He clearly thought getting into the bath with us was a marvelous idea. I stood up, grabbed my dog and marched through the apartment to put him in his crate.

"Bad dog," I said, unable to help my laugh. I was dripping wet and stark naked, not having had the forethought to grab a towel. Rocky didn't look one bit chagrined, in fact, he had a wad of suds atop his head that made him look ridiculously adorable. I was too busy laughing to sound stern. I shook my head and returned to the bathroom where Will was now in hysterics.

I reached down and splashed him with some water.

"Our dog has the worst timing in the world," he managed to say through his laughter.

I grinned wide. "Yes, yes he does."

"But he's the best."

My expression softened. "Yes, he is."

Will let out a sigh. "I guess our bath's ruined."

"Well, there is a silver lining."

"Oh?"

"We get to go back to bed and have more amazing sex. And this time *I'll* be using the handcuffs," I replied, and shot him a saucy smile. Will's expression transformed into one of carnal anticipation.

"In that case, I'm your willing participant. Also, you do realize that's the first time you haven't whispered the word *sex* around me?"

I placed a hand on my hip, thought on it, then smiled. "Do you know what? I think you're right. Yippee! Look at me, sex, sex, sex, sexy, sexified sex," I joked.

Will climbed out of the bathtub, grabbed a towel and wrapped it around my body while I sing-songed variations of the word sex.

Without warning, he picked me up, threw me over his shoulder and carried me back to his bedroom.

If this was how things would be with William Moore, then I was more than willing to sign up for a lifetime.

TWENTY-TWO
WILL

@WillthebrickhouseMoore to @JoseyInHeels: What do you want for dinner tonight? I'm stopping by Listons.
@JoseyInHeels to @WillthebrickhouseMoore: Chocolate syrup and honey, and whipped cream.
@WillthebrickhouseMoore to @JoseyInHeels: You are so fucking awesome.

I awoke sometime before dawn, startled to find a warm, soft body curled against mine. But then I remembered. Euphoric contentment flooded my chest and I exhaled quietly, part in relief, part in wonder.

Josey.

Light filtered through the door of my room from the hallway, illuminating her in a swath of pale gray, desaturating the colors of her captivating face. She looked like a black and white photo, timeless, classic perfection.

Something in me shifted, two heavy weights clicking into place. This was where I wanted to be. The rest of my life, I never wanted us to be separated.

Maybe for a day, maximum.

Like, twelve hours tops.

On the weekends, less than that. Three hours at most, but usually only one hour or less, and only if necessary.

The weight seemed to grow, increase in volume and mass, cusping the base of my throat. I swallowed against the sharp ache. For some reason, I reminded myself that Josey loved me. She wasn't leaving, she was here to stay.

. . . But for how long?

A sudden urge to wake her and ask caught me by surprise. I shook myself, blaming the impulse on sleep inertia, and laughed quietly at the temporary insanity. Returning my head to the pillow, I pulled her closer and she turned in her sleep, giving me her back and pressing her bottom against my front.

But my chest was still tight, and my throat still ached, and I couldn't stop thinking about it.

How long?

I tried to breath normally. I tried to close my eyes and go back to sleep. I couldn't. It didn't matter that my common sense told me the question was premature, that we'd *just* admitted our mutual feelings mere hours ago, that there were so many other pressing questions—namely, was Josey still my employee? Or . . . what was the plan there?—uncertainty clawed.

However, unlike our time together in Australia, the uncertainty was not accompanied by dread. Anticipation and a need to have things settled, defined, clear—yes. But definitely not dread.

I don't know how long I lay there, wrestling this need, but sometime after daybreak Josey stirred with a little sigh.

Slowly, I lifted my head, propping it on my palm, my elbow resting on the pillow behind her, and took several moments to appreciate the beauty of Josey in the yellow and golden sunbeams of a new day.

So beautiful.

My chest constricted, and I decided I could deal with my need for structure later. I wanted to take advantage of right now.

I slid my palm from her shoulder, down the curve of her side to her hip, pushing the covers lower as I exposed the luscious expanse of bare skin for my eyes. She should always sleep naked, I decided. I moved my hand between her legs as though to prove the practicality of this decision. Lifting her leg gently, I shifted it back and sifted through her soft curls to find the slick center of her.

She sighed again.

I smiled, watching her face, the way her brows moved up and then down, making me wonder if she was incorporating this—my touching her—into a dream. Eventually, though I thoroughly enjoyed the watching, I bent my lips to her neck and placed a licking, biting kiss just under her ear.

She groaned, turning towards me and onto her back, but her eyes remained shut.

Hmm.

I bit then kissed her shoulder, collarbone, and breast. Josey arched her back just slightly and made a sweet and short humming sound. She didn't open her eyes.

"Josey?" I leaned further over her, placing a knee between her open legs, sliding my hand up to her hip, stomach, and breast.

Lifting her hands, she settled them lightly on my back, murmuring something incoherent. Pressing forward, stroking her sex with the length of mine, I took her lips.

She shivered, opening her mouth instantly, and I was surprised to find she tasted like mint. Specifically, toothpaste.

I leaned away, squinting at her still closed eyes. "Did you. . . when did you brush your teeth?"

She opened one eye. "What?" she asked breathlessly.

I was over her now, our bodies touching almost everywhere. "You brushed your teeth. When did you do that? I've been up for at least an hour."

Josey scrunched her face, hesitating, and then said in a sleep-roughened voice, "Would you believe I always have minty breath in the morning?"

I laughed, shaking my head and lowering my lips to her neck. "I guess I'll be back after I brush my teeth."

Her fingers dug into my back. "Don't go. You have perfect morning breath, you taste like heaven." She arched beneath me, curling a leg around one of mine, which caused her thighs to widen. "Stay here." She placed a light kiss on my neck, but then returned to the same spot and sucked my skin into her mouth.

She'd found the spot that had me going stiff and painfully hard in seconds. "Josey." I struggled to say the single word.

"Fuck me, please," she whispered, rolling her willing pelvis against my erection, her hands grabbing my back and sides and torso.

Her words lit a flame and her roving hands fanned it. Yet, I resisted.

Reaching for her wrists, I pulled Josey's grasping hands away from my body, tangling our fingers together and holding them in place on either side of her face. I pushed myself up. She chased my mouth and I gave into her with slow kisses. She sought to quicken them. I also gave in with measured pressure against her slick and eager pussy. She sought rough strokes and invasion.

"Will." Her voice was strained, frustrated, as her gaze captured mine. "What are you doing?"

"You're gorgeous."

I slid my cock against her entrance. Her breath hitched. I pulled away. She whimpered.

"Are you trying to torture me?" Josey shifted restlessly, clearly attempting an irritated glare. Instead, she just looked damn sexy.

I shook my head, rubbing our noses together softly. "No. I'm trying to make love to you."

She groaned.

"Slowly," I added.

She groaned louder.

"Relax." I grinned down at her, and then lowered my lips to her chest, kissing the valley between her breasts.

"You know what would make me relax?"

"Hmm?" I skimmed my lips to her right breast, swirling my tongue around the stiff nipple and sucking. Her body jerked in response.

"Your penis in my vagina."

I smiled against her skin as her legs moved impatiently. She strained upward, moaning, "Please."

I relented, but I did so unhurriedly, hovering above to watch her face as I entered her body. Her lashes flickered, her eyes on mine. Her lips parted. Her breathing was somehow both light and labored, and her entire body had grown still.

I watched her reactions, the cadence of her breath as I began to move, giving myself to her gradually, claiming each inch of her body by degrees rather than a quick thrust. I wanted to memorize every sensation, every second. I was met with an erotic heat, a constricting resistance I'd never noticed before when we'd fucked. Her walls squeezed, a reflexive tightening, and I nearly came right then.

Our gazes locked and Josey looked a little lost, hazy, her hips tilting in time with my languid movements.

She swallowed thickly.

I noted a light sheen of sweat on her forehead and upper lip, so I bent to kiss her. She was hot there too, hot and lush and tasting of both heaven and depravity. I could not stop drinking from her, sucking and licking and biting her tongue and the yielding pillows of her lips.

This time, when I lifted to look at her, Josey's eyes were closed and her brows were pulled together, like she was concentrating.

"Oh God," she panted, her hips jerking to meet mine. "It hurts."

I hesitated. "Do you want me to—"

"Don't you dare! Don't stop, don't stop, don't stop," she pleaded in a high-pitched, breathy voice.

"Open your eyes." I needed to see them, the window inside.

She did. They collided with mine, wide and defenseless and a little scared. Josey bowed forward abruptly, her mouth open on a soundless cry, and I felt her come, her body tightening and releasing around me.

"I love you," she said, collapsing back yet still straining, still shaking. Turning her head to bite my forearm. "I love you, I love you. It hurts, it hurts so good."

I quickened my pace, going deeper, thrusting harder, giving her every inch with each stroke, and I felt another shudder course through her.

"Oh God," she moaned, shaking her head with a mindless sort of desperation. "I can't, I can't— oh fuck!"

She came again. And this time I followed, losing control at the end, my movements graceless and severe.

Bending my arms at last, I kissed her again and again, still hungry for her, still insatiable. Rolling us both to the side, I released her hands and pulled her completely against me. She was breathing as though she'd just sprinted, and so was I.

Though we'd barely moved, I'd never felt so close to flying.

This was where I wanted to be. The rest of my life, I never wanted us to be separated.

And I needed to know she felt the same.

* * *

"How do I convince Josey to marry me?"

Bryan choked.

He'd been drinking from his sports bottle, and now he was forced to lean against the wall as he struggled to breathe, finally rasping, "Excuse me?"

"How do I—"

"I heard you." He waved away the rest of my question, his glare moving over me as though I'd grown pig ears. "What the hell is going on? Last I heard, you were calling everything off and going back to business as usual."

We were in the long, cement hallway leading to the locker room, and we were alone. Everyone else had left, but both Bryan and I had appointments with physio and the team's orthopedist.

As anxious as I was to get home and see Josey after everything that had happened the day prior (and this morning before breakfast), I was thankful for a moment alone with Bryan. I trusted him to give me good, honest advice.

After our enjoyable morning in bed, I'd left her to doze while I showered, walked Rocky, and left for work. Therefore, nothing between Josey and me had been resolved, other than we agreed we were in love last night. I assumed—based on nothing concrete—that we were dating. And. . . that's it. No commitment beyond that, no discussion of expectations, no structure.

I tried letting it go.

I couldn't let it go.

So I filled Bryan in on the happenings of the last few weeks, Kean's emails, Aideen's visit, ending with a pared down description of the conversations I'd had with Josey the previous night.

When I was finished, he was still staring at me like I'd grown pig ears. "Wow."

"Yeah."

"So, you two. . . and that lady, she sounds like a real—" He shook his head, heaving a sigh. "Her husband, jeez." His eyes lost focus.

Eventually, since he stood staring without speaking for almost a minute, I had to interrupt his silent contemplations. "When do I ask her?"

"Huh?" He blinked at me, shaking himself a little. "Ask who what?"

"Josey. To marry me."

Bryan's gaze narrowed. "You're . . . kind of intense."

"What do you mean?"

"Exactly what I said. Listening to you, you're kind of intense, about all of this, about Josey."

"Of course I'm intense about Josey. I love her."

"Yeah but—" Bryan considered me for a long moment before saying, "I love Eilish like mad, Patrick too, but everyone needs space, to succeed or fail on their own. My job is to be the support staff, you know? Or, in terms that might make more sense to you, provide the assist."

Taking a drink from my sports bottle, I considered Bryan's words. *Provide the assist.*

"You said in Australia that she didn't want to get married, right?"

I scowled against my will at the memory. "That's right."

"Then give her time. Eventually—I'm talking months from now—tell her what you want, ask her for a more permanent commitment. And maybe, in the meantime, you work on accepting the possibility that you guys might not ever get married."

I stared at my friend, because his words weren't the ones I wanted to hear. "I need something now, more of a commitment."

"No. You don't." He grinned. "You're exclusive, right? You're living together, right? You love her, she loves you, right?"

"Right." I studied him, waiting to see where he was going with this.

"Then she's already there, mate. She's in. Josey might not want to walk down an aisle, but she's not going anywhere anytime soon."

I grimaced. "How can I be sure?"

Bryan shrugged, huffing a laugh. "You can't be."

I gritted my teeth.

"No. Listen. You can't be sure. No one is ever really certain. You have to trust her to stay, and trust yourself."

"Trust myself? Of course *I'll* stay."

"That's not what I meant." His grin widened again, and the way he was looking at me—like I was fucking *adorable*—inspired a glare in return.

"Fine. Then what did you mean?" I grumped, trying not to roll my eyes.

Looking dramatically over one shoulder, and then the other, Bryan took a step closer and lowered his voice to a theatric whisper, "You have to trust yourself that you're worth sticking around for."

TWENTY-THREE
JOSEY

@JoseyInHeels to @WillthebrickhouseMoore: If we were otters I'd hold your hand while we sleep to make sure we don't drift apart #otterlove
@WillthebrickhouseMoore to @JoseyInHeels: ~~If we were penguins, I'd give you a pebble #penguinproposal~~ I love you.

"So, let me get this straight," said Eilish, bringing her cocktail to her lips for a sip. "The wife was the one behind all the stories?"

"Yes," I exclaimed, not yet tipsy but definitely getting there. "It was her all along. Poor Will thought he was going mad trying to figure out where it all came from, but apparently, she paid a prostitute to corroborate the story. It's so bizarre. I'm just glad the poor woman got paid for having to do something so low."

"She lied for money and you're glad for her?" Ophelia asked. She sat next to Eilish, and seeing them side by side, the similarity in their looks was striking.

Since the double date, Ophelia and I became online friends. I looked up some of her music (which was incredible, by the way), messaged her to say how great I thought it was, and after that we started chatting regularly. Surprisingly, after I initially touched base, she'd been the one to pursue me. I must've made a good impression, though how, I had no idea. I'd been a mess the night we met. Anyway, when Eilish invited me out for drinks with her two pals, Lucy and Annie, I'd taken a chance and asked Ophelia if she'd like to come along. Since she already knew both Lucy and Annie through Broderick, she readily agreed. My friend group was starting to feel like the six degrees of Kevin Bacon.

"We're all the underdog in our own story," I said. "What she did might not have been the right thing, but maybe she had her reasons. Maybe she was fighting for something and the money Aideen paid her was just another step on the ladder to where she needed to be."

"The underdog in our own story," Ophelia mused. "I like that. Do you mind if I put it in a song?"

"Of course not! I'd be honored," I replied enthusiastically. Besides, I was definitely the underdog in my story. Nobody could've expected I'd end up with William Moore. We were champagne and fried chicken. We didn't make sense, and yet, we worked perfectly together.

"How would you feel about convincing Will to find her?" Annie asked, snagging my attention. "The sex worker, I mean. I ran the idea by him in our initial phone call, but he was adamant he didn't want to. I really think he should reconsider."

I thought on this. "Um, I don't know. She probably doesn't want to be found. But why?"

"Well, I think if we can convince her to retract her story, then perhaps it will help restore Will's good standing. It might also convince The Dream Foundation to let him work with them again. I know he's been unhappy about them letting him go."

"Yes, he has been, but I can't see him reaching out to her. He's focusing on moving on from all that now."

Annie's face was sympathetic. "I understand, but maybe run it by him. I'm confident I could find out who she is and convince her to come forward."

I didn't doubt she could convince the woman, whoever she was. Annie was one of the best PR people out there. She had a way of making you feel at ease, drawing you out of yourself when you didn't even realize she was doing it.

"After all," Annie went on, "she got her money from Aideen, so what's to stop her from saying it was all a lie? Especially if we offer her more money in return."

"How much money?"

"A few thousand, probably. Not much in the grand scheme of things."

I worried my lip, thinking about it. "I'll ask Will and see what he says."

"It can't hurt," Annie said, and then cleared her throat. "On an unrelated note, I actually have some news to share."

We all brought our attention to her. She pursed her lips and clasped her hands together, looking nervous.

She hesitated so long that Lucy clapped her on the shoulder. "Come on, woman, out with it. You're making me worry."

"Yes," Eilish agreed. "Is it bad news? Don't be afraid to tell us."

Annie shook her head. "It's not bad news. It's just…it's big." She widened her brown eyes meaningfully, and somehow Lucy managed to read her mind. Her eyes wandered from the glass in Annie's hand, then back to her face. "Oh my God, shut up! You're not!"

Annie nodded and flushed. "I am."

Lucy squealed in excitement.

"What? What am I missing?" Eilish questioned, perplexed. I was just as confused as she was.

Annie turned to her. "I'm pregnant."

Eilish almost spilled the drink she was holding. "Oh em gee!! You are? I can't believe it, I'm so happy!"

"That's great!" I added. "Congratulations."

"I'm going to be an auntie," Lucy beamed, as she and Eilish got up to cuddle Annie, telling her what a great mother she was going to be and what a great dad Ronan would make. As I watched them, I couldn't help but wonder if Will and I would ever have kids.

What would they look like? Would they have his personality or mine? Or both? Or neither?

The idea made my stomach fizzle with a mix of excitement and wonder. Maybe we would have kids. Maybe we wouldn't. Hell, maybe we'd just get three more dogs and call it a day.

The excitement lay in the fact that it was all ahead of us. Who knew what would happen. We still had a whole lifetime worth of new things to experience together.

Lucy and Eilish were still fussing over Annie, asking her a million questions. "How have you been feeling? Have you had any morning sickness yet?"

Annie nodded. "Yes, it's been unpleasant, but not the worst. I've heard stories of women having it all day every day, so I'm relieved mine has only been in the mornings. My biggest fear is labor. I'm terrified of something going wrong." Her hand went to her stomach.

Lucy waved away her fears. "You'll be fine. I'm sure my brother already has the best doctors money can buy lined up. And you can bet your arse I'll be flying home for the delivery."

"He should also make sure he starts investing in some good expensive cheeses," I added jokingly. Everyone stared at me in confusion.

"They used to call it groaning cheese," I elaborated, lifting my cosmo for a sip. "It was the Medieval version of an epidural. My dad wrote about it in one of his books. Husbands would give cheese to their wives to soothe them during labor."

Lucy chuckled. "That is the weirdest thing I've ever heard, but it also makes complete sense."

"Yeah," Annie agreed. "Cheese makes everything better."

Eilish shook her head, smiling fondly. "You and your fascination with old-timey facts and words."

I grinned, thinking of the time I told Will I was the voyeur to his varlet. The titles didn't apply anymore, but I still thought the "varlet's voyeur" had a good ring to it. Now I was just his plain old girlfriend. Funny how the thought still sent a flutter through me.

Lucy, Annie, and Eilish talked baby names while I turned to Ophelia. "So, how's everything going preparing for the big move?"

She sucked in a breath and made a face. "It's going."

"I take it that means it's been stressful."

"Yeah, my mam's been making a fuss. She thinks I'm not ready for such a big step. I think she's just terrified of missing me."

"Will you miss her?"

She thought about it. "Yes and no. I love my mam and all, but it's always been just the two of us, so she's a little overprotective. Broderick says she's acting crazy because she loves me so much."

Broderick. I'd almost forgot about the intense connection those two shared. Even though he was supposed to be on a date with me, and Ophelia was supposed to be with Will, it was obvious they only had eyes for each other.

"How are things with Broderick?" I asked coyly. "Has he gone back to New York yet?"

Ophelia nodded. "He left two weeks ago. I fly over in a couple of days and he's going to collect me from the airport."

She didn't give details on their relationship, but I didn't prod. Maybe they really were just friends. Or maybe they were both trying to ignore the fact that they liked each other, quite like Will and I had done.

"Speaking of," Lucy put in. "I'll be flying back next week, too, so if you want to get together I can show you around. I know all the best food places."

Ophelia smiled wide. "Yes, that'd be great. I'm going to be a duck out of water. Broderick's been such a great help, but I could definitely use a girlfriend over there."

Lucy and Annie shared what appeared to be a conspiratorial smile. Did they know something we didn't?

"Yep, old Rick's got a heart of gold. Always too happy to help," Lucy agreed.

My phone buzzed in my pocket and I pulled it out, my heart fluttering when I saw there was a text from Will. I was still getting used to the idea that he was mine, that of all the women out there, beautiful, funny, charismatic women, he'd chosen me. I wondered if he thought the same way, that of all the men out there, I'd chosen him. Though it definitely wasn't a hard choice to make.

> WILL
>
> Heading out to meet the guys. Let me know if you want me to pick you up on my way home.

He was going out for drinks with Ronan, Bryan, and Sean, and I wondered if, like Annie, Ronan planned to reveal the news about the baby to his friends tonight. I made sure not to mention it so as not to ruin the surprise. Look at me, thinking before I spoke, or well, texted. I really was maturing.

> JOSEY
>
> I've already had 3 cosmos so I probably will need picking up…and taking to bed ;-) Go easy on the tequila tonight. You know you're a messy drunk.

> WILL
>
> I'm a delightful drunk.

> JOSEY
>
> You get real handsy. Most people don't find that delightful, for example Sean might object to your advances F.Y.I.

I loved teasing him. He was surprisingly easy to rile sometimes, especially via text.

> WILL
>
> Lies. Sean would be so lucky. Plus, I'm only handsy with you when I'm drunk. And only when you wear the green dress.

> WILL
>
> Okay…maybe it doesn't matter what you're wearing, but I promise, no amount of tequila could make me feel up Ronan or Bryan tonight.

> JOSEY
>
> Oh, but Sean's fair game?

There was an extra-long pause before his reply came through. I could just imagine him chuckling to himself. I loved making him laugh.

> WILL
>
> He's very pretty.

That cracked me up and I had to roll my lips between my teeth to keep from snorting.

> JOSEY
>
> Yes, he is. Also, totally off topic, but I have a question for you.

I bit my lip, wondering how he'd react to Annie's suggestion. Putting it to him over text was definitely the safest option.

> WILL
>
> Ask me.

> **JOSEY**
> Annie wants to reach out to the woman Aideen paid to lie about you. She thinks she can convince her to retract her statement, and that would help to restore your reputation, maybe convince The Dream Foundation to take you back. So, I guess my question is, do you want her to do that?

I was nervous after I hit send, wondering if maybe I should've waited to ask him in person. I knew he wouldn't be too keen on the idea, but I also knew how much he missed his charity work. When he didn't immediately respond, I sent another text.

> **JOSEY**
> And if they still don't want to work with you, it's their loss. But a retraction could help in convincing other charities to let you work for them. I know you miss helping people.

Still there was no response. I hoped he was just mulling it over and not mad at me for bringing up something he was trying to move on from. I was about to send another text when he finally replied.

> **WILL**
> I haven't wanted to go this route from the beginning, and I still don't like it, but you're right, I do miss the work I used to do. Tell Annie she can try.

I exhaled in relief. He was willing to try.

> **JOSEY**
> Okay, I'll tell her. Have fun with the guys, but not too much fun. I'll see you later, and maybe we'll try out the handcuffs again <3

> **WILL**
> I'll hold you to that.

I slid my phone back in my bag, and gave the waiter a nod to bring over another round of drinks.

* * *

It was a month later, almost to the day, that my first semester results were in. I'd been studying so hard, pulling late nights and early mornings. I just really hoped my work paid off.

I opened my laptop with Rocky curled up beside me, and nervously logged on to the college website. Just before I navigated to the results page, I got a ping in my email, alerting me to a recent news story.

Okay, so I may have signed up for "William Moore" Google alerts. I'd told him as much and he'd shaken his head indulgently, telling me I shouldn't care about what people were writing online. But I cared about him, and I didn't want more false stories circulating.

I brought up the page, a knot in my belly until I read the headline: **Money for lies: Woman retracts story about Ireland rugby player, William Moore**

My heart leapt. I'd almost given up on Annie's plan, having not heard from her in weeks, but she'd done it. I couldn't believe she'd actually done it!

"Will! Will!" I shouted, leaping up and carrying the laptop into his bedroom. He lay in bed, glasses on, e-reader in front of his face.

"What is it?" he asked, pushing his glasses down his nose, all Clark Kent sexy.

"It's Annie, she managed to get the retraction. I can't believe it," I exclaimed, dropping down beside him on the bed and handing him the laptop.

He pushed his glasses back into place and scanned the screen. First, he frowned, then his brows rose, then his eyes widened as he continued to read.

"Isn't it great," I said as he rubbed his chin.

"Annie is very talented at her job," he said at long last. "This actually reads pretty well."

I gaped at him. "Is that all you're going to say? This cleans up your entire reputation. You can do your charity work again. Aren't you happy? You should be jumping for joy."

"That's not exactly how it works," Will replied. "Once something like this comes out, it stains you, no matter if there's a retraction. The Dream Foundation aren't likely to backtrack, but it may help with future endeavors, so for that I am thankful."

I deflated a little. Will was right, any kind of scandal stuck, no matter if it was true or false. "Well, look on the bright side, you have all those sponsorship deals coming in thanks to your new bad boy image. Maybe you could use the money to start your own charity. Turn a negative into a positive."

Will gave me a tender look and reached out to caress my cheek. "You always manage to see a silver lining."

I shrugged. "I try."

He bent close and pressed a kiss to my lips, then said, "You know, that's not a bad idea, to start my own charity."

"Exactly, and you could decide exactly where the money goes, make sure it's benefitting the people who need it most."

Will gave me another loving look, then glanced back at the laptop screen. Noticing the other tab, he asked, "What's this?"

I pulled the laptop away from him. "Oh, it's nothing. Just some results from college." I hadn't wanted to check them in front of Will in case they weren't as good as I'd been hoping. I usually did pretty well academically, but only if I absolutely killed myself with study. And though I'd been going hard at it, I'd admittedly been distracted of late, thanks to the big sexy rugby player I was now sharing a bed with.

"They're your test results? How did you do?" Will asked.

"I haven't checked them yet. I got distracted by the article."

He gave me a look. "Well, check them now."

"I might not have done so well. I probably should've studied more in Australia. Plus, the whole new living arrangement kind of screwed with my usual study routine. Normally, I'd sit in the nook in my dad's office, but there's no nook here, and the environment you study in really does affect how you…"

I stopped speaking when Will kissed me quickly. "Check the results. If you failed anything, you can always repeat the class."

Even the idea of repeating plunged a brick to the pit of my stomach. It was just that I'd finally found my calling. I was passionate about animals, about becoming a qualified vet. It might've been overly ambitious, but I wanted top marks. I wanted to do the best I possibly could. Swallowing tightly, I brought my attention to the screen and clicked on to my personal dashboard. My heart sped as I scanned the module numbers on one side and the results on the other. There were six altogether and…

And I'd aced them. I blinked to make sure I was seeing correctly. I'd gotten four As and two Bs.

"Well?" Will prompted. I turned the screen to him so he could see for himself. His smile was wide. "You did amazing. I knew you would. Congrats, sugar."

I was still processing the fact I'd scored so highly when Will pulled me to him. He wrapped his arms around me and pressed a kiss to the curve of my neck. Involuntarily, I shivered.

"I think you deserve a reward for being such a good student," Will murmured, his hand sliding down to cup my backside.

"Do you know what? I agree. I do deserve a reward," I said, my chuckle transforming into a sigh when Will sucked my earlobe in his mouth, his lips curving in a sexy smile, his voice a husky caress.

"Well then, let's see what I can do about that."

I smiled, too. And then I reclined and allowed him to have his way with me.

Will's reputation had been restored.

I'd gotten top scores in all my courses.

And, I was pretty sure I was on my way to a spectacular orgasm.

Once again, everything was coming up Josey.

EPILOGUE
WILL

I'd never been invited to a baby shower before.

In the States—at least where I was from—baby showers were a strictly female event. But as I stood along the sidelines of Ronan and Annie's big living room, watching all my teammates and their significant others, wives, girlfriends, and partners, I decided that I'd want a baby shower like this one.

First of all, Sean Cassidy was trying to suck three ounces of apple juice out of a baby bottle, and was in a dead heat with Ronan Fitzpatrick to be the first one finished. They kept glaring at each other, all the while their heads were tilted back, clutching their glass bottle, sucking and sucking and sucking through the microscopic hole at the end of a clear silicone nipple.

I'd been given a bottle with three ounces of apple juice, so had Bryan—who stood next to me—but we were too busy laughing at Sean and Ronan, as was everyone else.

"Oh my God, I hope someone is recording this." Eilish wiped at tears of hilarity pooling in the corners of her eyes. "I will never let my cousin live this down."

"He better win." Josey was holding her stomach from laughing so hard. "If he wins, at least he'll have bragging rights. No one wants to take second place at a nipple sucking contest."

This statement had Bryan, Eilish, me, and everyone nearby launching into another fit of hysterical laughter.

Lucy—Ronan's sister and Sean's girlfriend—was standing behind Sean, rubbing his shoulders and whispering encouragement into the big guy's ear.

Meanwhile, Annie was sitting next to Ronan and rubbing her swollen belly as she laughed and laughed.

"Oi! Ronan. Look at Annie. All this excitement might cause her to go into labor." Finley drew everyone's attention to the mother-to-be.

"Ronan already knows how important it is to stimulate the nipples!" Lucy shouted back, and everyone roared with laughter.

I shook my head, looking at Josey. Her smile was beaming and her eyes were bright, but something about the way she held her stomach drew my eyes and sobered me. What would she look like, pregnant with our baby?

Prior to now, I couldn't have imagined a scenario where I would have willingly sucked anything at all from a baby bottle, and especially not in front of a crowd.

Longing stirred within me, deep and low and secret. I swallowed the desire to speak, to ask her what she was thinking. Instead, I gave her a quick smile and returned my attention to the debacle. I was already nervous enough about my plans for Josey after the shower was over.

The last several months had been—without a doubt—the best of my life. They'd also been the most frustrating. I'd taken Bryan's advice and I'd decided to wait. I hadn't pushed, I hadn't asked for assurances. I'd tried to trust.

So far so good.

So far so fucking fantastic.

But I'd been restless. I wanted . . . something more with Josey. And I needed an outlet for this energy.

So I'd bought her parents' house, swore them to secrecy, and had been fixing it up while Josey had been busy at school and work.

I'd taken Rocky over, to run around in the backyard, while I replaced the paper-thin hardwood with brand new walnut floors throughout, painted all the rooms white in anticipation of Josey picking new colors, remodeled the kitchen, two of the bathrooms, replaced the pipes and worked with an electrician to update the wiring.

The roof was done by contractors, and I tried to leave as much of the original fixtures as possible, sanding down doors and windows to their original wood finish. I didn't want to change the house. I wanted to give her a blank canvas that she could make her own, but also a place she could look at as a real home. One she'd hopefully want to share with me.

Working on the house had helped, and I'd enjoyed it, but I couldn't stay silent about my wishes any longer. The time had come to act.

A sound at the center of the room drew my attention. Everyone cheered as Ronan finished first and stood in triumph, pushing fists of victory into the air.

Sean was grinning, but he dipped his chin to his chest and shook his head as though disappointed by his defeat. If I didn't know better, I would have guessed he'd lost on purpose. He'd been way ahead until everyone dropped out but him and Ronan.

Eventually, Sean stood too and turned to Ronan. "Congratulations, Fitzpatrick." The big blond man offered his hand in a shake, lifting a sardonic eyebrow and adding, "You suck the most."

Everyone laughed, including Ronan. And to everyone's surprise, he pulled Sean into a quick hug, both men smacking each other on the back once or twice before leaning away and finishing their handshake.

"All right, all right, that's enough of this sordid affair. Cake is served, and I've been told by my sister that presents are next."

I felt Josey slide her hand against mine, drawing my attention. I glanced first at our entwined hands and then at her upturned face.

"Hey, my sexy beast," she whispered. "Don't even think about trying to steal a bite of my cake."

Unable to help it, a smile burst forth and I turned to her, leaning to her ear and licking her earlobe. "You know how much I love eating your cake."

She shivered, her hand not holding mine coming to my chest and curling around my shirt. But before she could speak, I felt a hand hit my arm.

Scowling, I glanced over my shoulder, finding Ronan, Bryan, and Sean smirking at us.

Sean lifted his chin. "Hey you two dirty birds—"

"It's lovebirds, eejit," Ronan corrected.

"Not with these two," Bryan mumbled, earning him a glare from me.

"Whatever, same difference." Sean smoothed a hand down his impeccable suit, sounding bored. "We're setting up a match, partners versus players. Are you two in?"

I gaped, unable to process the words he'd spoken. They wanted to play a match? Against our partners? Were they crazy?

What the fuck?

"You can't be ser—"

"Hell yes!" Josey cut me off, her words loud with excitement. "Count us in. We're totally down. Abso-fucking-lutely."

Sean's gaze moved down and then up Josey's form, a grin pulling one side of his mouth upwards. "Excellent."

I fought against a growl. But before I could protest, Josey pulled away, capturing Eilish's hand in hers and charging off, making a beeline for Lucy.

This was unbelievable.

I brought my scowl to Sean and said through gritted teeth, "If she gets hurt, I'll ruin your other knee."

Ronan's hand came down on my shoulder, drawing my attention; he looked like he was endeavoring to hold in laughter. "Lighten up, Will. It'll be fun."

Fun?

Were they nuts?

* * *

Ronan was right. It was fun.

It was ridiculous.

Most of my time was employed defending Josey from my teammate's grabby tackles, which was how all of us seemed to be spending our time, keeping each other away from our women. Or, in Donovan's case, his man.

Sean elbowed Finley in the face for putting a hand on Lucy.

Bryan knocked the legs out from under Donovan before he could reach Eilish.

Everyone wanted to ruck with their own partner, so—unsurprisingly—there were a lot of rucks.

Pretty soon, the ladies figured out that all they had to do was give Annie the ball. One look from Ronan and she was untouchable.

We were so focused on sabotaging our teammates that we were soon annihilated. But to be fair, Josey and Eilish were decent players. Josey was tough, focused, and had a good eye and aim. She stayed low and maneuvered quickly around Finley when he tried to catch her in a hold.

For the record, I would make sure he paid for that later.

When it was all over, I had the beginnings of a nasty bruise on my jaw—courtesy of Sean for when I attempted to intercept a throw from Lucy—and Ronan was limping—courtesy of Bryan for when Ronan deflected Eilish's kick.

But, yeah. I had fun.

Josey jogged over to me, a big, cocky grin on her face. But it quickly dissolved when she spotted the swelling mark.

"Oh my gosh! Are you okay?" Gentle fingers came to my face and she brushed her lips over my jaw, her arms sliding around my waist. "Let me take care of you. I'll get some ice."

Josey leaned away, concern and love in her gaze, and gave me a sweet, parting kiss before hurrying back towards the house.

I stared after her, silently thinking Ronan, Sean, and Bryan were geniuses.

Not a second later, a hand clapped over my shoulder and I turned, finding Sean giving me a little, knowing smile.

"Did you have fun?"

I nodded, dazed, my mind still on Josey.

His grin widened. "That's good. But the best part—the *real* fun—is what comes next."

I was about to question him when we were interrupted by Lucy, sliding next to Sean and cupping his jaw. "My poor handsome man. Look what they did to your eye." She sighed sadly, her gaze on a small cut just above his eyebrow.

She pressed her body closer, giving him a fiercely affectionate kiss, and he spared me a quick glance as though to say, *See what I mean?*

But then his expression completely changed as he looked at Lucy. "It doesn't hurt too badly. But maybe you could kiss it? In the bathtub tonight?"

I rolled my lips together to stop a disbelieving exhale and glanced around me. Couples everywhere were huddled together, fawning over each other, kissing and giving comfort. My eyes were opened.

What a bunch of sneaky fuckers.

Man, I was clueless sometimes.

These guys.

These guys were the real pros.

* * *

JOSEY

"When we get home, I'm running you a bath," I whispered seductively to Will as we headed for his car. I'd had such a fun time at Annie and Ronan's baby shower, but after that rugby game I was exhausted. I hadn't played since I was at school, so I was definitely rusty, but I'd still enjoyed it. I especially enjoyed how Will glared daggers at any of his teammates who tried to tackle me.

Will opened my door for me, then walked around to the driver's side. "I actually have somewhere I'd like to take you first."

Hmm. . .

He sounded nervous. And, now that I studied him, he looked nervous. Why was he nervous? His lips were tight, his jaw stiff. He was keeping some kind of secret because those were his tells.

I folded my arms and narrowed my gaze. "Where do you want to take me?"

He started the engine and pulled out of the parking space. "It's not far," he said, avoiding the question.

"Will, tell me where you're taking me."

"It's a surprise."

"I don't like surprises."

"Yes, you do. You love them."

"Okay, that's true. But I don't like this surprise. You look nervous. You're never nervous."

"I'm nervous sometimes."

"Will."

"Josey, please just trust me. It'll take ten minutes and then everything will become clear."

It was the exasperated look on his face that shut me up. Ten minutes into the drive I started to think the worst, and then, suddenly, the scenery became familiar. Will pulled to a stop outside my parents' house. Except, it wasn't my parents' house anymore. They'd moved out months ago into a cozy two-bedroom apartment after selling the house to some property developer. Whoever it was, they'd already done a lot of work on the place. There were new triple glazed windows installed and a fancy new front door.

I looked at Will. "What are we doing here?"

His gaze fell on me, so tender and full of love. "I thought you'd like to see our new place."

There was a vulnerability in him now, and I had to catch my breath. *Our new place?*

No, he couldn't have.

Surely not.

I tried to keep my voice steady and failed. "Will, did you b-buy my family's house?"

He nodded. "For us."

Tears sprang forth. I loved this house. It broke my heart when Mam and Dad told me they were putting it on the market. And Will had. . .he'd bought it for me. For us.

It felt like too much.

But then, we'd been together almost six months, and already I couldn't remember a time when he wasn't with me. It felt like he'd always been there, even though logically I knew he hadn't. He just fit into my life so perfectly, and I in his.

Will leaned closer to study me. "Are you crying?"

"Nobody's ever done anything like this for me before."

"Well, when you love someone, you'd do anything to make them happy."

"Like buy them houses?"

He shrugged. "Sure."

"Will, have you any idea how crazy this is? It's so much money. Too much."

He caught my chin in his hand and looked deep into my eyes. "It's our future. No amount of money is too much."

Our future.

I was quiet for a moment, letting it all sink in. "I really do love this house. I've lived in it my whole life."

"And now it's yours," Will breathed. His eyes were big, absorbing all the emotions on my face like he was etching them into memory.

I shook my head, flabbergasted, touched and completely blown away by this gesture. No, it was more than a gesture. It was a declaration. By buying this house, Will was saying something BIG. He was telling me that our lives were entwined now. What was his was mine, and what was mine was his.

If he didn't know me, this would just be any old house to him. But he did know me, loved me, and because it meant something to me it, in turn, meant something to him.

Turning away from him, I looked back at the house. "You've been keeping this a secret all this time. How did I not know?"

"You were studying, and it's the off-season. I've had a lot of time on my hands."

"Well, you've certainly been busy," I said, and sniffed, trying not to cry and failing. I wiped at my tears with the backs of my hands. I was overcome.

"Okay, I guess you better show me what you've done with the place, but be warned, if you screwed it up, we're over," I teased, my voice watery.

Will smiled and led me out of the car. "I think you'll be pleased."

He was right. I was pleased. He'd done an amazing job. All the walls had been stripped of old wallpaper and repainted, the rickety staircase had been replaced with a new, modern design, and the entire kitchen had been remodeled. The builders knocked through the back wall to create a giant window looking out into the back garden, giving the effect that there was no gap between modernity and nature.

I was stunned by the sheer extent of the work in so short a time. It still wasn't finished, but what had been achieved was incredible. I barely recognized the place, and yet, it felt like home. It had that feeling of comfort, like slipping into an old pair of well-worn, soft cotton pajamas after a long day at work.

"I wanted to wait for your input on the furniture," Will said, coming to stand next to me. "But overall, what do you think?" Again, he looked unsure. I felt like he had more to say, but was holding back.

I exhaled heavily, came to stand in front of him, and wrapped my arms around his big shoulders. "I think it's amazing. You're amazing. And the fact that you did all this for us? I don't deserve you."

"Yes, you do. We deserve each other. We've earned it."

That got a chuckle out of me. "Go us. Wosey for the win!"

Will's brows drew together, a smile tugging at his lips. "Wosey?"

"It's our couple name. Will and Josey makes Wosey. I've been waiting for a special occasion to reveal it."

His deep, throaty laugh gave me a warm feeling in my belly. "I fucking love you."

I went up on my tiptoes and pressed a soft kiss on his lips. "And I love you."

He brought his mouth to my ear and whispered, "What do you think about getting married?"

I blinked, sure I'd misheard, but no, Will gazed down at me like he'd just casually suggested we should have beans on toast for tea. Like asking me to marry him was the most natural thing in the world. I opened my mouth, then closed it. My throat ran dry.

"What did you just say?"

Will tugged my arms from around his shoulders and stepped back. "You once said you didn't think you'd ever get married."

I blinked at him, trying to recall the conversation, and remembering our walk in the Botanical Gardens in Sydney. "Yes, I guess I did."

He nodded, his eyes solemn and serious. "I want you to know, this is *your* house. I bought it for you. No matter what happens, it belongs to you. I understand if you don't ever want to get married, and I'll accept that." He paused here to swallow, a hint of sadness and longing shading his expression. "I'll always want to be with you, regardless of whether I'm your husband, or not."

New tears pricked my eyes and I captured his face with my hands. "Oh, Will. I love you. And whether or not we get married—which I am not against, for the record—and whether you'd actually bought this house or not, I'll always want to be with you, too."

Will's gorgeous brown eyes seemed to grow larger as I spoke, and they bounced between mine. "In that case. . ."

He lowered to one knee. My heart somersaulted, my belly flipflopped, and my lungs filled up with too much air. He reached around to his back pocket, pulled out a small, velvet box, and opened it up to reveal a white gold ring sparkling with the most beautiful diamond.

What the...

WHAT?

First the house, and now this. Was he trying to *kill* me?

And great, now I was crying again. Over the last few months, I'd imagined where our lives would lead, wondered and hoped, but there was always one constant: Will at my side.

I wanted to spend the rest of my life with him, I had no doubt.

His eyes met mine, his full of love and affection, mine full of love and tears.

"I hope those are happy tears," he said as he held out the ring.

I swallowed back the lump of emotion in my throat. "They are."

As soon as I said it, his face transformed. He beamed pure joy at me. It hit me square in the chest as he took my hand in his. "Josey Kavanagh, will you marry me?"

I blinked back more tears, cleared my throat, and just about managed to find my voice. "William Moore, abso-fucking-lutely."

THE END

ABOUT THE AUTHORS

L.H. Cosway has a BA in English Literature and Greek and Roman Civilisation, and an MA in Postcolonial Literature. She lives in Dublin city. Her inspiration to write comes from music. Her favourite things in life include writing stories, vintage clothing, dark cabaret music, food, musical comedy, and of course, books. She thinks that imperfect people are the most interesting kind. They tell the best stories.

Come find L.H. Cosway-
Facebook: https://www.facebook.com/LHCosway
Twitter: https://twitter.com/LHCosway
Mailing List: http://www.lhcoswayauthor.com/p/mailing-list.html
Pinterest: http://www.pinterest.com/lhcosway13/
Website: www.lhcoswayauthor.com

Penny Reid is the *New York Times*, *Wall Street Journal*, and *USA Today* bestselling author of the Winston Brothers and Knitting in the City series. She used to spend her days writing federal grant proposals as a biomedical researcher, but now she writes kissing books. Penny is an obsessive knitter and manages the #OwnVoices-focused mentorship incubator/publishing imprint, Smartypants Romance. She lives in Seattle Washington with her husband, three kids, and dog named Hazel.

Come find Penny -
Mailing List: http://pennyreid.ninja/newsletter/
Goodreads: http://www.goodreads.com/ReidRomance
Facebook: www.facebook.com/pennyreidwriter
Instagram: www.instagram.com/reidromance
Twitter: www.twitter.com/reidromance
TikTok: https://www.tiktok.com/@authorpennyreid
Patreon: https://www.patreon.com/smartypantsromance
Email: pennreid@gmail.com …hey, you! Email me ;-)

OTHER BOOKS BY L.H. COSWAY

Contemporary Romance

Painted Faces

Killer Queen

The Nature of Cruelty

Still Life with Strings

Showmance

Fauxmance

Happy-Go-Lucky

Beyond the Sea

Sidequest for Love

The Cracks Duet

A Crack in Everything (#1)

How the Light Gets In (#2)

The Hearts Series

Six of Hearts (#1)

Hearts of Fire (#2)

King of Hearts (#3)

Hearts of Blue (#4)

Thief of Hearts (#5)

Cross My Heart (5.75)

Hearts on Air (#6)

The Running on Air Series

Air Kiss (#0.5)

Off the Air (#1)

Something in the Air (#2)

The Rugby Series with Penny Reid

The Hooker & the Hermit (#1)

The Player & the Pixie (#2)
The Cad & the Co-ed (#3)
The Varlet & the Voyeur (#4)

The Blood Magic Series
Nightfall (#1)
Moonglow (#2)
Witching Hour (#3)
Sunlight (#4)

St. Bastian Institute Series
Foretold

OTHER BOOKS BY PENNY REID

Knitting in the City Series
(Interconnected Standalones, Adult Contemporary Romantic Comedy)
Neanderthal Seeks Human: A Smart Romance (#1)
Neanderthal Marries Human: A Smarter Romance (#1.5)
Friends without Benefits: An Unrequited Romance (#2)
Love Hacked: A Reluctant Romance (#3)
Beauty and the Mustache: A Philosophical Romance (#4)
Ninja at First Sight (#4.75)
Happily Ever Ninja: A Married Romance (#5)
Dating-ish: A Humanoid Romance (#6)
Marriage of Inconvenience: (#7)
Neanderthal Seeks Extra Yarns (#8)
Knitting in the City Coloring Book (#9)

Winston Brothers Series
(Interconnected Standalones, Adult Contemporary Romantic Comedy, spinoff of Beauty and the Mustache)
Beauty and the Mustache (#0.5)
Truth or Beard (#1)
Grin and Beard It (#2)
Beard Science (#3)
Beard in Mind (#4)
Beard In Hiding (#4.5)
Dr. Strange Beard (#5)
Beard with Me (#6)
Beard Necessities (#7)
Winston Brothers Paper Doll Book (#8)

Hypothesis Series
(New Adult Romantic Comedy Trilogies)

Elements of Chemistry (#1)

Laws of Physics (#2)

Irish Players (Rugby) Series – by L.H. Cosway and Penny Reid

(Interconnected Standalones, Adult Contemporary Sports Romance)

The Hooker and the Hermit (#1)

The Pixie and the Player (#2)

The Cad and the Co-ed (#3)

The Varlet and the Voyeur (#4)

Dear Professor Series

(New Adult Romantic Comedy)

Kissing Tolstoy (#1)

Kissing Galileo (#2)

Ideal Man Series

(Interconnected Standalones, Adult Contemporary Romance Series of Jane Austen Reimaginings)

Pride and Dad Jokes (#1, TBD)

Man Buns and Sensibility (#2, TBD)

Sense and Manscaping (#3, TBD)

Persuasion and Man Hands (#4, TBD)

Mantuary Abbey (#5, TBD)

Mancave Park (#6, TBD)

Emmanuel (#7, TBD)

Handcrafted Mysteries Series

(A Romantic Cozy Mystery Series, spinoff of *The Winston Brothers Series*)

Engagement and Espionage (#1)

Marriage and Murder (#2)

Home and Heist (TBD)

Baby and Ballistics (TBD)

Pie Crimes and Misdemeanors (TBD)

Good Folks Series

(Interconnected Standalones, Adult Contemporary Romantic Comedy, spinoff of *The Winston Brothers Series*)

Totally Folked (#1)

Folk Around and Find Out (#2)

Three Kings Series

(Interconnected Standalones, Holiday-themed Adult Contemporary Romantic Comedies)

Homecoming King (#1)

Drama King (#2)

Prom King (#3, coming Christmas 2023)

Standalones

Ten Trends to Seduce Your Best Friend